ALSO BY MANDY BAGGOT

One Last Greek Summer

One Christmas Star

Mandy Baggot

HEAD of ZEUS

An Aria Book

First published in the United Kingdom in 2019 by Aria,
an imprint of Head of Zeus Ltd

9 7 5 3 1 2 4 6 8

A CIP catalogue record for this book is available
from the British Library.

ISBN (PB): 9781789544329
ISBN (E): 9781789544282

Typeset by Silicon Chips

Printed and bound in Great Britain by
CPI Group (UK) Ltd, Croydon CR0 4YY

Aria
c/o Head of Zeus
First Floor East
5–8 Hardwick Street
London EC1R 4RG

WWW.ARIAFICTION.COM

For Justin Edinburgh

One of my first romantic heroes.

Sleep tight. Shine bright.

One

Late November

Concentrate. Con–cen–trate. You are a crafting guru...

Emily Parker's tongue was out of her mouth, pressed to her top lip, eyes narrowed and focused as she held the tiny crown made from modelling clay between a pair of tweezers. She moved her lips and blew upwards, hoping to rid her eyelashes of her slightly too-long auburn fringe.

It was before 8 a.m. and her classroom, for now, was currently quieter than a chapel of Benedictine monks. Her hand was shaking, like she was performing open-heart surgery and not simply adding the finishing touches to a 'What Christmas Means to Me' tableau. Yesterday, her Year Six children had made sensational sparkling stars with glitter and tin foil, attaching them to wire coat hangers that were now suspended from the ceiling. They twirled and whirled and decorated the painted walls with shimmering lights. Emily was still slightly terrified one (or all) of them were going to drop onto this precious model she was helping to construct.

'Don't squash it, Miss Parker, 'cause it's good again now.'

'I know,' Emily breathed. 'You made it really, *really* well, Jayden.' The encouraging words were for one of her pupils who lived in the ironically named Riches Tower – an awful seventies-style building that housed some of the poorest members of their Greater London community. This latest sculpture was Jayden's second attempt at the model, under her guidance before the school day began. The first model had succumbed to Jayden's fist-happy father who had thrown it at the wall of their kitchen. Emily had been to the Jacksons' flat only once, when she was worried about a 'sick bug' that was keeping Jayden off school for over a week. She had only made it as far as that dated kitchen – the first room after the front door – before Mr Jackson had pushed past Mrs Jackson and ordered her out.

Emily took a breath, her fingers trembling. Positivity. *Something* had to go right for this boy. It was almost December, the festive spirit was rapidly arriving. Emily flashed an eye to the ceiling, and the swaying mobiles, before blowing out the breath she'd been holding so intensely. She was determined to fix this crown on without incident. Lowering her implement, she reached her target, pressed… and then, finally, released.

'Wow,' Jayden exclaimed, scooting his chair closer to his work of art. 'D'you think I'll win the competition, Miss Parker?'

Emily swallowed. He couldn't win. He *shouldn't* win. She had helped him quite significantly over the past week. But, out of her class of thirty-three, Jayden was one of the students who probably deserved the chocolate selection box prize the most…

'I think,' Emily said, looking to the ten-year-old, his greasy dark hair clinging to his forehead, eyes under his fringe so full of hope, 'you have an excellent chance of winning.'

Jayden smiled then, poking the last portion of the cream cheese and bacon bagel she'd brought in for him into his mouth. 'Look at my dad.' He laughed, pointing at the scene. 'He looks wasted even in Plasticine.'

What did you say to that? There were no words. But she had to come up with something. Something positive. 'Maybe your dad will be proud he's taking centre-stage in your tableau.'

'He won't see it,' Jayden announced, through chewing. 'He can't come to the presentation. He'll be working.'

'He's got a job!' Emily exclaimed. 'Jayden, that's wonderful.' Mr Jackson worked about as much as Jeremy Kyle's lie detector did now.

'It won't last,' Jayden answered in matter-of-fact tones. 'My mum says she gives it a fortnight.' He grinned then. 'I didn't know what a fortnight meant before she told me. I thought she was on about the game.'

'Well,' Emily began, taking a tissue from her pocket and wiping at the corner of Jayden's mouth to remove cream cheese. 'You know, in this class, we listen, and we don't judge, and we give everyone a second chance, don't we?'

Jayden made a begrudging noise, shaking his head away from Emily's attempts to clean him up. 'Rashid's on his third chance with me now.'

'Has he been mean to you again?' Emily asked. Rashid Dar came from a seemingly wealthy family who owned a chain of Indian eateries. She had wondered, ever since Rashid joined her Year Six class in September, why he

3

didn't go to the local private school instead of Stretton Park. Maybe creating phall feasts wasn't quite as lucrative as it appeared to be or, perhaps, they simply didn't want to shell out on private education. But, like with her class rules, it also wasn't *her* place to judge anyone. However, it *was* her place to try and ensure *all* her pupils worked at being the best version of themselves. She was their teacher for that last important year before they left for secondary education. Emily had always thought that was the time when they really changed. The time when she watched them going from infants to tweens, finding out who they really were and who they wanted to be...

'Rashid said there was so much grease in my hair,' Jayden said, 'that his dad could probably deep-fry samosas in it.'

She felt herself bristle. Despite her best efforts, Rashid's self-confidence did come across as cocky and arrogant and at ten years old it was slightly worrying. 'Did he now?'

Before her cogs began whirring as to how she could attempt to tackle Rashid's verbal bullying, the door of the classroom burst open and in walked the headteacher, Susan Clark, arms full of heavy files, glasses slipping down her nose, lipstick a fluorescent pink, too-tight skirt straining with every step.

'Good morning, Miss Parker. What seems to be happening here?' Susan marched towards the table Emily and Jayden were working on with all the determination of an army general about to engage in battle. One of the star mobiles suddenly came unstuck, dangling precariously now from one small sliver of Sellotape.

'We were...' Emily began tentatively. She stopped speaking then and internally cursed herself. What was it

4

about this woman that constantly made her feel inferior? She *wasn't* inferior. She should actually be heading up a school herself now. She re-started, trying to project more confidence. 'Jayden got here early to hand in his "What Christmas Means To Me" project.'

Emily could see Susan's blouse literally weep for mercy as the headteacher dumped the files she was carrying on a table and then took a deep breath, sniffing the air around Jayden's model.

'Have you made it out of cream cheese?' Susan asked, pushing her glasses up her nose, the amber-beaded chain they were attached to catching the light.

'No, Mrs Clark,' Jayden was quick to answer. 'That was from the bagel Miss Parker gave me.' He grinned. 'It was banging.'

Emily bit her lip. She'd be encouraging a cold sore if she wasn't careful. And now she was going to be in trouble. Susan had told her – twice – that she wasn't to give food to impoverished students as it set a precedent and, apparently, a bad example. *Besides, they already get free school meals and there are things called food banks...*

'I see,' Susan answered, recoiling from the project and setting her eyes on Emily. Susan saying 'I see' really meant she didn't see at all.

'Jayden,' Emily said, taking control. 'Why don't you go out into the playground now? It's eight o'clock, you can play some football until the bell goes.' Perhaps she would get a tick against the food faux pas by encouraging physical activity...

'Alright,' Jayden answered, never needing much of an excuse to turn to sport rather than education. He got up from his seat, picked up his rucksack with the broken strap – held together by gaffer tape – and made his way out of the room.

Emily figured then she may as well head things off with Susan as best as she could.

'Before—'

'*You* made this model, Emily, didn't you?' Susan interrupted and the volume of her boss's voice cancelled out the fact that Emily had even started speaking at all. Another star mobile came unstuck, dangling right over Susan Clark. If one hit her head, Emily knew she could kiss goodbye to promotion thoughts for this whole school year. She swallowed, her mind drifting away to a memory. A memory of Simon. Simon had always been her biggest supporter in her campaign to achieve headteacher status...

'No,' she said immediately. Except she was pretty sure potential headteachers weren't meant to lie.

Susan gave her a look through her lenses that said she believed her as much as anyone believed that the UK trying to leave the EU had been easy.

'I didn't,' Emily continued. 'I mean... I may have... made suggestions to perhaps... enhance the overall aesthetic but...' Why was she bothering? Susan knew. Susan always knew. Whether it was some sort of dark magic, or simply her infinite years in teaching, there was literally nothing that got past her.

'OK,' Emily started. 'His horrible, aggressive, nasty father threw his original tableau at the kitchen wall. Then he stamped on it.' She knew her face was reddening, and she also knew that when Jayden had come to her and told her about the incident, tears spilling from his eyes, she had wanted to throw Mr Jackson against a wall and stamp on *him*. Not that she condoned violence at all. Nor was she attached to any of her pupils. Because attachment wasn't allowed. It was up there with budget restraint and political correctness... and, apparently, buying bagels.

'I see,' Susan said.

She still didn't see. And she didn't want to see either. Oh well, Emily could handle any reprimand that was coming, as long as she kept her job. With her flatmate and best friend, Jonah, moving out, her boiler making noises like it was an expensive coffee machine and Christmas on the way, she really *did* need to keep the money coming in. The smallish lump sum she'd received unexpectedly wasn't going to last for ever, unlike the devastation that had come before that bank transaction...

'I've been you, Emily,' Susan said, sliding her bulk onto the table, hips almost catching the side of Jayden's sculpture. 'I was you for almost twenty years. There wasn't a nose I didn't wipe or a knee I didn't put a plaster on. But, Emily, as much as it saddens me, and it *does* sadden me... those days are gone.' Susan leaned forward, her large face determined to force its way into Emily's sightline. 'You understand, yes? Because it isn't as if we haven't had this conversation before.'

Softly, softly and then the death punch. It wasn't the first time. Emily was bending the rules. Not listening to Ground Control...

Susan turned her attention back to the structure on the table, adjusting her glasses as if to magnify what she was looking at. 'What exactly is it? Because it doesn't look like any sort of manger to me.'

'It isn't a manger,' Emily answered. 'I didn't go for wholly

Christianity as a theme this year.' She hadn't wanted to go for just Christianity as a theme *last* year, or the year before that but as the primary school was Church of England governed, and Susan had drummed it home that the visiting diocese were expecting all things Biblical, she hadn't had much choice. 'As I said, it's a "What Christmas Means to Me" tableau. Or rather, "What the Holidays Mean to Me", for those who don't celebrate Christmas.' She swallowed. 'Frema is doing both because of her interfaith upbringing.'

'Is that… a man holding a pint glass?' Susan continued, studying Jayden's creation even more closely.

'Yes,' Emily said. 'Yes, it is.' She sighed, looking at Jayden's work. The tiny crown she had placed so delicately wasn't for the head of a sleeping Baby Jesus, or for one of the Three Wise Men, it was for the roof of Mr Jackson's favourite public house, The Rose & Crown.

Susan stood up, springing away from the desk like what she was looking at was a prop from Sky's *Chernobyl*. She picked her files back up. 'Don't forget the budget meeting after school tonight,' she said, backing towards the door. 'And, Emily, this *pub*—' she said 'pub' like she was saying 'Judas' in front of the bishop '—can't possibly win the competition.'

Emily didn't reply. She knew her place. Twenty-nine years old and not even the deputy. Susan whisked from the room, the door shutting with force behind her. As it closed, two of the star creations fell to the floorboards trailing tinsel like exploding comets.

Two

Well-Roasted Coffee House, Islington

The music being played was all Nat King Cole and Dean Martin with a smattering of Mud and Band Aid. Way too cheerful and nothing in a minor key. Musician Ray Stone hated all that festive schmaltz. 'Nothing festive' had been one of the clauses he had demanded be added to his last contract with Saturn Records. Absolutely no Christmas albums. Not even if the actual Saturn froze over.

It was literally a few weeks before December and the whole of London already seemed to have turned into a festive wonderland. Lights were being switched on by Z-list celebrities, every shop seemed to be advertising an 'advent sale' and eateries had started adding cinnamon and nutmeg to everything. Like this coffee Ray was drinking. He hadn't asked for whatever syrup was swirled into its rich dark colour, but it was there and… he really wished it was something else. Something distilled by the team at Jack Daniel's, Tennessee.

'Are you listening to me, Ray?'

He looked up then, his eyes adjusting to the razzle-dazzle of tinsel, baubles and flickering LEDs, wound around a real fir tree sitting in the snug corner just behind his agent, Deborah. He should have worn sunglasses. Yes, it was November, and perhaps it would draw *even more* attention, but the cold, crisp morning had a blue sky and a bright sun sitting low down in it and here, in Christmas Coffee City, everything was lit up like Vegas.

Ray took a swig of his coffee, the sweetness feeling unwelcome on his tongue. 'You look tired, Deborah.' When hungover and in doubt about your own fatigue, point the finger somewhere else...

His comment prompted her to fuss with her always immaculate black bobbed hair. She sat a little straighter, adjusting the sleeves of her grey corporate jacket. Only when those tasks were complete did she make a response.

'I don't think you should be concerning yourself with how *I* look or how *I* might be feeling. Ray, we have a shitload of work to do if you're going to survive this latest article.'

'Are you not sleeping?' Ray carried on, avoiding the topic they were supposed to be discussing. 'That dog of yours still keeping you awake?'

'Tucker is actually going to canine therapy now,' Deborah informed him.

'Oscar then? Talking in his sleep again, is he?' Ray knew Deborah's husband was always doing something that annoyed her.

'Oscar doesn't talk in his sleep. He snores… a bit… but I got him nasal dilators for his anniversary gift.'

Ray couldn't contain his laughter, even though it made his headache throb inside his skull. 'Sorry,' he apologised, putting a hand to his grey woollen beanie hat, his dark brown hair escaping over his forehead and around his ears, a little shaggy, in need of a trip to the barber. 'I'm sure more sleep allows you both to be… more romantic at other times.' He thought for a minute. 'What did Oscar get you for *your* anniversary gift?'

Deborah began toying with the serviette her cup of masala chai was sitting on. 'An introduction to making greeting cards on DVD.'

He shouldn't laugh again. But the image of his ball-breaking agent watching a programme on crafts before sitting around a table with ribbons, sequins and a glue gun just didn't fit. He tried to squash the rising humour, but he knew his expression was already giving him away.

'It was something I asked for,' Deborah clarified. '*Very* romantic.'

The laugh escaped and Ray picked up his coffee, needing something to put his mouth to no matter how cinnamon-infused.

'Anyway, Ray, this meeting isn't to discuss *my* private life, it's to discuss yours. And yours is, as we know, a very public life that is currently splashed all over the tabloids.'

From somewhere beneath the table, Deborah produced a newspaper and thwacked it down in front of him. Even the thud of paper stomped all over his hangover like a flat-footed chorus girl. And he had no need to re-read the headline. He had seen it all earlier, on every social media channel. And he had heard it again through the lips of Piers Morgan on *Good Morning Britain*.

He took another swig of coffee and met Deborah's eyes, shrugging. 'I don't know what you want me to say.' He didn't want to talk about this. He simply wanted it not to be happening...

'I want you to tell me the truth,' Deborah said in low tones. 'I'm your agent, Ray. Your best friend in all this. But I cannot defend you unless I know what's real and what isn't.' She took a breath. 'Do you understand?'

'I understand that this article says nothing at all.' He wasn't going to acknowledge this latest report, like he hadn't acknowledged the previous stories sold to the press by his ex-girlfriend, Ida. He'd ridden the waves before. Granted, the other articles hadn't been quite so damning as these were, but he'd got through it.

'It calls you, and I quote, "controlling and obsessive" and "a man in love with all of life's vices".'

'What can I say?' Ray asked. 'I like a drink.' He swallowed, somehow keeping the smile on his face. Inside though it was a whole different story. Inside he was keeping a tight lid on his real emotions. *Keep centred. Be strong.* 'And no one publicly persecutes David Beckham for liking Haig Club.'

'Ray, this is serious. Work for you is drying up quicker than laughter at a really poor comedy club. Saturn Records are on my back to make this go away and I admit, I don't even know where to start.'

'And I still don't know what you want me to say.' This

had been his stance since the beginning of Ida's quest – keep his head down and say nothing. Hope any story would be eclipsed by another celebrity falling from grace or *EastEnders* being cancelled. Except Ida seemed intent on whipping him with this. Every few weeks there was another 'revelation' he had to deal with. Maybe she needed the money. She was clearly still hurting from their break-up last year. Certainly, Ida had a number of issues. Perhaps it was again time to reach out to her himself. Except every time he thought about it, his instincts woke up like a sore bear rising too early from hibernation...

'The story doesn't *say* that you were violent to her,' Deborah carried on. 'But it implies it. Just close enough to put those thoughts in the public's minds, but not close enough for us to think about suing. Although I can call the lawyer if you would like me to. Get his take on it.'

Ray shook his head. He didn't want to sue. Where would that get him? Although he really could do with the cash... This was Ida. She was a struggling artist. If she had got money from these newspapers, she probably needed it. There had to be more to it than her simply wanting to persecute him. Didn't there?

'Unless,' Deborah said, leaning forward a touch, 'there is a certain truth to this... I mean, I know Ida is highly-strung. And no one would blame you for being overwhelmed by the pressure of the music industry. It's been a rollercoaster ride these past few years. From zero to... well, top of the charts and...'

'Back to zero again,' Ray reminded with a sideways glance. Was it his imagination or was the Christmas soundtrack playing in the café getting louder? And he wasn't hearing any real words of solidarity from Deborah, or affirmations contrary to his statement about being at the bottom again… Had things got that bad? Were they set to get even worse?

'I'm not going to beat around the proverbial bush, Ray but, making both main channels' breakfast news *and This Morning* for something like this, well, it isn't going to win you any BRIT awards any time soon.'

He blew out a breath then, realising that he did have to do *something*. But what? He put a hand to his chin, his getting-rather-bushy, completely undefined beard pricking his fingertips.

'Ray…' Deborah began again.

'There's no truth in it,' Ray said, seriously. 'There's no truth in any of it, at all. That's all I can say.' He pushed his coffee cup away. 'Come on, Deborah, you know me. You know I may drink a little too much. You know I have taken advantage of most of the excesses this opportunity has given me, but I would never do anything like these interviews are suggesting I would.'

'So, Ida is simply lying to whichever hack will listen.'

'Well…' Even now he didn't want Ida to be in the firing line. Even when it came to saving his own skin. What was wrong with him? His dad would say he was soft, weak, not the boy he had raised on greyhound-racing and belly-busting breakfasts. A belly-busting breakfast wouldn't have gone amiss right about now.

'Ray! Please! Give me something here!' Now Deborah was raising her voice above Frank Sinatra's dulcet tones and a young couple, holding hands over a frosted cupcake complete with a golden star on top, turned to look at her. Ray reached forward and clasped Deborah's hands in his. His agent immediately withdrew, snatching her hands back with an irritated tut.

'You asked me to give you something,' Ray stated.

'I didn't mean another story for the press to latch on to that highlights any of the traits mentioned in this morning's news.' She doffed her head towards the steamed-up window of the café. 'You know there are reporters across the road. They might be demolishing bacon baps right now, but when they're done murdering the morning rolls, they're going to be snapping shots of you in here with me.'

Ray wiped his hand over the condensation, looking through the constantly moving traffic to the adjacent pavement. There were definitely two journalist types, steaming cardboard-cup coffees resting on a frosty metal broadband cabinet, hands on cameras around their necks. He looked back to Deborah.

'I can't pay my rent,' he admitted. 'And my credit cards are maxed out.'

'What?!' Deborah exclaimed.

'You know how it's been,' Ray continued. 'The split with Ida and... the Sam Smith factor.'

'You cannot blame your credit card spending on another singer's success, unless you've been splashing the plastic *with* Sam Smith.'

'He's stopped returning my calls.' Ray answered, forcing a grin. The truth was, his financial situation, even this situation with Ida, was not what was concerning him most. He had a hospital appointment that afternoon and he was still in two minds whether to turn up. Things came in threes and well, what you didn't know couldn't hurt you, right?

'OK, I'm going to be really blunt with you now, Ray, because I'm not going to waste my day sitting here listening to you talk around the houses.' Deborah puffed a sigh. 'I'm going to deal with only cold, hard facts from now on.' She inhaled deeply. 'You have two options here. You bury your head in the sand hoping all this will go away and face losing what's left of your music career. Or, you make a statement, refute everything Ida has said and give your side of the story.' Deborah picked up her tea. 'I can get you on *Loose Women*.'

'*Loose Women*,' Ray said with a shake of his head.

'It's the perfect place for you to tell everyone there isn't an ounce of truth in any of these stories. But you go at it from the right angle. Say that you respect Ida's opinion of your relationship, but that she is... deeply troubled. *Deeply troubled* says you are "caring" and "compassionate", but it also alludes to Ida being "slightly batshit crazy".' She sipped at her drink. 'And then you say you hope Ida reaches out for the help she needs. That will imply to everyone that she's one step away from a psychiatric ward.'

Many true words were spoken in jest. Or in this case, in spin. But Ray's gut was telling him this was all wrong. Ida *did* need help, but, in his heart, he knew this wasn't the right way to go about it. Forcing her hand in the public arena might lead her to do something nuts and, despite what she was doing to him, he couldn't have that on his conscience.

'I don't know,' he answered.

'You don't know?' Deborah replied. 'You don't know! Ray, if you don't do something, *say something*, the world is going to draw its own conclusions based on *The Sun* and the *Daily Mirror*.'

He pushed the coffee cup away from him. 'The one thing I do know, Deborah… is I am *not* going on *Loose Women*.'

Three

Stretton Park Primary School

'*Tangfastic?*'

Before Emily had a chance to reply, the sharing-size bag of Haribos was pushed under her nose by Dennis Murray, the forty-something teacher of the Year Five class. He shook the plastic and all manner of gum, sugar, sweet and sour flew into Emily's sinuses in one mammoth rush. She picked out a sweet simply to get the bag away from her nose. Popping it into her mouth, the bitterness hit her taste-buds straight off, contorting her expression. She watched, one eye squinted, as Dennis put five sweets into his mouth at once, double-chin wobbling. He was a walking, talking pick 'n' mix addict but still his capacity for sugary sweet treats astounded her. Simon had liked sweets – Maltesers, Minstrels, Mars Bites, *all* the chocolate. Simon had liked chocolate the way Emily liked cheese...

'So, what do you think the budget meeting is going to be about this time?' Dennis asked, nudging Emily's arm as the other teachers joined them in the main hall used for assemblies, performances, lunch and meetings such as these. 'Christmas cancelled? No unnecessary expense until we're back in January?'

'I don't know,' Emily answered. 'But no matter what it is, I can't protest.' She lowered her voice and leaned a little into Dennis's personal space. 'Susan caught me giving Jayden Jackson help with his project this morning *and* I bought him a bagel because I know he isn't getting breakfast at home.' She wasn't getting breakfast at home herself, but only because the cupboards always seemed to be bare now Jonah had gone. Plus, really strong coffee almost counted as a meal, didn't it?

Dennis sucked through his teeth, bits of gum crushed between his canines. 'A double-whammy.'

'I know,' Emily said with a sigh. 'I only narrowly managed to avoid the proverbial third thing because the Sellotape on the Christmas stars held out just long enough until Susan had closed the door behind her.' But she knew she was under scrutiny and it made her nervous. She pulled at the sides of her maroon corduroy skirt, shifting her bottom on the too-small chair. Had she picked one of the children's chairs and not a grown-up one? That was exactly how her luck was right now…

'Definitely no extra baubles for the Year Six Christmas tree this year then,' Dennis remarked, chewing on more sweets.

Emily's phone erupted, tweeting like a bird, from inside her all-colours vintage carpet bag. It had been a bargain. Well, actually it had been quite expensive, but it *was* a genuine 1950s artefact. And she'd been quite emotional on that particular visit to the antique boutique. Emotion and her love of vintage were a heady mix…

'You'd better turn that off before Susan arrives,' Dennis instructed, crunching up the now empty bag of sweets and shoving the wrapper into the pocket of his polyester suit trousers.

Emily checked the screen of her phone. It was Jonah. Jonah texted her even more now they weren't living together. She wondered if he was worried she would remember to feed herself if he wasn't there to cook for her. It was fortuitous that he didn't know about the bare cupboards...

Jonah was a great cook, a chef at a nearby hotel, and she almost missed his hotter-than-hot chilli and jerk chicken more than she missed his company.

What time are you getting home tonight?

Emily furrowed her brow. Was it her imagination or did the 'home' part of the message seem collective? As in, *their* home? Maybe Jonah had already changed his mind, come back, unpacked and was preparing a Caribbean recipe right now! That thought immediately cheered her up.

'Emily,' Dennis said.

'In a second,' Emily replied, tapping out a message.

Meeting at school. Hopefully 6 p.m. Are you moving back in?

She had asked him if he was absolutely sure about the decision at least ten times after he had announced he was moving out, and at least ten times more since he'd actually left. She was still adjusting. To Jonah leaving and to losing Simon. Mainly, if she was honest, still to losing Simon.

Don't be late. I'll make Thai ☺

Jonah *was* making food. Jonah was going to feed her. The excitement was real. She should send a Christmas emoji. Then Jonah might also bring the festive chocolates they would have started to put on the pillows at the hotel, for after the divine green curry he was going to concoct—

'Miss Parker!'

Oh God, it was Susan's voice at louder-than-Twickenham-on-match-day level. She looked up from her phone to see the headteacher glaring at her from the platform at the front of the room. The front of the room was only ten rows of chairs away because it really *wasn't* Twickenham.

'Sorry, Susan... I mean, Mrs Clark.'

'As I was saying... budgets.' A breath was sucked in, the blouson briefly relaxed. 'I'm afraid that budgets are at the very heart of a modern school. Gone are the times when we could just order a hundred rubbers because they were on offer... or extraordinarily pretty or... they smelled nice or...' Susan took a breath. 'Or they smelled nice.'

'I'm glad we're talking about erasers and not glue,' Dennis commented under his breath. 'Or Sharpies. I heard from my friend at the secondary school that permanent markers are the thing to sniff now.'

'Gosh, really,' Emily whispered with a shake of her head.

'I, as your Head,' Susan continued, 'have to account for every *single* item we spend on. Not every *ream* of paper. Every *sheet* of paper. Even the toilet paper.'

'God,' Dennis gasped. 'I should have brought more sweets. This is dire. This is like a good drama going a season too far... and changing the setting to Pluto.'

Emily couldn't disagree. They were already working against such stringent budgets already. She had decided, after Halloween, that anything festive she bought for her class she would pay for herself. Jonah was always telling her what a soft touch she was. Her parents were always telling her she would get nowhere with compassion and everywhere with a confidence-building seminar. And Simon was no longer here to have her back...

Susan cleared her throat. 'I am going to be doing a thorough inventory of your classrooms this week and, I'm afraid, I will have to start considering *extremely* carefully *any* requests for new supplies of anything until after...' The pause seemed to elongate forever. 'February.'

'What?!' Emily didn't realise she had exclaimed so loudly or that she had got off her chair to do it either. Maybe she didn't need those confidence-building classes after all...

'Do you have something you wish to say, Miss Parker?' Susan asked, clicking the pen she was holding on, then off, then on again.

She should stay quiet. She should toe the line. For all Dennis's talk about a good TV show going bad, *he* hadn't stood up and, in fact, was currently shrinking down into his adult chair, folding his body into his Parka coat like it was camouflage.

'I just wanted to say,' Emily began, before hesitating. What *did* she want to say? That counting every sheet of paper was madness? That no one could work properly if they were worried how fast they were running down the ink in the pens?

'I just wanted to say,' she pushed on, 'that I know how

hard it is to juggle everything you have to juggle, Susan...
Mrs Clark. And I'm sure none of us envy your position...
not the position of Head, I mean, I am positive almost all of
us envy that.' She swallowed. This wasn't coming out right
at all. 'Well, perhaps envy isn't quite the right word but...
anyway... it's Christmas coming. The children have worked
really hard already this school year. I don't think, in my very
humble opinion obviously, that we should cut any more
corners... in this term in particular.' Emily could practically
hear the tension fizzing off the skin of her colleagues. A
quick side-eye to Mrs Linda Rossiter (Year Three) gave
her nothing but the sight of a tightly wound, greying bun.
The woman's face was trained on her lap, hands clasped
together as if in prayer. No one was going to agree with her.
They were all too good at sitting on the fence. Worried they
could be stage-managed out of the school and back on to
the job market.

'Why *this* term in particular?' Susan queried sharply.

'Well,' Emily said, trying to maintain her calm alongside
her conviction. She pulled down the sleeves of her cream
cardigan. 'It's Christmas, isn't it? The children love this term.
They love making things, adding sparkle to everything. And
there's the Christmas lunch with the giant trifle and crackers
for everyone and then there's the Christmas play...'

'Ah!' Susan said, smiling then and holding up a finger as
if to stop Emily from talking further. 'The Christmas play.
I'm glad you mentioned that.'

'You're not going to cut the Christmas play, are you?'
This *had* come from someone else. Dennis had got to his
feet, half in his coat, half out of it, a pair of thick mittens

falling to the floor. 'I mean, I know we've lost Mr Jarvis and his fantastic piano-playing skills, but that shouldn't mean we lose the show completely. That's what smart speakers are for these days, isn't it? You know... Alexa, play an instrumental version of "Silent Night".'

'I'm not cutting the play,' Susan responded. 'In fact, despite the need to conserve funds in the everyday running of this establishment, we are going to be shaking up the Christmas show this year thanks to some very generous sponsorship.'

'Sponsorship?' Emily queried.

There was murmuring and movement in the hall now, her colleagues all raising their heads and opinions out of their arses and coming to life.

'Yes, Ahmer Dar from Dar's Delhi Delights is one person who has given us a substantial sum to put on what I hope is going to be a wonderful culmination to everyone's hard work and dedication this term.'

Rashid's dad. Emily closed her eyes. How was she going to broach Rashid's bullying of Jayden if his dad was sponsoring the Christmas show? It was utterly impossible for this day to get any worse...

'The children won't all have to wear T-shirts with the restaurant logo on, will they?' This question came from Linda Rossiter, a panicked look on her face. Her husband, Ralph ran the local fish and chip restaurant and rumour had it that Ahmer Dar had added deep-fried Bengali fish and fries to his menu to steal customers from Ralph's Plaice. Then Ralph had quickly countered, serving giant bhajis with curry sauce on a weekend special offer...

'No, of course not,' Susan replied, waving her

comment away. 'Although they will get a large mention in the programme and... perhaps a couple of lines in the performance.'

The murmuring increased in volume and Emily took that as a cue to sit back down, while Susan was distracted...

'Quiet!' the Head ordered. 'You all sound like the children!' She shook her head. 'This is a good thing. A *wonderful* thing. Particularly in light of everything I've just been telling you about having to do a little bit of penny-pinching.' She let her eyes rove over each and every one of them until all the teachers looked like they felt exceedingly uncomfortable. 'This year's show has the chance to pull the whole community together. Because that's what we have always tried to do here at Stretton Park. Be part of something bigger. Yes?'

Community spirit. This was making it sound a bit better. So, they might have to work around the fake Pritt-Sticks for a while. They were going to have a lovely Christmas show. Perhaps she could help with the costumes...

'And, Miss Parker,' Susan continued, 'I'm so glad you asked about the show because... I want *you* to be at the forefront of it.'

At the forefront. What did that mean? Emily needed quick clarification. 'I'm sorry, what?' She swallowed. 'What does that entail exactly?'

'I'd like you to be the one to organise a festive extravaganza the diocese can be really proud of this year. A strong Christian theme throughout, with all original songs. Proper singing and dancing. You know, like... *The Greatest Showman* or *Mamma Mia* but with... more... more Jesus.'

Emily tried to swallow again, but it felt like there was

a Terry's Chocolate Orange stuck in her windpipe. This couldn't really be happening. *Festive extravaganza. The Greatest Showman.* She might sing a little bit, when no one was listening, but she had zero musical ability really. The only instrument she had ever played was the recorder and the only excelling she had done with it was annoying her parents. Somehow, she remembered, the instrument had got broken…

'Mrs Clark, I don't think…' Emily began. She couldn't do this! The eyes of all her co-workers were on her, looking expectant like she had suddenly morphed into Andrew Lloyd Webber.

'Fantastic! You have until 20th December to get your little darlings' show ready! Right, if there's no other business we'll head off. See you in the morning!' Susan announced, already halfway to the door.

Emily was dumbstruck. How the hell was she going to create a *brand-new* Christmas show in weeks, with *original* songs and dances, performed by the children whose skills at coordination were limited at the best of times. She wanted to burst into tears. She equally wanted to down a bottle of elderflower tonic water and really, *really* pretend it was full of gin.

'Well,' Dennis said, voice close to her ear, 'that was unexpected. But I have every faith in you, Emily. Even though one of Mr Jarvis's original songs did almost get picked as a UK Eurovision entry.'

Emily closed her eyes, wishing she hadn't even mentioned the end of year show. The only saving grace was that this was the third thing. Things happened in threes not fours, everyone knew that. Her day had finally reached its lowest ebb and she had Thai food to look forward to. And she was sure, as soon as Susan realised the low level of her musical expertise, she would give the role to someone else. She just needed to keep calm... Except then Dennis doffed an imaginary top hat and began to whistle the tune to 'This Is Me'.

Four

Harley Street, Marylebone

It was early evening in Central London and Ray was glad no semblance of Christmas had leaked into the office of Dr Crichton yet. It had been enough walking through a festive Marylebone High Street on the way, while listening to Deborah's voicemail suggestions for him turning holiday lights on. It would be a miracle, though, if his agent were able to find a London borough that hadn't had them either turned on already, or someone who was happy to have *him* anywhere near their brand after this latest press story. Still, he was here now, in the familiar leather bucket seat, staring at the equally familiar bubbling tank containing the shoal of black fish that all looked like they had teeth. He'd had one pet growing up, a gerbil called Soot. It hadn't lasted long.

He swallowed, eyes moving to the mid-distance, hands either side of the green chair, tapping on its arms as he waited. What he really wanted to do was pick at the leather to distract himself from the waiting, but he suspected, like with most things in this office, it was antique. He didn't want to add criminal damage to the press furore. Deborah would probably drop him as a client... or make him do obedience lessons like her dog. He wasn't sure which would be worse.

The door behind him finally opened and Ray turned his head a little. In strode a beaming Dr Crichton dressed in his trademark three-piece grey suit. The man was either always extremely happy with life, or existing on the verge of being a raging psychopath. Ray hadn't decided which yet. But, as he was his doctor, he was really hoping it wasn't the latter.

'I am so sorry to keep you waiting, Ray. You know what it's like with these celebrity types.' He laughed at his own joke before throwing himself down in the bigger green leather chair that sat behind his large desk. Dr Crichton picked up a glass paperweight and began moving it from hand to hand like it was a cricket ball he was weighing up before a bowl.

'Ariana Grande?' Ray asked with a smirk.

Dr Crichton guffawed, slamming the paperweight into his palm. 'This one would like to be. But it will take quite a lot of my magic to achieve that.' He tapped his nose with a finger. 'But don't say I said so.'

The reality of his visit here scratched at Ray's conscience while that now all-too-familiar ache in his neck scratched at his throat.

'So, to you,' Dr Crichton said, finally putting down the paperweight and leaning over his desk, elbows on the wood, palms together. 'Well, Ray, I'm afraid it's not good news.'

He'd known. Something was *really wrong*, and he had ignored it, for far too long. He had kept it from Deborah. He hadn't even let himself acknowledge it fully. And now...

'But I don't think it's bad news either,' Dr Crichton continued. He manic-grinned, pushing his gold-rimmed spectacles up his nose. 'The endoscope suggests there's nothing that can't be fixed by some rest and an operation.'

'An operation.' He had meant the statement to be in his head, but he'd said it aloud and his voice had cracked on the last word. Immediately, Dr Crichton was up out of his seat, a small torch he'd snatched up from somewhere now in his hand, its light flicking on.

'Open your mouth,' he ordered. 'Is that happening more often?'

Ray was caught between opening his mouth as if he were at the dentist and replying to his doctor's question. 'Does what happen often?' He widened his mouth as the torch came closer, the doctor stooping over him, face close to his as he looked to inspect his throat's inner workings.

'Your voice breaking like that. Hold still.' The doctor put a hand on top of Ray's head as he continued to look, before flicking the torch off and leaning back against the desk.

'I don't know,' Ray answered. 'I suppose... it does sometimes... I just put it down to, you know, maybe when I've had a rough night.'

'Hmm,' Dr Crichton said. 'It all looks inflamed again, Ray. Have you been singing since our last appointment?'

Ray threw his hands up. 'I'm a musician. It's what I do.' He was working on a new album, while he still *had* a record deal. And it was a challenge trying to make this one as good as his first. It also had to be different, somehow more soulful. Not as in the soul music genre, as in actually *coming* from his soul. His best songs always came from a very personal place. They were always stories of who he was, where he had come from and where he wanted to go to. He stayed one step above the very darkest places, but some lyrics had skimmed closer to those places. And, at the moment, with his voice not being on its A-game – plus all this controversy with Ida's claims – inspiration and creativity was taking a battering.

'How about the drinking?' Dr Crichton asked, one eyebrow seeming to raise of its own accord. 'And, so we're clear, I don't mean Aquafina.'

Ray said nothing. Alcohol was sometimes the only thing that made him feel better when the songwriting wasn't hitting the spot. But it wasn't a problem. It was just a tool. Like the breathing techniques he was supposed to be using...

'Ray, this is serious. If you don't listen to my advice and take it on board, there's a chance you won't have a voice at all. And I don't simply mean for singing,' the doctor told him. 'I mean real life-altering issues.'

And there came that pain right between his ears again, as if reminding him that this was affecting every part of his ENT connections.

'So you say,' Ray answered gruffly. God, why was he being so antipathetic? Was he letting the press attention get to him? He'd had years of media scrutiny and usually it ran off him like melting ice from the roof of his three-storey modern townhouse. Except, this time, it felt very different.

'You want a second opinion?' Dr Crichton asked, looking far more maniac than Mr Happy now. 'Because I've discussed your case with three other colleagues already.'

'No,' Ray said, shaking his head, fingers still desperate to pick at the leather on the chair. 'No, I didn't mean that.' What he wanted was some of that alcohol he wasn't meant to be drinking that totally wasn't a problem for him...

'You need rest, Ray,' Dr Crichton continued. 'Your voice needs rest.'

He nodded. He didn't know why he had nodded because Deborah was currently trying to line him up with more appearances to counteract the tabloid stories and save his career. One person saying he needed to sing to distract the press from his personal life and keep his career on track. Another telling him if he *did* sing, he was putting his voice in real jeopardy. And his voice was literally all he had left.

'My advice,' Dr Crichton continued, 'is to stop drinking alcohol completely. Stop singing *completely* for the next week. Practise the breathing techniques we went through last time. Do you need me to print you off another sheet?'

He hadn't looked at the last one. It was screwed up in the fruit bowl that only contained plastic fruit on his coffee table at his house. He shook his head. 'No, I remember.'

'I'm telling you,' Dr Crichton said, fixing Ray with what seemed like a well-practised look of authority. 'You *are* going to need an operation. Lifestyle changes will help, but I strongly suggest you clear your schedule for December. I'll see you here again next week and we will talk about getting you in for surgery before Christmas.'

Ray swallowed, feeling all the tension, but well-practised in not letting it show. He smiled at his doctor. 'No singing, I promise,' he stated calmly. 'Not even in the shower.'

Five

Crowland Terrace, Canonbury, Islington

The bright purple miniature Christmas tree overloaded with silver, gold and a clashing red tinsel in the communal hallway of the period house conversion made Emily smile. She knew it would be the work of Sammie, the little five-year-old who lived in the apartment on the ground floor. Emily had stumbled into a conversation between Sammie and his mum, Karen at the beginning of November when Sammie was insisting that now Halloween was over it was definitely time to start Christmas. Kudos to Karen for hanging out this long. The tree was a little something to make Emily smile as she took the stairs to the top floor apartment she had once shared with Simon, had recently shared with Jonah and now shared with no one but a wardrobe full of vintage apparel she had been indulging in slightly too much to combat the loneliness...

Through the closed door of the flat she could smell the delicious fragrances of Thailand. She closed her eyes.

Definite coconut milk and lemongrass with a hint of spice. Jonah still had his key and had obviously let himself in. Like everything was normal. Like she really still wanted it to be. She sighed. She thought she had done quite a reasonable job at acting pleased Jonah was taking the plunge and moving in with his boyfriend, the lovely Allan – nicknamed Two L's. It had started out as something to avoid spelling confusion but it had stuck. The two men shared a gorgeous apartment not too far away, but Emily still wished she could share Jonah. For a moment she had considered suggesting a scheme whereby he lived with Allan four nights of the week and with her for the other three, but she had never got up the courage to put it out there. Plus, it would have made her look very needy. And women of almost thirty should not really be needy.

Putting the key in the door, Emily let herself in, hurriedly unbuttoning her coat as tropical temperatures assaulted her. This was way too hot. There had to be something wrong with the heating system, because yesterday the climate was definitely North Pole and now it was halfway to the Bahamas.

'Before you say anything!' Jonah called, voice coming from the direction of the kitchen. 'I did not do anything to the heating. And I'm sweating like Bradley Cooper's ex-girlfriend watching *that* Oscars performance just so you know.'

She threw her coat on the blanket-covered sofa, taking a second to enjoy the stars twinkling through the large full-width window that lined the main wall of the spacious lounge room, then went towards the kitchen. Leaning on the doorframe she looked at her best friend at work; he was in his element. Black hair slicked back into the tiniest of ponytails at his nape, apron on over jeans and a slim-fit designer jumper in a coral colour. Jonah was stirring something in her large cooking pot with one hand, while flicking sizzling vegetables in a wok with the other.

'How was work?' he shouted as if she was still in the other room.

'I'm right here,' Emily answered, stepping into the tiny kitchen with only room for the smallest of small tables and two chairs. Jonah seemed to have laid out placemats, glasses of water and cutlery, even added tealights.

'Oh, sorry,' he replied, laughing. 'So, how *was* school? Or are you already at the we-don't-do-anything-but-eat-chocolate-make-christingles-and-watch-*Elf*-on-DVD stage?'

'Rude!' Emily doffed his arm with her hand, her hip nudging one of the chairs as she attempted to shuffle round the slightly too-small space. Yes, the kitchen did leave a lot to be desired, but she could always move the table out into the lounge if she needed to. Except she liked the light and space in the lounge and, now it was just her here, she tended to eat her meals curled up on the sofa in front of Davina's *Long Lost Family*.

She picked the wooden spoon out of Jonah's hand and tasted the culinary creation. Closing her eyes, she revelled in the mix of tastes, all heavenly and perfect, all reminding her of summer evenings out on the roof terrace, Jonah and Simon barbecuing, her trying to get the solar-powered fairy-lights to work before it was too dark to find the wine.

The roof terrace was her favourite part of the apartment. It wasn't huge but it was private and decked and gave her a gorgeous view over the city. And, with the benefit of patio heaters it could be used all year round which more than made up for the limited kitchen space. She gave the spoon back to Jonah before more reverie took hold. 'It's so good,' she said, sighing. 'And it's just what I need after today.'

'Oh?' Jonah asked, putting down the wok, turning off the gas and reaching above the hob for plates.

Where did she start? With Susan having a go about feeding Jayden and helping him with his project? With the cost-cutting? Or the Christmas show…?

She watched Jonah, plating up this spectacular meal, expertly wiping off stray sauce like he was in the hotel kitchen or appearing on *Masterchef*. He was acting like this was some sort of special occasion. Had she missed a date? It wasn't his birthday, that was in March. Or was there really something wrong between him and Two L's? She might have wished for Jonah to return, but not at the expense of his happiness. She loved Allan.

'What's going on?' Emily asked, suddenly really concerned.

'Have a seat,' Jonah said. 'I'll just get out the roti bread.' He bent over, bum hitting a chair. 'You might have to move the table a tad.'

'You made roti bread?' Emily exclaimed, pulling at the table until it shifted an inch, then sitting. 'Now I know something's *really* wrong. What's happening, Jonah?'

'Did you see the cute Christmas tree by the front door. I

thought Sammie did an excellent job.' He still had his back to her, was now avoiding her questioning.

'Jonah! I'm not going to eat anything until you tell me why you're back here cooking Thai food in my minuscule kitchen you moaned about for years, when I know Two L's has luxury granite and Belfast sinks and a built-in griddle.'

Jonah finally turned around and faced her as he lowered an immaculately presented dish to the mat in front of her. 'Dinner is served.'

'You want something,' Emily guessed. 'You realise you really wanted the TV unit you paid half for and you don't know how to tell me. Well, it's yours, Jonah, just like I said. I can fix the telly to the wall or prop it up on a chair, *this* chair in fact, until I find something else.'

Jonah sat down and demolished his carefully constructed dome of rice, forking that and a selection of vegetables and curry into his mouth.

'You can't chew for ever,' Emily reminded, her plate untouched, her eyes on her best friend.

'Don't be mad,' Jonah said, looking tentative about whatever was coming next.

'If you've left Allan I *will* be mad... but, we'll talk about it calmly, until you realise what an idiot you're being.' She gripped her fork. 'It's not that, is it?'

Jonah shook his head and smiled. 'Of course it's not that.'

'Then...' She stopped talking, eyes widening. 'No! You haven't invited my parents over, have you?'

'I don't have a death wish,' Jonah answered.

Emily put a hand to her chest. She never invited her parents over. They knew all the synonyms for 'small' and they used every one of them about *every* room in her home, including the gorgeous roof terrace that her mother, Alegra, had called 'uber bijou' when Emily had first moved in. It had been a stupid guess that they were on their way here. Neither William nor Alegra had approved of her friendship with Jonah since the very first time they'd met at one of her mother's fundraising initiatives. Usually Alegra only put her professional clout and money behind such schemes, not her actual presence. However, back when Emily was ten and she had tonsillitis keeping her off school, Alegra was unable to get out of visiting a less illustrious area of the city where disadvantaged adults were being re-schooled at a community centre. Jonah's dad, it transpired, was taking a qualification in engineering and Jonah had been there outside the centre, on his bike, drinking a high-sugar fizzy drink Emily could usually only dream about. Whilst Alegra talked about the benefit of higher education and how it should very much be available to all – i.e. lied through her teeth – Emily and Jonah had bonded over taking it in turns to do tricks on his bike up and down the skateboard ramp. Despite coming off, tearing her jeans and the skin of her knee open, Emily had loved every minute of it and, quickly swapping addresses, the two friends made a pact to keep in touch. And they had. All this time.

'You need someone to take my room,' Jonah continued quickly.

Emily sighed. 'We talked about this. I'm managing at the moment.' She had that money in the bank. She had a wardrobe full of vintage clothes she didn't really need that she could sell if push came to shove...

'Em, there was literally *nothing* in the fridge and the freezer is empty apart from garden peas and ice cream.'

'I haven't had a chance to go shopping this week.' It was more like this month, but she wasn't going to tell that to Jonah. Beans on toast never harmed anyone and they did all sorts of flavours these days. Plus, it was hard moving on from living with someone who loved creating delicious home-cooked dishes most evenings – several different ones if he wanted to try something new or they needed to stock up that freezer...

'You've taken some of the lightbulbs out.'

She had done that. She read online that if you took some of the lightbulbs out of lamps and ceiling roses you simply got used to prioritising on light and energy, and with that large window in her lounge there was usually more than enough ambient light until at least five o'clock. Well, she hadn't fallen over anything yet...

'I'm saving energy,' she countered. 'We all have to do our bit for the planet.'

'You're cost-cutting,' Jonah stated. 'Because you don't have my rent money for the room. You need the rent money for the room.'

'I really don't want to share my space with anyone else.' She quickly carried on. 'And before you say anything, that wasn't meant to make you feel guilty in any way. I am completely adjusting to you not being here... well, you know.' She inhaled the aromas of her fragrant dinner then dug in, putting some into her mouth and relishing every fine sensation.

'I put an advert up in the hotel,' Jonah admitted.

'What kind of advert?' Emily asked, taking a sip from her water glass.

'The kind that advertises a large double room in a bright and airy apartment in Islington with a compact kitchen, bathroom with bath *and* power shower and a pretty roof terrace with far-reaching views.'

Her apartment. Jonah had taken it upon himself to advertise for a lodger. Suddenly the curry didn't taste so nice. She put down her fork and blinked back rapidly arriving tears.

'Before you say anything,' Jonah began, 'anything at all, this comes from a good place. The best place.' He reached over the table and took hold of her hands. 'I love you, Em, you know that. But you can't carry on living this half-life, hiding from the world and not accepting change.'

She wanted Jonah to stop talking now. Because this was dangerously close to becoming not about his moving in with Allan but about her losing Simon... So why couldn't she think of a thing to say now? Jonah had advertised her space. Without her knowledge. What if someone replied to the advert? Had Jonah given out her mobile number? She took back her hands, eyes watery but currently still contained.

'You should take the advert down,' Emily told him, almost composed.

'It's too late,' Jonah told her. 'Three people called me in response to it.'

'What?!'

'And they're all coming here tonight to see the space.'

'Jonah! You can't do this! This is not who a best friend is.'

'Em, it's exactly who a best friend is! Yes, we're there for the gin and the giggling over *Car Share*, but sometimes we have to do the tough stuff too.' Jonah sighed. 'And this is tough. I know it's tough. I *see* it's tough.' He took another breath. 'Let me try and help to ease the financial burden at least. While I can't be here anymore to stop you wallowing in Paul O' Grady dog programmes.'

People were coming to look at her apartment. She didn't want them here. She was fine on her own. She didn't mind eating baked beans and the occasional still vaguely inside its sell-by-date seafood risotto.

'Listen, they all sounded really keen on the phone... and nice... you know, normal. Normal people looking for a lovely London apartment to live in. And, I promise, if any of them or all of them are really unsuitable, I will be the first one to kick them out of here... but not just because they might come from the wrong side of the city. Everyone deserves an equal chance, right? And I'm not your mum. No offence.'

Why was she still not talking? She should be saying something. She should be mad at Jonah. She should be telling him that there was no way she was going to be spending her precious evening interviewing lodger candidates she didn't want instead of curling up with a litre bottle of flavoured tonic water goggling 'how to create a Broadway-style show on a non-existent budget'.

Jonah took one of her hands back in his and fixed his dark brown eyes on her, adopting that serious, soulful expression he was so good at. 'So, I've bought some new Christmas decorations to spruce the place up a bit and give it that homely, welcoming festive feel and… I took down five of the framed photos of Simon.'

Emily felt her cheeks begin to flame and she tried to remove her hand from Jonah's grip. This was too much. This was not what she wanted at all!

'Let me go!' Emily begged, tugging at her arm. 'You shouldn't have done that.' Tears were falling now. 'Why did you do that?'

'He's gone, Em,' Jonah said, holding on fast as the table wobbled under the duress of their grappling. 'And he's somehow taken most of you with him.'

Jonah needed to stop talking. The nostalgia was gaining momentum now and that was the very last thing she needed after the day at work she had had.

'Em, you don't need photos in every room to remind you who Simon was or how much he meant. You've got all that in here.' He put one hand to his heart and Emily felt another piece of her own heart wither a little as those tears plopped onto the front of her cardigan.

'Shit,' Jonah said. 'I didn't mean to make you cry like this. Allan and I talked about it last night and he said I had to go gentle with you, but we both agreed this is what you need.'

'You should have talked to me about it,' Emily finally spoke. 'You went behind my back.'

'You wouldn't have listened to me, Em. I've been suggesting this since before I moved out.'

She knew he had a point. Jonah was her best friend for a reason. He knew her better than she knew herself. And she also knew that this 'moving forward' scenario he was putting out to her would not have moved at all if he had discussed it with her first. She had two choices now. She either met these potential flatmates or she told Jonah to cancel them before any of their feet hit the natural floorboards.

Emily took an edifying breath. 'OK... so... tell me... do any of the candidates cook?'

Six

Earl of Essex, Danbury Street

The first pint had gone down quickly, coating Ray's throat with a pleasing fizz. The second delivered that slightly blurry-at-the-edges feeling where real life seemed to matter a little less, problems diminished and headlines in the tabloid newspapers weren't quite as scary as they had appeared at eight o'clock that morning.

He had the newspapers in front of his eyes now, sitting on a bar stool in the most dimly lit corner, the dark duck egg painted walls sadly enhanced by hanging silver bells and posters announcing the new festive menu. *Fucking Christmas*. He knew he shouldn't be adding to his misery by reading any of these false stories – literal fake news – but Deborah always banged on about forewarned being forearmed and she had texted him earlier telling him *Loose Women* wanted him on tomorrow's show. She had also said that to 'get out in front of this story' was probably the only way they were going to be able to kill the controversy.

Ray took a gulp of his pint and looked at the photos the press had used. Great, there was one of him appearing less than his best after a concert after-party. He had definitely been drunk that night. He barely remembered getting home. In fact, he'd fallen asleep at the piano.

And then there was a photo of Ida. Was it one a photographer had taken recently? Had they interviewed her at his former home? Who had initiated the contact? A journalist pressing for any hint of disgrace to fuel a story, offering wads of cash or opportunities for Ida's art? Or had Ida herself gone looking for this? For monetary gain... or simply to hurt him?

He ran his finger over the ink on the page, tracing the light blonde hair of his ex-girlfriend. She looked sad in this photo, frail. Was that who she was now? Was that regret in her eyes about how things had ended for them? He swallowed. Whatever it was, there was no going back. No matter what the media did to try to destroy him, his life with Ida was over.

Ray's phone vibrated in the pocket of his jeans. It would be Deborah. Asking him again to consider the daytime chat show. He couldn't do it, could he? Sit in front of a live audience, being scrutinised by a panel of celebrity women asking him about his private life. *His life with Ida.* He reached for his drink and took another large swig. He looked at the glass in his hand, the lick of white foam clinging to the inside. Was this how his mother had felt? Had *her* life been in some way out of control like his and no one had really realised? He missed his mum. No matter how much of a screw-up she had been, he'd loved her. And she had loved him. He'd really felt that, despite everything.

Perhaps what was happening in his life now was simply his own fault. Maybe he should have considered all the trappings of celebrity before he'd got caught up right in the middle of it. But, then again, it had been such a virtual whirlwind, there had been little time to think at all. One moment he'd been playing weekly sets at a tiny pub in Camden Town and fitting busking around bricklaying, the next, he'd been catapulted to fame on TV's *Lyricist* – the songwriting equivalent of *The Voice*. That had been three years ago and, up until now, he had managed to keep his star, if not on a constantly constant rise, at least holding its own amongst his contemporaries. And Ida had been there for most of it. Seeing him grow from show contestant to singing at the Royal Variety Performance for the Queen.

When they'd met, Ida had had no idea who he was. He and a couple of the other acts on *Lyricist* had been asked to perform at the opening of an art gallery. It was a small affair but publicised a great deal more because of the attendance of the *Lyricist* contestants. And, after his song, Ray had looked at the paintings and the – mostly phallic – sculptures, wondering what any of them really meant. Ida had stood next to him, seeming to sense his difficulty in comprehending exactly what he was looking at and she had described what turned out to be *her* painting. It had been a magpie on top of a high-rise building not dissimilar to the Shard, one wing spread wide, the other somehow buckled. Ida said it represented modern-day life. *We are all aspiring to reach the highest of levels, but to get there sometimes we have to break a little bit.* Ray had listened all the more intently then, longing for her to carry on talking, this blonde, ethereal-looking girl dressed in a ruby red ballgown with Vans on her feet. *And when you get there, broken, no one usually wants you anymore.* Her words had really hit home, her eyes had called to him and that had been their beginning…

The sound of smashing glass made him jump on his stool. He held his breath, his gaze going along the bar to a group of women. One of them had dropped a wine flute to the floor. They were laughing, happy, fine. The barman was already coming around with a dustpan and brush. He steadied his breathing, and then he felt the vibrations start again. His mobile. Not a message this time but a call coming through. He pulled his phone out and checked the screen. *Gio.* His landlord.

'Hey, Gio,' Ray greeted, on answering. 'Listen, before you say anything about the rent…'

'There is nothing to say about the rent. Nothing at all,' the Italian voice galloped. 'I have been saying all that I need to be saying for the past eight weeks.'

'Gio, I know, I know, and I apologise, but I'm between situations right now. I'm waiting to untie funds that are bonded and…' God, he really needed that advance from the record company. Gio had been patient. The credit card companies were unlikely to afford him such grace for much longer.

'I see the newspapers. And I see it all before,' Gio carried on.

Ray could visualise him right now, round face turning red, hands waving around in the air. He almost sensed what was coming and he braced his core as he focused on the sign for Christmas party nights with stuffing balls *and* cranberry sauce…

'I have given you warning, Ray. *Written* warning last

month. I am sorry, Ray, I like you, I really do. I do not want to believe what they write in the news, but I have my business to think about.'

'Gio, I will get you your rent money. Just let me call my agent. We can sort something out.' His hand tightened around the pint glass, preparing to take a hit.

'*I* sort things out,' Gio responded. 'This morning I arrange for all your stuff to be taken to storage. I have emailed you the details. The locks of the house, they have been changed. I have someone new moving in tomorrow.'

His stuff had been taken to storage! The locks had been changed! He should have gone home between coffee with Deborah and the meeting with Dr Crichton. He shouldn't have come here for an alcoholic crutch to lean on... The blurry-edged bit of him said he should shout, tell his landlord that he had no right moving any of his stuff. The still-hanging-on-to-sober half of him said there was nothing he could say to change the end result. Gio had made his decision.

'You are still there?' Gio asked. 'You listen to what I tell you?'

'Yeah,' Ray answered. 'Yeah, I'm here. And I hear you.'

As days went, being torn apart by the British press, finding out you need an operation and now being homeless, it was pretty up there on the shite scale. All it needed to really top it off was a festive Cliff Richard song...

'Well, you know, no hard of the feelings,' Gio said, voice slightly less punchy. 'You have a good Christmas.'

'Yeah,' Ray answered with a sigh. 'You too.'

Seven

Crowland Terrace, Canonbury, Islington

'Any hobbies, Anthony?'

It was Jonah asking the question because Emily was still sitting in horror-stricken awe that Anthony, who had seen the advert for the spare room while he was delivering bottled water to the hotel Jonah worked at, had eaten almost all of the Tesco Finest Mature Cheddar and Red Onion crisps she'd planned to make last a week. *And* he also didn't seem to care that when he talked, he was spattering crumbs over her sofa. Jonah had always been very careful with snacks. Jonah was neat and tidy. Damn Two L's and his courtship with her friend...

Anthony also looked like he had been dressed head-to-toe by Sports Direct. Not that there was anything wrong with tracksuits and box-fresh Adidas, but the style and the scattergun crisp-eating seemed slightly at odds.

'Hobbies?' Anthony queried, as though he didn't understand the word.

'Things you do at the weekend?' Jonah elaborated.

'I have to tell you what things I like to do at the weekend to get a spot here?' Anthony asked.

'No,' Emily said, leaping up off the sofa and almost knocking over the black and silver Christmas tree Jonah had pitched on the lamp table. It was really very Habitat and she wasn't quite sure how she felt about it. 'No, of course you don't.' She picked up the bowl of snacks, cradling them protectively like a newborn. 'I think we've asked you lots of questions already.'

'So, I get the room?' Anthony asked, all smiles.

'No,' Emily said firmly. 'I mean… we don't quite know yet.' She took a breath. 'We have a couple of other people to see and then there's the… two months' rent we will need up front.' She had said 'we' deliberately, even though it was 'I'. And she had made up that clause on the spot. She knew she couldn't live with Anthony. Just like she knew she couldn't live with the first potential lodger to come through the door. He'd been called Lee and he had talked non-stop about London's Murder Mile walks…

'Two months up front?' Anthony and Jonah said this sentence together and then looked at each other like they were twin spirit animals.

'We have your number,' Emily said. She had no idea if Jonah had Anthony's number or not and she didn't care. 'So, we will let you know.' Yes! He was getting to his feet! As soon as he was out of the flat, she was going to get the Hoover out.

'To be straight up with you I don't think I can pull together two months' rent straightaway,' Anthony said.

'No, oh, well, that's a shame. Sorry,' Emily said, sighing for effect. Jonah was looking pretty cross with her now. Her best friend got to his feet and flashed her a dark look.

'I'll show you out,' Jonah said.

No sooner had Jonah and Anthony left her lovely lounge, Emily was up, going into the cupboard that housed Hoover, ironing board, a small collection of bags for life and the old Christmas decorations right at the back. There was limited storage space in the apartment, but it did help achieve minimalism... except in her bedroom wardrobe. Minimalism no longer had a place there now it was bursting with vintage clothes she hadn't worn yet. The ones she should wear before she had to sell them to prevent sharing her space with someone like Lee or Anthony.

Plugging the vacuum in, she moved the end over the crisp bits on the floorboards, then, detaching the stick, she set the brush onto the upholstery. The cleaning was lately almost as therapeutic as the compulsive clothes shopping...

A side-eye to the door told Emily that Jonah was back in the room and he was mouthing words she didn't want to listen to. She did what anyone would do. She pretended she could neither see him nor hear him. She kept on brushing with the hand-held section of the vacuum.

Finally, after at least ten strokes forward and back she could no longer ignore Jonah who had stood directly in front of her and was now flicking off the vacuum switch causing an immediate heavy silence until...

'Emily, you can't do that to everyone who comes to view the place.'

'Do what?'

'Judge them with higher standards than Judge Rinder!' Jonah exclaimed. 'Demand two months' rent up front! No one normal has that sort of money, especially at this time of year!'

'Well...' Emily said, hands still on the Hoover, eyes on half a crisp peeking out from under the sofa. 'They do if they are serious about finding a nice place to live. Decisions like that should come with saving up and a lot of thought. Before I took on this place I had to save up for ages.' Even though her parents had offered to buy her a flat for a birthday present. That's what Alegra and William were like. Happy to throw money around like it was confetti. And accepting anything like that from them would have come with some sort of hidden clause. A monthly dinner maybe or, even worse, a family holiday. So, she had decided to rent, and her agreement allowed her to take in a lodger.

'Well,' Jonah said, 'some people haven't got the means to save up, have they? I didn't when I moved in.' His hands were on his hips now and he was still looking less than pleased with her.

'I know,' Emily said, 'but you're my best friend. You have years' worth of credentials on your side. Like... knowing the best chip shops and... all the wi-fi codes for every coffee shop in the borough so you can instantly connect me.'

'Did you think either of them were attractive though?' Jonah asked slightly too quietly, like it was a sentence meant to drift into her subconscious.

'What?' Emily asked. She lifted her head then and reattached the wand to the Hoover's motor section with a snap.

'Anthony and Lee,' Jonah reminded. 'Both very good-looking guys in my opinion.' He sniffed. 'And I am an aficionado on good-looking guys.'

'Why would it matter if they were good-look...?' Then Emily suddenly got it. The next person due to come walking through the door was called Raul. Jonah had said he was twenty-eight, had Portuguese heritage and was currently working the bar at Jonah's hotel. This wasn't simply about getting a new person in her spare room, this was also about letting a new person into her knickers. Now *she* was the one who was mad.

She shook her head at Jonah, gripping the vacuum rod like she wanted it to turn into a jousting lance. 'I don't believe it. *That's* why you wanted to take down the photos of Simon.'

'Now, Em, it isn't quite like that.'

'Isn't quite like what?' Emily snapped, stomping to the cupboard and shoving the vacuum cleaner back in. 'Isn't quite like you trying to matchmake me with someone while they move right into my personal space as well?! Cereal packets abutting mine. Mixed washing in the machine. Then what were you hoping for? An adjoining door from my room to the spare? Followed by king-size mattress-dancing?'

'No,' Jonah said defiantly. 'No... not really.'

'See! I'm right!' Emily exclaimed, blowing her fringe upwards off her forehead. 'None of the applicants are female. Why is that?'

Jonah shrugged but he looked deeply sheepish now and Emily knew him inside and out. Why hadn't she seen this coming? Maybe this had been Jonah's plan for a long time. Perhaps he and Two L's had discussed it. Move Jonah out, move a Mr Single in...

'Pure chance,' Jonah offered as an explanation. 'I mean, if none of these guys end up being suitable, although I have high hopes for Raul, I'll put the advertisement up again and who knows what gender will respond.'

'You won't put the advert up again!' Emily exclaimed, raising her arms in frustration. 'Because I didn't want the advert up in the first place. I'm fine! I miss you and your gorgeous cooking and maybe our weekend film marathons, but you're only a few Tube stops away and... you'll come over on Christmas, won't you?'

'Yes,' Jonah said. 'Yes, of course I will, but that isn't it, is it?'

Emily sniffed the air. 'Did you leave the cooker on?' She took a step towards the kitchen. 'I think I can smell something burning.' Jonah took her arm before she could escape the talk she knew was coming.

'Em, you need to get back out there. You know that, right?'

'Back out where? To cringy dating scenarios that are more awkward than... wondering if it's a double kiss greeting or a single kiss greeting at one of my parents' cocktail parties?'

'When was the last dating scenario you actually had? Cringy or otherwise?'

She hadn't had any since she lost Simon. She needed to make one up quickly.

Emily rolled her eyes. 'This photocopier repair man at school... his name was... Willy...' Her lips were somehow desperate to form the word 'Wonka'. 'Willy Wallace,' she continued. 'And he offered to share his cheese and pickle sandwich with me. I mean,' Emily rolled her eyes again. 'What a chat-up line.'

'Em,' Jonah said, softly. 'I don't believe you.'

'Well!' Emily said, folding her arms across her chest.

'If there *had* been a photocopier repair man called Willy who offered you his lunch box, you wouldn't have even noticed the invitation.' Jonah sighed. 'You're not being open to opportunity.'

'I am,' Emily said insistently. Why were her eyes tearing up? She focused on the newly acquired Christmas tree, knowing she would be taking it down later and replacing it with the trusty old one. The trusty, old one she had bought with Simon. It was ridiculously hard to put together, with more sections than an Ikea warehouse, but it held memories. Memories of the times they had sipped mulled wine and eaten mince pies while sorting the branches into colour-coded piles. Some years it had been a two-night task.

'I know it's really, *really* hard, but it's been a year now...'

And it still feels like yesterday. 'I'm fine,' she said, one stray tear making its way down her cheek.

'I know you're fine. But I want my best friend to be more than fine. I want her to be ready to... scale new heights and achieve all her dreams.'

Jonah drew her into a hug and she breathed in the scent of him. Thai spice and the sculpting clay he used on his hair. Was Jonah right? Was she walking around like she had a 'do not approach' sign around her neck? When *had* she last looked at life with wide, excited eyes and a fire in her belly?

'Do I have to see Raul?' Emily muttered into Jonah's comforting shoulder. Tired, still slightly sweaty from the seemingly out-of-control heating, Emily simply wasn't ready to face a new beginning tonight.

'Yes, you have to see Raul, because it's too late to cancel.' Jonah held her away from him and wiped the tear from her cheek. 'But, if he really isn't suitable, then maybe I'll rethink this flatmate-matchmake plan.'

'So, there *was* a plan!' Emily exclaimed.

Jonah sighed. 'It was Allan's idea… OK, that's unfair, it was *my* idea, but he signed off on it. Sorry. We just want you to be happy, Em.'

'Well,' Emily said. 'If you want me to be happy, help me get the old Christmas tree out of the cupboard and tell me you know *someone* with musical ability who can help me organise the school Christmas show this year.'

'They put *you* in charge of the show?' Jonah put a hand over his mouth, stifling a laugh.

'Yes,' Emily answered. 'And this Christmas it's not simply singing a few carols and dressing everyone in tea-towels. No,' she said, 'this year Susan Clark wants a festive Broadway production with new music John Lewis will commission for next year's *special* advert.'

Jonah pointed a finger at her, a wry grin on his face. 'Opportunity,' he said. 'You might not feel it yet but maybe this performance could be a whole kind of life-changing.'

'Yes,' Emily agreed with a nod, heading towards the cupboard-of-household again. 'The kind of life-changing that sees me ejected out of teaching for ever.' She looked at Jonah, feeling slightly smug. 'How's that for positive?'

'Well,' Jonah mused. 'Leaving teaching would please your mum. She would have your head measured for that barrister's wig before you'd stuck on a Christmas Day paper hat.'

Emily checked her watch. 'What time was Raul due? I'll

tell him there's been a mistake. That the spare room is really with two lovely guys just a few Tube stops from here.'

'You wouldn't dare.'

'No,' Emily answered. 'You're right. I'd just advertise it in the staff room at school. Dennis *has* been living with his mother since for ever.'

The doorbell rang and they looked at each other, neither moving to answer it.

'Shall we pretend we're out?' Emily suggested, one eyebrow raised.

'We can't,' Jonah said, heading towards the door. 'He has the cutest puppy dog eyes. Any letting down will have to be done *extremely* gently… by me.'

Eight

New North Road, N1

Ray had had two choices after the third pint with no home to go to. He either phoned Deborah, agreed to do *Loose Women* and asked for a bed for the night. Or he phoned his dad. Neither of those choices immediately appealed so he hadn't called anyone. And he'd made no decision about anything at all until after the fourth pint. Then he had got on a Tube and ended up here, New North Road, looking up at the high-rise block of flats he had spent his childhood in. It looked no different to how it had looked back then. It was still an ugly Kit-Kat of a building. Two fingers of towers with a slightly sunken inset section in the middle. When he was younger Ray and his friends had all joked the location looked like the worst of settings for re-enactments on *Crimewatch*, but then there were three muggings and a stabbing within two weeks, and no one laughed anymore. The community had rallied though. Instead of closing their doors and hiding away from it, the residents had set up a neighbourhood watch scheme and invited the police to meetings to share information, together hoping to help combat the drug and gang culture that threatened to swallow up their desperate youth.

So, here he was, back, looking for a roof over his head, when he had spent most of his life trying to escape the place. It was the fullest of circles. Ten floors up, his dad, Len, was still in the same council flat he'd been living in for the past thirty-plus years probably still smoking his way to lung cancer. Hands in the pockets of his dark three-quarter-length coat, Ray took a long slow breath of the freezing cold night like it was the last chest full of fresh air he was going to get, then he headed for the lobby and the urine-impregnated bank of lifts.

It was a bed for one night. He could make amends for one night. He couldn't even remember what he and his dad had argued about in the first place. He just knew that in six months neither of them had been man enough to pick up the phone and make the first move towards reconciliation... or simply agree to forget whatever-it-was that had riled them up in the first place.

Getting out of the elevator, Ray walked from the lobby and onto an external corridor until he was standing outside number 1021. The shiny, gold, numbers were bright on the centre of a newly painted green door. Gone was the old, seventies-style, cheap door sticker number. Was the brightening up his dad's doing? Or was this the council spending some of their budget on making the building look less war zone and more up-and-coming?

Ray raised a hand to knock, then hesitated. There seemed to be a doorbell now. There hadn't been a doorbell the last time he was here. He pressed the button and, through the door, even *he* could hear the chimes of 'Jingle Bells' announcing his arrival. His dad not only had a doorbell, it was a doorbell you could apparently program with festive tunes...

As that thought went through his mind, the door was heaved open and a woman in her fifties greeted him. Big hair the colour of Guinness – dark curls, creamy on top – huge gold earrings in her ears and a purple sequinned dress over the rest of her.

'Deliveroo?' the woman asked, looking Ray up and down.

'Who?'

'Where's the kebabs?'

'I don't know,' Ray answered as the woman stepped out of the flat and began turning a circle around him as if she was looking to find an insulated bag about his person. She was so close, her expression accusing. He took a step back away from her. 'I'm not delivering food, I...'

The woman beat a hasty retreat back inside the house and folded her arms across her chest, about to draw the door closed. 'If you're gonna pretend to read the gas meter before rooting through our stuff for our life savings, I can save you the bother. We ain't got nothing!'

She was making to shut the door. She hadn't recognised him. He didn't even know who *she* was. Had his dad moved? Not told him he'd moved? Were things *that* bad between them?

'Brenda, is it the kebabs or not? You're letting the cold in and I didn't turn this new fire on for nothing, did I?'

His dad's voice. He *was* still here. So, who was this woman, Brenda? He needed to find his voice.

'I'm Ray,' he said quickly, before the door could move another inch. 'Ray Stone.' There was not a flicker of recognition in this woman's eyes. Was she a home help? Had his dad's health deteriorated? No, a home help wouldn't be organising the delivery of kebabs, would she? Or wearing sequins… 'I'm Len's son.'

That seemed to hit the spot. The door stopped creeping to a close and, such was the cold, Ray really did long to be invited in for some of whatever this new fire had to offer. He shivered, shoving his hands into the pockets of his coat.

Then, suddenly, he was sucked into Brenda's bosom, the purple sequins of her dress crinkling against this coat, her hair getting in his mouth.

'Why didn't you say so? I should have recognised you! You've grown a beard. You didn't have a beard on those photos they were putting up with Piers Morgan this morning. Ooh, it's so good to finally meet you. I kept saying to Len we should have you round. See what we've done to the place. I've got one of your CDs somewhere. Would you sign it for me?'

All the 'we's' being thrown in there were more distracting than the asking for a signed CD. Did Brenda live here? With his dad? Was she ever going to let him go? Finally, there was a release and Brenda stepped back and ushered him with both hands.

'Come in! Come in! Len, your Ray is here!' she bellowed, letting Ray step over the threshold before her.

He held his breath as he stepped into the narrow hallway that was the corridor to all the other rooms. Before, it had always been painted a rather gruesome shade of red. The paint had been discounted at the shop and his dad had said it wouldn't show up any marks. Now though it was wallpapered, a soft, creamy colour with a fluffy dandelion head pattern. Brenda was behind him now, a hand at the small of his back.

'Go on. Go on through. Your dad is in his usual spot in that bloody old reclining chair. I said to him, I said, that thing must have fleas living in it by now and it doesn't go with anything else we've done, but he insisted on keeping it. Go on through, love.'

Such was Brenda's insistence he keep on moving into the lounge, there was no time for thinking about what he was going to say once he was face-to-face with his dad. In seconds there was Len, sitting in the ancient chair, its white, heavily embroidered upholstery stained and faded. The rest of the lounge was transformed like the hallway. It was muted greys and light yellows with a new sofa and fluffy cushions. It was very different to how it had been before.

And his dad didn't even turn his head to greet him. He remained stoic, eyes on the television showing the Challenge channel, bald head covered by slithers of silver, swept back with Brylcreem, cigarette between his fingers. He looked a little thinner, Ray decided. Was he ill? Was this why Brenda was here? Was she just a friend? Or was she a girlfriend? He didn't know how he felt about that last idea. He had never thought his dad would want to share his life again. *Naïve, Ray. Always still so naïve when it came to matters of the heart.*

'It's Norway, you berk, not Iceland!' Len took a draw on the cigarette, puffing out a cloud of smoke that seemed to expand quickly into every inch of the room. 'I don't know where they drag these contestants in from, Brenda.'

So, Len didn't appear ready for reconciliation. He didn't seem to want to acknowledge Ray's presence at all. This wasn't a good start and Ray was beginning to regret coming here.

'Turn that bloody thing off!' Brenda ordered, striding past Ray and grabbing the remote control from the arm of Len's chair. She pointed it at the television like it was a Taser set to maim and Bradley Walsh and *The Chase* disappeared from the screen.

'I was watching that!' Len exploded. 'Now I won't know who wins or what money they end up with!'

'Your son is here!' Brenda said, pointing at Ray.

Ray wanted to step backwards, out of sight, down the corridor and back out into the cold. This was definitely a mistake.

Len forcefully stubbed his cigarette out and picked up a newspaper.

'Len!' Brenda exclaimed. 'Speak to your son!'

'Tell him I've got nothing to say to him,' Len growled.

'Leonard!' Brenda shouted.

'It's OK,' Ray said. 'I'll go. I shouldn't have come.' He was going to find the nearest pub and top up his alcohol level before finding a hotel for the night. One of his credit cards had to have something left on it. Or, even if it didn't, he could go old-school, find an all-night café or a park bench. His mum had often been found asleep on more benches than London had cabs.

'No, you won't go!' Brenda ordered him. 'You'll sit

down, and I'll make us some hot chocolates. We've got the one from Whittard's with coconut in.'

'That'll be wasted on him unless it's filled with whisky,' Len remarked. 'Just like his mother.'

'Leonard!' Brenda snapped straightaway. She looked at Ray, her eyes soft. 'I don't know what's got into him today,' she said. 'I ordered us the kebabs as a treat as well.'

'It's OK,' Ray said. 'There's actually somewhere else I need to be so...'

He wasn't going to let his dad's words hurt him. His dad had always blamed his mum for everything. Except Ray had seen both sides of things. It hadn't been a perfect marriage by any means, and he believed his father's long working hours, no matter how desperate they were for cash, had definitely contributed to his mum's drinking hobby. She was bored. She wanted more from life. She found solace at the bottom of a bottle. Maybe everyone was a little bit to blame...

'Oh, I bet there is,' Len said, hands on both sides of the chair, pushing himself up to a standing position. He did look a little weaker than Ray remembered. 'A pub, is it? Then back home to beat your girlfriend?'

He should feel anger and disappointment. But, looking at Len's expression of disgust he just felt sad. Len had shut him out when his mum had died. And in the end, music and Ray's fame had driven them further and further apart. There was no pride in what his son had achieved, only disdain that Ray hadn't pursued plumbing. *No one made anything of themselves by forgetting their roots.*

'We don't believe what they're saying,' Brenda said

quickly. 'I said to your dad earlier that everything on the news these days is faker than those handbags on Camden market.'

'You don't have to apologise for him,' Ray said, through gritted teeth. 'My mother always said he'd been angry at the world since Tottenham lost the 1987 FA Cup Final.'

'Your mother,' Len snarled, 'has been facing the world with a vodka in her hand since about the same time!'

'Had,' Ray said coolly. 'She *had* been facing the world.'

'Lovey,' Brenda said, all diplomatic envoy. 'Take a seat. Let me make a hot chocolate."

'He's only here 'cause he wants something,' Len carried on, picking up his cigarette packet then selecting a fag with his lips and pulling it out. 'Mark my words.' He lit up the cigarette and sucked greedily. 'He'll have pissed his money down the urinal at The Black Dog and his career's in the shitter because he couldn't keep his fists to himself and he's probably heard about our luck on the gee-gees.'

'Still down the betting shop every day then,' Ray commented.

'Piss off!' Len shouted, arms flying out. 'Don't you come here thinking you're better than us. I've told you before, having your fucking name on a sign at the Palladium doesn't make you fucking Frank Sinatra.'

'And spending all day studying form in Ladbrokes doesn't make you Sheik Mohammed!' He took a deep breath and faced Brenda. 'Listen, you seem really nice, but you're deluding yourself if you think you can change him into a half-decent human being. It was good to meet you and...' He was running out of things to say but he knew he was leaving before the takeaway arrived or before the hot chocolate could be offered for a third time. 'I like what you've done with the flat.'

'Yeah, that's right,' Len shouted as Ray made his way down the hall towards his escape. 'Fuck off when the going gets too tough for you. As I said, just like your mother!'

'Ray, love, please, don't go yet,' Brenda called as Ray rushed down the corridor and quickly opened the front door.

He wasn't stopping. The freezing cold air blasted him as he stepped outside, and he almost barrelled into a girl on a bike wearing a Deliveroo tabard.

'Kebabs?' she asked, holding them out to Ray.

'Inside,' Ray replied roughly. 'And if you've forgotten the chilli sauce, I wouldn't hang around waiting for a tip.'

Nine

Crowland Terrace, Canonbury, Islington

Raul had had the most gorgeous dark eyes. But he had also talked at a million miles an hour, mainly about his endless number of cousins who Emily had suspected would all have been visiting her apartment over Christmas singing *Feliz Navidad* if she had accepted him into her spare room. Working at a primary school, she didn't have a complete aversion to noise, but her flat was her sanctuary, it was where she came to escape the models of 'What Christmas Means to Me' and Orange Justice dance routines in the playground. It was where she had cosied up with Simon.

Leaning a little from her curled-up position on the sofa she reached for one of the photo frames she had put back in place as soon as Jonah had left. She brushed a finger over Simon's mousey-coloured hair, down his cheek then over his bright smile. Simon had smiled more than the average person smiled. It might be a cliché, but it was true, he really had been one of life's beautiful people, inside and out. And their meeting had been so completely random there could have been every chance they might never have met at all... if her Oyster card had worked like it worked on every other day.

That fateful evening, Emily had tapped her card on the pad and made to push on through, but the barrier had remained closed and she had banged into it with such force it had prompted an audible grunt, which was most unlike her. She'd taken a step back and tapped again, very aware that at rush hour on a Friday she was holding up a long queue of commuters all equally desperate to make it home or to their favourite pub. Still the gates remained shut. She turned around, looking at the large man stood very close behind her waiting for his turn. She either had to try for a third time or she needed to shimmy out and try an alternative gate. But then Simon had arrived, asking very politely for people to move out of *his* way. He'd slipped through the not-really-there space between gate and large-man-behind-Emily and handed her his Oyster card.

'Thank you. Ever so much. But, I can't take that,' Emily said. 'How will *you* get through the gate?'

'Ah,' Simon had said, a twinkle in lovely deep blue eyes that she'd noticed instantly. 'If you don't use it you won't get to find out.'

'Come on! This is madness! Some of us actually want to get home tonight!' The large man was getting beetroot cheeks despite it being November cold.

'Go on,' Simon urged. 'Honestly.'

Emily had pressed his card to the pad and the previously unmoving grey gates had flipped open almost joyously. Through to the other side, she turned, preparing to give her saviour back his card, only to be greeted by the sea of travellers edging backwards again. Simon had dropped to the floor and was commando-crawling underneath the gate, his smart grey trousers and thin-knit cream jumper rubbing the floor of the Underground like a human mop. He was going to be filthy when he got up. He was ruining his clothes to save her an extra fare.

Simon had got up now, brushing down his dirty clothes like it was inconsequential. 'Well,' he said, smiling so genuinely. 'It's been a while since I've done that.'

Emily hadn't been able to help smiling back at him. His good nature had always been so infectious. 'So, you make a habit of helping female commuters in distress?'

'Oh no,' Simon had replied. 'I don't limit it to females. The last time I went under the gate it was for a Hungarian weightlifter who was on his way to a tournament, carrying actual barbells.'

Emily had giggled. She vividly remembered everything about their very first conversation and how it had instantly made her feel light inside.

Simon had smiled again. 'I know you're meant to ask someone for assistance but at rush hour there never seems to be anyone around *to* ask... and, what can I say? I'm English, we don't like to make a fuss. We keep calm and carry on.' He pumped a fist in the air.

'Or keep calm and crawl under a gate,' Emily had answered.

'And long for a cup of properly brewed tea,' Simon had added.

She had longed for a cup of tea from the moment Simon's suggestion had hit the air of the Underground. The simplest of ideas, practical yet oddly romantic. And he had continued the theme...

'Would you like a cup of tea? Or a coffee? Or beer?' He had pushed up one sleeve of his jumper and looked at his watch. 'It's officially past five o'clock so we Brits can have a beer without feeling a modicum of guilt.'

Emily had laughed again. 'Actually, a cup of tea would be lovely.'

'Great!' Simon had replied, seemingly elated. 'I mean, very good.' He brushed more dust from his jumper. 'I'm Simon by the way.' He had held out his hand.

'Emily,' she'd answered, shaking his offering rather formally.

'It's nice to meet you, Emily.'

'You too.'

They'd both nervously smiled and lingered, the rush of the Friday commute carrying on around them. It was like they portrayed in those romantic films, two people connecting, unaware of anything else in the moment...

'I have to say,' Simon had begun, 'just for the record, I didn't offer the Hungarian weightlifter a cup of tea.'

Emily had laughed and Simon had laughed, and they'd walked side-by-side out of the station and into a cosy coffee shop where they'd ordered tea and two slabs of a chocolate fruitcake. And that's how two entirely separate people had become an 'us'.

Emily sighed now, replacing the photo frame on the lamp table. She was still sad. It was still so hard to move on when part of her thought that making that transition would be putting Simon and what he had meant to her in a box along with their memories...

The phone rang and Emily got up to answer it. It could only be one of two people. Either Two L's under instruction from Jonah to try and cajole her into giving renting out her spare room proper consideration, or it was the woman from the diet plan who had phoned last night and had been very persistent about ringing again at a more convenient time.

She answered. 'Hello.'

'Julian, I can't do Tuesday or Wednesday, I told you that already.'

Emily sighed. It was her mother. Multitasking as usual. Alegra Parker making a call while chatting to one of her minions at the same time was par for the course and Alegra saw no problem with it. Emily always thought it was the height of rudeness but even when she pointed this out – diplomatically of course – it went straight over her mother's court wig. She should say hello again, prompt her mother into realising she had actually picked up. But sometimes it was more fun to listen…

'The Nobles are anything but, Julian. These people think because they own a house in Madeira it puts them right up there with the Duke of Westminster. We need to remind them that isn't the case every now and then.'

Emily bit her lip. Her mother the snob. There was never any change there. She had definitely heard enough.

'Hello,' Emily greeted again, this time super-loud. She took the phone back to the sofa and sat down, pulling a blanket up around her. The tropical climate had changed to sub-zero now and despite much button pressing on the boiler the appliance seemed to have developed a mind of its own. She had tried to phone her landlord – three times – and it had kept going to voicemail. She hadn't left a message yet.

'Oh, Emily, you're there already,' Alegra answered.

She could imagine Alegra in her barrister's chambers, one hand on the phone, the other at her diary – manicured fingernail running down a list of appointments – eyes calling her assistant to get her a coffee or bring her a file she could peruse while she was having a conversation with her daughter.

'Yes, I'm here,' Emily said. She really didn't have the energy for this conversation after the day and evening she'd had. She needed to conserve a little oomph in order to remove all the modern Christmas decoration props Jonah had put up and replace them with ones she actually liked. And, just for tonight, she was completely ignoring the fact she had been put in charge of the school's Christmas show…

'I can't talk for long,' Alegra began. 'But keep a week next Friday free.'

'What?' Emily asked, sitting forward, the blanket falling from under her neck. 'Why?' A deep chill invaded her bones now. Her mother wasn't coming here, was she? Near to Christmas her parents did usually, in some sort of fit of guilt, decide to phone more, turn up more, engage better… but it never lasted through to the new year.

'Why, she asks?' Alegra replied with a tut. 'Emily, we have this conversation every year.'

Oh God! Emily now knew what was coming next. She couldn't believe she had forgotten. It was the only time her mother really needed her and admitted to it… that was, *almost* admitted to it.

'It's the St Martin's Chambers Community Day Planning Committee's get-together. It's the one day this side of Spring free in all our diaries. Would you believe it?'

And, of course, Emily's diary was completely free of

anything all the time unless it involved sticky back plastic. 'Day?' Emily checked. 'I work in the day.'

'We all work in the day, Emily. I meant the one "date". So, pencil it in. A week next Friday. Dinner with Mummy and Daddy and all of Mummy and Daddy's clever friends planning our doing good day for next year.'

Still, how they hated doing good. Like when she was ten, they only did good to *look* good, in the eyes of the law – literally all their colleagues and other counterparts – and in the media. Emily had long since stopped worrying about their reasoning for charity work. It should matter, but ultimately it was more important to her that they used some of their wealth for worthy causes no matter how they spun it in the press. And any chance she got to see her mother and father in overalls with rubber gloves on was a bonus she didn't hesitate taking photos of. It had been her suggestion they spent a day at the dog shelter, and she made sure to let the manager know how keen her parents were to really muck in... or actually, muck out.

'Pencil it in?' Emily asked. 'As in, the date isn't officially, 100 per cent decided yet?'

'No, it's decided,' Alegra said pointedly. 'I said it was decided. The only date we all had free in our calendars. Aren't you listening to me?'

'You *also* said "pencil in" which means "to tentatively or temporarily schedule something".'

'Emily,' Alegra said, using her 'addressing the accused' voice. 'You do realise you're not talking to one of your schoolchildren, don't you?'

She knew that, but she also knew that her class knew the difference between pencil and permanent marker, although, to be fair, not always the difference between a tissue and a jumper sleeve...

'Sorry,' Emily said. Why was she apologising? Apologising gave the other person power. Alegra had taught her that aged six when she had said sorry, on instinct, to a boy who had barrelled into *her* at the exclusive soft-play centre for professionals who didn't want their children to mix with children in soft-play centres *not* for professionals – ones that didn't have a waiting list, hand sanitiser or a parents' lounge area that served caviar blinis.

'A week on Friday. 7 p.m. the usual venue. Don't be late.'

Emily grimaced. The usual venue was a very upmarket cocktail bar with sharing platters that cost more than a family of four's weekly shop. An ordinary family of four, not a family whose children went to the exclusive soft-play centres. It was nice in some ways, all dim lighting and bare lightbulbs on ropes with larger-than-average filaments, subtle piano music and mixologists with subtle beards, but it was like being part of an artsy film set. Emily much preferred cosy and soft to expensive and pretentious. She had once wondered if she had been swapped with another baby at the hospital and somewhere in London was a twenty-something female in a bedsit wondering why she couldn't afford the Prada she felt formed part of her soul...

'Did you hear me, Emily?' Alegra repeated.

'Yes. A week on Friday at seven.'

'Right, got to dash. You know how it is.'

Yes, she knew. *All* about Alegra. She never even asked about Emily. Her life had been pretty much inconsequential to her parents since she turned down law school. It jarred a little, more so at the time, but jarring was comparable to not owning her choices.

'It was nice to—'

Alegra cut her off literally, by disconnecting the call, and Emily was left looking at the receiver in her hand. Oh well, sometimes predictability was comforting. She returned the phone to its dock and looked around the lounge, taking in Jonah's Christmas decorations anew. She supposed the small chains of silver stars weren't that bad. Her eyes went back to the photo of Simon. He would have liked the new decorations, simply because Jonah had bought them to cheer her up. Maybe they should stay after all.

Ten

Stretton Park Primary School

It was officially freezing, a full-on frost coating the playground as Emily wrapped her glove-clad fingers around her coffee mug. There were a whole collection of children running from one length of the Tarmac to the other, sliding like they were ice surfers, despite her warning them of the dangers. She had gone out with one of the bags of salt saved for these occasions in a bid to alleviate the worst of it, but it was still considerably slippery. Still, kids would be kids. Her breath was visible now, like it had been in her Arctic apartment when she woke up. Today the boiler was refusing to do anything – no lights on the panel, no pipes groaning – and if the shower was as cold this evening as it was first thing, she was going to have to call her landlord every hour until he was compelled to pick up.

'Cola bottle?' Dennis asked, a brown paper bag arriving in Emily's face.

'Eew! No! I mean, no thank you, Dennis. Not this early.'

Emily put her mouth to her coffee mug and virtually inhaled the rich creamy goodness like she had digested a much-nicer sweet by suggestion alone. She turned back to him. 'Is that really your breakfast?' That sounded a bit judgemental for someone who had only eaten half a crumpet because she'd run out of margarine to coat the whole of it. She'd pop into Sainsbury's on her way home and see what Taste the Difference meals were on special offer. Or maybe there would be some marked-down expensive cheese...

'Of course not,' Dennis answered. 'This is my...' He pushed up the sleeve of his Parka coat to check his watch. 'I was going to say nine-ses but it's not quite nine yet so, early morning interlude shall we say? Mother made me leftover corned beef hash with two fried eggs this morning. You were meant to go to work on an egg back in Mother's day.'

Emily had to admit eggs did sound good. She did like eggs, particularly scrambled eggs. She hadn't had them in ages. Simon used to... She urged her brain to stop. She really did have to stop every instance relating back to something Simon had done/made/vaguely once referred to. She was noticing it far more now Jonah had called her out on the whole 'living in the past' vibe. She knew Jonah meant well but it wasn't that easy to move on. It wasn't as if Simon had just got bored one day and dumped her for a Holly Willoughby lookalike. Although Simon *had* liked Holly Willoughby. Emily wasn't simply recovering from a broken heart, she was trying to recover from a broken life. A future changed in an instant, her long-term boyfriend of two years killed just like that. There had been no warning, no chance to say goodbye or hold his hand and whisper how much she loved him. Just a policewoman at the flat, telling her the news and offering her a Murray mint. Surely everyone's grieving timescale was different... and a year wasn't really that long, was it?

'Mind you,' Dennis continued. 'In my mother's day, people actually went to work on trams.'

'How old *is* your mother, Dennis?' Emily asked him.

'Eighty-five years young in January.'

'Goodness!' Emily exclaimed. 'She's very... mature.'

'She's a miracle, is my mother. Still got all her own teeth, own hair *and* her own hip and knee joints. She'll probably outlive me.' He shoved another palm full of cola bottles into his mouth and chewed. 'She'll probably outlive you.'

'She probably will,' Emily said, sighing. 'If Susan has anything to do with it.' Her attention was then drawn away from Dennis and his sweets, to a corner of the playground that had darkened from a line of red-faced children skidding across the icy terrain to an ominous huddle. She took a step forward, eyes seeking out any familiar heads of hair or stand-out coats of members of her class. Was that Jayden at the centre of it?

'Could you hold my coffee?' Emily asked, handing Dennis her mug.

'Where are you going?' Dennis wanted to know as Emily walked away from him. 'I was going to tell you about my mother's other secret to longevity!'

Emily could hear about how you got to eighty-five later; right now she was intent on finding out what was going on in this close collective that was verging on appearing a little sinister in the misty half-light. As she neared, the raised voices were in complete contrast to the whoops of delight from ice sliders and some girls skipping and singing 'I Wish It Could Be Christmas Every Day'.

'I said that isn't yours.' That was Rashid's voice, taunting.

'Well, it ain't yours either.' Definitely Jayden. Emily quickened her pace, wanting to head off this situation before it escalated.

'You don't have money for football cards,' Rashid continued. 'You don't have money to even wash your hair.'

The group laughed and Emily felt her insides turn nuclear. *Horrible little brat.* But she had to maintain some level of teacher decorum.

'And what's going on here?' she asked, slipping in between twins Charlie and Matthew from her class and facing Rashid. 'Talking about the football at the weekend? Who's playing?' She had limited knowledge about football apart from the names of the teams and a few of England's key players… the men and the Lionesses.

No one answered her. The group of four all look decidedly sheepish, eyes now on the ice-covered floor. Emily willed Jayden to look up and tell her what this was about. If he said that Rashid was being unkind, she could take some sort of action.

'No one watching the football?' Emily asked. 'Who is your favourite team at the moment? Is it Chelsea?' She forced a smile.

'You don't *choose* a favourite.' Rashid had raised his head now and was all but snarling at her. 'My Dad supports West Ham, so I support West Ham.'

'I support Fulham, Miss,' Charlie piped up, snot bubbling from his nose.

'I don't,' his twin answered. 'They're rubbish. I support Arsenal.'

And then Emily saw something. Just poking out of Rashid's coat sleeve was a glimmer of silver. Was this what he was goading Jayden about?

'What's that in your hand, Rashid?' Emily asked him.

'Nothing.'

'Rashid, I can quite clearly see you have something in your hand, and I would like you to show it to me, please.'

'I don't have to do that. My dad told me.' Rashid adopted a smug look she had seen once too often in her classroom. It seemed he and his parents knew the school protocol handbook off by heart and weren't afraid to pull out sections of it whenever it suited them.

'It's a football card, Miss,' Matthew informed, his finger curling around a piece of his ginger hair poking out from underneath his woollen hat.

'It's Jesse Lingard,' Charlie added. 'A superstar limited edition Match Attax card.'

'Oh really,' Emily said, really none the wiser. 'I would love to see that, Rashid.' He had challenged her authority once, but would he *really* dare to do it again?

'It's not Rashid's card,' Matthew said boldly.

'Really?' Emily said. She was saying 'really' a lot and she wanted to get closer to Rashid and intimidate him a little. However, she had to remember he was only ten, and in her care and she was a teacher with a strong set of morals and guidelines to adhere to. She also wasn't good at being intimidating and she didn't relish confrontation. Apart from that one time when she and Simon evaded concert security blocking a shortcut to one of their favourite eateries after a show…

'It's Jayden's card,' Matthew stuttered a little, eyes roving to Rashid.

'It can't be his card,' Rashid erupted. 'They're rare. You don't find them in ordinary packets. And he said he had Leroy Sane too and he's a gold card.'

'I see,' Emily said, her gaze falling on Jayden now. Jayden's head was still bowed, looking at his very scuffed black trainers. They weren't meant to be allowed to wear trainers to school, but Emily had long since suspected they were probably the only shoes Jayden had. It was obvious Jayden didn't want to engage in this conversation at all. He seemed to have run out of energy for even standing up for himself in the playground and her heart ached for him.

'Jayden,' Emily said softly. 'Is this your card that Rashid is holding but refusing to show me?' If Jayden confirmed it was his she was going to wrench it from the arrogant little bully and get him cleaning the whiteboard at lunchtime after she had written today's lesson planning in bubble writing and deeply coloured it in using *all* available space. Jayden was still, unmoving, unspeaking.

'It *is* his, Miss.' This came from Matthew. Brave little Matthew who she had just about differentiated from his brother by the fact he did love to play with his hair.

'Rashid,' Emily said, her tone no nonsense. 'Give me Jesse Lingard right now.' She held out her hand and beckoned with her fingers. If he *dared* to not give up the football card immediately, she would be sending him to Susan Clark before lessons even began.

She glared at the boy, watched the defiance dying in his dark eyes. He very reluctantly slipped the card down from the sleeve of his coat, into his hand and curtly plonked it in Emily's palm. She looked at the card. It wasn't much to write home about for a so-called 'rarity'. It wasn't even a particularly flattering photo of the England player...

'Right,' Emily said, looking up at Rashid, Matthew and Charlie. 'Mrs Rossiter is just about to blow the whistle, so I suggest you pick up your bags and line up.'

'But there's five minutes until we have to go in,' Rashid complained.

He was really testing her nerve this morning and she hadn't drunk enough of her coffee to be mellow yet. 'Rashid,' she half-hissed. 'I've asked you to line up... now line up!' She'd shouted. Reasonably loudly. Loud enough to draw attention from the group of children who like to poke at worms with sticks. She cleared her throat and calmed. 'I'll be taking you inside as soon as the whistle goes.'

Jayden picked up his bag and went to make a move too, but Emily stopped him. 'Not you, Jayden.' She waited for the other three boys to leave them before she said any more. Jayden's chin was still resting on his chest, the top of his head the only thing at Emily's eye level. He really did need a shot of self-confidence from somewhere. He wasn't the brightest student in her class but, equally, he wasn't the least academic. Given a chance, and a bit of a helping hand, she was sure he could find his way to achieving more than average at secondary school.

'What's going on, Jayden?' Emily asked him. 'We talked

about Rashid yesterday and I thought you were going to tell me if he was mean to you again.'

Jayden didn't respond or even lift his head. This wasn't good at all. Yesterday he had seemed much brighter. His dad had a job. The 'What Christmas Means to Me' project was almost complete...

'Jayden, is this football card yours?'

No response.

'Jayden, I don't want to get cross with you, but you need to look at me.'

'I don't want to.'

'Jayden, come on, I want to help you.'

'You can't help me, Miss.' Finally, he lifted his head from his view of his trainers and Emily took a sharp breath inwards. Jayden had a huge painful-looking red bruise on his cheekbone. She swallowed. She mustn't jump to conclusions, but she was already seeing Mr Jackson and his more-than-ready fists...

'Jayden, what happened to your face?' Emily asked him.

'I fell up the stairs,' Jayden said robotically. 'I was running. I shouldn't run up the stairs. Especially when it's icy. My mum's always telling me not to run.'

It was so practised, Emily winced. She needed to speak to Susan about this. That's all the power she had. To raise her concern with the headmistress again. Not that that had changed anything the last time.

'Jayden,' Emily said. 'You know, if someone did that to you, you know, if it wasn't the stairs, you can tell me.'

'I fell up the stairs. I was running and...My mum is always telling me not to run.'

This was getting her nowhere. Jayden would no doubt keep blanking this out until she stopped asking. She held up the football card. 'Is this yours?'

Jayden nodded. 'My nan came to visit. She got them off of eBay.'

'Why didn't you tell Rashid that?'

'He doesn't believe anything I say.'

Emily nodded. 'Well, Jayden, I believe what you say and, like I said before, if you have any trouble from Rashid or anyone else in the school, you come to me.'

'My dad says no one likes a grass.'

'Your dad isn't here at Stretton Park. And telling me that someone is being mean to you, isn't being a grass,' Emily assured. 'OK?' She needed to get this point across. She couldn't be present in every corner of the school every day protecting the weaker children and she really shouldn't have to be, but she was a realist.

'OK,' Jayden said, the words not really filtering into his eyes.

'Here,' Emily said, handing Jesse Lingard over to him. 'Maybe it's better if you keep the football cards at home.'

Jayden accepted it and slipped it back into his pocket just as Mrs Rossiter blasted the whistle to indicate it was time for the children to line up to go into the school building for lessons.

'Miss Parker! Miss Parker!'

Emily turned around to the calling of Alice Monroe. Alice was a bright girl in her class, always neatly turned out with her dark hair in plaits and polished Clarks shoes. She did have an odd fascination with death though. Like the time she took the class stick insects home and they all died except one, who Alice attributed the blame to...

'What's the matter, Alice?' Emily asked as the girl got to her, cheeks pink, hat falling off her head.

'There's something in the shed... like a ghost... or a badger or something.'

'The shed?' Emily put a hand to her head. Her class had been working in the shed last thing yesterday. They'd tidied it up and were preparing for it to be part of the Christmas bazaar. They were going to be dispensing hot chocolates and homemade shortbread for £1 a time to raise funds as part of their class initiative. How could a badger, or anything, have got in there? She'd padlocked the door herself and, although the wood had seen slightly better days, there were no gaps even the smallest of animals could have squeezed through, was there?

'The padlock wasn't on the door,' Alice announced. 'And there was shuffling.'

'Shuffling,' Emily said. 'What kind of shuffling?' She didn't really believe she had asked that question. Were there different kinds of shuffling?

'Like something's half-dead,' Alice replied, bottom lip trembling a little.

'Miss Parker!' It was Susan Clark's voice now and Emily looked across the playground to where her children were lined up ready to go in. They were the last class to still be standing on the freezing Tarmac, their combined breath creating a blanket of mist.

'Miss,' Alice said pleadingly. 'What if it's a half-dead body of a badger?'

'OK,' Emily answered. 'Listen, we'll go inside, we'll do

the register and then we'll come straight back out and check out the shed, OK?'

'OK,' Alice replied. 'I'll tell everyone to bring their phones. I've not seen a half-dead badger before.'

It seemed today was going to be just as wonderful as the day before.

Eleven

This was ridiculous, but she couldn't leave the children unattended and she wasn't going to tell Susan something was nesting in the shed. The Head's opinion of her was pretty low as it was. And gone were the days when schools had janitors they could call on to help with this sort of thing. The cleaner only came every *other* day now.

Emily put an ear to the wooden door of the shed. It wasn't padlocked anymore, but the door *was* closed. She was *sure* she had locked up yesterday. She could hear nothing from inside. Was this another case of Alice's imagination running away with her?

'Maybe it's something Newt Scamander forgot,' Frema suggested.

'Or something from *Hotel Transylvania*,' Matthew suggested.

'They don't have vampires in Islington,' his brother told him matter-of-factly.

'My mum says *she's* a vampire,' Cherry Wheeler piped up.

There were gasps amongst the group and Emily watched Alice actually grin.

'She works for the NHS Blood Donation Service,' Cherry clarified. 'Did you know, if you give blood, they give you crisps and chocolate and coffee for actual free.'

'But what if they take too much and your blood runs out and then you die?' Alice asked her.

'They don't take *all* your blood, stupid,' Rashid snapped.

'Thank you, that's enough, Rashid,' Emily ordered. And then a bang came from the shed and everyone squealed and drew back a couple of feet. There was definitely something in there.

Emily took a deep breath and prepared to pull at the door. What was the worst it could be? An angry swan with babies it was protecting? Well, it was the wrong time of year for cygnets and they weren't that close to the river. Other than that, she was really at a loss to what could have crept inside. But standing here, letting her class come up with frightening suggestions was a pointless exercise. She needed them inside, in the warm, giving her ideas for this Christmas show she was in charge of...

'Right, stand back a bit everyone, I'm going to open the door,' Emily stated.

'What, now?' Alice asked.

'*Right* now?' added Lucas Jones.

'Yes,' Emily said. 'There's probably nothing even here. Something's probably fallen down from the tidying we did yesterday.' She took a breath. 'OK, here we go.'

Emily grabbed the handle and pulled open the door.

Immediately she gasped and fell back as her class screamed simultaneously, some running away, others snapping photos on their mobile phones.

'It's a man! It's a man!' Felix, a boy who lived with his aunt and uncle announced, running round and round in circles while Emily tried to catch her breath.

It *was* a man. He was sitting in the shed, surrounded by the sheets she had neatly folded onto the racking yesterday. He had a cotton bag-for-life on his head and what looked like a tea bag hanging from his beard. A down and out in the school shed! Did he really have nowhere better or warmer to be?

'I know who that is!' Rashid announced, mobile phone snapping away. 'It's Ray Stone. The singer. He's been all over the news. My mum used to like him, but now she says he's a drunk and hits girls.'

'Sshh!' This came from the man in the shed. 'Keep your voices down!'

'I know him!' Cherry declared. 'He was on the Royal Variety Performance after Lost Voice Guy.' She took a photo with her phone.

Emily was so taken aback she was in danger of losing control of this situation. Was this *really* Ray Stone? He had a thicker beard than usual and he was currently half-sitting, half-lying on a thick pad of gymnastic mats wearing a cotton shopper as headwear. Despite the odd attire, anyone could see he was ridiculously attractive. Emily could certainly see he was ridiculously attractive…

'Sshh!' the man said again, struggling to get to his feet. 'You're going to frighten her.'

'He's drunk!' Jayden announced. 'My dad always talks nonsense when he's drunk.'

'Stand back, Frema, the news told us all yesterday how he gets when he's drunk,' Rashid said warningly to his classmate.

She needed to do something. 'Year Six, you need to quieten down,' Emily urged as the man stumbled out from the shed, pulling something out from under his Luther-esque coat.

'He's got a gun!' Rashid yelled. 'Everyone get down!'

There was screaming and half of her class dropped to the floor in hysterics. She had had enough of this!

'Listen,' she said, addressing the man. 'I don't know what you think you're doing in here, but this is private property. This is a school and I'm afraid you're trespassing.'

'I tried to make a splint,' the man said. His voice was rough, a little like he was trying to hold back a cough. 'But she wasn't having any of it. So, I wrapped her up as best I could... and then I must have fallen asleep.'

Was this man delirious? None of what he was saying made any sense. Until Emily saw what had been under his coat, what he was cupping gently in his hand. It wasn't any kind of weapon. It was a...

'It's a hedgehog! Aww! Look, Cherry, it's a hedgehog,' Angelica Anderson said, rushing forward, past Emily to the bearded man cradling an animal in his palms.

Her whole class started to surge forward and Emily was pushed closer to the stranger from the shed. He smelt of whisky and oddly enough, Plasticine. His large hands were holding the rolled-up ball of spikes so tenderly, thumbs rubbing over its body. He had large, strong-looking hands...

'Her leg's broken,' the man told Emily. 'We should call an animal hospital or something.'

'Aww, can't we keep it?' This came from Frema. 'It's so cute and we don't have the stick insects anymore. Do we, Alice?'

'Is it going to die?' Alice asked, muscling her way through the growing throng of children keen to see the hedgehog.

'It's a wild animal,' Emily stated. 'Wild animals need to be in their natural habitat.'

'Are you really Ray Stone?' Rashid asked, snapping photos. 'Because, if you are, you really need to get your beard trimmed, innit.'

'Rashid!' Emily exclaimed. 'Apologise right now!'

To a man who had been sleeping in the school shed. Someone who was trespassing. Had he spent all night in there? She needed to remember who was in charge here. This was already set to be an even more bizarre day than yesterday...

'And, all of you,' Emily addressed firmly. 'Put away your phones. You know you're not allowed to have them out of your bags in school hours.'

'But I want to take a Boomerang of the cute hedgehog,' Frema stated.

'Before it dies,' Alice added.

'What's its name?' Matthew asked, seemingly directing his question at the stranger from the shed who may or may not be a singing sensation. Emily was reserving judgement. He looked like Ray Stone but there were a lot of good lookalikes these days and she had never been much of a celebrity spotter. She wouldn't trust herself to pick Elton John out of a line-up.

'I told you,' Rashid said, phone still in his hand. 'It's Ray Stone, the singer who won that talent show.' Rashid did seem super-insistent and the man did have all the singer's handsome…

'I meant the hedgehog,' Matthew said with a tut. 'What's its name?'

'I don't know,' the man said. 'But we should take her inside.' He looked directly at Emily then. 'Do you have a cardboard box and maybe a bowl of water?'

What was happening here? Did she really have a pop star and an injured hedgehog in the school shed, both seemingly looking to come into the school building? She was going to get fired if this continued and none of it was actually her fault… unless she *had* left the shed unlocked. Then it was possibly *all* her fault.

'We have loads of cardboard,' Cherry announced, bouncing up and down. 'We've been making projects. Come on, it's this way.' She beckoned the man towards the school. That stranger danger talk obviously really needed repeating again.

'Hold on a minute,' Emily said. 'Listen, we can't do this like this. Stop moving.' She held her arms out and leaned forward, her classic move for making the children listen and obey. She didn't really know why her creating a pose like the statue of Jesus looking over Rio De Janeiro worked but it did.

'The hedgehog is cold, Miss Parker,' Frema said with a sniff. 'And the pop star looks cold too. Are you cold?' She studied the man as if she was looking for signs of frostbite.

'Well…' he began, voice still a little rough.

He *did* look cold. Freezing in fact. He was shivering, the hedgehog in his hands bobbing up and down a little with the tremor of his fingers. But he was on school property, they didn't really know who he was and he smelled like he'd spent the night in a pub not in a supplies shed.

'Miss Parker! It *is* cold,' Lucas said.

'I'm frozen,' Jayden agreed.

'Listen,' the man who was allegedly Ray Stone said, his words jolting with the shivering vibrations of his body. 'I'll go. If you just take the hedgehog and call London Wildlife Protection or the RSPCA or something.'

'It's going to die,' Alice bleated. 'I knew it.'

'No one is going to die, Alice.' Why didn't she know what to do? Perhaps because this wasn't in the average teacher's workday or in any of the university course notes. *Common sense. If in doubt, apply common sense.*

'OK, right.' Emily put her arms down and nodded at her pupils. 'Everyone into the classroom, get some pencils and paper, sit in your places and draw me pictures of hedgehogs while I work out who to call about its injury.'

There was plenty of cheering then rushing towards the doors to inside. They were supposed to be running through a maths challenge this morning... before she told them about the Christmas play and they all got carried away with things they could do that were beyond their budget and her capabilities.

'I could carry the hedgehog in if you like,' Alice offered, all smiles. 'I promise not to squeeze him too hard.' She made her fingers into steeples and looked slightly too keen.

'I think it's a girl,' Ray informed her.

'I won't squeeze *her* too hard,' Alice said.

'Thank you, Alice,' Emily said. 'I'll take it from here. You go inside.'

Seconds later and Emily was left with the apparent pop star and a hedgehog with a damaged limb.

'Sorry,' the man said, body still shaking. 'For ending up in your shed. I was heading back from... the pub... late, well, you know, early, and I found this one who was walking less straight than me. I headed for the first place I thought might have something to help her and...'

'I don't know what to say,' Emily admitted. 'I mean, you being here is probably breaking a million rules and if Mrs Clark finds out that will be me fired and I really *really* don't need to be fired right now. And she *wants* to fire me. She really would use anything she could. I think a stranger sleeping in the shed would definitely do it.'

'Sorry,' the man said again. 'I'll go.' He handed out the hedgehog.

'Eww! No! I can't take that. I don't do... things like that.'

'Animals?' the man queried.

'Well, it's not really an animal, is it? I mean, it isn't a cat or a...'

'Lion?'

'Quite.' She was sure she had read somewhere that hedgehogs had fleas. She didn't want fleas getting involved in the lovely three-coloured striped cardigan she was wearing under her coat. She really should go back to that little shop on Holloway Road...

'So, what shall I do?' the man asked.

He had a point. She wouldn't take it. It needed to be inside until someone came to get it... and she needed to be with her children.

'Bring it in and I'll see if I can get you a coffee.'

'You don't have to do that,' the man answered.

'The way my week is going, if I let you leave without a warm drink, you'll probably collapse on school grounds and I'll be to blame and I'll get fired anyway.'

'OK,' he answered, clearing his throat.

'OK,' Emily replied.

'I *am* Ray by the way,' he said with half a smile. 'The singer who needs his beard trimmed.'

'Emily,' she introduced. 'The teacher who needs this job to pay for someone to repair her central heating seeing as her landlord has disappeared off the face of the Earth.'

'Nice to meet you.' He smiled and, again, Emily could immediately see why he would be easy-on-the-eye star material even with the un-neat facial hair.

'Right, well, let's get this hedgehog inside… just, don't let Alice touch it. She's the one in the red hat… with black hair in plaits, looks like Wednesday from *The Addams Family*.'

'O–K,' Ray replied.

'Believe me, if she gets hold of it, we won't be needing the London Wildlife Trust.'

Twelve

Ray couldn't believe he was in a school. When he was of school age, he had spent most of his time trying to avoid going into the place. It wasn't that he hadn't been bright, it was that academia simply hadn't ever interested him. Music was where his passion had always lain and in music lessons, despite his talent in that area, it had been all *Peter and the Wolf*, introducing the orchestra and understanding scores. That wasn't his bag at all. His mum had loved to dance, and it was listening to the music she played that had inspired him. Queen. Led Zeppelin. Fleetwood Mac. Those guitar riffs, the composition of the songs, even as a young teen he had been intrigued by how it all happened. How these musicians decided which notes to put together. What worked and what didn't. His mum had never got to see how he put music together…

Sitting at the back of this classroom now, his hands around a steaming hot mug of black coffee, he began to realise exactly how bad his hangover was. How much had he consumed after the scene at his dad's flat? He'd been angry and deflated and he had no home to go to. Yes, perhaps, if his platinum card had managed to offer him some sway at the nearest Hilton, he could have holed up in a suite with a dressing gown, slippers and the mini-bar, but the thought of a declined card and the press attention that would have drawn had been enough to keep him walking... until he had stumbled over Mrs Tiggywinkle or... Olivia Colman as the children had named the hedgehog. He shouldn't have bothered. It was a hedgehog. Natural selection would decide whether or not survival would follow. But he'd looked at the creature, amid his half-drunk stupor, and felt a kinship with it. Two slightly prickly, injured individuals, simply wanting somewhere to stay. And here he was, sitting under precariously placed coat hangers with Christmas tat attached to them, spinning in his vision and catching the light from the window like very basic oddly shaped glitter balls.

'OK, Year Six, that's enough thinking time now,' Emily said from the front of the room, whiteboard marker in her hand. 'Let's have some of you tell the class what you do on Christmas Day. Frema, thank you, you can go first.'

These children were all a lot more enthusiastic than Ray had ever been and it was apparent they all had a great deal of respect for their teacher. He wasn't going to lie. Teachers had never looked like Emily Parker in his day. Even at ten years old, if he had had a teacher that looked like Miss Parker, he might have been a lot more interested in study. But there was something ultimately serious and restrained about her. As good as she was with the children, there was something else going on. Perhaps she had really meant it about being worried for her job. Even in his position he could totally empathise with the whole 'running out of cash' scenario. He had no idea how he was going to settle up with Dr Crichton if he had to go through with this operation. Or actually how much each consultation was costing his account...

'Well, my dad is Jewish, so his religion doesn't celebrate Christmas, but my mum is Christian and she does. My parents want me to choose my own religion when I'm older, so we practise bits of both religions. We have a Christmas tree and we have presents and lights and sometimes I go to church and sometimes I go to the synagogue. I like doing both things.'

'Thank you, Frema. Rashid.'

Ray took a sip of his coffee and watched on. It was strangely nice just sitting here in the calm, listening to the children talk. He wondered how long the wildlife sanctuary would take to arrive...

'I'm Muslim, Miss,' Rashid said. 'You know that.'

'I do know that, Rashid. But I also know that you have before, taken some time during the school holidays in December to visit some of your family you don't usually get to see, so why don't you remind the class of that?'

Miss Parker was no nonsense. She also had quite striking eyes and a quirky dress sense. No, quirky wasn't quite the word, 'individual' was a more accurate description. She was wearing a dark green corduroy skirt with little brown boots and a striped top. It was smart but also playful... God, either there was something in his blood stream he didn't remember taking last night or there was something in the coffee.

Rashid sighed heavily and rolled his eyes for good measure. 'We all get in the car and travel to Birmingham and my nan makes horrible food which we pretend to eat and then we get McDonald's on the way home.'

Some of the children laughed.

'That sounds better than my Christmas,' Nathan piped up. 'My mum and dad are both in the police so they always have to work. And my Auntie Ann is a vegetarian so all I get to eat is fake turkey.'

Ray was beginning to realise that his Christmases up to now hadn't actually been that bad. Granted, his dad ordinarily found something to have an argument about, but the food had always been plentiful and he'd got good gifts. His mum had even bought him his first guitar. He still had that. Well, Gio had it, in whatever storage unit his stuff was now in. He needed to get Deborah on to that. Christmas with Ida, however, had always been less upbeat. She had never been a Christmas person. She blamed her mother. She had blamed her mother for a lot of things. They had had that in common, mothers who weren't perfect. But that wasn't exactly something to keep you in a relationship, was it?

'What are you doing for Christmas, Ray Stone?' Rashid asked loudly.

Hiding out at the back of the room, enjoying blending in amongst the collages of bonfires from the History of Guy Fawkes board, keeping an eye on Olivia Colman who had snuffled at the water they'd put in the cardboard box, he'd forgotten he was in the midst of a lesson, an interloper into their routine…

'Rashid, I'm sure Mr Stone doesn't want to tell you what his Christmas plans are.'

'Are you singing for the Queen again?' a girl with a crop of ginger hair asked.

'Do you eat meat?' Nathan inquired.

'Do you believe in Jesus?'

Ray shifted in his seat. It was very small, making him a little hunched. He had been interviewed by almost every journalist the UK had to offer, and some from the States, but none of them had made him feel this uncomfortable. Even having his private life on breakfast television was dropping in the significance ranks a bit.

'Year Six…' Emily said.

'No,' Ray called out. 'It's OK.' He cleared his throat and undid a button on his coat as he finally began to thaw. 'I don't know what I'll be doing this Christmas.' He looked at Nathan. 'I do eat meat. Love the stuff. Love turkey.' He looked at the boy who had asked if he believed in Jesus. 'I've never been 100 per cent sure about Jesus.'

There was a collective intake of breath he hadn't expected.

Emily cut through it. 'Year Six, please, remember one of our fundamental rules of the class. We don't judge anyone. We are all entitled to speak freely and we are all accepting of everyone's opinion.'

'Fun and mental. Fun and mental.' He remembered from the playground this boy being called Felix. He seemed to like repetition.

'Sorry, Mr Stone.' Emily was addressing him. 'Despite

accepting all faiths at Stretton Park, we are a Church of England school, which means it's kind of at the backbone of everything because of the financial support from the diocese.'

'I believe in Father Christmas though,' Ray said quickly. 'Obviously.'

Rashid snorted. A few other children laughed.

'What?' Ray asked, all innocent, spreading his arms out. 'Don't tell me you don't believe in Santa.'

'I believe in Santa,' Cherry said, chewing on her pencil. 'He *has* to be real because when I asked my mum and dad for a Barbie Dreamhouse for Christmas they said there was no *way* they could afford that. And then on Christmas morning there it was, next to the Christmas tree.' She grinned. 'It was that big it couldn't even fit *under* the actual Christmas tree.'

'What are you going to ask Santa for then?' Rashid asked. 'A new career?'

'Don't be so rude, Rashid,' Frema ordered. She smiled at Ray. 'I think you're a very good singer.'

'Thank you,' Ray replied.

'Will you sing for us now?' Cherry asked. 'Please.'

He didn't want to sing. He wasn't even allowed to sing.

'How about a Christmas song? I love "Rudolph the Red-Nosed Reindeer".'

'Me too!'

'I like "Jingle Bells".'

'Year Six, that's enough,' Emily interrupted.

He should go. He had almost finished his coffee. He was warmer. Someone was going to come for the hedgehog. He should call Deborah, organise somewhere to stay from tonight, find out what she had managed to achieve with regard to picking his career out of the gutter...

He stood up, ready to make his exit.

'Mrs Clark is coming! Mrs Clark is coming!' It was Felix again, the boy's voice like a wailing siren.

Within a split-second Emily had made it down the room towards him and was grabbing hold of his arm, pulling him into the corner of the room.

'Get in the cupboard,' she whispered, eyes wide with what appeared to be fright. 'God, I know how that sounds but please, please, just get in the cupboard.'

Ray opened his mouth to appeal this idea as a door was opened and all manner of stationery was revealed along with a couple of brooms, a dustpan and brush and what looked like a very old vacuum cleaner. 'I...'

'Please,' Emily begged again. 'I did give you coffee.'

What could he say? She looked positively desperate. He stepped into the space and before he could offer up anything else Emily was closing the door and plunging him into darkness.

Thirteen

'Listen everyone,' Emily said as quickly as she could get the words out, rushing back to her position at the front of the classroom. 'No one mention Mr Stone... or the hedgehog.'

'Why?' Rashid asked, a glint in his eye. 'Will you get in trouble?'

'I just think that... Mrs Clark has enough to worry about with running the school. She doesn't need to worry about a hedgehog or—'

'An actual pop star,' Cherry remarked.

'Jayden,' Emily addressed. 'Why don't you tell the class what you're going to be doing for Christmas this year.'

The classroom door banged open without a knock of courtesy and in walked Susan, a man in a dark blue uniform following. Of course Susan was already going to know about the hedgehog. Emily had phoned the RSPCA from her mobile. The first port of call for their officer would be reception and reception would ask the Head if she knew about an injured animal...

'I've been to all the other classes and they all looked at me like I was a clown at a funeral so please, Miss Parker, tell me you know something about a hurt hedgehog.'

'I do,' Emily said, forcing a smile she hoped spoke of utter professionalism and control. 'It's just back here.' She walked towards the rear of the room, shimmying between the children's tables.

'It's a she, Mrs Clark,' Frema informed her as the headteacher and the man from the RSPCA came into the middle of the room.

'How do you know?' Makenzie asked. 'It might not have decided its gender yet. We should say "they" if we're unsure.' Makenzie had been a surrogate baby and had two dads who were both amazing supporters of the school fundraising initiatives.

'It doesn't have a willy though, does it?' Nathan announced loudly. The class descended into laughter and red faces.

'Thank you, Nathan,' Susan replied. 'The man from the RSPCA is here now and I'm sure he's going to look after it no matter what body parts it owns.'

'A hedgehog's willy comes out of its belly button. I drew it on my picture,' Charlie announced, holding aloft his piece of paper.

Emily swallowed as her cheeks flamed. What was she doing with a man in the stationery cupboard? She couldn't ask her children to lie about it. She'd never asked them to lie about anything... apart from the one time she hadn't read them something the diocese had sent through on modern day Christianity before the special assembly. She just had to hope that Susan left with the RSPCA man and the hedgehog quickly and she could then get Ray off the school grounds as fast and stealth-like as possible.

'Her name's Olivia Colman,' Alice announced, getting up from her seat and rushing to the cardboard box. Emily eyes caught on the coffee mug Ray had left on the table. She sauntered forward rapidly, hoping to remove it before Susan could make comment.

'When she's fixed can we keep her?' Matthew inquired, joining the group of children who were all rushing to crowd around the animal's temporary home.

'We talked about that, Matthew, didn't we? How hedgehogs are much better in their own, natural environment. They aren't pets,' Emily said.

'We don't have a class pet anymore though, do we?' Cherry said.

'I loved the stick insects,' Alice replied.

'Say goodbye to Olivia Colman, Year Six. She's going to be in good hands now with the RSPCA,' Emily offered loudly.

'Will you make a splint for her leg?' Lucas wanted to know as the RSPCA officer picked up the box and observed the animal. 'That's what Ray was going to do.'

Emily felt sick. Like Jonah's Thai from last night was going to make a rapid reappearance all over Olivia Colman's box. Lucas did have slight hearing difficulties, but since he'd had grommets put in, he'd been much better. He couldn't have not heard her say 'don't mention the singer in the cupboard'.

'Ray is Lucas's uncle,' Jayden said quickly. 'He messaged him when we found Olivia Colman by the bushes in the playground. He asked what to do to make her leg better and Ray said a splint. Right, Lucas?' Jayden jabbed an elbow into the other boy's side.

Lucas looked completely bewildered while Jayden had proved he was extremely accomplished in telling lies. Emily wanted the day to be over and it wasn't even half past ten. She picked up the coffee cup and set it down on the windowsill out of sight.

'Does your Uncle Ray like singing, Lucas?' Rashid asked.

'She wasn't in the bushes,' Charlie stated. 'She was in the shed.'

'Children,' Susan interrupted. 'I think this hedgehog has had more than enough attention for one morning. Let's let the man take him now and...'

'It's a she!' Frema insisted.

'We're calling they they,' Makenzie reminded everyone.

'Bye, Olivia Colman. I hope your leg gets actual better soon!' Cherry called as the RSPCA officer headed towards the door with the hedgehog.

'Miss Parker,' Susan said, looking Emily up and down. 'In all my years of teaching, I've never been called to meet with the RSPCA about a hedgehog.'

'Oh, really?' Emily asked. 'I mean, I'm surprised. The children are very interested in all inner-city wildlife and they were worried about the little thing.'

'It's a hedgehog, Miss Parker, not a natterjack toad.'

'And did you know there used to be thirty million hedgehogs in Britain in the 1950s and now there are less than one million?' Emily informed.

'We're adding our sighting of Olivia Colman to a map on the internet,' Nathan explained.

'Hedgehogs won't win favour with the diocese at

Christmas, Emily,' Susan said through gritted teeth. 'Your focus should be with the show, as discussed last night.'

'About that,' Emily started. Now was as good a time as any to remind Susan about her lack of musical ability and perhaps suggest the task was given to someone else. Dennis seemed more than keen... and he could whistle in tune.

'The Christmas show could literally make or break this school, Emily. Do I need to make myself any clearer than that?'

It wasn't clear. What exactly did she mean? That the school itself was in jeopardy? She understood there needed to be budget restraint but was the Head hinting at possible *closure*?

'It's a headache I could do without,' Susan continued in whispered tones. 'There's only so much Nurofen one can take...' She sighed and adjusted another too-tight blouson. 'With Beaujolais Nouveau.'

'OK,' Emily said on an out breath. 'What else *could* she say? If she wanted the chance to be thought of for Deputy Head after Mr Simms's retirement, then she needed to keep Susan sweet. Mr Simms was currently on long-term sick leave... again. It was getting towards a case of 'if' he came back rather than 'when'.

'Right, thank you, I'll let you get back to drinking that coffee you're hiding on the windowsill, shall I?'

Before Emily could say anything in her defence – not that she had a defence – there was an almighty crash from the stationery cupboard that had some of the children screaming in alarm.

'What on earth is that?' Susan exclaimed, beginning a march towards the doors.

Emily suddenly had all the symptoms of a stroke come on at once. Tingling in her hands, numbness in her face, panic in her chest. She couldn't let Susan open the cupboard doors and find Ray in there.

'It's...' Emily started, darting ahead of Susan and backing up to the doors, defending them like she was an ancient warrior protecting castle fortifications.

'A rabbit!' It was Jayden coming to her rescue, but she really wished he hadn't. She wasn't sure suggesting there was a second animal in the classroom was going to stop Susan from opening the doors. Even the RSPCA man was showing significant interest.

'Did you say a rabbit?' Susan asked, staring at Jayden.

'No,' Emily said. 'He actually said "bracket", didn't you, Jayden?' She nodded extensively, trying to force his opinion like a suggestion technique from a mind-reader.

'Yeah,' Jayden answered. 'I said "bracket".'

'I noticed it was loose yesterday and I meant to do something about it, but we got very invested in our projects and... I forgot about it. But, I'll get someone to sort it out,' Emily said, back flush against the doors, fingers winding around the metal handles.

Susan rolled her eyes and thankfully took a step back. 'Please, if it's going to cost a fortune, I'll get Malcolm to come in and look at it. Let me know before the end of the day though or he'll have arranged a golf session.' She took a breath and looked at the man from the RSPCA. 'Right, let's leave before a protected species of pigeon comes down the chimney.'

Emily held her breath, body still against the door, watching and waiting for her boss to leave the room.

Finally, Susan departed and she breathed the biggest sigh of relief. Turning around she opened up the cupboard doors to find Ray with two of the once-fixed-to-the-wall shelves in his hands, the floor covered with paint pots, brushes, art sponges and all the easels.

'There's good news and there's bad news,' he said looking at her with those rather attractive brown eyes. 'The bad news is the bracket needs fixing. The good news is you weren't lying about it to your boss.'

Fourteen

The Breakfast Club, Camden Passage

Ray basically inhaled the giant full English breakfast he was tucking into. There might be festive Shakin' Stevens playing – a song he particularly loathed – and there were even tiny elves on strings 'climbing' up the yellow-painted window panes, but nothing was going to distract him from the plate of food in front of him. He was still cold from his hours overnight in Stretton Park Primary's shed and he was starving. He was glad the caff hadn't decided to 'festive-up' the all-day bacon, eggs and sausage.

'So, let me get this straight,' Deborah stated, sipping on her flat white. 'Since I left you yesterday you've been made homeless, you've been photographed looking like you're having a heated argument with a woman in a purple sequinned dress and a Deliveroo rider – that was in *The Sun* this morning by the way – and…' Deborah leaned over the table. 'What was the other thing you said?'

'I rescued a hedgehog,' Ray informed between chewing on a sausage. The breakfast really was top notch here and he'd always found a fry-up the best hangover cure there was. Never mind the cholesterol effects… It hadn't, after all, been a full-fat diet that had killed his mother. She'd never been one for breakfast at all and that probably should have spoken volumes at the time.

'Well,' Deborah stated. 'No one got a photo of that. Which is a shame, because that's the sort of good news story you need. I mean, imagine you on *Loose Women* then, photos of you cradling Sonic playing on a loop to some sentimental music. The Great British public love an upbeat animal story much more than they love a half-story about a celebrity's fall from grace.'

'Olivia Colman,' he said through a mouth full of beans.

'What?'

'The hedgehog. It's called Olivia Colman not Sonic.'

Being homeless and almost broke did make you appreciate the simple things in life. Like this plate of hot food and saving the hedgehog with the class of ten-year-olds. When was the last time he had had time to do something like that?

'Ray,' Deborah said softly, dipping her head as if she was trying to look deep into his eyes. 'I have to ask. Are you on drugs?'

He couldn't help the smile that formed on his mouth and he had to reach for a serviette and dab at the corners before bean juice met with his beard. The truth was he had never felt so high on normality before. 'Sorry, I didn't mean to laugh.'

'Ray, seriously,' Deborah said. 'You're making my job impossible. I don't want to have to abandon you, but you have to understand that I have a family to feed and Tucker's obedience classes do not come cheap.' She sighed. 'And I have a reputation to uphold. There's only so much damage limitation one agent can handle and…'

Now Ray was listening. He couldn't lose Deborah as his agent. She had been there from the start when the talent show had hooked them up together. Yes, she was a little bit more middle-class than he was sometimes completely comfortable with, but she understood him and she was excellent at her job. 'Debs, you know I can't do any of this without you.'

God, that sounded so pathetically unmanly. But he knew it was true. He hadn't handled the fame well. He still didn't know how to handle it. Deborah had always made him feel as OK as he could be with it. She presented everything methodically, reminding him this was a job like any other with tick-lists of things to complete. She had even bullet-pointed his last album launch so he didn't feel overwhelmed. In short, Deborah had always calmed the chaos. He swallowed at her lack of immediate reply, fork poised over his plate, fingers shaking a little. His throat was scratchy again. He needed to tell her about Dr Crichton and the possibility of an operation. Surely, she couldn't leave him if he was sick…

'But you're not doing it with me, Ray,' Deborah reminded him. 'You're not taking my advice. You're burying your head in the sand… or snow if the Met Office is right about next week.' She sighed, putting down her cup of coffee. 'I believe in you. You know I believe in you. I'm not the kind of agent who fills clients up with platitudes I don't mean. That isn't my style at all. I love your music. I love your voice. I think there's a whole lot more to come from you, but you have to do something about Ida… and your drinking.'

Ray put down his knife and fork, the fried foods suddenly no longer appealing. He felt uncomfortable because he knew that she was right. The echoes of his mother's voice were ringing in his ears already. He picked up his cup of tea, then, realising there was nothing in it, he put it down again.

'You have to let me do my job, Ray. You have to let me manage this situation.' Her tone was dead serious. 'And you have to do what I tell you to do.'

Doing as he was told had never been one of his strong points. But, at the moment, he didn't know *what* to do. It seemed any kind of stability and normality he had was falling away like an avalanche beneath his feet.

He nodded, accepting. 'Yeah.'

'So, we're agreed?' Deborah said, sounding more than a little surprised. 'You are going to follow my plan and we are going to get you out of this hole you're currently in with regard to the public and the press and relaunch your new clean, more wholesome than ever image.'

'Christ, you didn't say anything about wholesome.'

'The beard needs sorting out, Ray,' Deborah told him definitely. 'I know they're still trending, but it needs proper care and attention. I'll book you in with the barber.'

He couldn't help but run fingers down his face. It *had* got a little long, he supposed. It was something to hide behind a little though. He had gone through all the stages of facial hair over the past year.

'And, if you can *promise me* you'll be nothing but civil, I think we ought to set up a meeting with Ida.'

His heart sank then. Like it had been dropped into the Atlantic. He knew that would have been on Deborah's agenda. How could it not be? Ida had sold this non-story to the press and they were spinning it around like a DJ with one of his records. It needed to stop. He *wanted* it to stop. He just didn't know at what cost that would be and that scared him. It really scared him. Suddenly all he could hear was the clattering of pots and pans in the kitchen. Loud. Heavy.

'Ray?' Deborah said. 'I'm not hearing anything from you.'

'OK,' he replied quickly, shaking the noises out of his head. What else was there to say?

'OK?' Deborah checked.

'Yeah, OK.'

'Good,' Deborah said, taking a sip of her drink. 'Right, then we need to find you somewhere to live and get your things moved over there. I'll call Gio for the details of this storage locker. Bloody cheek of him if you ask me. So, is there anything else I should know? Absolutely anything else that's going to hit the fan in the coming days?'

Ray thought back to the pubs he'd been in after his altercation with his dad. He didn't remember being obnoxious to anyone. No matter how wasted he got he usually remembered later if he had been out of line. But then his thoughts went to Stretton Park Primary and all those children with their mobile phones. That could definitely come back to haunt a new wholesome image. He might have had hold of a hedgehog, but, fed into the arena by uncontrolled means, the journalists could make it look like he had harmed the animal. Plus, he had felt rougher than new guitar strings this morning so he could guarantee the photos would be full of heavy-lidded, red-rimmed eyes at the very least…

'Ray?' Deborah said. 'This is serious. Is there anything else I need to know about? Anything that could blow up in our faces at a later date?'

Ray shook his head and planted a fork in his piece of black pudding. 'No, Debs. There's nothing else.'

Fifteen

Stretton Park Primary School

Emily had never craved gin as much as she was craving it now. It was a year since she had gone tee-total, and until now she hadn't really missed it. The odd occasion when she breathed in the scent of Jonah and Allan's Waitrose red wine maybe. It was more like she missed the *idea* of alcohol, the thought that she could drink something that would soothe her woes or relax her to sleep. But now she wanted some to blot out the rest of the festive countdown. Hedgehogs. Rashid being a little twerp. The Christmas show.

She had told the children about the Christmas performance that afternoon and, as predicted, they had got all bulbous-eyed with excitement, chattering with ideas of dressing up as robots (Felix) or doing a tribute to *Frozen* (Cherry and Alice). Most of the other boys had declared the show idea 'sick' and Emily was so out of touch she couldn't remember whether 'sick' meant 'bad' or 'good' these days. What she also didn't know was where to start? She didn't want to phone Mr Jarvis and see if, at seventy-five years old, he would like to pen songs for a Christmas performance. Was he even still alive? He'd had a nasty bout of pneumonia before he left…

'Bloody hell!' she blasted as she caught her finger under the nail she was trying to hammer in. That hurt and it was starting to bleed. Emily put her finger to her mouth and sucked. *This* sucked! No money in the budget to call a repair man and she wasn't going to ask Susan's husband to abandon a golf day because she was incapable of replacing a couple of shelves. It was a couple of shelves! Anyone could sort that, couldn't they? Without a trip to A&E…

'Hello?'

Someone was still here. But she'd checked the whole school before she embarked on this DIY crusade. Dennis had flitted off minutes after the bell had rung with talk of faggots for tea. Linda Rossiter had lingered for a while, wrapping empty cardboard boxes with Christmas paper to put under a quirky and frankly rather scary looking tree made from recyclables. Emily wasn't sure how festively attractive empty Heinz cans, Pringle tubes and Walkers packets could be… ever. There had been no one else. So, who was here?

She stepped out of the stationery cupboard and there was her answer. Standing in her classroom, beard freshly trimmed to nothing more than a light coating of stubble, no hat and shaggy brown hair tamed and swept back behind his ears, wearing black jeans with boots and a maroon jumper under that thick winter coat, was Ray Stone. In his hands were two tool bags.

'Hiding with the paperclips again, Miss Parker?' he commented with a grin.

'What are you doing here?' she half-whispered like Susan had bugged the room. Maybe she *had* bugged the room. When times were slightly less lean there had been talk of every class having its own Amazon Echo Dot…

'You're bleeding,' Ray said, dropping the bags and hastening towards her. 'You got a first aid kit in this place?'

'No,' Emily said. 'I mean, yes. But it's nothing.' Ugh. It had dripped a bit on her skirt. And her skirt was hand wash only. Everything vintage was hand wash only unless you wanted it in pieces or fit for no one but a six-month-old baby.

'Let me see.'

He had reached to take her hand and she found her insides boiling up at the very thought of his skin touching hers. She'd gone mad! It must be some sort of reaction to doing shelf repairs or being in a confined space. She quickly put her finger in her mouth again, the metallic taste a bit grim, but if she sucked hard enough surely it would stem the blood flow.

'You shouldn't be here.' She had said the words through a mouth full of finger and it hadn't sounded quite as clear as she had hoped. She withdrew the digit and carried on. 'You need to be DBS checked to be here.'

'I've been DBS checked,' he replied.

He didn't smell of alcohol or Plasticine anymore. He smelt of something possibly made by Radox with undernotes of Givenchy.

'I've done some music workshops with schoolkids before.

Older than yours. More into Drake songs than my songs. Definitely not into "Baby Shark".'

Emily couldn't help but raise a smile at that comment. The Baby Shark song had been the bane of her life last year.

'Come on,' Ray said. 'Let me fix those shelves.'

Now she was suspicious. Why on earth was this singing sensation back in her classroom armed with tools like a handyman?

'What's going on?' she asked him, waving her finger in the air in a bid to dry it of her saliva. 'Is this some new reality TV show you're part of?' Or maybe Susan Clark was behind this. She could have set this whole thing up in a bid to catch Emily out. First a superstar in the shed and now he was back with everything except overalls. What was the Head going to throw at her next?

'I knocked down the shelves. I've come to fix them. That's it.'

'I don't believe you,' Emily said.

'You *and* all the British press,' Ray commented with a sigh. He followed it up with a smile. 'But I've learned to ride that choppy ocean like the very best surfer. So, put me in the cupboard again, Emily.'

'I've been doing perfectly well on my own, if you must know.' She sniffed, watching a blood droplet slide its way down her forefinger.

'Really?' he queried, stepping into the storage space. 'You're using nails to hold up the shelves?'

'What else would you use?'

'Is there any more of that coffee going?' he asked. 'Because I'm confident, by the time you've made us both one, I'll have these back in place stronger than ever before.'

She swallowed. What to do? Accept this unexpected help

or order him off the premises again? Was he really DBS checked? Did it really matter if there were no children on the premises?

'But, do me a favour,' Ray said. 'Put a plaster on that cut *before* you make the coffee. I don't like my Nescafé with an extra shot of plasma.'

Sixteen

The shelves were proving a little trickier than Ray had envisaged. The walls of the inside of the cupboard were crumbling every time he tried to fix something to them. He was currently plugging them with a combination of tissue paper, Rawlplugs and Blu Tack. And now, Emily had just put festive music on her phone.

'It's still November you know,' he called out.

'What?' Emily replied over the strains of 'Do They Know It's Christmas'.

'You don't have to play Christmas music just because all the shops and cafés are.'

The volume decreased suddenly, and he heard her boots on the linoleum floor, coming closer. He turned his head a little, holding a screw into the flaky wall as she appeared.

'If you must know, I'm seeking inspiration.'

'You play the xylophone?'

'Glockenspiel actually.'

Her face was so deadpan he didn't know if she was

serious or not. A sigh left her lips and he forced the screw into place with a hard push.

'I'm in charge of the Christmas show this year,' she said.

'Yeah?' Ray answered, steadying the half-up bracket. 'You do a nativity with tea-towels and donkey suits and stuff?'

'I wish it were that simple,' Emily said. She commandeered a high stool from the edge of the room and climbed up onto it.

'When I was at school,' Ray began. 'I was always the innkeeper. I was the tallest and apparently that meant the role was mine.' He smiled. 'I never did find any Biblical evidence that the innkeeper was a six-footer.'

'Well,' Emily said. 'This year Mrs Clark wants a show to end all shows.' She sniffed, hands at full stretch as she made adjustment to the hanging display on the ceiling. 'I think she would actually love it if I could get Hugh Jackman to star in it.'

'I hope he's DBS checked,' Ray answered.

'Oh!' Emily exclaimed. 'I'm so sorry. That was really, really rude of me!'

Her hands were at her face now, looking embarrassed. She really was very attractive. He picked up another screw. 'It was only a joke,' Ray said. 'I'm sure Hugh Jackman has all the right credentials.'

'I know, but here I am saying in a roundabout way that he's a singing star and you're here, an *actual* singing star…'

'In a cupboard,' Ray said. 'Mending your shelves because I knocked them down in between trespass and animal protection.' He picked up the screwdriver. 'And you've seen the news, no one is really wanting me to appear in anything at the moment. Well, anyone apart from *Loose Women* who would probably want to pick over the bones of my former relationship like it's leftover Christmas turkey.' Why was he telling her this? Because he needed to broach the subject of the children's mobile phone photos of him…

'I don't watch shows like that or really read anything but the BBC Breaking News on my phone… except I really should turn off the alerts because it keeps making the dramatic music noise in the middle of class even if I put it on silent.' She was up on her tip-toes now and the stool didn't seem particularly stable.

'Did my news get an alert on the app?' Ray asked.

'Should it have?'

He sighed, refocusing on the task in hand and using the screwdriver hard to vent his frustration. 'Some people seem to think it's more important than anything.'

'Some people are stupid,' Emily answered.

He looked back up at her then and she was smiling down at him.

'Sorry,' she said. 'I always try to teach my children to be all-accepting. Treat everyone equally and don't be quick to judge. There's so much miscommunication in the world, so much pre-ordained directioning – from politicians to *Strictly Come Dancing*. I want my Year Six's to know their own minds and walk their own paths.' She smiled again. 'But don't tell Mrs Clark that. I think she'd rather they just followed the rules without thinking too much. Which is hard when you're ten and want to know everything about the world.'

She was animated now, not in her movement – thank God, given the stool situation – but in her manner. There was a light in her eyes when she talked about the class of individuals he had encountered that morning, a very deep affection. He didn't remember any teachers he had giving off anything like that vibe. And, Miss Parker was serving all this with a side-order of sultry he could almost guarantee she knew nothing about…

'They like you,' Ray commented, putting the wood back in place and reaching for a spirit level. 'The kids.'

'Well, I'm not sure that's true of all of them. I have a job to do and that involves making everyone try the hardest they can. Some try more than others, shall we say?'

'You listen to them,' Ray remarked, standing back from his work and looking hard at the bubble sitting in the trap of the level. 'Not everyone listens these days.' Like the press. Like his dad. Had his mum really listened to him like he thought she had? Or had she been far more wasted than he liked to remember?

'I can't disagree with that. My flatmate – *ex*-flatmate I should say – never listens if it opposes some grand plan of his. And my mother never usually hears, let alone listens.'

'Families, eh?'

'Yes,' Emily answered. 'More trouble than they're worth. Although don't tell the children I said that. Not that you're likely to see them again, but… whoa!'

Ray looked away from the shelves to see the stool starting to sway and Emily, on top of it, rocking back and forth attempting to maintain her balance. He acted fast. Jumping out of the cupboard, he got to her exactly as the stool finally gave way and she came tumbling towards the ground. He caught her, mid-air, steadying her in his arms.

'Oh, my… I don't know what happened,' Emily breathed, shock coating her words, shaking a little.

'You stood *en pointe* on top of a stool that's seen better days.' He swallowed, as she gazed up at him. 'You could have really hurt yourself.' Holding her close was doing the strangest things to his insides right now. He seemed to want to brush away that fringe of auburn hair that was almost in her beautiful eyes...

'We don't have the budget for... big, strong...' Emily started.

His heart was beating faster wanting to know what she was going to say next.

'Ladders,' Emily finished. She jumped down out of his arms and brushed her hands together the way British people do when there's not the remotest chance of their palms actually being dusty, but they need to do something to move the situation forward...

'Well,' Ray said, stepping back over towards his handiwork. 'Those shelves aren't going to be moving any time soon.' She moved to stand next to him. 'You know, if you have to hide any other men in there ever.'

'Oh... well... actually this morning was a first for me.'

She was blushing now. It was sweet and also somehow incredibly sexy. He cleared his throat. Holding her had definitely done something to him. 'Listen, Emily, I'm not going to lie, this press attention is difficult at the moment and my agent is doing her best to fight fires but, well, she's not Captain Marvel, you know what I'm saying?'

'I think so. She can try and help, but she can't work miracles?'

'Yeah,' Ray answered. 'Exactly that. So, I'm going to need to know that none of those photos the kids took of me this morning are going to end up on the internet.'

'Oh… I see.'

'I'm not saying they're the kind of kids to do that but, at the moment, the whole world seems out to get me.' He put his hands up, knowing he sounded particularly pathetic. 'Not that I'm asking for anything like sympathy but…' He was. A bit. And he hated asking for anything. 'OK, so, my agent needs to know that nothing is going to hit the fan while she's busy trying to…'

'Emulate Captain Marvel,' Emily suggested.

'Exactly that,' Ray agreed.

'I understand,' she answered with a pragmatic nod. 'I'll speak to the children in the morning and I'll ask them to delete any photos.'

It was the best he could hope for. What had he been expecting? For Emily to visit the kids at home? Demand their devices and check their Snapchat history? 'Thank you,' Ray said sincerely.

'No, thank *you*,' Emily said. 'For… breaking my fall just now and for fixing the shelves.' She smiled. 'As much as I hate to admit it, I probably couldn't have done it on my own. If I knew anything about home improvements I would be fixing my own central heating right now.' She shook her head. 'It's either going to be as cold as Siberia when I get home or roasting hot like… jalapeños dancing in Death Valley… with a fever.'

'Your heating's still broken?' Ray asked.

'Yes. Apparently. Perfect timing with Christmas coming and the flatmate going and this school play to coordinate.' She sighed. 'But, first world problems, right? I'll work it out.' She started to stack chairs on top of tables and tidy up.

'Well,' he began. What was he doing? What was he going

to say? He didn't have time for any of this… but he did have the experience. 'I could take a look at it for you, if you like.'

'Oh, that's OK,' Emily said immediately. 'I'll struggle on for a bit, extra jumpers when it's cold and bikini tops when it's not. See if I can track down the seemingly uncontactable landlord.'

'Seriously,' Ray found himself continuing. 'My dad was a heating engineer before he retired. I know almost all there is to know, without the qualifications but, I promise I won't blow your place up.'

'That's awfully kind of you but…'

Walk away, Ray. You fixed the shelves. You asked her about the photos. You have no other reason to offer anything else. She might have felt amazing in your arms, but you don't do relationships and Emily is nice. Too nice for someone like you. Now he could hear someone else's voice in his head. He needed to banish that and quickly.

'Listen, what sort of man would I be if I left here with all these tools knowing that they could have been put to more use.' He lifted up one of the bags he'd brought – items from his stuff in Gio's storage locker Deborah had managed to secure him access to.

'I don't know.'

She looked a little awkward. Like he was pushing this on her. What was his motivation here? Obviously, it was nothing but the idea of pure distraction. Filling his evening with anything but going to the nearest pub and waiting hopefully for a text telling him he had a new rental to go to, whilst avoiding scrolling through social media and ignoring the judgemental looks from other bar patrons…

'Listen, you'd be doing me a favour,' he admitted. Now

he was the one who felt awkward. 'I'm at a really loose end tonight waiting for something from my agent and your central heating issue is arousing the unfulfilled engineer in me. If I go now, I won't be able to stop thinking about this problematic boiler and then the paparazzi are bound to catch me, head in my hands or a frown on my forehead and it will be with tomorrow's headline…' He made quotation marks with his fingers. '*Stone At Rock Bottom*. And all it will be, will be a photo of me thinking about your heating dilemma, and you not letting me help you will just keep this bad press going.'

'OK,' Emily said, a curve of a smile on her mouth.

'Thank God for that,' Ray replied.

'But you must let me pay you if you manage to fix it,' she insisted.

'Seriously?' Ray asked. 'For all this fun I'm going to have?'

'I'll finish packing up,' Emily said.

Seventeen

Islington

Emily had no idea what she was doing right now. It was as if this week had turned into an episode of *Wayward Pines* and someone else was controlling what happened in her life. Why had she agreed for Ray Stone – celebrity known to the entire planet – to come to her flat and look at her central heating? And, come to that, why had he offered? Yes, he had said he needed a distraction from the fallout of his life that was almost-BBC-Breaking-News-alert-worthy, but, surely, someone with his connections had more available to him than tinkering with her thermostat. What did celebrities do when they weren't being celebrities? Were they ever really *not* celebrities once they hit a certain ceiling? If the Tube ride home had been anything to go by, she already knew the answer to that.

'I'm sorry about that,' Ray said as they burst into the freezing air, fresh out of the station.

'It's OK.'

It wasn't OK. Emily had felt for him. They had been

packed into a carriage hurtling away from Stretton Park towards Angel and commuters had started getting out their mobile phones and taking photos of him. It was subtle at first, twisted screens and surreptitious looks and then it was more obvious and uncaring. The moment it had started, Ray had ceased all conversation with her, turning sideways as he gripped the bar above his head. He had said nothing. Not to her. Not to anyone violating his privacy. The behaviour of the British public had made Emily cross. Was this how his life was? Unable to just get on a Tube without someone snapping a shot of him?

'It wasn't that I didn't want to continue our conversation about Christmas. I just didn't want them to take photos of you... with me. I'm not a good look right now and if your headteacher is really intent on making your life hell like you said three stops ago, then I'm not going to win you kudos.'

'You might,' Emily replied, her breath visible in the night as they turned a corner and she led the way through Canonbury towards her home. 'If you fix my central heating. Because the constantly changing temperature alters my mood. One minute I'm Mary Poppins, the next I could be Tywin in *Game of Thrones*.'

'Shit,' Ray said, exhaling with a throaty laugh.

'I didn't realise it was quite so bad,' Emily admitted as they strode on, past the upmarket terraced houses and patches of iron fenced parkland.

'Bad?' Ray asked. 'That was just normality. Bad is the paparazzi on your tail. They can be relentless and ruthless and they really don't care what they do or how they do it.' He turned his head to smile at her then. 'Everyone wants to be famous, right? Glitz, glamour and invites to all the red-carpet events.'

'It's not at all like that?'

'It is in the beginning. When it's all new and fresh and *you* are all new and fresh and not jaded by the endless exhausting round of being nice to everyone when they ask the same questions over and over and over again.' He shook the two tool bags in his hands with a good degree of frustration. 'God, I sound like the most ungrateful bastard in the world.'

'Everyone has parts of their life they want to change. There must be good things about being a musician though, or you wouldn't keep doing it.'

'What parts of your life do you want to change, Emily?'

This had thrown her. She had been more than happy to hear about his life. It was interesting and diverse. It wasn't making festive shoeboxes to send to Bulgaria or trying to stop rap battles in the lunch queue.

'I'd settle for a change in my apartment's climate control for now,' she answered, giving nothing. What did she have to give? She didn't understand her parents and the love of her life was dead? That would kill the mood. And she did feel strangely upbeat. Like this diversion from her routine was welcome.

'That will be sorted within the hour,' Ray replied. 'So, after that? Do you want your headteacher's job? Is that why she has it in for you?'

Emily shook her head immediately, slowing a little as she prepared to lead them across the road. Christmas had begun on this street. There were bright coloured lights and reindeer all along the eaves of half a dozen houses, hanging garlands in the large windows, Christmas card collections beginning on ledges. Families with children were more than ready. Families *without* children would be catching up in a week or so. If it wasn't for her thirty-three pupils she'd be struggling to make any effort at all…

'Being a headteacher is the goal for most teachers when they start out. It's like working your way up to becoming the CEO.' She sighed. 'Except I've done what you shouldn't do as a teacher. I've become attached to Stretton Park.' She smiled then, leading the way over the road to the opposite pavement. 'My Year Sixes this year, I've known them since they were in Reception. Not all of them. Some of them joined the school late, but Jayden and Frema and Felix and Angelica and Alice, they've all been familiar faces for so long.' She felt herself blushing despite the cold temperatures. 'That sounds ridiculously sentimental, doesn't it? And I know they're leaving in July, to start a whole new life at secondary school, but, well…' She took a breath. '*I* feel comfortable at Stretton Park.'

'So, you *are* after the Head's job,' Ray said with a smirk.

Emily shook her head. 'No, you don't usually get the top managerial position at the school you're already working at. Susan is a good few years away from retirement and I *should* get experience at another school to widen my abilities but…' She'd stopped talking because she didn't know if she really wanted to say any of this out loud, to Ray, or even so she could hear it herself.

'But…' Ray prompted.

'I'm not ready to leave yet.' She sighed. 'What I'd really

like is the Deputy Head position at Stretton Park until I *am* ready to move on.'

'Have you applied?' Ray asked.

'No,' Emily said. 'Because it hasn't been advertised yet. And the longer it goes on not being advertised and Susan carries on talking about budget restraint and cutbacks, I'm thinking she's going to say we don't need a Deputy Head at all. Or she'll give the position to Linda Rossiter as some sort of un-paid promotion. And Linda Rossiter is the type of person to take that, for no more money, and be ridiculously grateful.'

'And I thought *I* had problems,' Ray said.

Emily laughed. 'I can't wait to show you my boiler.' What was she saying? That had sounded like a euphemism, which it definitely was not. This was such a bad idea. She should have simply asked her mother for a few hundred pounds when she'd called earlier. A few hundred pounds was a couple of rounds of drinks at her father's members' club. No, she would have to be literally about to become destitute before she would ask for help. And even then she might consider crowd-funding her weekly food shop before she asked her parents. And her landlord should be sorting this!

'Your boiler won't know what's hit it,' Ray replied with a wink.

Emily put her key in the door and pushed while Ray checked out the view across the street from the landing window. This was a nice area. It was in the thick of things, but it was also tranquil with its tree-lined streets and large park across the street. He imagined that in summer those bare boughs would be plump with greenery and the bitter-cold park they had walked through would become a haven for picnickers or office workers on their lunch breaks. It wasn't anything like New North Road and it also wasn't like Gio's rental property with its high metal gates you had no chance of seeing the property through and decked outside space for low maintenance. He had never changed anything at that place, not even to add photos or personal items. Because it was a rental? Or because it wasn't a home? He already suspected that behind Emily's apartment door would be more 'home' than anything else...

'Surprise!'

Emily let out a scream and on instinct Ray dropped the tool bags and stepped forward from behind her. The sound of festive Andy Williams singing 'It's The Most Wonderful Time Of The Year' struck up and there were party poppers popping, the paper foliage hitting him in the face. The entrance hall suddenly felt crowded with two men bursting from the inside to greet them with this unexpected revelry. Hadn't Emily said she had an *ex*-flatmate earlier?

'Shit! It's Ray Stone! Jonah, are you seeing this? Emily's brought home Ray shitting Stone.'

Ray put his hand forward to this same-height-as-him ginger-haired man. 'Hi, Ray shitting Stone, pleased to meet you.'

'Sorry,' the ginger man replied, cheeks turning almost the same colour as his hair. 'I didn't mean to be rude. It's just Emily bringing any man home is big news around here and you're...'

'Here to fix the central heating,' Ray replied.

'Jonah. Allan. What are you both doing here?' Emily said. Her hand was still clasped to her chest.

'Forget that,' Jonah said. 'What are you doing with Ray Stone?'

Emily turned to face Ray directly then. 'I am really sorry about my ex-flatmate who I am considering depriving of his second key rights. This is Jonah and his partner, Allan.'

'Hello,' Ray greeted, picking the tool bags back up.

'It's amazing to meet you,' Allan picked the conversation up. 'Are you really real? Can I check? Would it be OK to squeeze your arm?'

'Allan, for God's sake,' Jonah said, rolling his eyes. 'I'm right here.'

'I'm so sorry,' Emily said again. 'They're usually such normal individuals. I don't know what's got into them and I don't know what they're doing here in *my* flat with…' The music changed to 'Rocking Around the Christmas Tree'. '… With Brenda Lee on the stereo and… playing with things that should be saved for Christmas Day.' She picked a piece of party popper plumage out of Allan's hair.

'Allan had some good news at work and we wanted to celebrate so we bought festive eats at the shop and we thought we'd celebrate with you.' Jonah beamed.

'Have you lost *your* job?' Emily asked him as she checked out her watch. 'Because most hotel restaurants require their head chef to be in the kitchen at this time of night, doing whatever head chefs do.'

'I've got a couple of days off before the real Christmas madness sets in,' Jonah informed.

'Well,' Emily said, bustling past them, 'you should

be spending it doing something productive or having a Brighton mini-break. Not worrying about me.' She turned to Ray again, her cheeks flushed. 'The boiler is this way, but if you've decided to take your tools and run in the opposite direction, I won't blame you.'

'I'd be a bit miffed,' Allan admitted as Ray followed Emily inside. He took in the large windows and the cosy furnishings. *Soft. Comforting. A real home.*

'Could you sing the chorus of "Loved By You"?' Allan giggled. 'Just a snippet would do.'

'No, he couldn't,' Emily called as they reached the kitchen. 'I don't ask you to read me lawyer contracts when you come round. Neither do I expect to stand and narrate the lesson I taught to the children for your pleasure. I don't ask Jonah to cook.' She stopped talking and turned around. Ray watched the two men squeeze into what was a rather compact kitchen space. 'OK, that last one was a bad analogy,' Emily admitted. She sighed. 'Why don't you two open a bottle of wine, if you've brought wine, and I'll come through in a minute?'

'Oh, we're not having our little soirée in the lounge,' Allan informed. 'We've set up the roof terrace.'

'The patio heaters are on, the table is ready, the lights are glowing and any second now the timer on the oven is going to go off telling us the first batch of hot snacks is ready.' Jonah smiled. 'I haven't handmade them all. We went to Iceland for some of it. Don't tell anyone. Especially your mother.'

'Fine,' Emily replied. 'I'll be out in a second.'

'We got you a bottle of the Morello cherry fizz you like,'

Allan informed, opening the half-glazed door that seemed to lead from tiny kitchen to outdoors. 'And the elderflower tonic.'

When the men had left them alone Emily let out a heavy sigh. 'I'm so sorry about them.'

Ray shook his head. 'I'm just the repair man.'

'Jonah used to live here. He seems to forget he doesn't still live here sometimes.'

'On the plus side, they've brought you food that does smell good,' Ray replied. His stomach was starting to need something now. He hadn't eaten since the breakfast of earlier.

'You're welcome to join us,' Emily said, putting her bag down on the small table for two. 'Part payment for looking at the boiler. Even if you can't fix it.'

'Oh, no, it's fine. I'll just take a look at this beast and I'll be out of your hair,' Ray said, stepping towards the boiler on the wall.

'Would you like a coffee?' Emily asked.

He would actually have killed for a beer, but he found himself nodding. 'Yeah,' he said. 'A coffee would be good.'

Eighteen

The roof terrace, Crowland Terrace, Canonbury, Islington

'Jonah! Get the girl a glass of Morello cherry fizz right now! Come here! Come and sit right down here and tell me everything!'

Allan's words were so loud Karen and Sammie could probably hear in the flat below and, balancing a tray of snacks on her arm, Emily quickly shut the door to the kitchen where Ray was currently wrist deep in her boiler...

'Sshh!' she insisted, heading quickly to where Jonah and Allan were sitting beneath her two ancient-but-still-working patio heaters in a cosy, festive snug of candles and fairy lights they had created. There were lights entwined round the pergola and round the evergreens in pots that had taken the place of the summer blooms they'd had earlier in the year. Despite the cold temperatures, it felt warm and inviting and she put the snacks down and hurried to take a seat on a vibrant cushion Jonah had obviously got out from her lounge cupboard. Should she reset boundaries now he definitely wasn't living with her? Or was she just worried he might have noticed one of the photos of Simon he had put away was back out again…

'Never mind "sshh"!' Allan continued at full volume, unrelenting. 'You've brought a fucking pop star home! That needs to be discussed!'

'Yes, it does,' Jonah agreed. Her best friend didn't look quite as excited as Two L's. In fact, he looked a little concerned. What had happened between yesterday and today? Yesterday he was pushing men at her hoping for awkward flatmate dating scenarios. Now he didn't seem to like it that she'd bought someone in to look at her heating. It made no sense.

'There isn't a lot to tell,' she answered. That was a lie. More had happened to her in these past few days than had happened in her entire career.

'Oh, so, you were just there at school, teaching about Good King Wenceslas or whatever, and in walks Ray Stone and then you ask him to mend your central heating?' Allan announced, verging on hysterical. 'Jonah, are you getting this? Ray Stone is currently in the kitchen, metres away from us, getting all oily trying to fix a boiler. I mean, what universe are we currently living in? Forget the whole EU debacle! This is off the scale!'

'He saved a hedgehog,' Emily said, picking up a glass of red liquid from the table and taking a sip. 'At school. He was there, in the playground, with it in his hands and it had a broken leg, or something.'

'I might pee myself!' Allan announced, hands flapping. 'I might actually pee myself!'

'And you asked him to fix the boiler?' Jonah asked, frowning.

'No... well, yes... after he had mended the shelves that he knocked down... after I...' She stopped talking, considering for a second whether she really wanted to end the sentence and be responsible for the potential wetting of Allan's underwear... She cleared her throat. 'Hid him in the stationery cupboard.'

Allan yelped and leaped up, almost knocking into the patio heater. He grabbed his crotch and squealed. 'Oh my God! Jonah, make her stop!'

Emily watched Jonah take one of the cranberry and feta pin wheels and eat it very slowly and deliberately. He wasn't musing whether the shop-bought snacks were inferior to his own creations. He was thinking. Deeply.

'This is *the* most exciting thing that's happened to me since... I don't know... since...' Allan exclaimed, hopping from one foot to the other like he was dancing on hot coals.

'Since Jonah moved in?' Emily suggested in a bid to divert attention to her concerned-looking friend.

'Oh, natch!' Allan answered quickly. 'Natch to that.' He sat down close to Jonah and draped an arm around his shoulders, pulling him close. 'That was the best day of my life up to now.'

'Emily, I don't mean to douse this man situation with cold water but you have read the news lately, right?' Jonah asked.

Emily dipped her lips into her drink again before making response. 'I stopped reading the news ever since that article about shops selling wonky cucumbers. There isn't anything of interest for me lately.' She'd actually stopped reading the news after one particular article a year ago. The article that had made her heart break a second time.

'Well, I know what the press can be like but... I wouldn't

be your best friend if I didn't mention that Ray Stone is all over it at the moment... and not in a great light.'

'Oh, Jonah, shame on you!' Allan announced. 'Have you been reading the *tabloids* again? Honestly, the trash these sous chefs read when they're not chopping up quince.'

'What does it say?' Emily asked. She didn't really want to know. But she had the feeling that Jonah really needed to tell her. He had been so excited about introducing her flatmates/dating opportunities last night it seemed very off for him to be this cautious now. She needed to know why.

'Well,' Jonah said, 'it kind of suggests, in a roundabout way... that he was less than a gentleman to his ex-girlfriend.'

Allan coughed, returning to his seat. 'Well, what does that mean? Because I've enjoyed quite a lot of less-than-gentlemanly pleasure in my time.'

'It means... I think,' Jonah continued cautiously. 'Well, the articles say that his ex-girlfriend says he has a temper. There's talk of raging rows and smashed glasses and neighbours complaining about the noise and... Em, I wouldn't want you to get involved with someone like that.'

'If any of it's true,' Allan added.

Emily adjusted her position on her cushion. 'I'm not *involved* with him. He's trying to stop me freezing to death or sweating into a pool of perspiration before Christmas arrives. I wouldn't have had to ask *anyone* if the landlord had answered my millions of calls!' She took a breath. 'Ray is doing me a good deed. And he's been nothing but pleasant and interesting to talk to and... he was so gentle with Olivia Colman.'

'Jesus!' Allan wept. 'You met Olivia Colman too? She's a fucking queen... literally.'

'Em, I worry about you,' Jonah said. 'That's all. I worry. And I worry because I'm not here anymore and I know you're still struggling and… I just care.' Jonah wrapped his hand around his glass of wine and took a sip.

'She knows that,' Allan told him. 'And I care too. You know that too, don't you? And if you didn't know before, you know now.'

'I know,' Emily answered. 'Of course, I know. And I appreciate the concern, really I do.'

'But you're not one of your ten-year-olds, right?' Jonah said, shaking his head. 'And I'm acting like an annoying younger brother right now, aren't I?'

Emily smiled. 'No. You're acting like an annoying best friend who I love very much. But, I've got this. I'm a good judge of character and I make those decisions based on how *I* find people, not what other people say. I mean, otherwise, you and I would never have been friends.' She laughed then leaned forward and ruffled up Jonah's carefully crafted hair. He batted her away.

'Oi!' Jonah said, hurrying to flatten it back down.

'So, just mending your heating then and saving the local wildlife. That's all there is to it,' Allan asked, popping a spring roll in his mouth.

'Yes,' Emily replied. 'That's all there is to it.' She swallowed, remembering how it felt to be held in someone's arms again, even if it was only to save her from dropping to the floor. Ray's solid frame, bearing her weight so effortlessly, his gorgeous ombre eyes…

'Shame,' Allan breathed.

Nineteen

The interior thermostat wasn't working properly. Ray had thought that was going to be the case from Emily's description of the issues she was having. The good news was he had diagnosed the problem. The bad news was he couldn't immediately fix it. It would need a new part and there was no chance of getting one just like that. It wasn't something that could be sourced from the corner shop.

He wiped his hands on a tea-towel Emily had given him for that exact purpose and looked around the tiny kitchen space. He could possibly have fit fifty of this size room in the kitchen of Gio's rental property. But all that rental property had *had* was space. It didn't have kitsch egg timers or a set of Russian nesting dolls or three whisks in rainbow colours... Who needed three whisks? But again, it was as homely as it got, despite its small proportions. Or maybe because of them.

Ray took a sideways step, avoiding the table and looked through the partial glass door. He could see Emily and her two friends out on the roof terrace. Apart from the generous lounge area the terrace was probably the next biggest part of this apartment. The bathroom definitely wasn't spacious. He'd almost got up close and personal with the shower curtain while using the toilet. But it did have a bath, he'd noticed.

Under patio heaters, surrounded by the glow of fairy lights, the friends were talking, sharing snacks and glasses of wine. He swallowed. *Wine.* Wine would be great right now. His mother's favourite had been a Merlot called Turner Road. He still remembered the orange and white bird on the bottle…

His phone buzzed in the pocket of his coat, which he had hung over one of the little chairs. He reached in, drawing it out and looking at the message. It was from Deborah.

> Two things. One, I've lined you up with a spot on City FM tomorrow morning. You need to be there at 6 a.m. Not a second later. They have solemnly promised this will be about your work on your new album and they want you to sing 'Let It Be Me'. They will have a keyboard. Two, I haven't been able to find you a house yet. I'll try again in the morning. Stay in a hotel tonight but make it low-key. And keep your chin up. I've got this. D

Ray's eyes blurred a little as he studied the words. He had to sing tomorrow. On live radio. Early in the morning when his vocal cords would be cold, no matter how many voice exercises he performed. He had no new house to go to tonight. He should have told Deborah exactly how dire his financial situation currently was. Even a low-key hotel might be an issue. And he should definitely have told her about Dr Crichton. He ought to leave here now, try his luck at the nearest Travelodge. There was no way he was going back to his dad and New North Road. He picked his coat off the chair and put it on before heading to the door.

'Can you get us tickets for the Christmas show?' Allan asked, crying with laughter. 'I have to see it. It's going to be truly spectacular in all the wrong ways.'

'That's very rude,' Emily responded. 'The children are extremely creative. They've come up with lots of ideas already.'

'And you're the one who's going to have to implement them,' Allan reminded. 'You sing "Jingle Bells" out of tune!'

'I do not!' Emily insisted, cheeks reddening despite the cold. She took a sip of her drink and noticed Ray coming out from the house. 'Oh!' she exclaimed, standing up. 'Is it unfixable? Is it going to cost me thousands of pounds?'

'Come and sit down next to me, Ray Stone,' Allan ordered, patting a red cushion to his left.

'It's the thermostat inside the tank,' Ray informed. 'It needs a replacement.'

'I knew it,' Emily said with a heavy sigh. More money to be shelled out. Yes, she could claim it back from the landlord but the last time he hadn't been quick in reimbursing and she had had to withhold rent money to compensate herself. 'Is it going to be terribly expensive?'

'I don't think so,' Ray said.

'And what is a successful pop star's idea of expensive, we ask,' Allan remarked, smiling at Ray.

'Allan, you're an embarrassment,' Jonah remarked with a tut.

'I would think it's under fifty quid,' Ray told her.

'Really?!' Emily said. She could cope with that. Things were suddenly looking up.

'Would you like some wine?' Allan offered, standing up and picking up a bottle and a glass.

'I should probably get going,' Ray admitted.

A mobile phone began to ring and Jonah got to his feet in a panic. 'It's the hotel,' he stated, looking at the screen. 'I'm on holiday. Everyone knows I'm on holiday. This is bad news.'

'Well, answer it then!' Allan urged. 'Away from us, so we don't have to listen to talk about chopping techniques.' He rolled his eyes. 'Honestly, the lengths these chefs go to to make food like a piece of art. If I want something that looks like a Salvador Dali I'll go to a gallery not a restaurant.'

'Hello,' Jonah spoke into his phone before moving across the terrace.

'Would you like a glass of wine?' Emily asked Ray who was still hovering and looking a little uncomfortable. 'Or there's Morello cherry lemonade.'

'Your pretend rosé Prosecco,' Allan teased.

'I'll—' Ray started before he was interrupted.

'Shit, Allan, we have to go. The restaurant's in meltdown. Two of the hobs have broken down and Hillary's in tears. The manager has begged me to come in and he sounds like he's on the verge of a nervous breakdown himself.'

'Oh, Jonah, that place! You don't own it, you know!'

'I know but this job is going to lead to even bigger things. Like you with your promotion,' Jonah reminded.

'Is that your job news?' Emily asked Allan excitedly.

'Put your coat on, Allan, I'll order an Uber,' Jonah said.

'Yes, that's my news. Promoted to manager. Underlings to be mean to now… I mean, colleagues to train and inspire.' He grinned as he put his jacket over his shoulders.

'Congratulations,' Emily said. 'I'm so pleased for you.'

'Not that I get a minute to announce it or celebrate it,' Allan said, frowning at Jonah.

'I'll make it up to you,' Jonah said.

'Ooo, is that a promise?'

'Yes, just, please, hurry up before my kitchen's never the same again.'

'It was lovely to meet you, Ray,' Allan said. 'Please do not leave on our account. There are snacks to finish and plenty of wine Madam here won't touch.'

'Allan!' Jonah hissed. He waved a hand at Emily. 'I'll call you tomorrow, OK?' He looked to Ray. 'Bye.'

'One more sausage roll,' Allan said, snatching one from the platter and stuffing it into his mouth with aplomb. 'Night all.'

And whipping up like a frenzied, winter whirlwind, the two men left the roof terrace.

'One glass of wine?' Emily offered Ray. 'To thank you for diagnosing my boiler's ailment?' She gasped. 'Where do I even buy this thermostat thing from?'

'I can have a look online,' Ray suggested. He took his phone out of his pocket like he was going to begin a search and moved to sit down opposite her. She poured him some wine into a glass. He hadn't accepted but the open wine had to be used up, didn't it?

'Sorry, you must think I'm the neediest person you've

ever met. I can Google it later... if you tell me what it's called... and spell it out.'

'No problem,' Ray said.

She held the glass out to him and he accepted it, immediately taking a drink.

'It's a nice place you've got here,' he remarked.

He was gazing out over the rooftops of Canonbury now. It was the view from the roof that Emily liked the best, because you could see a little bit of everything. Office buildings mixed with old-fashioned terracotta chimney pots. There were roof gardens, some with actual grass and even wooden hives for urban bee-keeping... London was far more than just a grey steel city, there were portions of diversity at every turn. In some ways she hoped the predicted snow was going to happen. A light dusting of white would give it all a magical Christmas topping. She might even start to get enthused about the season...

'I do love it,' she said. She did. Despite her future not being what she thought it was going to be on this street, she still loved her home.

'How long have you lived here?'

'Three years now.' A whole twelve months on her own without Simon. She regrouped. 'I don't own it. I mean to own it would be the most amazing thing in the world. But, even with a headteacher's salary it would be completely out of my reach.'

'Well, you never know,' Ray replied, drinking more wine. 'There's always the National Lottery.'

'I don't play that,' Emily admitted. 'I used to, but now I put the money I would have spent on tickets in a big vase in the lounge.' She smiled. 'I've been doing that since we moved in and I've never counted it. Jonah used to say it was probably the most valuable thing we had in the flat, but no burglar would be able to shift it.' She took a sip of her drink. 'Whereabouts do *you* live?'

Ray sighed, eyes looking into his glass. 'There's a question.'

Emily didn't know how to respond. He suddenly looked a little sad and she wondered if she'd asked too much. He *was* this well-known figure whose life got constantly shared with the world whether he liked it or not. She really shouldn't have been so nosy.

'I'm sorry,' she apologised. 'I'm being like Two L's... sorry, Allan, that's his nickname. Sometimes he loves it, other times he says it makes him sound like a rapper.' She cleared her throat. 'Sorry, it's none of my business where you live.'

'It's not that,' Ray admitted. He gulped down the rest of the wine and replaced the glass on the table. 'I... don't really live anywhere right now.'

'Oh,' Emily said, a little bit shocked.

'Yeah. I know. Tragic, right?' He sniffed. 'This supposed star everyone wants to snap a picture of on the Tube and he doesn't have a roof over his head.'

Emily gasped. 'Was that why you were in the school shed with Olivia Colman?'

He laughed then and shook his head. 'I don't think so but, you know, I don't know. I was drunk, maybe the shed with a hedgehog was preferable to a park bench with the press pack getting it all on their SD cards.' He picked up the bottle of wine and went to put some in her near empty glass. She hurried to put her hand across it.

'No… no, thank you.'

'You're going to make me drink alone?' he queried. 'You know that's equally as tragic as sleeping in a shed?'

'I… don't drink,' Emily informed matter-of-factly.

'Ah,' Ray said. 'I forgot it's a school night.'

Emily shook her head. 'No… I don't drink…' She took a breath. 'At all.' She shrugged quickly, as if it was nothing. It wasn't nothing. 'I've been totally tee-total for a year now and… not missing it at all.' She swallowed. 'OK, I might miss it a little bit, but these new flavoured lemonades and J2o Spritzs are pretty good.'

'Why?' Ray asked simply. 'If you don't mind me asking.'

She took a deep breath of the night air and looked into his gorgeous eyes again. She should tell him why. Basic gut feelings told her he was being honest with her about his housing situation, no matter how unlikely that might seem to the world at large.

She smiled. 'Health reasons.' She carried on quickly. 'Jonah talked a lot about liver when he had a spate of making his own pâté. It made me think about the damage I was probably doing to my human one with all that wine and gin and… well, you know.'

'They say it's sensible to have a couple of units a night,' Ray stated. 'Everything in moderation.'

'Well,' Emily said. 'I suppose we're all going to die some day no matter what the cause.' Why was she talking about death? And why hadn't she just told him the real reason she didn't drink? It wasn't like she was ashamed of it. She had the greatest of reasons for it and she was actually pretty proud of it. It wasn't too late to admit it if she spoke now…

'Yep,' Ray agreed, nodding. 'That's true. One minute you

could be going for a really simple procedure at the hospital and the next gone for ever.'

Emily looked at him again then. He was staring into the mid-distance. At the rooftops again? Or somewhere else entirely? Somewhere not even on this planet? Who was the real Ray Stone? The celebrity being depicted as a raging monster by the tabloids according to Jonah? Or someone else? Someone definitely troubled, but human nonetheless. *Real.*

'Where are you staying tonight?' Emily's lips blurted out. Should she have asked that?

'Listen, with all these great snacks and wine and—' he looked towards her bottle of red lemonade '—not wine… let's not make it into a pity party.' She watched him pick up two sausage rolls and pop them into his mouth.

Was she going to do this? After what Jonah had told her *and* after saying that she didn't want anyone in her spare room. But, on the other hand, he *had* fixed the school shelves *and* he'd found out what was wrong with her central heating. She should give him something…

'No pity,' Emily said deftly. 'Just the offer of my spare room for the night… or for however long you need it.' She nodded, picking up her glass and swirling around the dregs of the soft drink. 'It's spare, you know, a spare room, doing nothing much but being spare.' She blew out a breath. 'I mean, it isn't luxury and it's small but it's maybe better than…'

'A shed?' Ray suggested.

'Even with the heating doing its crazy thing at the moment I'd like to think that it was better than a shed.'

'I don't know what to say,' he replied.

'Say yes,' Emily said. 'Then I'll feel better about that oil you still have on your hands.'

He looked down at his fingers and cursed at the black streaks that lay there. 'Lucky it's radio in the morning not television.'

'You're on the radio?' Emily asked.

He nodded. 'City FM. I've got to be there at 6 a.m.'

'Well then,' Emily said. 'You need somewhere decent to sleep before that.' She stood up. 'I'll go and make the spare bed.'

'Emily,' Ray said, calling her back.

She turned around to face him. His expression told a story that looked like what she had offered him was not an empty room but a lifeline, something worth the world.

'Thanks,' he told her.

Twenty

Blurry-eyed, Emily woke up to the sound of water running in the bathroom. Her first thought was that something was now leaking and she had another boiler issue to deal with. But then, as she turned over in bed and reached for the switch for her bedside lamp, she remembered last night. Ray Stone had stayed the night. He could even be her new flatmate until she found a suitable paying party or got her promotion...

Glancing at the clock she saw it was only 5 a.m. Well, he had said he was meant to be at the radio station for 6 a.m. and City FM was over in Leicester Square. Usually she *got up* at 6 a.m., but once she was awake there was no nodding off again. She clambered out of bed and reached for her dressing gown – a 1940s peach silk with four little buttons in the middle to fasten it. Another piece of her inheritance money chipped away at in the name of melancholy...

As she opened her bedroom door the running water stopped and before she could take the few steps across the hall to the kitchen, the bathroom door burst open and there was a dripping wet Ray, completely naked.

'Oh... I...' Emily exclaimed, closing her eyes then opening them again, then not really knowing what to do. It took milliseconds for the taut physique to be ingrained on her brain. Broad chest, washboard abs, that deep muscular V to his... Eyes up – was that a scar on his shoulder?

'Sorry,' Ray apologised. 'I left the towel you gave me in my room.'

She couldn't proceed past him. He couldn't proceed past her. She had never had this small walkway scenario with Jonah. The only option she had was retreating backwards and letting him go past her to his room.

'Sorry,' she apologised again, eyes to the floorboards, catching sight of the water droplets falling to the wood. 'I'm not usually up this early so we won't... have this happen again.' Just how awkward was this?! And she still hadn't stepped back into her room... She shuffled backwards.

'Cheers,' Ray said, voice breaking a little as he headed back to his new abode.

When Ray came into the kitchen, dry and dressed, Emily was plunging the top of a cafetière down into inky black steaming coffee on the tiny table. There were two cups and saucers on placemats and a silver rack holding triangles of toast and the very last crumpet. He was in the same clothes but after the shower he definitely felt fresher.

'Good morning,' he greeted. 'Again.'

'Oh, hello,' Emily answered, turning to face him. Her fringe was a little stuck up and the gown she was wearing was on one shoulder far more than her other. The colour of the gown wasn't too dissimilar to the glow of her skin...

'I'm sorry about that before,' he said. Should he try and sit? It was a very snug space. 'I'm not usually a man-up-at-five-in-the-morning kind of guy.'

'It's fine,' Emily replied. 'Me neither. As I said. Not that I'm a man. I mean the five o'clock bit.' She poured the coffee into both the cups. 'Please, have some toast. Or the crumpet. I'll just get the margarine... do you like margarine? I don't have butter... but I have Nutella... or it might be out of date. Or there's Marmite. That never really goes out of date, does it?'

'I'm good,' Ray answered. 'The coffee's great.'

'Do you take milk?' Emily asked, hovering a small jug over his cup.

'Yeah... but not right now.' He picked up the cup and sipped some of the coffee. It was good coffee.

'Oh,' Emily said. She sniffed at the milk in her jug. 'It's not gone off, has it?'

'No,' Ray replied. 'It isn't that. It's dairy. I have to sing on the radio and dairy... it's not good for the voice.'

Neither was alcohol, but that hadn't stopped him from finishing up all the wine last night. And he hadn't done one breathing exercise since he'd left Harley Street... Had a night in the spare room of this apartment really made him wake up focused and half-sensible?

'Gosh, I'm so sorry,' Emily said, putting the milk jug down as if it was toxic. 'You must think I'm a very poor host.'

'I think the complete opposite,' Ray replied. He decided to keep standing, lean slightly on the worktop behind him.

'I think it was very kind of you to offer me your spare room for the night and as soon as I have an alternative, hopefully later today, I'll leave you in peace.'

'Oh, well, that's fine,' Emily said. 'But... wow, I'm still thinking about dairy. I could never be a singer in that case. Not that I have any ability in that area whatsoever. But, I do like dairy... cheese and... cheesecake... and well, cheese.'

Ray smiled. 'Chocolate's a no too.'

'Goodness,' Emily said, picking up her coffee cup. 'I could have the talent of Jennifer Hudson and I'd have to hide it from the world if it meant giving up all that.'

'Not giving it up,' Ray said. 'Just not eating it or drinking it a couple of hours before a performance.' He checked his watch. He was apprehensive. For the singing and for the interview. Deborah might have said there would be no questions about what was being talked about in the papers, but the radio show was live. Once the presenter asked the question over the airwaves there was no taking it back. And what if his voice cracked or broke the way it had done recently at the studio? There was nothing like not hitting the perfect notes to really compound the tale that his career was on its way to being over.

'I should get going,' he said, slurping the rest of his drink and putting the cup down again.

'Good luck,' Emily answered. 'Oh, is it OK to say good luck? You don't have any superstitions about that, do you?'

'No,' he said. 'Good luck works for me.'

'Oh,' Emily said, turning towards the worktop and moving multi-coloured tins, magazines and one of the three whisks. 'You should take this.' She held out a key on a small keyring made of acrylic with a pink pressed flower inside.

'Simply in case your alternative doesn't happen... not that I think it won't. But if it doesn't, you can get in if I'm not here before you... get back... maybe.'

'Emily,' he said, not reaching for it. 'That's really kind of you but I can't pay you anything for the room just yet so...'

'I've Googled the thermometer thing you told me I needed for the boiler. I was hoping, if it wasn't too much of an imposition, that you would perhaps fit it for me if I ordered it.' She carried on holding out the key. 'That would be payment enough for now. But I understand you'll probably get a better, much bigger place and that's fine if you do but... if you don't...'

He shook his head. Why was this virtual stranger being so nice to him? He was sure he didn't deserve it. And he definitely wasn't used to it.

'Thermostat,' Ray told her. 'Not thermometer.'

'Crap. See! I'll probably order the wrong thing.'

'I'll get one,' Ray told her. 'I'll try and get one today. After the radio thing.'

She offered the key again. 'Well, if that's the case then you'll need a key to get in to fix it.'

He looked at the brass attached to the ornate keyring. She was offering him her home for the price of an hour's work... He reached out, picking the key from her palm. 'Thank you.'

'No problem. I'll look forward to a flat that doesn't give me Caribbean cruise one minute and Northern Lights the next.'

He felt emotional in this moment. Perhaps it was the stress of the worry about this interview and singing live on radio. Or maybe it was the story Ida had sold to the newspapers, or his run-in with his dad last night. Or the threat of an operation looming. Maybe it was everything. He breathed deeply and tried to take control. 'I should go.'

'Yes, good luck,' Emily said. 'And, well, see you later.' She flapped a hand in the air. 'Perhaps.'

He picked up his coat from where it was still draped over the kitchen chair. 'See you later.'

Twenty-One

Stretton Park Primary School

'Rumour has it, Penny is pregnant.'

It was Dennis, sucking on something that smelled like rhubarb and custard. Emily found it surprising she could smell his sweet – or probably sweet*s* – over the lingering aroma of macaroni cheese that was clinging to the air and probably her silk shirt with real mother-of-pearl buttons. She couldn't remember where she had bought this one, but Simon had always said it was his favourite. It was always noisy in the hall at dinnertime and today was no different. All the children were either crashing knives and forks against plates or crinkling up tin foil from their lunchboxes.

'Did you say Penny is pregnant?' Emily asked, as loudly as she could without fear of being overheard. Penny was the cook. Emily knew she worked for next to nothing because her daughter was in Year Three.

'I said,' Dennis said, ducking his head a little closer, that half-sweet half-sour aroma ripening. 'Rumour has it she's pregnant.' He dipped a hand into the pocket of his trousers and pulled out more sweets. 'I wouldn't want to start a story that isn't true, but she lives near us and Mother saw her buying three packets of ginger biscuits the other day.'

Emily scoffed. 'Maybe she just likes ginger biscuits.'

'They're good for morning sickness, Mother says. And,' Dennis carried on, 'she's put on a bit of weight, don't you think?'

'I can't say I've noticed.' And Emily didn't scrutinise her colleagues like that… except maybe Mrs Adams before she left. She'd had a rather unmissable case of elephantiasis.

'Mark my words,' Dennis said. 'They'll be looking for a new cook soon to cover maternity leave. Mother's quite excited.'

Emily frowned. 'Why?'

'Well,' Dennis said, crunching up the hard-boiled sweets now. 'Mother's started to get a bit restless at home. I think she needs a part-time job.'

'Dennis,' Emily said. 'I thought you told me she was eighty-five.'

'Eighty-five in January.'

'Well, goodness, she should be enjoying life and…' What did Emily want to be doing if she made it to eighty-five? She mused for a moment. 'Going on a cruise or… drinking gin in the middle of the day.' Some people didn't make it to eighty-five. Some people didn't even make it to thirty. What would Simon have wanted to be doing at eighty-five? Eating his way through boxes of Cadbury's products probably. Watching classic rom coms while they nibbled, curled up on the sofa together. She took a breath and focused on Dennis again.

'Hmm,' Dennis said, sounding thoughtful. 'She did have a good few years doing those things, but she seems ready for a new challenge.' He offered Emily a paper bag he'd got out of his pocket. 'A bit like you and the Christmas show.' He giggled. Actually giggled.

'Yes, well, I've got lots of ideas for the show already. The Year Sixes are extremely talented when it comes to taking a concept and running with it.' In reality she had a ton of rather ridiculous, over-the-top ideas they didn't have the budget or the health and safety certificates for and very little else.

'If you believe the rumours, some of your class are quite good at taking stuff off the shelves of the local shop and running with it.'

'Who?' Emily asked, in full-on maternal mode.

'I'm not one to name names.'

'If you don't tell me who it is then I'll tell Penny you're telling everyone she's pregnant.'

Dennis shoved the now empty paper bag back into his pocket. 'Everyone will see for themselves in a few months' time. Mother has an intuition about these kinds of things.'

'Dennis, if one of my class is shoplifting then I need to know about it.'

'I haven't seen anyone do it. Someone else told me,' Dennis backtracked.

'Well, who was it?' Emily snapped, getting more annoyed by the second. It was going to be Jayden. She knew it. She shouldn't immediately think it, but he had nothing, it stood to reason he would be the most in need of treats out of financial reach in the shop. She hoped to God it wasn't football cards he'd taken, that would mean he had completely lied to her over that spat in the playground...

'Rashid Dar,' Dennis informed matter-of-factly. 'And you didn't hear that from me.'

Emily was gobsmacked. 'No, Dennis, that can't be right.' Rashid's family were wealthy, she was sure of it. She'd been to Dar's Delhi Delights several times. It was buzzing and busy and it had just had a brand-new makeover. She knew they also paid for Facebook advertising because their deals were forever coming up on her timeline. Rashid had the latest iPhone, new shoes every term, school trousers from Next... He wasn't Jayden with his Shoezone trainers and his falling-apart rucksack.

'He was seen, a couple of times, slipping those fancy chewing gum pots into his pockets. The person in question called him on it the last time, gave him a chance to put it back on the shelf. He denied all knowledge. I'm just saying, if it happens again, she said she's going to tell the owner of the shop.' He sniffed. '*I* wouldn't have hesitated.'

And Emily couldn't blame this person. She would be doing the same. But everyone deserved a second chance. Perhaps if she spoke to Rashid herself. She had ear-marked this afternoon, when her pupils were a little jaded and full of macaroni cheese, to get them to delete any photos of Ray. She could throw in a talk about taking things that aren't yours. It wouldn't come so out of the blue having had the football cards incident...

'Leave it with me,' Emily said to Dennis. 'Tell... your source that I'll handle it.'

Dennis crunched up the sweets in his mouth again.

'Quite the busy bee, aren't we? I hear Susan's going to put you in charge of decorating *this* space tomorrow. The diocese is visiting next week apparently. It's all hands to the Christmas pump.' He indicated the large hall currently filled with chattering children, then clapped his hands in front of Emily's face. 'Showtime.'

Twenty-Two

Marylebone

'I don't understand,' Ray said, struggling to keep up with Deborah's hectic pace as she rushed down one of London's main shopping streets. 'Where are we going?'

'I'll explain when we get there,' Deborah answered. She had thrown the comment at him, over her shoulder as she hurtled past other pedestrians. She looked back for a second. 'Did I tell you how brilliant you were on the radio? How well you handled yourself?'

'Yeah,' he responded with a sigh. It was raining. A cold, freezing rain making him wish he had his hat with him. It wasn't in the pocket of his coat, so he knew it was most likely at Emily's apartment. He looked up at the stores around him, all bedecked with glittering tinsel and round shiny baubles. Even in the daylight it was Festive 101. He could only guess how bright the 'Christmas is Calling' signs strung across the road from one side to the other would look when night fell. There were even giant reindeers suspended on strings that looked like they were flying. All this, he decided, would be much better viewing if he was pissed.

'So, do you think I was good enough to get a rental property without anyone looking too closely at my finances? Maybe people who read *The Independent* not the *Daily Mail*.'

He hadn't been amazing. He had been scared to death. And, in some ways, he had been right to be. The DJ had asked about work on his new album but then, at the very end, just before he was due to sing, he asked his final question.

We've all seen the newspapers. We've all jumped to our own conclusions. Tell us, Ray, have you got anything you'd like to say to Ida if she's listening?

For a second, he had almost fallen into the trap set beautifully by the interviewer. A vision of Ida had sprung up, kicking at his brain, and those thoughts were tumbling out of his mind and down towards his lips. And then one of the crew had spilt boiling hot coffee over the desk just as he was about to reply. It brought back a vivid memory of another cup, a just-boiled kettle and the bubbling water flowing through the air.

This time, as the steaming liquid headed his way he'd scooted back, standing quickly. The interruption and the DJ's need to explain what had happened to the listeners, gave him enough time to regroup. He'd sat back down and smiled at the interviewer before responding.

You shouldn't believe everything you read in the press, Milo. And, I'd really like to sing for your listeners before we run out of airtime.

He'd then slid along to the seat behind the keyboard and played a chord to signify that talking was most definitely over.

'I asked Saturn about an advance on your advance,' Deborah said as he caught up to her at last.

'And?'

'Ray, you haven't been in the studio for over two weeks. They're worried you aren't going to complete before the deadline.'

He sucked in a breath. How could he get back in the studio when Dr Crichton had told him not to sing? The singing on City FM hadn't been without a hitch either. He'd really needed to hit a high note if he wanted to impress, but the ache had been so immense at the last minute he'd dropped an octave. Thankfully it had sounded OK and no one seemed to notice it was less than perfect. But, to him, it was average. And you didn't stay in this industry by being average.

'I will finish the album,' Ray answered. 'They know that, right?'

'You need to get back recording,' Deborah said sternly, powering on, crossing a road and side-stepping someone selling *The Big Issue*. 'When can I tell them you're going to book more time?'

He didn't have an answer. Dr Crichton's words about an operation next month were ringing in his ears. He knew what he should say. He should be truthful. But he also knew what Deborah wanted to hear. She had bills to pay too. He was holding on to their client/agent relationship by a thread. It was only the money he had brought her in the past that was keeping her from giving him up now. Despite what she might say about having faith in him, even his own father had zero faith in him anymore.

'I don't know,' Ray answered. 'Maybe next week.'

'How about *definitely* next week?'

'Would you tell me where we're going?' He stopped walking, the rain getting worse and battering his not-so-much-covered-in-beard-now face. 'Or I'm going to stop right here.' He looked to the shop he had halted next to... The Disney Store. He could see a red wagon and Minnie Mouse in a Santa suit from the pavement. He shuffled a little bit further away. Definitely a scenario that would be made better with alcohol...

'We're going to a rather nice café in Seymour Street.'

Ray shuddered. He didn't want a nice café. He couldn't afford a nice café. He couldn't really afford a *not* nice café. Or a pub. And why did Deborah always need coffee to talk with him? He stayed where he was... listening to a festive mix of songs from *The Lion King* emanating out onto the street.

'Ray, please, come on, or we're going to be late.' Deborah pushed the sleeve of her coat back and looked at her watch.

'Late for what?' Ray asked.

'Late for our meeting.'

'A meeting with who?' He felt his chest tighten. Someone from Saturn Records? Was all this talk about getting more time in the studio what Deborah was building up to? A meeting with the record company and an ultimatum. Suddenly he felt backed into a corner.

'Come on, Ray, I've got another client meeting at 6 p.m. so I've literally got two hours max.'

'It's not with the press, is it?'

'No,' Deborah answered with a sigh. 'It's not with the press. And I'll pay.'

He dug his hands deep into the pockets of his coat. It didn't seem like he had a choice.

When they arrived at Seymour Street it was to a quirky-looking establishment with two chairs and a table on Astroturf outside of a large white wooden-framed window. Above the door was the name 'Daisy' in lights. Ray could see from the entrance that there were paper balls and real flowers in a myriad of colours hanging down from the ceiling inside. It looked like someone had gone crazy creating a rather eccentric garden theme and, for the festive vibe, there were neon-coloured gifts along the windowsills.

'What are we doing here?' Ray asked, following Deborah across the parquet floor.

'Hello there, Deborah Michaels, I made a booking for a private space.'

Deborah wasn't talking to him. She was addressing a server behind the counter. There was a board stating they served Detox Boxes but, to counter that health, were Bottomless Brunch Parties. Perhaps this *was* his sort of place after all. Did they serve lager?

'Come on, Ray,' Deborah said, urging him forward as another server led the way into the bowels of the café. Suddenly they were heading downstairs, like they were destined for a basement and Ray wondered exactly what his agent had in store. It was all going a little bit *Homeland* if he was honest…

White walls, a low ceiling and art painted over the bricks – pastel daises and hummingbirds and… Carmen Miranda.

There was more fake grass on the floor and mismatched chairs at a long rustic wooden table. But what shocked Ray the most was who was sitting there waiting for them. He stopped in his tracks as his heart pulsed, the beat travelling to his neck, his vision swimming.

'Hello, Ray,' Ida greeted.

Twenty-Three

Stretton Park Primary School

'Cherry, we never run with scissors, do we? Come on, Year Six, these are things you were told in reception class,' Emily called as her class hurried round the classroom tidying up before home time. This was always a manic time of day. The children were tired. She was tired. She liked to get them to pack up, then have the last twenty minutes or so to impart important information, possibly information she wanted them to pass informally on to their parents before a news bulletin went out on the email system.

'Did you fix the shelves, Miss Parker?'

Emily looked to the stationery cupboard then. Matthew was poking his head out, PVA glue still all over his hands despite her best efforts to peel it off earlier.

'Shelves! Shelves!' Felix called out, head waving from side to side.

'Er, no, I didn't.' She clapped her hands together then made the Jesus in Rio stance until silence prevailed. When all was calm she spoke again.

'Now, Year Six, remember when we had that conversation about online safety and—'

'You said that even if someone says they're ten and into *Miraculous Tales of LadyBug and Cat Noir* they could be aged fifty and a man called Brian,' Cherry informed brightly.

'Yes,' Emily said. 'Well, today I just want to talk to you a little bit about privacy.'

'Privacy,' Makenzie said, sounding out pry-vacy not priv-acy.

'That's usually the American way to say it,' Emily said. 'In the UK we tend to say privacy.'

'My nan says baff for bath,' Jayden offered. 'She's from Yorkshire.'

'I suppose there's not really a right or wrong way to say these words,' Emily told them. 'It's simply different dialects... anyway, back to privacy or pry-vacy, however you like to say it, it means the same thing. Now, remember when Ray Stone was here and—'

'You locked him in the cupboard,' Frema added.

'Yes... well...'

'And he saved Olivia Colman from certain death,' Alice said, grinning.

'And you didn't want Mrs Clark to know,' Rashid stated, stony-faced yet somehow smug.

'Yes, but this isn't about that,' Emily said. 'It's about Mr Stone's right to privacy.'

'What do you mean?' Matthew asked, toying with a strand of his hair.

'Well, I know, that despite me telling you not to get your phones out and take photos yesterday, that you all got very excited about the hedgehog and about having a musician in the playground, and you did take some snaps that probably showed the hedgehog and Mr Stone.'

'I did,' Cherry admitted.

'Me too,' Makenzie said.

'Well, Mr Stone has asked me if we can delete any photos of him, because if those photos go on the internet it will be a breach of his privacy.'

'What does that mean?'

Why was this so difficult? Maybe she should have just rifled through their schoolbags at lunchtime, got the phones out and deleted the pictures herself. Except there was fingerprint technology now. And passcodes. Her students probably knew multiple number combinations better than the maths she tried to teach them. 'It just means that if any of you have used those photos on the internet, on social media, that you could get in trouble.'

There was a collective gasp of near-terror that left Emily in no doubt that somehow this chat was too late.

'Snapchat isn't actual social media though, is it?' Cherry asked, eyes wide, bottom lip trembling a little.

'Of course it is, dummy,' Rashid snapped with a scoff. 'I was going to put my photo on Instagram, but my mum said the way the newspapers are feeding on this story now I could probably make money from it.'

Emily swallowed. Rashid had told his mother. His mother would be talking to Mrs Clark. Asking her why there was an apparently disgraced pop star in the playground of her son's school…

'She didn't believe me that it was him though,' Rashid added. 'She said he looked like a really red-faced fake lookalike.'

Emily didn't know whether to feel aggrieved on Ray's behalf at this description, or pleased that Mrs Dar wasn't going to be on her back. And had Cherry only sent it to a friend on Snapchat? If her friend wasn't someone from the Fox Corporation then it could still be OK.

'Well, what I would like you to do,' Emily began, 'so that no one gets in trouble over this, is to get out your phones and we are going to all delete any photos we have with Mr Stone in them.'

There was a bit of moaning and groaning and over-the-top sighing now.

'Year Six, I'm doing this for your own good. No one wants to get in trouble, do they?'

'Could we get in trouble? Like with the police?' Angelica asked.

'Nee-naw! Nee-naw!' Felix blurted out, jumping up from his desk and spinning around like he was an out-of-control helicopter.

'Felix, sit down please,' Emily ordered. 'So, before the bell goes, everyone get out your phones and I will come over to each of you and make sure any photos of Mr Stone are deleted.'

All the children scurried about, dipping fingers into rucksacks and satchels, searching for their devices and putting them on to the table. One child remained completely still. Rashid.

'Rashid,' Emily stated. 'Did you hear what I said?'

'I heard you talking about privacy, Miss,' he answered. 'But isn't making me delete a photo I took an invasion of *my* privacy?'

As she looked at Rashid she could almost see the triumph shining in his expression. Why was he such a difficult child? Where did this sense of self-importance and need to be one up on everyone really root from? She took steps towards his table as everyone else began fiddling with their mobile phones calling up photos.

'Rashid,' Emily said firmly. 'I would like you to delete any photos you have with Mr Stone in them. He did not give you permission to take any photos.'

'Probably because he was wasted,' the boy retorted.

'And saying things like that, Rashid, is defamation of character. You could get into a lot of trouble over that.' Emily took a breath. 'Just like you can get into a lot of trouble for stealing from the mini-market.'

For one brief second she saw a flash of something like lessened bravado, almost – but not quite – fear. And then it was gone as he made his reply.

'I don't know what you mean, Miss.'

'I mean, Rashid, that when your parents come to see your "What The Holidays Mean to Me" tableau, I will have to speak to them about your behaviour inside and *outside* of school. Anything you do when you're dressed in school uniform, Rashid, is a reflection on the reputation of Stretton Park. And we all know how much Mrs Clark wants a great reputation for the school.'

'And we all know that my dad is sponsoring the festive play,' Rashid reminded.

'And *I* am in charge of the festive play,' Emily said. 'Executive director. In charge of script-writing and songwriting and costumes and… deciding who will be taking part in it.' She smiled. 'Basically, I am the Stephen Spielberg of Stretton Park right now.' Good grief, now she sounded so full of self-importance she was close to channelling her mother. She drew a determined breath. 'Phone, Rashid. On the table. Right now.'

He slowly drew his mobile from his rucksack and put it down in front of him.

'Good,' Emily said. 'Now, let's start with deleting your photos, shall we?'

Twenty-Four

Running away was what children did. It wasn't what grown men who already had the world scrutinising their every move did. Ray had struggled to breathe as he'd rushed from the café the second he realised Ida was in front of him and that this set-up of Deborah's had involved his ex-girlfriend. Why? Why had his agent done this? Without warning. Sure, she had loosely mentioned the idea that meeting with Ida *might* be an idea, but he hadn't expected it now. Right now. When he was nowhere near ready. And Deborah had no idea what was really going on with Ida. That was why he was here, outside a betting shop. It wasn't a pub. That had to be some sort of progress. Really, he wanted to pretend the past thirty minutes hadn't happened and focus on something he could be in charge of.

Taking a deep breath, he looked at the red and white branding-matching Christmas tree in the window display. What was going to be inside? Inflatable Santas with racehorses or greyhounds pulling a sleigh? *Fucking*

Christmas. He pushed opened the door and hoped he would find what he was looking for in here…

The air was warm inside and smelled slightly of sweat, beer and possibly last night's vindaloo. Since the smoking ban had come in, there was no longer a thick fog of emissions from Marlboros or roll-ups like there had been when he was younger, there was now even a drinks machine. Apart from that, the place looked the same. Same carpet, same walls with today's race meetings pinned to the boards, definitely more flat-screen televisions and some faces he recognised. Only one in particular interested him.

'Hey, Wilf,' Ray greeted a man in his sixties, wrapped up in a thick polyester coat that could have passed for a sleeping bag. He had a fisherman style hat on, wisps of grey sprouting out from underneath it. The man stuck a small pen in his mouth and growled a greeting. 'How do.' The man's attention then fell back into the betting slip he was writing on.

'You keeping OK?' Ray asked, sliding himself onto the stool next to the man. 'Still winning?'

'Yerp,' the vague reply came. Wilf had never really been one for long or in-depth conversations. Two syllables was even a novelty.

'So, I'll cut straight to the finish line,' Ray said. He cleared his throat then lowered his voice. 'Do you still have a lock-up full of parts for heating systems?'

Wilf looked up from his writing then and eyed Ray with suspicion. 'Who's asking?'

'Er… I am.'

'Who for?'

'Um, well… me.'

Wilf sat back a little on his stool, looking Ray up and down as if he suddenly considered him a threat of the highest order. 'And who are you working for?'

'Listen, Wilf, I'm not working for anyone. I just need a part for a Worcester boiler. I've written down the make and the part number and...'

As Ray got the piece of paper from the pocket of his coat Wilf slid backwards, completely off the stool, lumbering towards the counter, mumbling to himself and making shooing motions with his hands. He walked straight into a hanging glittery horse with an elf in the saddle, making it bounce and swing like a clock pendulum.

'I don't know nothing,' Wilf finally said, shaking his head. 'And why are you asking me? You should be asking him.'

Now everyone in the bookmaker's was looking at Ray like he was an unwanted outcast. He swallowed. First the paparazzi. Next the radio station. Then Ida. Now here.

'Ask *him*,' Wilf repeated, pointing to the darkest corner of the room and Ray followed the direction of his finger to the person getting down off his stool and heading across the carpet towards him. *His dad.*

Suddenly Ray wished he had taken his chances in the café with Ida. He dug his hands into the pocket of his coat and waited for the next round of harsh words...

'What's the model?' Len growled, unlit cigarette hanging from his lips.

'What?' Ray asked, taken aback the question hadn't been yelled at volume.

'The model of this boiler,' Len repeated.

'It's a...' Ray paused. He was flustered and he couldn't have felt more pathetic. It was like he was thirteen years old again. He drew out the scrap of paper and held it out to his father.

Len sucked through his teeth as he scrutinised at the numbers in front of him. 'Your place has got this model?' He shook his head. 'Bet it's the thermostat you're wanting, ain't it?'

Still no shouting. Ray answered quickly. 'Yeah, it is.'

His dad started heading towards the door and Ray felt the eyes of all the customers still on him as if this was pre-racing entertainment.

'Well, don't just stand there,' Len called, looking back to him. 'I've got one in my van.'

It was bitter outside now, although it *had* stopped raining at least. The sun was making a weak attempt to break through the thick cloud, but all Ray could feel was the icy wind as it whipped around him. Standing outside his dad's seen-much-better-days white transit van, the doors open, his dad somewhere in the middle of the back, rifling through boxes of parts, sighing, cussing and coughing every few moments was not where he had ever imagined being when this day started. His phone vibrated in his pocket again. He wondered when Deborah was going to give up hunting him down. When he gave her some sort of intelligent reason for running from the café he assumed. He wasn't sure that was going to happen today. It was all too much.

'Do you need help?' Ray called to Len as his dad's head disappeared completely and the backside of his brown trousers became all that was visible, shoes buried ankle-deep in cardboard.

'You're joking, aren't ya?' Len retorted. 'You ain't got a clue of my system.'

This pile of crap was actually in some sort of order?! Unbelievable.

'So, are you going back to heating then?' Len shouted, voice muffled by products.

There was pride in his tone. And hope. If he wanted an easy time of it he should just lie and say yes. Although, given the situation with his vocal cords, saying yes might end up being a reality if he lost his voice…

'No,' Ray answered. It seemed his voice still had some sort of control, even over his brain. 'I'm just… helping out a friend.' His thoughts quickly went to Emily Parker. A virtual stranger who had given him her spare room without any judgement on what he was doing with his life. A *beautiful* stranger he really needed to make sure he kept proper boundaries with.

'You've still got some friends then,' Len commented. 'After all that stuff in the papers.'

And there it was. His father's quick judgement yet again. He bit down his immediate urge to bite back. Where had biting back ever got him? If you bit back, everything simply escalated to a whole different level, one he usually didn't understand and couldn't easily manage.

'Tell you what, I'll sign that CD for your new girlfriend next time I'm passing. How were the kebabs?' he offered instead.

'Fucking fantastic,' Len answered. 'They always are from Mehmet's.' He appeared from the van, a piece of parcel tape stuck to his coat and bubble wrap hanging from his neck like a scarf. 'You used to love 'em.'

He had loved them. His mum had loved them too. Mehmet had to be at least a hundred years old now. Friday night had been kebab night and he and his mum and dad had sat at the same tiny table in the very corner of the bijou Turkish grill house, stuffing their faces and watching whatever foreign football match Mehmet was showing on the ancient old television, held to the wall by an engineering feat of a wooden pallet and electrical flex.

His parents had drunk Efes beer and he'd been allowed a sip, and it was always a time where the family dynamic just worked. It was in those moments where young Ray could see why his mum and dad had fallen in love. They talked and they laughed, and they asked Ray about school. His mum dressed up, even though it wasn't really a place you dressed up for, and she was almost sober when they arrived, like she wanted to be really present on those nights. It was as if Mehmet's restaurant was their safe haven, a place where real life was suspended for one night a week. It was a shame it hadn't been enough.

Len held a box out to him. 'There you go.'

'What?' Ray asked, looking at the pristine package.

'It's the part you need. A thermostat for the boiler.'

'What? The exact one?' He looked at the box again, doubtful.

'That singing malarkey has addled your brain, boy! Yes, the exact one, the model number you gave me.' He pushed the box towards Ray again. 'Now, do you want it or what?'

'Yeah... I do but...'

'What's the matter?' Len snapped. 'You're happy to ask Wilf for a part, but you can't take one from me?!'

He really didn't want an argument. 'No... I... thanks, Dad.' He took the box. 'Can I pay you next week?'

Len tutted and shook his head. 'I don't want any money for it, you daft sod. It's cleared a space in my van, hasn't it?' Len closed the van doors then dipped a hand into the pocket of his trousers for a lighter and lit up the cigarette, taking a long draw before exhaling a cloud of smoke into the cold air. 'Wilf's probably got a dozen of these in his lock-up, but he's under scrutiny from the local law enforcement. That's why he almost pissed his Y-fronts when you asked him.'

It was at that moment a car drove past, festive Slade blaring from its partially open windows.

'Fucking Christmas,' Len commented, shaking his head. 'It starts earlier and earlier every year, don't it? And now I'm living with a woman who wants to decorate the place like Santa's fucking workshop. It's not even December.'

So, Brenda *was* living there. Well, Ray had surmised that already. The other non-festive decoration – new wallpaper and frilly fripperies – were a giveaway. His dad had always hated most forms of DIY, mainly because after working hard all day repairing central heating systems, he didn't want to be back using tools in the evenings or at weekends. Ray could understand that, and his mum had never been worried about the latest home fashions. She had only really been worried about where her next drink was coming from…

'Hard at Christmas, ain't it?' Len stated soberly.

Ray looked at his dad then, saw a poignant expression cover his features. Was this Len trying to open up a dialogue?

'Yeah,' Ray answered. Was that really all he had? *Knockout, Ray.*

'Not the same without her, is it?' Len carried on, eyes in the mid-distance.

So, this *was* about his mum. 'No,' Ray replied. 'But...' He didn't really know what he was going to say. Nothing he said was going to bring his mum back. Len was moving on with Brenda and, if that made him happy, then it was OK. He had been a long time a widower. And had it only been his mum's drinking that had made the relationship strained? Or was it the working-class life in general? A chicken and egg situation. Where you drank to escape because you had to work so hard, and worked so hard to afford to drink and escape... Except his dad had managed not to drink so much that his liver gave out.

'But what?' Len asked.

'I don't know,' Ray said, letting a breath go, visible in the cold air. 'Ask me again after a couple of pints.'

'The sun's hardly over the yardarm, boy,' Len told him.

'It's always five o'clock somewhere,' Ray answered.

Len shook his head. 'Don't say that.'

There was an awkward silence, his dad smoking, Ray's hands in his pockets, toying with a stray thread in one of them.

'Don't fall down that hole, Ray,' Len eventually said, his voice uneven. 'Don't do what your mother did. Because booze, it can take over.' He cleared his throat. 'And I know what you're thinking. You're thinking I'm some sort of old, stupid bugger who couldn't stop his wife from dying but...'

'I don't think that,' Ray interrupted. 'That's not what I think at all.'

'I'm just saying that... the booze, needing it like, it can sneak up on you and quickly. One time you might just be having one too many a night, the next it's all you can think about to get you through the next day.'

'Dad...'

'Listen,' Len said, taking another drag on his cigarette. 'I'm just saying... you don't need a drink to solve your problems. Drinking, well, it will only add to them. Your mum, she was testament to that.'

Ray couldn't speak. This was about as open as his dad had ever been with him before. His throat was choked, and it had nothing to do with his vocal condition. It was pure emotion.

'And, well, I didn't mean what I said, you know, at the flat, about what they're saying on the telly about you and in the newspapers.'

'Yeah?'

'You're this year's Ant McPartlin, that's all,' Len said with a nod of authority. 'Journalists love nothing better than a good, clean and honest person going to the darker side of life. Not that I'm saying that's what you've done... I don't know what you've done. Or haven't done. It's none of my business. You're a grown man and...'

'I didn't do anything, Dad,' Ray finally said, the sentence somehow crawling up his throat independently.

'Alright,' Len said quickly. 'Alright, let's not be getting too sentimental on the high street. You don't know who might be watching.'

He *was* getting sentimental though. Ridiculously so. One mention of Mehmet's kebabs, his dad actually talking about his mum, it was more than enough.

'Well, I'd better get back in the bookies or Brenda will be

calling, asking me why it took so long for me to grab some chicken cordon bleus from Nisa.'

Ray nodded and held the box containing the thermostat aloft. 'Thank you for this, Dad.'

'S'alright,' Len answered, stubbing out his cigarette on the ground.

He should mention Christmas despite it being the worst of 'c' words for their family. He could suggest they at least thought about spending it together... if he wasn't going to be in hospital. Except he didn't have anywhere to host a Christmas Day meal which would put the onus back on Len. Still, someone had to make the first move...

'Dad...'

'Drop that CD in some time,' Len interrupted gruffly. 'You know, if you're passing. Might earn me some brownie points with Brenda.'

The moment had gone so Ray nodded and forced a smile. 'Sure, Dad.'

Twenty-Five

Crowland Terrace, Canonbury, Islington

Emily's apartment was freezing. In fact, it was so cold she had turned the oven on and was sitting huddled around it in her dressing gown wondering whether she should actually put something in it to cook while she was using it as a heater. But instead of cooking she was staring at the instruments on the table. She had taken a recorder, a xylophone and a triangle from school, determined to make a start on the Christmas show tonight. She was not going to be Little Miss Last Minute. She was a super-organised, worthy-of-a-headship teacher. She picked up the recorder and gave it a blow. Ugh! It was such an awful sounding instrument. How was she going to compose festive songs on that? She lifted up the triangle and gave it a tap. Nothing but a dull thud... oh, you needed to hold it by the string, didn't you? Ching! That was better. Then her phone vibrated and she checked the message. It was from Jonah.

Sorry about yesterday. Allan says I was being Judgy

Jonah. We love you that's all. I averted crisis at the hotel and Allan mixed tacos with too much tequila again. Hope the boiler is fixed and I have a very nice South African called Caleb interested in your spare room if you're still up for it. #newstarts xxx

Oh no! Jonah was still keen to get someone in her space. She swallowed, easing herself back from the table a little as if to distance herself from the text. Would her best friend turn all Judgy Jonah again if she told him Ray was using the room? She checked her watch. But, then again, Ray wasn't here. He did say he might have other options. Perhaps he had found somewhere bigger or sleeker without someone to bump into his naked form on the landing. Not that she had thought about his naked form for one second today... OK, that was a lie. She had thought about it and refreshed the image like he was a hot fireman on Facebook holding the cutest of puppies. But that was normal, wasn't it? Jonah said she ought to try normal again, not grieving nearly-widow hiding from everything connected with moving on...

Why hadn't she grabbed a tambourine? That's what she needed. Something nice to beat, with little cymbals. She put the triangle down and picked up the recorder again. Could she remember anything from her own school days? 'Three Blind Mice' even? She blew, and the instrument let out the most high-pitched of squeaks that Emily was surprised a pod of dolphins didn't swim in and start a conversation.

'Whoa!'

And suddenly there was Ray, fully-clothed, in his coat, putting a box on the table, then moving his hands to try and muffle his ears. She had to admit that *Luther* coat was almost as hot as the bare display that morning. Emily took the recorder away from her mouth. 'Sorry.'

'What are you doing?' Ray asked, seeming to only gingerly remove his hands from the sides of his head. 'Is this a teacher's homework?'

'No,' Emily answered. 'Well, actually maybe yes.' She sighed. 'The diocese are coming next week and remember I said I was in charge of the Christmas show? Well, I haven't even begun to think about a script, let alone songs to go with the script and Susan *really is* expecting something like a festive, Christian version of *West Side Story* with more camels than gangs and... I don't even know where to begin.'

'And because you can't get Hugh Jackman you thought a recorder could help?'

Emily looked up at him then and he quirked an eyebrow upwards, a smile playing on his lips. God, he really was frightfully good-looking. She dropped her eyes again, ignoring the awakening of her libido that was probably as dry and stale as an out-of-date yule log by now.

Ray took the recorder from her, observing it. 'I don't think anyone has ever written a song on a recorder.'

'Well, that can't be true,' she answered. 'We have books and books of recorder tunes at school.'

'I meant something contemporary,' Ray elaborated, still looking at the instrument. 'It's not like a guitar or a piano. It's not versatile enough.'

Emily watched him put the recorder to his mouth and play a selection of notes she instantly recognised as 'O, Holy Night'. He drew the instrument away and shook his head, laughing.

'God, it sounds terrible.'

'How did you do that?' Emily asked, dumbfounded. He had played a song, just like that, with no sheet music to follow and he had made it sound like the recorder was the forgotten cousin of the wind section of an orchestra.

'How did I do what?'

'Play "O, Holy Night" without, you know, notes to read or instructions telling you which holes to put your fingers in.' The realisation of how that last sentence had sounded crept up on her cheeks like she'd developed Slapped Cheek Syndrome instantaneously. She had had it once. It had done the rounds of Stretton Park.

'Once you know music you know music,' Ray answered with a shrug. 'I didn't do a degree in Recorder Recitals if that's what you thought.' He smiled. 'God, I really hope that isn't a real thing.' He shrugged his shoulders. 'It's freezing in here.'

'I know,' Emily answered. 'That's why I'm sat round the cooker.'

Ray picked up the box then and shook it gently. 'Well, I have good news. I've got a part for the boiler so, in no time, we'll have this place warmer than…'

If he said warmer than her cheeks, she was probably going to put her head *inside* the oven and hope it cooked her quickly.

'The coffee you're going to make me while I get my tools out.' Ray grinned then hesitated. 'Shit, I should have bought some coffee. Do you have more coffee? I can go to the shop… I'll go to the shop.'

'No,' Emily said, standing up. 'I have coffee. Plenty of coffee.' Nothing much to eat apart from sharing-size packs of crisps she didn't usually share and maybe some frozen potato waffles. When had she got so utterly poor at catering for herself? Oh yes, when the chef moved out… 'I'll make some. And, thank you, for getting the part. You must let me know how much I owe you for it and for your time and…'

'Well,' Ray said, toying with the box in his hands and looking a little awkward. 'I was wondering… and tell me, you know, if it's not OK, because that will be OK.' She watched him pause before carrying on. 'My other place to stay hasn't come off yet so, could I take up the offer of staying here for a bit longer?'

All of what Jonah had alluded to about Ray's current issues came flooding to the forefront of Emily's mind, joining hands and dancing with the reports from the quick look she'd done on Google after deleting the children's photos on their phones when school ended. The press was delivering a hard-faced, angry, uncompromising individual who would do anything to get his own way. But here in her minuscule kitchen, his tall, broad frame taking up almost all the space, he was holding a boiler thermostat for her central heating in his hands and looking like he needed a break…

'Of course,' she replied quickly. 'But on one condition.'

'I'll get you some rent money. As soon as I get my next payment from the record company. I promise you that. I'll write an IOU. I'll…'

'It isn't that,' Emily told him. 'I think I'm going to need your musical expertise more than I need the cash.'

'Listen, the recorder really isn't my speciality.'

'No, but songwriting is, isn't it?'

'Well, I'd like to think so but…'

'I'm in trouble,' Emily said frankly. 'With this Christmas show. I don't have a clue when it comes to tunes. I can't even sing.'

'Everyone can sing,' Ray answered.

'Seriously,' Emily said, wide-eyed. 'I really can't sing.'

'I'm telling you everyone can sing. Some more in tune than others I admit, but everyone can make a sound with their voice.'

'Well, my sound is apparently a blender grinding up rune stones.'

'Someone said that to you?' Ray queried.

'My mother,' Emily replied. 'She was going through her pretending-to-be-interested-in-the-occult stage. It's surprisingly helped her on a good few of her cases. She's practically a black magic legal expert.' She smiled. 'Anyway, I'm begging you. If you could just help me a little bit with a song before the diocese visit next week, I would be eternally grateful.' She batted her eyelashes. 'I'll even borrow Jonah's second Dolce Gusto machine, stick it under my coat the next time I go round, he'll never notice. And then I'll buy the Starbucks coffee pods to go in it… and I'll do a shop… lots of non-chocolate, non-dairy produce to not coat your vocal cords.'

'Alright, stop,' Ray said, shaking his head with a smile. 'I don't want you to get the wrong impression of me.'

Was it coming? Was now when he was going to admit that he was the Ray the newspapers had been depicting? Was this when he admitted that some of what the stories were alluding to was true? She really, really hoped not…

'I like coffee in whatever form it comes. And I might know the inside of a heating system, but the coffee machine

I had at my last house looked like a robot and I swear, I was too scared to touch the widescreen display in case it called an Uber instead of making a macchiato.'

Emily laughed. 'OK, no coffee machine. Tesco's Finest?'

'Honestly, as long as it's hot and wet it's good with me.'

Hot. Wet. Now Emily *wanted* someone to slap her cheek to get her out of this conversation... 'OK,' she answered. 'Noted.'

'One more thing,' Ray said seriously.

'Yes?'

'There's no way I'm writing a song with a recorder.'

'The triangle?' Emily asked, reaching to pick up the metal shape.

'Songs have to have more than one note, Emily. There's your first lesson.' He laughed. 'I'll get my stuff tonight. I don't suppose you've got room for my piano.'

A piano! Where was she going to put a piano?! She had got Simon to measure the bookcase in the living room three times before she allowed herself to be satisfied it would fit without destroying the overall ambience of the space...

'I'm kidding,' Ray said. 'I'll bring over a guitar.' He clapped his hands together. 'Right, let's get this heating working, oh, and I'll have a couple of sugars in that coffee you promised.'

Twenty-Six

Chips out of the paper, covered in salt and vinegar, had never tasted so good. The temperature in the flat was an even twenty degrees thanks to the new thermostat and Emily had finally taken off the thick fleece dressing gown that had been over her clothes. After repairing the boiler, Ray had headed to Gino's storage locker by foot to pick up whatever he could carry. Clothes mainly, and two of his guitars, one electric, one acoustic, plus whatever he had been able to fit into the largest of his backpacks. It didn't say much for his superstar lifestyle that his possessions could fit into one large rucksack and instrument cases. He pushed another lightly crisped-outside-fluffy-inside chip into his mouth, watching Emily fighting with branches of a Christmas tree across the lounge. He had bought her chips too, with the last actual real cash he had in his wallet, but she hadn't eaten very many. Instead she had nibbled at a few then headed into the depths of the cupboard to begin hauling out a box that contained this fake evergreen monster.

'What are you doing?' he asked, reaching for the bottle of supermarket own-brand ketchup Emily had placed on the coffee table.

'I'm going to decorate.'

Ray's eyes went to the smaller, more modern Christmas decorations that were already around the space. Was he missing something? It was already done in his opinion.

'I know what you're thinking,' she answered, as if she had mind-reading powers. 'But those tokens of Jonah's aren't really my style. They're all very... Oxford Street and I prefer... Swiss chalet or German Christmas market. Traditional. Nothing like my parents would buy to impress their friends.'

He was coming to the rapid conclusion that she had a difficult relationship with her parents. When she'd eaten the few chips with her fingers she had made a comment about how appalled her mother would be that they were eating out of paper with not even a deli fork between them. She'd then told him there were actually seven different types of fork...

'It has a lot of branches,' Ray commented, inhaling more food. He hadn't realised just how hungry he was. Had he even eaten today? He wasn't sure the vinegar the guy had splashed about like he was filling a swimming pool, was doing his throat any favours though. He mentally added vinegar to the irritants he probably shouldn't ingest before singing.

'Fifty-three,' Emily answered, putting them into their colour-coded piles. 'It's meant to have fifty-five, but Simon got it heavily discounted and, well, when you have fifty-three branches already, you're really not going to notice a couple missing.'

'Who's Simon?' Ray asked. 'Your boyfriend?'

'Oh… yes… I mean, no. Well, actually… yes.'

He watched her. She looked suddenly uncomfortable and now so was he. Chips were poised in mid-air in his fingers, salt making his skin sore. He didn't know what to say and neither, it seemed, did she.

'Simon was my boyfriend,' Emily said, picking up a branch and fanning out the twigs. 'He… passed away… last year. November. The beginning of November. A few weeks ago… last year.' She swallowed. 'I said last year already, didn't I?'

'God, Emily, I'm sorry,' Ray said, dropping the chips back into the paper and putting the paper down next to him on the sofa. He felt like he needed to stand. But when he got to his feet, he had no idea what to do next. Go to her? Comfort her? Who was he to really do anything? He was the lodger paying her in engineering skills and songwriting… when he wasn't even supposed to be singing.

'It's OK,' Emily said, flapping the tree bough in the air and pulling her legs tighter into her body. 'I mean, it's not obviously OK, it's not OK at all, but it happened and everything changed and… there's nothing I can do about it.'

There were a million things Ray wanted to ask. Like, how old had Simon been. What had he died of. How long had they been together. Instead he looked at a photo on the windowsill, strode towards it and picked it up. What was he doing?

'Is this Simon?' He should put the picture down. These were her memories he was thumbing now. Emily looked different in this photo. She was still wearing something unique – a blouse with a print of small brown birds all over it – but her face was a little fuller, her hair lighter. Simon was a good-looking guy and the way he had his arm around Emily's shoulders, drawing her close so genuinely, relaxed, un-posed, told its own love story...

'Yes,' Emily said. She was getting to her feet now and she crossed the room to stand next to him. She took the photo frame from him and gazed at the picture. 'We were so drunk in that photo. I blame the rhubarb gin.' She was smiling as she looked at the image and then she folded the arm that had propped the photo up. 'I should put this one away,' she said. 'Make room for more Christmas things on the window ledge.'

'Only the good die young,' Ray commented. If there was a prize for the most inappropriate comment, he would have just claimed it. 'I mean, there has to be something in that, doesn't there?' What was he talking about? There was nothing in it. Nothing. Death was never good no matter how old you were.

'I wonder what that tells me about Dennis's mother?' Emily said, sighing. 'Sorry, it's just Dennis, he's one of the other teachers at work, slight addiction to sweets, he told me his mother is almost eighty-five. I was automatically assuming she was good but...'

'Do you want some help?' Ray asked. 'With the tree?'

'Oh, no, that's OK. It's an awful job really. You have to put all these branches into colour-coded piles and then you have to start with the red ones and then the blue ones and... you must have other stuff to do.'

'Eating chips I've already eaten too many of and avoiding looking on social media. Yeah,' he said. 'My night is lit.'

He watched her laugh. There was that light he had seen in her eyes in that photo. It was still there, somewhere, just under the surface. She was even more beautiful when she laughed.

'Listen,' he began. 'I'll help you with the tree and then you can tell me what sort of lyrics you think will be acceptable to your priests or vicars or whoever is coming to school next week. Deal?'

She smiled softly. 'OK. Deal.'

Twenty-Seven

The Christmas tree was up. In under two hours. It seemed that perhaps Emily and Simon hadn't had the same skills in logical putting-together of the indoor spruce that Emily and Ray had. Mainly Ray, if she was honest.

Ray was now playing the acoustic guitar, ripped jeans, bare feet, long-sleeved grey sweater over the rest of him. It should have been a non-descript kind of outfit, but on him it looked like perfection. Relaxed, easy, uncontrived perfection. The sort of combination that took most people considerable time standing in front of a full-length mirror to get right. And when he stopped playing it was to catch her staring right at him. *Fantastic, Emily...*

'Sorry,' he apologised. 'I'm getting carried away. Inspiration strikes when you least expect it.'

'You're writing new music at the moment?' she asked. She was still on the floor, crossed-legged, her hands wrapped around another mug of coffee.

'Meant to be,' Ray answered. 'Should be.' He smiled at her. 'Won't get any money unless I make it happen.'

'I don't know anything about the music industry,' she remarked, taking a sip of her drink.

'Well,' he said, 'it's the same as any other business. It has to make money. It has deadlines and contracts and stipulations and if you don't meet all its given criteria then you're off the rollercoaster, back down on the ground.'

'That sounds harsh.'

'It's life.' He strummed hard. 'So, tell me, this class of yours, are they a musically talented bunch of kids?'

'God no,' Emily answered, almost spitting out her drink. 'And we lost Mr Jarvis. Bless him, he did try and get them to sing in time with a metro… metro-gnome, is it? But the ticking set Felix off into a frenzy.'

'OK,' Ray said. 'But your plan is to write a Christmas show in what? A month? And get them to learn their lines and all the words to the songs before a performance?'

'The 20th December,' Emily said. The date had come out all breathy. Like she was close to hyperventilation. 'That's when the show is.'

'It can't be done,' Ray said, playing one chord, then changing his finger position and playing another.

'What do you mean it can't be done?' Emily asked. 'It *has* to be done. There's literally no other option. I have to produce a show on 20th December. I've got parents throwing money at me for costumes and special effects. I can't let everyone down.'

And by *everyone* she really meant the headteacher. This was her chance to make Susan see she wasn't just another ambitious newcomer with no depth to her long-term plans.

'I don't give up,' Emily stated boldly. 'Not with anything. Not ever. Even if the outlook is hopeless, I will still refuse to give up. I'm a last grain in the sand-timer kind of person.' Except apparently when it came to picking up her life after grief and realising that she couldn't survive on coffee and Jacob's crackers alone... But Ray didn't need to know that.

'OK,' Ray said, nodding. 'Well, in that case, I just think you need to streamline your expectations a little.'

'What do you mean?'

'Emily, it's a tall order for anyone to learn a bunch of new songs in that timescale, but untalented ten-year-olds...'

'I didn't say they were completely untalented.' Had she? That was awful of her. The trouble was they didn't really have the time to perfect anything. It was all rush through the curriculum to make sure everything was covered – often inadequately and not particularly thoroughly – the time for plays or music or creativity had got less and less. Perhaps it was her fault they weren't musically gifted. Had her lack of ability hampered her children?

'I've got an idea,' Ray told her before she could dwell any longer. 'How about I help you come up with some new lyrics to *well-known* Christmas songs, songs the kids are already going to know the tune to, and then we'll work on one brand-new song for, I don't know, the grand finale or something. That way there's not quite so much work to do for them... or you... or me.'

'I don't know,' Emily said. She was hesitant because Susan had kept saying the words 'show-stopping' and 'original' all the time. Making up new words to old songs wasn't quite what she had had in mind.

'I think it's your best bet,' Ray said. 'If you want a show to put on at all on 20th December.'

She wrinkled her nose. Was it giving in? Should she really be capable of making new songs? Even with someone talented in the music industry telling her it was going to be supremely hard?

'OK, listen,' Ray said, sitting forward on the sofa and repositioning his guitar. 'Instead of—' he began to sing '—O, Holy Night…'

His voice… it was like someone had come in and poured warm, melted chocolate all over her spine. Emily sat up a little straighter and tried to temper down the feeling. It was all deep and rich and profoundly sexy…

'You could have…' He sang again. 'Here at Stretton Park, the holidays are coming.' He was singing and playing the music and Emily's mouth dropped open.

'Did you just make that up?' she gasped. 'Just now? On the spot?'

He laughed. 'It's one line.'

'But it fits!' she exclaimed. 'It fits to the tune *and* it's about our school.'

'You sing it,' Ray encouraged, playing the tune again.

'Oh no,' she answered, getting to her feet. 'No, you're the singer. I'll be the writer-downer.' She grabbed a notebook from the bookcase and a pen from a drawer and sat back down, scribbling the lyrics.

Ray continued to sing. 'And the nights are dark and clear.'

Emily looked up. 'Seriously! Two lines already?!'

He smiled at her again. 'I wish my record company was so easily pleased.' He played the next line. 'Your turn. What comes next?'

'I have no idea,' Emily said, shaking her head. 'I'm not a songwriter.'

'Come on,' Ray encouraged. 'You don't know that. Have you even ever tried?'

'Obviously not. I'm a primary school teacher not... George Ezra.'

Ray sang again. 'Here at Stretton Park, the holidays are coming. And the nights are dark and clear.'

Here at Stretton Park. Our... hearts are filled with gladness. Could that work? Ray was playing the next bit, humming along to the tune. Well, she couldn't sing it, not out loud and she wasn't sure it was even good enough to tell him. But this *was* her project. And she couldn't expect Ray to come up with everything. She had to have confidence. *You have to have more confidence, Emily. You are amazing. Believe it.* That's what Simon used to say when she was bitching a little about her non-promotion to Deputy Head. Confidence was also what Susan would be expecting when the diocese visited. She cleared her throat.

'How about...' Emily started to sing. 'Here at Stretton Park, our hearts are filled with gladness?' Emily put a finger in the air. 'No, not gladness. *Jesus*! Our hearts are filled with Jesus. It's for the diocese, the more Jesus we can fit in the better.'

'You have a great voice,' Ray told her.

'Ha, you're funny. I'm not singing any more lines by the way.'

'Hey,' Ray said, his eyes finding hers. 'I mean it. You've got a really great tone going on.'

Emily shook her head. 'You don't need to say that. You don't have to say you like my singing to keep your room.'

'You're speaking to someone who has lost one rental this week and roughed it in a shed. I'm unafraid of being evicted,' Ray replied seriously. 'Take the compliment, Miss Parker. You have a great voice. And now I know that, you're going to be pulling your weight in this songwriting.'

One of those pretentious large lightbulbs she was going to be seeing with her parents the following Friday had suddenly inhabited her gut and was shining at the brightest setting. Ray said she had a great voice. He said he meant it. It was one of the nicest things anyone had ever said to her. After her mother's criticism of her vocal abilities, she hadn't really sung very much – only to Jonah and Allan when she'd been a little inebriated, not really ever to Simon. Not that Simon would have ever criticised anything she put her hand – or voice – to. He was... had been... always so supportive.

Ray tapped the guitar with his fingers. 'So, are all the kids in your class Christian?'

'No, we have a wide mix. Muslim, Jewish, Humanist...'

'And they're all OK with the Jesus vibe?' Ray inquired. 'Does the show have to be a nativity? Or even, you know, religion-based?'

'Oh yes,' Emily said immediately. 'Definitely yes. Because we get funding from the church board and everyone knows that and the parents know that. I mean, they can, of course, ask that their children don't participate in religious aspects of school life, but I always try to teach things in a non-conflicting way. Like with the "What Christmas Means to Me" projects. Anyone who doesn't celebrate Christmas does "What The Holidays Mean To Me".' She took a breath. 'But this show, this Christmas show at a Church of England school, has to contain God. Because, to the diocese that's the whole point of Christmas. I mean, it is obviously the whole point of Christmas or there wouldn't be a Christmas but...'

'OK,' Ray interrupted. 'I get it. Angels and wise men and... innkeepers.'

'Yes,' Emily said, thinking of Jayden's project and his model dad outside the clay pub. That was about as unconventional as it got.

Ray sang the first three lines.

Here at Stretton Park, the holidays are coming
And the nights are dark and clear
Here at Stretton Park, our hearts are filled with Jesus

That didn't sound too bad! It actually sounded quite good, particularly Ray singing it. She wasn't sure how Year Six were going to sound singing it though.

Then Ray continued singing: 'And long ago... his birth did save the world.'

Emily held her breath. God, it was perfect. It was actually perfect. She scrabbled to get up off the floor, full of enthusiasm that needed to be released. 'Oh my God! Ray! It sounds *brilliant*! Totally brilliant! I mean, I know the tune isn't new, but maybe that really doesn't matter, because it *sounds* so different.' She punched the air. 'Take that Mr "I've Written Something for Eurovision: You Decide" Jarvis!' She gasped once more and then looked to Ray who was looking back at her. 'Sorry... sorry, too much celebrating when there's tonnes more to do, I know. Like a storyline. Elongating the nativity is easy enough, but it has to be funny... especially for the parents who have to sit on the tiny chairs for over an hour. I'll definitely need some well-placed jokes about the latest disgraced celebrity and…' She stopped talking, suddenly feeling sick. What had she just said?! She was a complete numbskull. 'Oh my God, I'm sorry, I didn't mean that. I really, *really* didn't mean that.'

'It's OK,' Ray answered, putting his guitar down.

'No, it's not OK. It's so not OK. I don't know what I was thinking.' She felt truly terrible. Who was this diva in charge of drama who had just descended like some sort of celestial critic deciding people in the limelight weren't really people? Was this what power did to you? Would this be what she would be like as a headteacher?

'Ray, I am so, so sorry. I got carried away and I promise, there will be absolutely no jokes about celebrities, whether they're in crisis or not.'

'I don't know,' Ray answered. 'Justin Bieber is usually good for it.'

Emily looked at his guitar. 'Can I move this down and sit? Or isn't it allowed to be touched by mere mortals who can't even hold a tune on the recorder?'

He picked the guitar up. 'This is a guitar I used to busk with before *Lyricist*. I've had it since I was twelve years old. It's still my favourite. It's funny how every instrument has a different feel to it, even ones of the same model.' He stroked the neck. 'Some you can instinctively feel are right for you. Others not so much. And there are the growers.' He moved his fingers over the strings. 'You *can* learn to love something you thought wasn't right to start with.'

Emily sat down on the sofa next to him. 'That sounds like people… particularly landladies who plead for your help then open their stupid mouths and say something insulting and moronic.'

'I never wanted to be a celebrity,' Ray admitted. 'I just wanted to make a living from my music. But, these days, you can't do one without the other. As well as listening to my songs, people feel they need to see where I buy my clothes, what I eat for lunch, know how often I go to the pub or pee and... it's exhausting.'

'I'd say that I can imagine but... I really can't.'

He turned his head and Emily was caught up in his amber eyes. They were extraordinary. Brown yet not brown. Some sort of glorious nearly tortoiseshell. He sighed, his shoulders raising then dropping with the breath.

'That verse we just wrote,' he said softly. 'That's the first thing I've written for months. I'm meant to have songs written. I'm meant to be in the studio finishing my new album but... I can't do it and now there's all this with Ida and the press and...'

'A stupid school Christmas show,' Emily added. She shouldn't have asked for his help. He was busy and important.

'No,' Ray said quickly. 'No, I'm not saying that.' He sighed again. 'I'm not saying that at all.' He turned his body towards her slightly. 'I'm saying that, maybe meeting you and staying here and doing this was... meant to be, somehow.'

'Well,' Emily said. 'Sharing my apartment with you has definitely prevented me from sharing it with Lee, Anthony, Raul or Caleb. All quite questionable housemates in my opinion.'

'When you started with Lee and Anthony I was waiting for the rest of the members of Blue.'

'As my mother hears in court on a daily basis... all rise.'

Ray laughed then, the whole of his face creasing up, fine lines appearing by those gorgeous eyes, his mouth widening, beautiful straight teeth appearing...

'So,' Ray said, picking the guitar back up. 'Are we finishing "Here at Stretton Park" to the tune of "O, Holy Night"?'

'Yes!' Emily replied excitedly, leaping up again. 'I mean, if that's OK with you. Would you like a beer? I'm sure Jonah left some Peroni at the back of the cupboard.'

'No,' Ray answered. 'That's OK. But, if you're going to make one, I'll have another coffee.'

Twenty-Eight

Emily opened her eyes slowly and immediately nothing felt quite right. There was daylight for a start, not much, but a definite lightening and not the pitch black it should be at 6 a.m. when she usually woke up... and her pillow was way firmer than it ought to be too. Eyes springing open she saw it wasn't Dunelm Mill bedding under her cheek, it was a grey sweater. And the firmness wasn't being brought to her by synthetic filling, it was Ray's abs. She was lying on Ray! Her head on his stomach... she hoped it was his stomach. She shifted, sitting up. She was on the sofa and Ray was on the sofa too and light was now streaming into her living room. What time was it? One glance at her watch told her 8 a.m. 8 a.m.! She should be halfway to school by now! She was never late! She never slept on the sofa, with or without a man's body as a pillow! As she got up and off the settee, she kicked something on the floor. The guitar made a loud and echoing twanging noise that had her companion stirring.

'Morning,' Ray greeted, blinking and yawning at the same time.

'Yes,' Emily answered, patting herself down as if to check she was wearing all her clothes. How could she be this clueless about how the night had ended when neither of them had had anything to drink. They had been singing. *She* had been singing. They had been singing *together* and coming up with lines for 'Here at Stretton Park'. 'Yes, it is morning. Late morning. I'm late. I have to be in class by eight-thirty and I have to get there and I have to shower and change and…' And she was dithering. Moving back and forth between her bag at the end of the room and the door to the kitchen, wondering what to do first. Did she have time for coffee?

'I'll make some coffee,' Ray said, unfolding his large frame from the sofa and getting to his bare feet, stretching his arms over his head. 'Sorry about last night.'

Oh God! What was he apologising for? What did he do? What did *they* do? She remembered singing, as abandoned as she had ever been, Ray encouraging her to increase her volume – God knew what Sammie and Karen downstairs must have thought. And they had mugs and mugs of coffee and she'd opened peanuts she hadn't even known she'd had and they'd eaten them by the handful and Ray had such lovely, lovely hands… and her thinking that was why she was now worried she might have made an indiscretion. She had never woken up this way before…

'I… er…' She really had nothing else.

'Just so you know, when I get into something I'm pretty dogged about finishing it. Even if it means it's a late one.'

The song. He was simply talking about the song. They'd finished it and they'd just...

'You fell asleep,' Ray said. 'I didn't want to wake you. I thought that might be bad etiquette for a new lodger.'

So instead he had let her sleep... on him. She shook her head and hoped sense would follow. 'I should get in the shower.'

'And I'll make that coffee,' Ray said again.

Ray watched Emily scurry from the lounge and he took a deep breath and padded over the bare boards to the Christmas tree they'd put up together. It was insane. Ray Stone putting up a Christmas tree in November but doing it with Emily, *for* Emily, had felt right. She had given him a roof over his head without judgement and literally everything she did or said came from the sweetest of places. He wasn't sure he had met someone so genuine before. And last night was about the most fun he had had in so long. *Simplicity.* Sitting on a sofa, drinking coffee not alcohol for Christ's sake... literally for Christ's sake, with all the Biblical terminology he had had to rhyme with. It had been extraordinary in its normality. He touched one of the bright red wooden reindeer hanging from one of the boughs and his phone vibrated in the pocket of his jeans. He knew it was going to be Deborah, but now he was ready to face his demons and take her call.

'Hey,' he greeted and waited for the onslaught he knew was coming. Closing his eyes, steadying his core, he moved to the window and prepared to take the verbal roasting heading his way.

'Did you just "hey" me? Like we're drinking buddies or something?' Deborah asked him. 'Don't "hey" me, Ray. I'm at the end of a very short leash right now. Very short. Shorter than the leash they use at Tucker's obedience classes.'

'Sorry,' he apologised.

'Walking out on Ida yesterday was a very bad move. You need to talk to her and fast.'

'I know,' he answered with a sigh.

'Oh,' Deborah said. She sounded taken aback as if she had been expecting resistance from him. Well, perhaps he needed to show that this leopard could change his spots.

'Yeah, I was a coward for walking out. I just didn't expect to see her and seeing her was… confronting… and I wasn't ready to deal with it but now… well, I can't say I'm absolutely ready but… I'm ready to try.'

Was he? After one evening of installing a boiler thermostat, making up new lyrics to 'O, Holy Night' and decorating the most hard-to-put-together Christmas tree that had ever been invented?

'Really?' Deborah sounded less than convinced and he couldn't blame her. He had been doing the doggy-paddle in self-pity since all this started. But, put simply, things seemed brighter now. He looked out at the dawn breaking over the frost-coated rooftops of Islington. He had somewhere to stay. He had a new project. He had spoken to his dad yesterday and neither of them had yelled. They had talked about his mum…

'Yeah,' Ray said. 'Fix up another meeting. Text me the time and the place. I'll be there.' He heard Deborah draw breath, ready to say something else, so he carried on. 'And, can you get me a gig? Like, something small and intimate, but with all the press there. I think it's time we showed everyone that I'm still here, still singing, and definitely not hiding.'

The words sounded far more resolute and resilient than he really felt. His stomach was quaking with panic already but, singing last night, albeit not his usual style, had given him a shot of confidence that his voice wasn't about to give out. Perhaps he *should* seek another opinion. Maybe his vocals couldn't manage a full-on nationwide tour just yet but a few gigs, time in the studio, could be possible, couldn't it? Dr Crichton might have looked down his throat with his fancy equipment, but it was Ray's body. He would be able to feel what was right and what wasn't, wouldn't he?

'Fan club members and a shout out on social media. I'll book something like a jazz club. This is great, Ray, really great. I'll speak to Ida and I'll talk to you later. What are you doing this morning?' Deborah asked him.

'This morning,' he said, taking a breath and facing the new day outside of the window. 'This morning, I think I'm going to write a new song.'

Twenty-Nine

Stretton Park Primary School

'I don't know whether this looks like Santa's grotto or an upper-class brothel.' Dennis was standing at the doors of the school hall, hand dipping a lolly into a Dip-Dab, eyes moving around the ceiling and the walls, taking in all the decorations Emily and her class had put up earlier. The whole room was now festooned in fat, fluttery, glittering tinsel, with bright baubles, strings of lights and hand-painted pictures of the nativity scene covering one wall.

'I don't think you would get paintings of Jesus in a brothel,' Emily said, getting down off the chair she had been standing on to pin the last picture in place. 'And there isn't one red light. We went for classic white and blue... well, it was all Poundstretcher had.'

'It looks... fuller than it did this morning, I'll say that.'

'"Fuller,"' Emily said. 'That doesn't sound like a compliment. My class have worked really hard this morning. And we've got the "What Christmas Means to

Me" parents' visit after school today. The only full going on is full-on.'

'Keep your baubles on,' Dennis said. 'It looks fine. The diocese will love it.' He scrutinised the Jesus portraits. 'Especially this picture where the good Lord looks like Tom Jones.' He furrowed his brow. '*Is* that Tom Jones? Because even the throne looks like a chair from *The Voice*.'

'Have you found out if Penny is pregnant yet?' Emily asked, changing the subject.

'I do teach a class too, you know,' Dennis said. 'I don't have all day to...'

'Stalk the dinner ladies?'

'I'm just taking a healthy interest in her welfare... and worrying that the quality of the meals might go down if we lose her. Unless Mother applies for the job, of course.' He sucked at his lollipop.

'Is she *really* interested in working, Dennis?'

'She needs something,' Dennis told her. 'And I'd rather it was here making meals where I can keep an eye on her. And she would be in a kitchen situation where she's completely comfortable.' He sighed. 'Yesterday she was watching re-runs of The Ryder Cup and talking about getting her old clubs out.' Dennis shook his head. 'I would worry about her re-joining the golf club. Driving those buggies around or falling in a bunker.'

'So,' Emily said, looking up at her beautifully crafted ceiling work with the decorations. 'What day are the diocese coming next week? And what time? Because if it's afternoon maybe we can wow them with scones... or mince pies and cinnamon spice coffees.'

Dennis clapped a hand to his cheek, lolly between his lips. 'Don't you know?'

'Know what?' She actually now felt sick. Maybe it was last night's peanuts. She hadn't checked the eat-by date.

'They're not coming next week now,' Dennis said.

Thank God! She had time to write a script and make up some new lyrics to Christmas tunes and get Year Six to learn them! There *was* someone or something up there looking down on her... possibly Simon or maybe an angel he had sweet-talked with an Oyster card for the pearly gates.

'They're coming today,' Dennis informed. 'I thought you knew! I thought that was why you'd got on and done the decorating this morning.'

Holy Christ. Today! The diocese was coming today! She wasn't ready! For anything! And why hadn't Susan told her? She already had parents coming in later. She couldn't deal with parents and vicars on the same day... What did she do? Her mind was racing like Mo Farah on the final sprint to the line. She had shared 'Here at Stretton Park' with the children that morning, but they wouldn't remember the lyrics for a performance later that day. But they *could* sing from song sheets for now. If she whipped some up on the computer...

'Are you alright, Emily?' Dennis asked her.

She mustn't flap. She mustn't look pale or overwhelmed or pretty much ready to faint. She wasn't a giver-upper. She could do this.

'Fine,' she managed to say. 'I'm absolutely fine.' She cleared her throat. 'It's good they're coming today. They can see the tableaus the children have made and...'

'See the start of the show you're creating,' Dennis added.

She nodded. 'Absolutely that.' And then another thought struck her. It was all very well getting the children to sing the song, but she had no one to play the music. Now she really was going to be sick. She put a hand over her mouth and headed for the door.

'Emily!' Dennis called after her. 'Are you OK? *You're* not pregnant, are you?'

Thirty

Ladurée, Covent Garden

Ray looked up at the stone building in the heart of Covent Garden, its sign in green and gold, matching the frames around the windows. This was typical Ida. This location would have been her suggestion, exactly like the *Alice in Wonderland* fantasy style of yesterday's eatery. Ida liked eccentricity as much as she liked excess and exuberance. She would think nothing of spending hundreds of pounds on a painting she liked but couldn't understand why their electricity bill was so high. She had always had a different, slightly skewed view of what was most important in life. And some of that was wrapped up in the lyrics of the song he had begun to write this morning. Since moving into Emily's apartment, he had managed to avoid the press, so, donning his coat and hat, he had taken his guitar out to the park and sat on the damp grass letting the grey and cold seep into his thoughts as well as his skin. As difficult as it was, really bringing out the honesty of your soul was the only way to write real music in his opinion. In the last few years the *only* honesty he'd shared had been in his lyrics.

Covent Garden was alive with tourists and shoppers taking photos of the well-known markets and arcades. Despite the late-November temperatures there were still street-performers drawing a crowd, still people sipping drinks from the balcony of the Punch & Judy pub. Large wooden wheelbarrows held planters containing winter ferns, hot dogs sizzled on stalls outside Jubilee Market Hall... He pushed open the door of the French café and headed inside.

Rows and rows of perfectly rounded macarons in all the colours greeted him. They were set on a black marble slab ready to be served for taking away, along with other elaborate-looking cakes that could have been put on display in an art gallery, such was their intricacy. The décor was soft and pastel and very French and, as he moved through the building, he hoped in the direction of the seating area, macaron trees bordered the way.

Finding the room he was supposed to be in, he saw the back of Deborah's sleek bob first and focused on that as he made his way to the table. Ida was there too, but he couldn't fully engage with that notion yet. *Keep on moving. Keep it civil.*

He put a hand on the red velvet-covered chair to steady his body, as well as his nerve, before dropping down into the seat next to his agent. He took in the pale green wallpaper and randomly placed pictures on the walls before he raised his head to look at his ex-girlfriend.

'You're early,' Deborah said, putting down her iPhone.

'Surprise,' Ray said. He took in the teapot on the table and a gold three-tier cake stand filled with circles of macarons. What even was a macaron? What was it made out of? 'You started without me?' If they had had tea and cakes before he'd even arrived, just how long had his agent and Ida been here? He needed to look at Ida now. He needed to own this difficult situation she had put him in.

'You won't like the tea.' It was Ida speaking and it forced his gaze to meet hers. 'It's Earl Grey. You don't like Earl Grey.'

She didn't look a bit different from the last time he'd seen her in person, not including yesterday's brief encounter. That last fateful day when he'd finally packed his bags and left. Her near-white blonde hair still looked as soft as dandelion fluff and she was wearing an off-the-shoulder dusky pink jumper that was somehow shapeless yet equally showed off her petite frame. She'd screamed that day and clawed at him, telling him, in one breath, he was worthless, a piece of shit, and in the other breath that she loved him and she was never going to let him go... He looked back to the macarons.

'The waiter will come,' Deborah told him. 'Ask you what you want to drink.' She lowered her voice. '*Not* champagne.'

'I'll have Earl Grey I think,' Ray said, settling in his seat and clasping his hands together.

He watched Ida roll her eyes and shake her head. 'Maybe this was a mistake.'

'What?' Deborah asked. 'We haven't even started talking yet.'

'No, but I can tell Ray is in one of his moods,' Ida answered.

'*I'm* in one of *my* moods!' That was rich. And typical of Ida to carry on playing the victim she had portrayed in the newspapers. Deborah put a hand on his arm. *Firm. A warning.* And she was right. Even though his agent didn't know the depth of their story, she *was* right. Riling Ida up was only going to be counterproductive.

'I'm going to make a suggestion to both of you before we get into this. We are all here to try to make progress, yes? There will be no raised voices. There will be no judgement. Everyone will get a chance to have their say and then we will try and work towards a resolution that suits everyone.'

There was so much Ray wanted to say. So much. But still now he couldn't. He was here at this meeting knowing he wasn't ever going to be able to be completely honest, in this room or any other, and Ida, she knew that too.

'Would you like something to drink, sir?'

It was a waiter at Ray's side. He looked up at him and nodded. 'Yes, please, I'll…'

'He'll have English Breakfast tea,' Ida ordered. 'And please bring plenty of sugar.'

He really *really* wished he could order the champagne.

Macarons, Ray had found out, were crisp, baked shells of sugar, egg white and ground almonds making the sandwich around a creamy ganache in a rainbow of colours and flavours. He had eaten five already, mainly to stop himself from speaking too much or, particularly, whenever Ida said something really offensive and he'd been tempted to want to hiss across the table at her.

'I think, Ida,' Deborah began again, 'and correct me if

I'm wrong, Ray, what we'd like is for you to stop speaking to the press.'

Ouch. That was to the point and Ray instinctively knew this would push all Ida's buttons. She had never liked being told what she could or couldn't do by anyone. She liked to be the one calling the shots. Always.

'I'm sure you would,' Ida replied. She picked up her tea cup with a forefinger and sipped silently before returning the cup to the saucer. 'But my free speech isn't something you can control.'

'It is if there isn't any truth in it,' Ray snapped. 'If it's lies.'

'Oh!' Ida exclaimed. 'So, you're saying that I've lied in the stories, are you? Perhaps I should have asked my lawyer to come with me today.'

'Come on, Ida,' Ray said, leaning forward. 'We're not stupid. *I'm* not stupid. You've said the bare minimum to kick the rumour mill into overdrive to try and nail my reputation to the wall.'

'Oh, that's what I've done, is it?' Ida asked, unmoving. 'It's all about you, Ray, is it? It couldn't possibly be about me? About my need to release myself from the past and forge a new future?'

Ray shook his head. This was going to be a waste of time. Ida saw things completely differently to anyone else he had ever met. Everything was always about the unfairness of her life. Her battle against the world…

'You leaving was incredibly stressful for me,' Ida continued. 'It worsened my anxiety, it brought out my OCD tendencies, I couldn't paint or sculpt…'

'And that's *my* fault?' Ray stated.

'*You* left me!' Finally, there was emotion from her. The

wild eyes, the cutting tone. Difficult memories arrived. He had seen that look in her eyes so many times, the anger bubbling away that showed in the line of her jaw and the downturn of her lips. It had always taken him by surprise. How someone so seemingly content in one moment could turn the complete opposite because of one misplaced word, one look in the wrong direction, the incorrect item bought from the supermarket…

'I had no choice,' Ray answered. His voice was calm, but inside there was a riot of emotions jockeying for position, all armed, some of them with petrol bombs ready to blow.

'There's always a choice, Ray,' Ida said. This time the voice was gentle and coquettish. It was a performance he'd seen too often. Now it only turned his stomach. He reached for another macaron.

'What would it take, Ida, for you to retract what you've said in the press and to not speak to them again about Ray?' Deborah was desperate for this to be productive but, as good as she was at conflict resolution and negotiation, she really didn't know Ida.

'I won't be retracting what I've said already,' Ida made clear.

'Why?' Ray asked. 'Because they'll all ask for their money back?'

'I've never been materialistic,' Ida stated, toying with a thread on her jumper. 'Money is simply paper with different portraits on. Some people like to collect it like it's art, but it will never make them truly happy. Like with you, Ray.' She picked up a macaron and smoothed her thumb and forefinger over it. 'You say you don't want fame, yet you couldn't survive if you were back to busking on the street or playing those tiny venues to a crowd of twenty. You crave attention. You always have. Losing a mother does that to a boy.' She crushed the macaron with her grip and watched the pieces crumble down onto her plate.

Don't react. She knows how to hurt you. She's always known. She had punched him, emotionally, in the deepest, darkest place, the place she knew would trigger a response. *His mother.* Veronica Stone would have hated Ida and everything she was. *Cold. Shallow. Fake.* Someone who showed you what you wanted to see, then revealed it as a desert mirage once you committed and got close. He rolled his tongue up inside his mouth, focusing on the texture of it, distracting himself from Ida's words and the way she was looking at him now, waiting for him to fall apart.

'Right,' Deborah intervened. 'Ida, if you won't retract what you've already said to the press, can we at least have your assurance that these stories will stop now? That we can all agree that what's done is done and we can move forward with a line drawn underneath it? No unwarranted or unwanted media surprises.'

Ray continued to watch Ida. She tilted her head a little, looking at him with a half-smile on her mouth. 'As I said, the stories were my therapy. I feel better now it's out there… for now. But I don't know how long that feeling's going to last.'

Ray shook his head. Here it came. Just how much money did she want to go away? Enough to buy her some rent in a smarter art studio? Except he didn't have anything to give her. And Deborah didn't have the money to sub him – she was already working for the bare minimum she got from Saturn Records.

'OK,' Deborah said. 'So, can I ask, do you have a figure in mind that might help you feel better for longer, ideally for good?'

'Money,' Ida whispered, like the word was poison to her ears. 'I don't want money. Haven't you been listening to me at all?'

'OK,' Deborah said again. 'If not money, then what? What can we do to make your life a little more comfortable, so you don't feel the need to share details of your relationship with Ray with the world?'

'Well,' Ida said, sitting forward. 'There's only one thing I really, really want.'

'Tell us,' Deborah said. 'We'll see if we can make it happen.'

Ray knew it was coming, but part of him wanted to hear Ida's audacity out loud, in front of his agent, to underline his ex-girlfriend's instability.

Ida smiled, playing with a tendril of her hair. 'Ray,' she said. 'I want you to come home.'

Thirty-One

Stretton Park Primary School

'How do I look?'

It was Susan Clark, fresh from the ladies' toilets where she seemed to have slicked a deep plum shade of lipstick over her lips and highlighted already quite prominent eyebrows with a kohl stick. What was the right answer? Emily was just glad she had worn her champagne-coloured blouse and taupe trousers today. She always felt ultra-confident in that outfit and thought it was a good mix of looking ready for business yet also maintaining an appearance of 'softly approachable'.

'You look ready for the bishops,' Emily answered finally. 'Or are they deans? I did tend to get them mixed up the last time.'

'One bishop,' Susan answered, fiddling with the amber beads on the string of her glasses. 'And two suffragans. As far as I know. But, last time there were representatives from other deaneries, so we could actually have the whole church shebang.'

'Except the Pope,' Emily added with a smile.

'Obviously,' Susan said, frowning. 'Because we are talking Church of England, not Catholic.'

Of course they were. Emily knew that. But the ins and outs of religion had never been her strong point. She hadn't been formally baptised. Allegedly, the story went, that off a yacht called *Destiny II* belonging to someone called Cassar, William and Alegra had dipped Emily in the crystal waters off the Ivory Coast and declared her godly with witnesses all drunk on dark rum. She was sure the diocese wouldn't have approved of that kind of christening. She had no everlasting candle or documents to prove it even happened. Only the testimony of her parents and occasionally the drunken rantings of her alleged godfather Marcus, who she used to see every other Bank Holiday Monday if her parents weren't working...

'I'm putting a lot of faith in you here, Emily,' Susan spoke, sucking in her chest and adjusting a button looking like it was keen to slip into an escape. 'Pardon my pun.'

'I realise that,' she answered. Did she? Was this actual faith Susan was putting in her? Or was it more the case of she had no one else she was capable of bullying into the difficult role of Christmas show organiser. Dennis wouldn't have done it. Linda Rossiter would probably have had a seizure if she was asked to do it. But, whatever her reasoning, Emily was now at the helm and therefore she would do her upmost to deliver. 'I won't let you down.'

'That's music to my ears,' Susan answered. 'And, speaking of music, we are going to give them all a cup of tea, or coffee, and biscuits and then we'll be straight into a taster for the Christmas show, yes?'

'Yes,' Emily replied. Why was she saying yes? She had no one to play any music whatsoever. But, if push came to shove, she would just have to play the Mariah Carey version of 'O, Holy Night' on Spotify – on her phone – and hope that her children could sing loudly enough over Ms Mimi.

She had texted Ray earlier, having thoroughly deliberated over even asking him for a whole hour before her fingers met the keys. He was helping her enough already. He had basically written the new lyrics and mended her central heating. But he *was* getting a lovely room in a bright and roomy apartment and, this close to Christmas, there wasn't going to be a lot else out there. So, she had done it. She'd messaged him.

HELP! Sorry! I know you're super busy and I'm already taking up lots of your time but I need a guitarist or a piano player this afternoon. At 2.30 p.m. To play 'Here at Stretton Park', I mean 'O, Holy Night', with the new words. Anyway, would you possibly in any way at all be around? This is Emily Parker by the way.

She wasn't sure she had ever sent a more pathetic text message in her life. And they had only just swapped numbers the previous night – a landlady/tenant thing in case emergencies occurred – and here she was asking for another favour. Needless to say, he hadn't replied.

'Miss Parker, Cherry says she feels sick.' Alice was suddenly in reception at her side, tugging at her champagne-coloured blouse. Why wasn't she in the hall with the other children? And why weren't Dennis or Linda, or one of her other colleagues keeping a closer eye on them?

'Oh, Alice, are you sure?' Emily asked. She had worked out quite a while ago that Alice quite liked classmates to be feeling ill. She would probably make a very good nurse... as long as her interest in death didn't continue. Although there *was* hospice care...

'She's really pale,' Alice said, stroking fingers down her own cheek. 'And her face looks like this.' Emily watched as Alice rolled her eyes to the roof of the sockets so almost all her iris disappeared, then she made her mouth into a replica of Edvard Munch's *The Scream*.

The last thing Emily needed was a vomiting child when the church representatives arrived. And she didn't want Susan to catch wind of this potential disaster. She shuffled away from the Head who was now preening a rather awful festive flower arrangement Linda Rossiter had popped on the reception table earlier. It was gold terribly spray-painted fir cones and deep, dark berries Emily was concerned were deadly nightshade.

'If Cherry is feeling sick, Alice, she really needs to come and tell me herself,' Emily whispered.

'I think she's too sick to move,' Alice said, blinking. 'That's why I thought I should tell you.'

Emily still wasn't convinced, so she took three paces towards the hall doors and looked through one of the small viewing windows. There was quite a lot of chatter going on amongst all the pupils gathered to greet their guests from the diocese. Dennis was eating more sweets! More! He had to be personally keeping that retro sweet shop on the high street going. Where was Cherry? If she was less than her usual vibrant self perhaps she would go in and speak to her.

'They're here!'

The announcement came from Susan, who was fiddling with her blouse buttons again. There wasn't time to check on Cherry. Anyway, if Cherry really *was* feeling ill she'd have to tell one of the other teachers. One of the other teachers who wasn't in charge of impressing the people with the money.

'Alice, please tell Cherry that if she's feeling really poorly she should tell Mrs Rossiter or Mr Murray. Now please, go back into the hall and tell the class to sit nicely and quietly until it's time for us to sing.'

'But…' Alice began.

'Please, Alice,' Emily begged, already sounding like she was losing control of the situation. 'I'll… let you play with worms in the playground this afternoon.'

'Really?!' Alice said, brightening up.

'If you're gentle with them,' Emily said. 'Now, please, go in and sit down.'

She made sure Alice skipped off into the hall before re-joining Susan at the door. She looked out of the window at a large black car pulling into a disabled space in the car park. It was smart, with privacy glass.

'They didn't have that car the last time they came,' Susan stated. 'It's very luxurious.'

'Well, they have given us money for the Christmas show so…'

'Not yet,' Susan answered, pursing her lips into a smile.

'Not yet?' Emily asked. Not that she had any grand plans

for costumes seeing as she didn't have a script or know what the play was actually going to be…

'We aren't the only school they look after. That's why I'm so keen to impress them, Emily. If we impress them they might give us more and then I can loosen up those budget restraints.'

Now she felt more pressured than ever. Literally the school's immediate financial future hinged on her getting this right…

'There's the bishop,' Susan breathed. 'No headdress today. Do you think that's a good thing or a bad thing?'

'I have no idea,' Emily replied. 'But I quite like his purple shirt.'

'I feel that's rather like wearing civvies for him. Maybe he's saving his hat for St Osmond's school.'

'Don't worry,' Emily said. 'It's going to be fine. Year Six are ready to sing their little hearts out.' Although Felix might repeat the repeating line twice more to balance out his OCD. And she didn't have anyone to accompany them on a real musical instrument, and she hadn't even tried to connect her Spotify account to the Bluetooth speaker yet…

Her phone vibrated in her pocket and she quickly took it out before the bishop and his companions got to the front door.

I'm outside Stretton Park. Front door or back? Could do without getting arrested. But ready to play piano if you still need me. I'm hoping you have a piano. This is Ray.

She had a pianist! She had Ray Stone as her pianist. And

he could help the children sing too! But if he was going to play in front of everyone she either needed to tell Susan, get him signed in, do everything above board or... she needed to put him in a disguise.

'Hello, Bishop Nicholas and... suffragans. It's so lovely to see you again.'

Susan was greeting their guests. Emily fired off a quick text and smiled at their visitors, ready to shake hands and win favour.

Thirty-Two

Ray wasn't entirely sure how his life had come to this. He was currently behind the stage curtain of the school hall, dressed in a Santa outfit, complete with a fluffy white beard that covered every inch of his face. He could barely breathe, let alone sing... and, of course, he wasn't even meant to be singing at all. Well, that wasn't going to happen anymore. Even more so not after the meeting with Ida going the way he knew it would go. He had no other choice now. He had to face everything head on, starting with getting back out there, being 100 per cent unfazed by what the media were saying. He had nothing to hide. He had done nothing wrong. Hiding away was saying the exact opposite and it needed to stop.

'I can't thank you enough for doing this,' Emily said, putting a red hat over his head and tucking in his hair so nothing of who he really was showed. 'I mean, really, thank you. You're basically saving my life here. My professional life at least.'

'Did I tell you I hate Christmas?' Ray said through the white nylon-y curls snaking around his mouth.

'No! Ray, you *can't* hate Christmas!'

'I can. And I do. I even have a no Christmas songs clause in my record company contract.'

'What? Well, that's silly. Because everyone loves a Christmas song.'

'I don't.'

'But… all the new words you made up for this song we're about to perform.'

'Yeah,' Ray said. 'I didn't say I couldn't *write* a Christmas song, I just wouldn't want to release one of my own.' He shuddered. 'All that talk about it being the most wonderful time of the year.'

'But it is! Christmas is all warm and cosy and…'

'Freezing and frosty.'

'Not now the central heating is fixed.'

He smiled at her. 'That is a very good point.'

'And you helped me put up a Christmas tree only last night,' Emily reminded, adjusting the hat on his head.

'And *only* under the influence of coffee,' he said. 'What are you turning me into?'

He was getting a little nostalgic. Some Christmases past *had* been warm and cosy, with brandy-laden trifles and presents his dad had worked every hour available to afford to buy. This was because of Ida's comment about losing his mother and seeing his dad yesterday. It was all bringing to the fore the loss he still hadn't quite dealt with yet. Christmas wasn't ever quite the same when you were a family member down…

'Sorry,' Ray apologised. 'Don't listen to me. I'm like The Grinch. Just thought you should know that in case…'

'You start to turn green and furry?'

'I'm wondering if that might be a better look than Santa Claus.' He put out his arms, indicating his attire.

'I have to go,' Emily said, straightening the collar of his Father Christmas jacket. 'I'll introduce you. As Father Christmas, obviously. And the children will love it, particularly the Reception Class. So, just wave, don't speak at all and play the music and we'll sing. Then everyone will clap – hopefully – and then I'll come backstage and help you out of your clothes.'

Even though she'd said the last sentence in a rush and it was all completely innocent, a smouldering crackled into life in Ray's gut. Emily Parker looking beautiful again in that pale shiny shirt that set off the colour of her hair. And the fit of those trousers wasn't lost on him either. They enhanced every curve she possessed. Emily would definitely be on his radar if romance was ever on his agenda again. But, right now, it was a pretty big 'if'.

She laughed, then cleared her throat. 'I meant, help you out of your costume.' Then she ran to the curtain and disappeared. Ray closed his eyes and let out a breath. *Romance*. He had had romance with Ida once, but that felt like a lifetime ago and, for the longest time, it had turned into a battle of control rather than an open, honest, two-way relationship. He wasn't sure he was ever going to be able to trust that it wouldn't happen the very next time he shared his heart…

*

'The bishop has eaten six mini-Christmas pudding bites,' Dennis whispered to Emily. 'Six! I've counted!'

'Best not let him near your bag of flying saucers then,' Emily replied.

'And those suffragans!' Dennis continued. 'I don't think either of them have spoken. Not one word.'

'Maybe they're not allowed to,' Emily suggested. 'Maybe they've taken a vow of silence or something.'

'That's monks, Emily. Not suffragans.'

'Well, they all seemed to like the portraits of Jesus.'

'How do you know? They haven't spoken!'

Emily caught Susan's eye and her head-docking towards the stage. It was time for the performance. Well, there was no going back now. Do or die. How hard could it be? One song, played by a professional musician and sung by her children who, having practised it at least fifty times on a loop this morning, should have it lodged as an earworm. And if they didn't, they had words on sheets of paper. It was fool proof.

'Right, I'd better get this show on the road,' Emily said, lacing her fingers together and stretching them out.

'Good luck,' Dennis answered.

Emily walked towards her class who were seated on the front rows, all chatting, shaking the sheets of lyrics in their hands. Makenzie seemed to be making a paper aeroplane out of his.

'Right, Year Six, are we ready to sing?' Emily asked. 'We'll go up onto the stage now and get prepared.'

'I'm not going to sing the God words,' Rashid told her.

'Rashid, that's absolutely fine. I told you that earlier. If anyone feels uncomfortable about singing any of the song, then you don't have to sing.'

'I don't really want to sing,' Matthew stated.

'Neither do I,' Angelica added.

'I don't want to sing either.'

'And I feel sick.'

The last comment came from Cherry. Alice was right. She did look very pale, with a slight ghoulish tinge to her features.

'Listen,' Emily said, trying her best to sound the epitome of calm. 'Year Six, I really, really need your help with this today. Because we really all want a wonderful Christmas show this year, don't we? With... sweets and... treats and... chocolate for everyone.' God, what was she doing? Bribing her children to get this done. It was an all-time low.

'Chocolate,' Jayden said, eyes lighting up. 'We'll get chocolate if we sing?'

'You'll get chocolate if you sing *well*,' Emily answered. 'So, let's go and sing. The sooner we sing, the sooner I can arrange chocolate.' She was counting on Dennis having something suitable for thirty-three children to share in his locker. If not, she would be off to the corner shop somewhere between after the song and before the parents arrived for the tableau exhibition. 'Come on, let's go up onto the stage.'

With thirty-three reluctant children, Emily finally made it onto the boards and behind the microphone. Suddenly, the hall looked huge, like a sold-out show at the O2 Arena. *Focus on the prize, Emily. Getting the funding for the school and that accomplishment leading the way to the Deputy Head position.*

'Good afternoon everyone and a special warm welcome to our esteemed guests from the diocese. Welcome Bishop Nicholas and...' She had no clue what the other two were called. 'Bishop Nicholas and... friends.' She smiled in what she hoped was a warm and welcoming fashion. 'My name is Emily Parker and I'm proud to be coordinating this year's Stretton Park Christmas show. And I can tell you, it's going to be the most fabulous and entertaining spectacle... in the world... ever.' What was she saying? Talk about making a rod for her own back... 'And to give you a small taste of what we are going to have in store on 20th December, my Year Six class are going to perform for you now. But first, let me introduce our piano-player. It's someone you all know really well. Let's give a hand for... Father Christmas!'

Thank goodness, there *were* the gasps of delight from the younger children she had been hoping for. Then Ray strode on, clutching his padded-out stomach and waving his hands. But where was he going? She'd told him to just play the song, but he wasn't heading for the piano at the side of the stage, he was heading to her and the microphone.

'Ho! Ho! Ho!' he announced in a rather convincing, been-at-this-Santa-lark-for-years cavernous voice. 'Very Merry Nearly Christmas to you all! You will be pleased to know that the elves and I have been working extremely hard in the toy workshop this year, so I hope you've all been good little boys and girls.' He spread out his arms.

'Have you? Have you been good for your mummies and daddies?'

Emily took ownership of the microphone back. 'Or good for your mummies and mummies or daddies and daddies or step-parents or other legal guardians. Thank you so much, Father Christmas.'

She was relieved when Ray did a final wave and headed towards the ancient piano. Then a sudden thought hit. Was the piano even working? Or tuned? Had anyone even touched it since Mr Jarvis's departure? Why hadn't she thought about that? The answer to that last question was because she was too busy thinking about *literally* everything else. But now she was praying. Sending up begging thoughts to whichever god was listening. After everything she'd had to do to arrive at this moment, please, for Stretton Park's sake, let the piano be in tune.

She stood back in line with her children and hoped they would all sing up nice and loud and confidently as well, so her voice didn't have to be on display too much. It was one thing singing aloud in the privacy of her own apartment but quite another to be doing it in front of church royalty...

Ray began to play and Emily felt a swell in her stomach. It sounded beautiful. It was perfectly in tune and the notes were nothing like the loud jabbing of the keys Mr Jarvis had performed. This was like piano-*stroking*. It sounded like Ray was gently and carefully caressing the ebony and ivory, the soft, yet rich sound floating up into the hall. She was so caught up in listening to the introduction that she almost forgot when to come in...

Here at Stretton Park, the holidays are coming
And the nights are dark and clear
Here at Stretton Park, our hearts are filled with Jesus
And long ago, his birth did save the world

They were doing it! Her class was singing! Most of them in tune, but Ray was singing too, making sure they kept in time.

… Our school, will come together
This night is ours to share
One night, the star a sign
One night, a baby came
One night, in olden time

Emily felt the tears prick her eyes as they finished the song. She had never felt more proud of her children than she did now. She looked around at their little smiling faces, so sweet, innocent and happy. Sometimes she forgot how young they actually were. And that was when the applause began. The classes watching the performance all cheered and clapped. The other teachers too. Emily looked to the bishop and the suffragans. They were applauding as well. The crosses around their necks actually vibrating with the force of their clapping. She wanted to bow. Perhaps they *should* bow. She bent her body slightly, looking to her children in the hope they would follow suit. And they did. Bending over and over, some of the others curtseying. The clapping carried on and someone shouted 'more'. No! No, they couldn't do more because they didn't *have* more. Emily suspected the heckler was Dennis. She was definitely going to him for chocolate…

'Thank you!' Emily said into the microphone. 'Thank you so much.'

Her thanks delivered, it was mere seconds before Cherry threw up all over the stage.

Thirty-Three

'I need you to stay in the Father Christmas suit.'

Ray had just taken off the hat that had been really itching his head. He looked to Emily. 'That's a joke, right? Because I told you how much I don't get on with Christmas.'

'No... I mean... you don't have to stay in the suit, obviously, if you have somewhere else to be... which you obviously do because you don't work here, and you have a life and... sorry.' She took a breath. 'I've got parents coming and Susan loved the fact I had Santa playing the piano and playing the piano so *beautifully* by the way, and it would just add to the whole festive atmosphere if Father Christmas was here. But, it's fine. I've asked too much of you already.'

Ray looked at the hat in his hands. 'How much longer would I have to stay in the suit?'

'An hour?' Emily said. 'Maybe an hour and a half. And you wouldn't have to talk to anyone... although I did notice you seemed to rather enjoy addressing the audience earlier. That was unscripted.'

'I told you, when I take on a role, I'm all in.' He grinned. And this *was* a brilliant distraction to the shit that was currently going down in the rest of his life. Deborah had also mooted once upon a time that he might consider acting should he want to diversify. It wasn't something he'd ever thought too seriously about, but given he seemed to be spending quite a bit of time avoiding truths with the people around him, maybe it wouldn't be a huge leap to get paid for pretending to be something else...

'So, you will?' Emily asked, her face lighting up. 'I'll buy the chips tonight. Or, not chips, something better than chips. Whatever food you want to eat. Processed... or not.'

'Deal,' Ray agreed, getting to his feet.

'Wait,' Emily said. She took the hat out of his hands. 'You need to put the hat back on.'

He stood there and let her guide it onto his head, her fingers again tucking in his hair. Here he was in a white fuzzy beard, dressed all in red, and he was getting a little hot under the big, black belt about Emily touching him. Well, it *had* been a while...

'There,' Emily said, stepping back and looking satisfied with her work. 'Come out when you're ready. And no ho-ho-ho-ing. Just mingle.'

'And jingle,' Ray replied, shaking his head so the bell on the end of his hat made a noise.

'And you say you don't enjoy Christmas. I think that myth is well and truly shattered now.'

He smiled at her as she disappeared behind the curtain again. He should check his phone. There was bound to be something from Deborah. Or some fall-out from his definite crushing of Ida's apparent dreams of reconciliation. He had been calm, but firm. He wasn't going to be blackmailed. And how could she even think of reconciliation after everything that had transpired between them? Because, he guessed, that was the world Ida existed in. A world *she* made the rules for.

He stood up and put his hands on the Santa belt. 'Ho! Ho! Ho!'

Who exactly was he trying to kid?

'Hey! Ooo, Emily, you're looking absolutely fabulous today. What colour is that shirt? Prosecco?'

It was Two L's, his mouth almost spilling the sausage roll he was nibbling on. What was he doing here?

'It's sort of that colour, isn't it?' Emily answered. 'What are you doing here?'

'It's the "What Christmas Means to Me" thing isn't it? Don't tell me we've got the wrong day because Jonah has been baking all morning and if it's not eaten then I'll have to eat it and, well, if I eat it I'll be as bloated as that Santa over there.'

Emily swallowed, looking to Ray who was coming down from the stage. She'd completely forgotten Jonah had offered to bring baked goods to the after-school showcase. He'd mentioned it before he'd moved out. He'd obviously remembered and she hadn't. She was turning into a very poor rememberer and an even poorer friend...

'Where do you want these?' Jonah asked. He was in full chef garb. His checked trousers, black restaurant shirt and apron, bandana over his hair. He had two large platters in his arms. 'And there's another three in the car.'

'Oh, Jonah, you didn't have to make all this,' Emily remarked. It all looked wonderful from what she could see under the film. Little pastries with festive piping – holly leaves and berries, silver stars...

'I said I would,' Jonah said. 'Plus, it gave me a chance to try out some new stuff. And I'm really happy with how it's turned out so the hotel will benefit... if they ever let me adapt the menu.' He smiled. 'There's smoked black pudding croquettes with apple sauce, the sausage rolls are turkey and cranberry, cod fritters with honey dip and fig and goat's cheese puffs. And I did some mini-mince pies.'

Emily felt tears prick her eyes. All these people helping her do life at the moment simply because they were wonderful, kind human beings. She wanted to hug Jonah, but she feared for the platters and his hard work.

'I don't know what to say,' she breathed. Simon had loved Jonah's sausage rolls...

'Tell me where to put them so I can set them up and go and get the others,' Jonah begged with a laugh.

'I'll get the others,' Allan offered.

'No eating them, Allan,' Jonah ordered him.

'I'll grab some more tables,' Emily said, rushing to the corner of the room.

'The tableaus are really impressive this year,' Jonah said as he walked around the hall with Emily a little later. The room was filled with parents looking at what their children had been making over the course of the past few weeks. There were sculptures created from clay like Jayden's, there were others made from recycling – cardboard, bottle tops, empty coffee pods – Felix's was a fishbowl with real goldfish swimming around inside. She had asked him what it represented, and he had simply said the word 'Christmas' twice.

'It's amazing what you can get the children to do when you offer chocolate as an incentive.' She really mustn't forget to buy the class its treat for singing.

'So, who's the sexy Santa Claus?' Jonah asked, nudging Emily with his elbow.

'What?' she exclaimed.

'Well, I know I can't see much of his face but he's six foot, broad... is this some new teacher you haven't told me about?'

'Er, no,' Emily answered. What was she going to say? Obviously anything other than the truth would be wrong...

'Em?' Jonah said. 'Are you holding out on me? Do you *like* the sexy Santa?'

'Sshh,' Emily ordered.

'So, you do!'

'No!' She looked over her shoulder, to see who, if anyone, was listening. Susan was talking to Alice's parents. Alice's tableau was of Jesus's tombstone with tinsel and red-paint-soaked bandages which Emily had thought was more of an Easter project than a Christmas one, but she supposed it was all open to individual interpretation. Makenzie's was nothing more than a Scalextric track... She turned back to Jonah. 'It's Ray.'

'Ray?' Jonah queried. And then all at once he got it. 'Ray Stone?' Now he just looked confused. 'Ray Stone is dressed up in a Father Christmas suit? Here at Stretton Park.'

Emily was momentarily phased at Jonah speaking the title of the song they had performed earlier. Then: 'Yes, sshh.' She swallowed. 'It's a bit of a long story. Listen, I just need to go and speak to Rashid's parents and then I'll tell you everything.'

'I will want everything,' Jonah told her. 'And Allan will want *more* than everything.'

Emily took a breath, straightened her blouse, then approached the table Rashid's project was resting on. Rashid's was good. It was an oval platter filled with small recreations of all the food he would be indulging in over the two-week break. She was in no doubt his parents had probably helped him with it, but it was absolutely worthy of being glazed and put on the wall of Dar's Delhi Delights. She also knew it was hard to take part in these festive activities when you didn't celebrate the season. She was always hyper-aware of that, despite Susan's insistence that school policy was school policy and the parents all knew the religious bent when they enrolled.

'Hello, Mr and Mrs Dar, I'm Miss Parker, we met at the start of the school year.' She held out her hand and the two parents took it in turn to shake it.

'Hello, Miss Parker,' Ahmer greeted. 'I hear you are in charge of the Christmas show this year.'

'Yes,' Emily said. 'Yes, I am. And thank you, for your kind sponsorship.'

'You are very welcome. I'm putting together a number of

advertisements for you to write into the play. Just around one hundred words each. That should manage to get the message across.'

Oh hell. Advertisements to work into a script she didn't have. One hundred words each. He had to be kidding, didn't he? 'Great,' Emily answered. 'That's wonderful. Now, before I talk to you about Rashid's fantastic project, I wonder if I could speak to you about something else.'

'Rashid isn't struggling at all, is he?' This question was from Mrs Dar.

'No,' Emily answered. 'No, nothing like that.'

'Because, if he is struggling, we can increase the amount of time he spends studying at home. Currently we have a two hour a night regime that increases to three hours on the weekends,' Ahmer continued.

Two hours a night. Three hours at the weekend. At primary school! It was all Emily could do not to shudder. She looked at Rashid. He didn't now look like the ultra-confident, show-off-verging-on-bully he portrayed for the majority of his school life. He looked anxious, wide-eyed, frightened even… Was this shoplifting something more than a boy acting out to impress his contemporaries? Was there some deeper significance she had missed?

'Well, I…' She really didn't know what to say. Rashid was looking at her almost pleadingly. His big, dark eyes welling up like the forming tears were a river set to burst its banks. There was *definitely* something more here. 'I just wanted to say that Rashid is progressing really, really well in all subjects. He perhaps just needs to work on his relationships with his classmates.' She could feel the scrutiny of the Dars. 'I mean, two hours a night of study is quite intensive for a ten-year-old. Perhaps spending a little more time after school with his friends might help.'

'Are you saying he's not a team-player?' Ahmer queried.

'No... I... Rashid works well in a group as well as on his own.'

'He will have plenty of time to waste with his friends when he's finished medical school,' Mrs Dar added.

Medical school. He was ten! Emily looked at Rashid then. 'So, you want to be a doctor, Rashid?'

He nodded, reluctant, the sign of agreement not meeting the rest of his expression.

'Of course he does,' Ahmer said proudly. 'I wanted to be a doctor myself, but I took on the family restaurants. Not Rashid though. He's going to take a better path. Help people.'

A loud rumbling noise distracted Emily from the Dars and, looking to the hall doors, she saw the Jackson family entering the room. Despite Jayden's insistence that his dad wouldn't be coming today, there was Mr Jackson, bumping into tables, red-faced and looking like he had spent his whole day in the pub Jayden had recreated so accurately.

'Excuse me,' Emily said, smiling at the Dars. 'I will be back.'

Thirty-Four

'I know it's you,' Jayden whispered to Ray, a grin on his face. Ray had been intrigued to find out Jayden's 'What Christmas Means to Me' sculpture was of the infamous Riches Tower and the local pub, the Rose & Crown. All the children's work was exceptional in different ways. It was definitely a cut above anything he had ever made at school. In his day they had made simple cards with glitter and glue and pom-poms made from wool. He remembered his mum helping him with the pom-poms. They'd cut cardboard out of the back of cereal packets that were still on the go and loose Shreddies had escaped all over the kitchen floor. They had laughed that afternoon. Laughed and laughed together… until Ray saw that Soot's cage door was open and the gerbil wasn't inside. They'd found him, under the sofa, but he'd passed away not long after that.

'Of course you know it's me,' Ray answered in pure Father Christmas tones, not giving up his role. 'I'm the man in red! Saint Nicholas! Kris Kringle! I live in the North Pole!'

'You're Ray Stone,' Jayden said quietly.

There was no fooling this kid. Did he carry on keeping up the pretence to him or come clean? Ray had a feeling, if he admitted it, he would be putting Emily in employment jeopardy again and, looking around the hall, there didn't seem to be a cupboard she could shove him in this time. Not that he could see much of the room around the literal wonderland of Christmas decorations coating every corner…

'I'm sorry, who?' Ray asked, all surprised. He put his hands to his belt buckle and gave a hearty chuckle. 'I've never heard of this Ray Stone. He doesn't sound very special to me. Anyway, young man, tell me, have you been good this year? What would you like for Christmas?'

Jayden gave a shrug then. 'Dunno.'

'Dunno?' Santa Ray repeated. 'But you must know what you would like.'

'My mum and dad don't have much money.'

A little piece of his heart melted. What was wrong with him? Dressed up in a beard and a red trouser-suit, talking about toy workshops and getting emotional about families who didn't have much. *He* had been part of a family who didn't have much. That hadn't stopped him having wishes and dreams. He was still wishing and dreaming now, having wasted most of the financial achievements he'd been given already. But at ten years old, he didn't want Jayden to think that life meant nothing, that he couldn't hope…

'Well, young man,' Ray stated. 'You are talking to Santa now. And it's Santa who brings the presents on Christmas morning.'

Jayden let out a laugh. 'I'm not a baby.'

'Would you like a rocking horse?' Ray offered.

'No,' Jayden said, still laughing.

'An Arsenal football strip?'

'I support Leyton Orient.'

'Oh dear,' Ray joked.

'Hey! They're good! In the football league now thanks to Justin Edinburgh!'

'Come on, young Jayden, there must be something you want to ask Santa for.'

Jayden hesitated for a moment. 'Well, there is one thing,' the boy began. 'It's sort of for me, but it's sort of for Miss Parker.'

'I see,' Ray replied, trying hard to keep his Santa voice together. It was starting to make his throat sore and that was the very last thing he needed.

'Her boyfriend died and she was really really sad and she had to be away from school for ages.' He sniffed. 'She's my teacher this year and she's really the only teacher that listens to me, so I don't want her to go away again.'

Ray swallowed… to soothe his throat… definitely not to quell the sentimentality. 'I see.' He had definitely lost all the Father Christmas bravado now.

'You see that man over there?' Jayden said, pointing. 'The one in the chef's outfit.'

Ray saw Jayden was picking out Jonah. Emily's friend was handing out food to the parents while Allan was pouring lemonade into plastic cups. It seemed to be on a pour one, down one himself cycle.

'I do,' Ray replied.

'Well, he comes here a lot to meet Miss Parker, but I don't think they're together, like boyfriend and girlfriend, because, well, she's still a bit sad sometimes, when she thinks we're not noticing. And I think if he was her new boyfriend, she wouldn't still be sad.'

'What are you telling me here, Jayden?' Ray cleared his throat and put on Santa tones again. 'I mean… what are you asking of Santa, young man?'

'Maybe Santa could help them get together. If Miss Parker had a new boyfriend, then she would be happy and then she won't leave Stretton Park.'

Ray took a breath. Wow. And he thought Jayden was likely to ask for the latest video game or the actual Nintendo Switch to play it on. 'Listen, I don't know if that is something even Santa can achieve,' Ray admitted.

'Well, have *you* got a girlfriend?' Jayden asked.

'What?!' Ray exclaimed, hand on his chest, eyes wide in shock, beard slipping a little. 'It is a well-known fact that I am married. Very happily married… to Mrs Claus who is, right now, making preparations for the big, festive day where we will eat turkey and stuffing and all the healthy Christmas vegetables… with the reindeer and the elves and…'

'Alright, Jayden?'

Ray stopped talking and looked to the man who had approached the table, his fingertips seeming to be needed to anchor himself to the edge of it to abate the swaying. This was behaviour Ray recognised immediately. The voice was slightly too loud, the stance wasn't steady, the eyes were heavy-lidded. The man was Ray's height, with dark hair, surprisingly clean-shaven, his complexion a little mottled. Ray also knew the expression on his face. He had seen it so many times, in the mirror of the gents' toilets in his own reflection and, in the past, on the face of his mother.

'Hello,' Jayden replied, instantly on edge, stepping away a bit until his back was at the wall.

'Show us what you've made then, Jayden.' This question came from a tiny woman Ray hadn't even noticed. She was standing next to the tall man, light-coloured hair swept back into a high ponytail, wearing jeans and a heavy knit black jumper.

'Is this the tower?' the man asked with a deep laugh, hands going to the clay sculpture. He surely wasn't going to touch it, was he? The man looked hardly capable of standing, let alone being in control of a precious piece of artwork.

'Whoa, there,' Ray said quickly, stepping into the man's space and blocking his waving arms aimed at Jayden's tableau. 'Santa suggests that you don't touch this most delicate piece of sculpture that could one day be auctioned for thousands of pounds.'

'Did you touch me?' the man questioned, his eyes narrowing at Ray.

So, this guy *was* far gone. He was going to treat every course of intervention as an attack.

'Nev, leave it,' the woman begged. 'Jayden, love, tell me all about what you've made. I like the tower and... is that the pub?'

'Yeah,' Jayden answered sheepishly.

'Let's have a look,' the man stated, side-stepping Ray and banging into the table, shocking the sculpture, which wobbled precariously.

A flashback of another table came to mind. *The aftermath*

of dinner with the plates and bowls stacked up, a painting almost tumbling to the floor...

'Listen, I think you should really step away from the table before you break something,' Ray warned the man.

Immediately, the man got up close and personal to Ray's padded exterior, glaring at him. 'The only thing that's gonna get broken around here, Santa, is you. If you don't get out of my way.'

'Oh, hello! Mr and Mrs Jackson!' It was Emily, gliding in effortlessly with her cheery demeanour, somehow straightaway able to take hold of the man's hand and shake it pleasantly *and* inch herself in between them despite the lack of space to do exactly that. She smiled at the woman too and shook her hand, instantly calming the intensity.

'It's so wonderful to see you again. Jayden's worked so hard on his sculpture over the past few weeks. I really think it shows wonderful attention to detail.'

'It's Riches Tower and the pub,' Mrs Jackson stated. 'Other kids have made churches and Christmas dinners.'

'Well,' Jayden countered, 'Felix has just got fish and Alice's isn't even about Christmas.'

'Yes, you're right,' Emily answered. 'They're all so unique, aren't they? I love how Jayden has made so much effort getting the detailing of the windows of the tower just right.'

'You do, do you?' Mr Jackson said. 'You love *this*?'

Ray's hackles were already up underneath his loveable Santa exterior. He didn't like Jayden's father at all. He was hard. He was bitter. It might be the alcohol. It might not. But what it definitely was was a father showing up his son in the same way Ray's mother had showed up him as much as he loathed to recall it. *Cornering the bottle stall at the school fête. Forgetting to make him lunch. Puking in public...*

'Yes,' Emily said. 'I do. Jayden has worked very hard on this representation. He's a very hard-working boy all round.'

Ray knew he shouldn't say anything. Staying quiet, just being a visual festive aid was what he told Emily he was going to do, but he couldn't help himself. 'I think he's depicted you extremely well.'

He knew his words would get Mr Jackson's attention, that the man's eyes would then train on the model and the figure, drunk outside the pub, a tankard in his hand. A reflection of how his son saw him. Maybe this man needed to see himself through the eyes of Jayden.

'This is me?' Mr Jackson asked Jayden, pointing a meaty finger at the angry man made out of modelling clay.

'Jayden said you're wearing your favourite shirt,' Emily said quickly. 'The one with the stripes you like to wear at Christmas.'

'D'you think this is funny?' Mr Jackson had both large hands on the table now, leaning across it, and the model, leering at Jayden.

'Nev, calm down,' Mrs Jackson said, putting a hand on her husband's arm. 'It's actually quite a good likeness. He's got your hair just right.'

Mr Jackson turned on his wife then. 'So, *you* think this is funny too, do you?'

'Listen,' Emily said. 'Why don't we go and get a cup of lemonade and some nibbles?'

'*You* dragged me here,' Mr Jackson carried on, pointing a finger at his wife. 'I didn't want to come. Why would I want to come to this?' His voice was getting louder and louder now, drawing attention from the rest of the people in the room.

'I didn't want you to come,' Jayden's voice burst out. 'Because I knew you'd be like this!'

'You little shit!' Mr Jackson yelled.

Jayden's father threw a fist towards his son and Ray lost it. How dare he go to hit his son! How dare he come to this school and spoil an afternoon everyone was enjoying! One second Ray was there, blocking Mr Jackson from reaching Jayden, the next he was aiming his own punch at the parent. But then, momentarily, the red mist lifted, and he caught sight of Emily in his peripheral vision. Her face was a picture of shock and concern. He couldn't put this afternoon in jeopardy for her. She was already so fraught. Quickly, he dropped his fist and instead grabbed the aggressor's arm, gripping his wrist tight. And then Ray did something he hadn't done since school. He dramatically ripped the skin both ways, as hard as he could, giving Mr Jackson the fiercest of Chinese burns.

Jayden's father let out a hideous yelp of agony until Ray eventually let him go, pushing him away from the group.

'Santa! Santa!' Felix shouted, twirling round and round in a frenzy.

'Miss Parker!' Alice called. 'Is Jayden's dad going to die?'

Thirty-Five

Crowland Terrace, Canonbury, Islington

'And I still don't know what you're doing here.'

Jonah was holding Ray's hand underneath the tap in Emily's kitchen. It seemed he had grabbed Mr Jackson hard enough to inflict an injury to himself. His finger joints were red and a little puffy. He was still wearing the Santa suit, but minus the beard now he was away from the school and didn't need disguising. Although he had considering hanging on to the outfit for avoiding the press the next time they were stalking him.

Emily had barrelled him out of the hall, and the situation, before he had even had time to process what had actually happened. He shouldn't have reacted like that, but what was the alternative? See Jayden get hit by his father? What then? What course of action was there after that? A boy would have been hurt and emotionally traumatised. Far better for him to take the rap, despite the shit he was in already. Besides, no one knew it was him. Except Emily... and Jayden... and now Jonah and Allan. OK, so, Father

Christmas giving a parent a Chinese burn at a primary school wasn't the best thing that could have happened, but it was preferably to the world finding out *Ray Stone* had assaulted someone. And he hadn't answered Jonah's question.

'I thought you were very gallant,' Allan said. He was leaning against the worktop in the tiny space, pulling apart a clementine and popping segments into this mouth. 'That man was an animal. And did you smell him? He didn't just smell like he'd been to the pub. He smelled like Guinness had distilled him for thirty-odd years.'

'I don't know what Emily's going to do,' Jonah admitted. 'She's been trying for forever to impress her boss so she can get the Deputy Head position and now this!'

'Ow!' Ray grimaced as Jonah pressed down on his hand. 'Watch it. I've got to play the piano and the guitar you know.'

'Is it broken, Jonah?' Two L's asked.

'It's not broken,' Ray said immediately. It might have been broken if he'd actually hit the guy like he'd wanted to. But he could move everything independently. It was just sore and a bit swollen. The likelihood was it would be worse tomorrow but, after that, hopefully it would start to loosen up a bit.

'Unlike Mr Jackson's wrist,' Jonah remarked.

'His wrist isn't broken!' Allan exclaimed. 'Is it?'

'Listen,' Ray said, taking back ownership of his hand and turning off the cold tap. 'I get this situation is unusual, but, believe me, I was there to help Emily. She asked me to be there, to play the piano and help her with this show she's got going on.'

'And the reason that she said for me to "take you home" and "home" appears to be her flat?' Jonah queried. 'What's that about?'

'We *were* hoping she would get another housemate,' Allan piped up.

'You've read the papers, right? Looked through Twitter? I'm a bit down on my luck right now. I needed a place to stay. Emily needed her central heating fixed.' Ray spread out his arms. 'Perfect temperature now.'

'And a good solution,' Allan said positively. 'For both of you. Helping each other in your hour of need, so to speak.'

'I'm not sure Emily had an hour of need until he ended up in the school shed,' Jonah remarked, folding his arms across his chest.

'Well, I'm going to come right out and say it,' Allan began. 'I think that nasty, vile alcoholic of a man deserved a good Chinese burn.'

'And I think,' Jonah said, 'that this is going to have caused Emily a whole heap of distress she doesn't need in her life right now.'

'I get it,' Ray said. He took a deep breath in and his Santa belt popped right open. He took it off and unceremoniously dropped it on the table. 'I'll make it up to her. I'll apologise again when she gets home. I'll help her with these songs she needs before 20th December. I'll…'

'Take her out to dinner?' Allan suggested, chomping down on his orange but looking directly at Ray.

'Allan, what are you saying? That's a terrible idea!' Jonah exclaimed.

'Thanks,' Ray said. 'For making me feel lower than Ted Bundy's morals.'

'It's not a terrible idea,' Allan continued. 'You said yourself that Emily isn't eating properly. What better way for her to pep up her diet than by going out for a lovely dinner with her new flatmate?'

Jonah slumped down into one of the small seats and put his head in his hands with a heavy grunt of frustration. Allan was quick to put fingers on his shoulders and started to lightly massage.

'Sorry,' Jonah said, his words a little muffled, his mouth directed at the floor. He finally lifted his head. 'I'm sorry, it's only because I care about Emily and she's had such a rough year. I'm trying to make it better for her, you know.'

'Emily's boyfriend died,' Allan informed Ray. 'Crossing over to the Tube station from his office. A driver lost control of the car and… well, that was it.'

'Allan!' Jonah said, his expression horrified. 'You don't blurt out someone's personal history like that. Emily might not have wanted him to know.'

'She told me actually,' Ray replied. 'That Simon had died. Not how he died or anything but… that he wasn't around anymore.'

'Did she?' Allan asked, wide-eyed. He started to perform a chopping motion on Jonah's shoulders. 'That's progress, isn't it, Jonah?' Allan looked to Ray. 'She spent many months not telling anyone Simon had even died. Karen and Sammie, her neighbours downstairs, they thought he was away on a business trip until Jonah broke the news.'

'Listen,' Ray said, undoing the top button of the red suit he couldn't wait to get off. 'I'm not here to cause any trouble or upset for Emily. Believe me, that's the very last thing I want to do.' He sighed. 'I'm not a believing-in-the-kindness-of-strangers type of a guy either, but she's been so good to me, for no other reason than because she's a great person. And I want to repay that by helping her with this Christmas show... if I'm ever allowed back in the building again.'

'Do you think that lout will try and press charges?' Allan asked. 'I mean, can you press charges for someone giving you a Chinese burn? He could ask Emily who you are. Or Mrs Clark could ask Emily who you are. I think Emily might cave if Mrs Clark threatened to put her fingers in the electronic pencil sharpener. Remember, Jonah, that was her greatest fear when we played that silly game in the summer.'

'I feel like I've let her down,' Ray admitted.

'Don't you regret hurting that swine!' Two L's insisted. 'He was about to wallop his own son. Someone who is younger than him, weaker than him. A typical bully!'

Ray swallowed. He didn't disagree at all, but he also knew that bullies came in many forms.

Allan shuddered. 'He should be drowning in his own shame right about now but, I expect, once he's had his wrist reset, he'll be back to drowning in real ale.'

'I know,' Ray sighed. 'But there isn't any excuse for violence is there?' Cue a number of recollections arriving like a Netflix recap you couldn't choose to skip.

'No, there isn't,' Jonah agreed. 'But Allan is right. It would have been worse if Mr Jackson had hit Jayden. I'm just not sure which scenario makes it worse for Emily.' He checked his watch. 'Allan, we have to go. I need to get to the hotel.' He got to his feet.

'That time already, is it? Time for me to eat all alone while you make delicious food for rich people.'

'You're going to eat more?' Jonah asked. 'You ate most of the food at the school.'

'I can't help it if you're the best chef a boy could have.'

Jonah headed out of the room and Ray caught Allan's arm, urging him to wait.

'So,' he said, less than confident he should even be asking this question. Dates were meant to be off his agenda. Except this was about repairing the damage he was at the centre of. Something to try and make up for the shit Emily was probably dealing with right now with her boss. 'If I did decide to take Emily out somewhere... just for something to eat... as flatmates... what kind of food does she like the best?'

Allan's lips widened into a delighted smile you might see on the face of someone who had just been told they had won Domino's pizza for life and their mortgage paid off. 'Well now, for Emily it's more about the ambience than it is about the actual food... but she does need to eat more than a bag of crisps and a Bovril. Nothing too fancy with half a dozen different knives and forks. She hates that because she was brought up with it. So, I'd say, for a *planned* treat think cosy and authentic. Or for a casual "I know, let's go out for supper" idea, then somewhere that serves hearty meats with sumptuous breads.' Allan gasped. 'God! This is making me hungry!'

'Allan, are you coming?' Jonah called.

'Coming!' Allan answered. He then adopted a more serious expression, one that a member of the Mafia might use if they were determined to get prime information on a rival faction. 'I have only one question. I think I already know the answer, but Jonah's mind needs putting at rest.'

Allan took a ginormous breath that seemed to inflate him like he had turned into Aunt Marge from *Harry Potter and The Prisoner of Azkaban*. 'You aren't the man they're depicting in the news, are you? You haven't and you would never hit a woman, would you?'

He shook his head straightaway. 'No,' he answered with as much pure honesty as he had. 'I haven't. And I would never, *ever*, do that.'

Allan smiled, then deflated, but in a good way. 'I knew it.' He winked then and gave a grin. 'I like you, Ray. And I think Emily likes you too. You should know that she wouldn't ever let me or Jonah touch that Christmas tree you've put up in the lounge, even when Simon was alive.'

'Allan!' Jonah shouted.

'Hearty meats… or actually, no, think *cheese*. Yes!' Allan exclaimed. 'I can't remember the last time Emily had good cheese that wasn't half-price or half-out-of-date. And she really does love good cheese!'

Then, leaping like one of Santa's happy little elves, Allan was gone from the kitchen and Ray was left clenching and unclenching his hurting hand.

Thirty-Six

St Martin's Chambers

Emily didn't really know what she was doing outside her parents' place of work, she just knew she was craving the pub and the largest gin and tonic in herstory. And she didn't want to ever give in to that feeling. She didn't really want to see her parents either, but in some way, a little tiny corner of her heart had been chipped away by the dressing down she had just received from Susan Clark. What she needed to know was that there was a life existing outside Stretton Park Primary if her teaching options were suddenly taken away. Not that she wanted to work in a chambers, or for her parents, or anywhere except at her beloved school, but if she kept messing up, she might not be the one who held the options cards anymore.

Her breath was a dense fog in the cold air as she stood outside the ancient stone building that seemed to emanate 'important' and 'rich list'. Stamping her feet against the pavement, she willed the circulation back into her toes. Her pale trousers weren't exactly outside attire and her coat, although a magnificent example of 1940s military chic, wasn't the warmest either. And she didn't even *know* her parents were actually still inside. If they weren't inside they could be anywhere. At their mansion. At the Court of Appeal. At someone else's mansion. On a boat called *Destiny III*... She'd texted her mother, an hour ago, but there was no reply. She should just cut her losses and head back to her flat. Although she didn't really know what to say to Ray yet.

'Emily?' It was Alegra's voice, clipped and beautifully enunciated. 'Emily, is that you?'

Your own mother needing closer visual confirmation that it was indeed the offspring she had birthed wasn't a great start. Why did she always convince herself that if she made the effort to reach out it was going to be absolutely any different to all the other times she had reached out and been disappointed?

'Emily, you're shivering. Oh! What on earth is that you've got on?' Alegra asked, grabbing hold but keeping her at arm's length. 'It looks like something they had on in the trenches.' She tutted. 'Is this what a schoolteacher's salary has come to now? Buying clothes from the Army surplus store?'

She was about to say it was actually vintage and from a lovely little boutique near Hyde Park, but what was the point?

'Alegra, what are you doing? Who are you talking to? Where's the car?'

It was her dad, William, trotting down the steps of the ancient building swathed in a black wool-rich coat, wearing a rather natty fedora Emily had never seen on him before. It actually quite suited him.

'It's Emily,' Alegra stated. 'Dressed in virtual rags.'

'Mum!' Emily exclaimed.

'Emily?' William answered, as if he had no recollection of anyone in his life circle with that given name.

'It's OK,' Emily said. 'I shouldn't have come here at such short notice. You're obviously busy and on your way somewhere so…'

'Emily!' William exclaimed suddenly as he reached them, as if he had only just noticed she was standing there. 'What are you doing here? We didn't know you were coming.'

'I… didn't know I was coming either.' Until an hour ago when she'd sent the text message. After at least thirty minutes of listening to Susan saying phrases like 'unprecedented debacle' and 'shocking, scarring scenes'. Her boss had obviously never watched an episode of *Killing Eve*.

'Is something wrong?' Alegra asked, eyes penetrating. Emily flinched as if she were a guilty party about to be found out in the courtroom. She would so hate to be up against her mother in court. 'Has something bad happened? Something bad that means you can't make it next Friday?' Alegra gasped then, as if Emily not making it was right up there with 'the Queen has died'.

'I…' Did she really want to tell her parents how she was feeling? About the incident at the 'What Christmas Means to Me' event and the pressure she was under with the show and pushing forward towards her career goal and… *everything*?

'No, nothing's wrong.' Only her entire life and everything

in it. Just for once it might have been nice to have some management over her existence. Emily longed for the one time when she might announce something she was off-the-scale excited about to her parents and have them throw their arms around her in a never-before-seen display of genuine thrill.

'And you can still make that Friday?' Alegra carried on. Her mother had reached into her handbag now – it was leather and glossy and dripping with gold nameplates she was probably supposed to recognise – found a lipstick and was sheening it over her lips as she spoke. Without a mirror it was impressive. Not a smidge out of place.

'Yes,' Emily breathed. 'I can still make the Friday.' Although she was going to hate every minute of it. Having your ideas of good for the community picked at like vultures over the corpse of a dead animal never got any better. Every suggestion she made was joked about to begin with. *You want us to actually make gardens for the nursing home? Dig with our hands? Touch soil?* Until they realised that what Emily had come up with hit every spot of their remit and would make them look extraordinarily caring, clever and celebrated.

'Jolly good.' This came from her dad. 'It wouldn't be the same without you. Right, are we done?' William clapped his hands together. 'Where's that bloody car? Are you sure you ordered it?'

'Yes, darling, I'm sure,' Alegra replied. She shook her mane of hair like a feisty polo pony invigorated for the sport. 'It's getting worse though, isn't it? All these people thinking they can get an exec car because the *other* ones aren't available.'

Coming here had been stupid. It was making Emily feel worse not better. How would her parents even begin to understand what was happening in her life when they had no concept of it, even now. Nor did they seem to want to. She started to back away, head towards the Tube that would take her home.

'See you a week Friday, Emily! Mwah!'

As Alegra aired-kissed the frosty night Emily let out a breath. What did she do next? Well, she really only had one choice, and that was facing the music.

Thirty-Seven

Crowland Terrace, Canonbury, Islington

Ray heard the key in the door of the apartment and his body reacted immediately. Since Jonah and Allan had left, he had gone through multiple scenarios in his head. What was Emily going to say to him? What should he say to Emily? Did he need to let her speak first, or should he offer a full, complete and deeply sincere apology before she could even get her coat from her shoulders. None of them felt quite right. It was overthinking. Except, he knew, if the roles were reversed and it was Emily who had Chinese-burned a parent in front of the whole class, he would probably insist that Emily packed up and left. Which was why his rucksack, one guitar and other possessions were behind the living room door.

He strummed at the acoustic guitar in his hands when Emily didn't appear in the living room. Was she going to avoid him completely? That would mean not coming into the lounge and therefore not getting to the kitchen. Had she gone into the bathroom or her bedroom? Or was she checking to see if all his things had gone from the wardrobe of his room. *His* room. It hadn't been his for very long.

Another line for the song came to him and he pulled the Biro out from behind his ear and wrote it down on the pad he was balancing on his knee in front of the guitar.

Still no Emily. Maybe she had collapsed in the hall. What had Jonah said about her having too much stress in her life already…

Ray got up and walked towards the door. Not barefoot tonight. His boots were on, ready to hit the pavement if he had to. When he got to the hall it was to see Emily, standing with her back to the wall, eyes closed. She hadn't even put on the light. He reached for the switch, then thought better of it. Should he speak? Or keep quiet? What would she want?

And then her eyelids snapped open and she was looking at him. He swallowed, suddenly deep-filled with regret like an over-stuffed mince pie.

'Emily,' he began. 'I just want to say, again, that…'

She held her hand up and he stopped talking.

'Don't say sorry, Ray, please.' She inhaled. 'I've said that word at least a million times this afternoon.' She breathed in again. 'I said it to Mr Jackson while Mrs Jackson held peas wrapped in a tea-towel to his burning wrist. I said it to Makenzie's dads and Frema's parents and Charlie and Matthew's mum and dad and gran and grandad and everyone else's relatives who had come to see what Christmas means to the children they have in my class.'

'Emily,' Ray started again.

'And, do you know what they all now think Christmas means to Stretton Park?' she asked. 'Do you?'

He didn't have an answer. He suspected that anything he did say wouldn't be the right thing. Was there even a right thing for this kind of situation?

'They think,' Emily continued, 'that Christmas means Santa Claus fighting in the assembly hall. They think that the man they still believe in, someone they practically idolise throughout the entire month of December, is someone who attacks parents.'

'I realise that,' Ray told her.

'Do you?' Emily asked. 'Do you really?'

'Of course I do,' he said, leaning back against the door frame. 'And I deeply and sincerely apologise for hurting him. I shouldn't have done that.'

'No, you shouldn't.'

'But I'm not going to apologise for intervening,' Ray said firmly. 'I'm not going to apologise for stopping him from hitting Jayden. Yes, I shouldn't have grabbed his wrist. I should have maybe… I don't know… got him in a headlock and taken him outside or something.'

'Got him in a headlock?!' Emily exclaimed, her arms going up as if exasperated. 'We weren't in a wrestling arena! We were in a school!'

'And a father was about to smack his son! You wanted that instead of this?!' Ray shouted.

'I didn't want any of it!' Emily yelled back. 'I don't *need* any of it!'

Ray watched the quick change in her expression. It happened in an instant. It was like that moment after the sun was all fierce and feisty, when the clouds blackened and the storm arrived and then the rain fell like a violent waterfall. Emily's face creased up and tears began escaping rapidly as full-on sobs racked her shoulders. It took him a micro-second to decide what to do. In one stride he was across the hall and he gathered her weeping form into his arms, supporting her frame, holding her tightly, taking her weight as she gave in to the emotional meltdown.

'You're OK,' he whispered, her sobs pounding at his own heart. 'You're OK.' He rocked her in his arms.

Still the crying came, loud and hard and soul-destroying. He clung on, his body sheltering her, as she seemed to lose the ability to keep upright, her body heavy and appearing like it wanted to sink to the floorboards.

'Hey,' he said softly. 'I've got you. It's OK.' He cradled her close. She was cold, shivering, despite the ambient temperature he had set the heating to. He wanted to wrap her up, give her his body heat, take away her pain... after all, he was to blame for at least some of it.

He stroked her hair and closed his eyes, willing her quaking to cease, for her to calm. Her hair felt like silk beneath his fingers and the scent she had – pinecones and winter berries somehow mixed with books and Biro ink – did crazy things to his brain. He wanted to protect her so badly, to soothe her, to make her feel better, but he wasn't sure who exactly needed who more in this moment.

Emily's heart actually hurt. It was a deep, swell of pain like she might never ever be the same again. What was this outpouring? Why was she crumbling here and now? *With Ray.* She came to a little, realising she had been properly howling like a fox might when finding nothing but soggy ramen in the bins, and stilled. Her eyes were pure fluid and so sore... and she was in Ray's arms... his body wrapped around her, firm and solid...

What was happening to her? She'd been to visit her parents too?! How had she thought that could help? And she was still enveloped in Ray's powerful embrace...

'Sorry,' Emily said, wriggling herself upright again.

'I thought "sorry" was banned.'

She couldn't look him in the eye yet. She had been so horribly angry and said some awfully accusing things. She didn't condone what he had done at all but Mr Jackson... that ugly-mannered man really would have struck Jayden if Ray hadn't stopped him.

'Listen, Emily, I'd understand if you wanted me to leave. I...'

'I don't want you to leave. That wouldn't change anything at all. And... I know I was angry when I came in, but I really don't think you did *entirely* the wrong thing.'

'No?'

She took a deep breath. 'No... I mean, Mr Jackson *was* going to hit Jayden. *Hit* Jayden. Again.'

'Again!' Ray exclaimed. 'He's hit him before!'

'Yes... no... probably.' She took a breath. 'It's unconfirmed.'

'His bruised eye,' Ray said with a knowing nod. 'His dad did it.'

'I don't know that. Not for sure. And I can't do anything about it. Not really.'

'I should have torn his skin harder. Sorry, no, not sorry.' He took a breath. 'I didn't mean that.'

'It's OK,' Emily said. 'I know what you meant.' She leaned

back against the wall again, touching it with the tips of her fingers.

'So, how were things?' Ray asked. 'After I left the school.'

Emily sighed, a vision of Susan in full-on intelligence gathering mode, reeling off all the questions the Head knew she was going to need the answers to if Mr Jackson made a formal complaint. 'Mr Jackson stopped screaming and Mrs Jackson took him and Jayden home. Mrs Clark then re-enacted several scenes from *Line of Duty* trying to get me to tell her your identity which led me to create a fictional company called "Rent-A-Santa". I told her I had hired you from there. I said I would call the made-up company, endeavour to find out who the Santa actor was if Mr Jackson formalised things.'

'Emily,' Ray said, shaking his head.

'I haven't finished yet,' she continued. 'Then, later, after I'd apologised to everyone in the room – on the microphone – and Dennis had ripped open another bag of liquorice wheels and Susan had eventually stopped calling all things "abominable", I went round to the Jacksons' flat.' She sighed. 'Mr Jackson had gone to the pub, so Mrs Jackson let me in, and I had a chat with her about Jayden and what had happened and my concerns. Although she was stony-faced to begin with, I think some of what I said got through. She was going to suggest that Mr Jackson *didn't* take things further by calling the police and I said that if she ever needed any help from me, as a concerned person and not as a schoolteacher, she only had to ask.'

'Emily, you didn't have to do that for me,' Ray said, shaking his head again.

'I didn't just do it for you, Ray. I did it for Jayden. The very last thing I want him to think is that school isn't a safe place for him. It's about the only place I think he *does* feel safe and I don't want the Jacksons to suddenly take him out of Stretton Park to somewhere that might not care as much as I do.'

The thought that Jayden's life could be made even more difficult than it currently was had been the driving force behind her daring to set foot in his home again after the last memorable visit.

'What can I do?' Ray asked her, his tone sincere. His eyes locked with hers. 'Tell me what to do to make this better for you.'

'Well,' Emily began, straightening herself up as a little strength returned. 'I told you I'm not a giver-up, and the other day I read something that said you can't change the things you've done, so you shouldn't dwell on them. You should, instead, focus on moving forward and affecting matters you *can* influence.'

'A fresh start.'

'Yes,' Emily said. 'That.'

'So…'

'So, it might seem like everything has changed, but really nothing has changed. Mr Jackson is still a bully. No one knows who Fighty Santa was. The bishop and the suffragans saw none of it. I still, very much, need help with the Christmas show.'

'OK,' Ray said.

'But, Ray, that can't happen again. Ever. It's a school. My children are all ten-years-old. I don't want their normal to be like an episode of *Jeremy Kyle*.'

'I get that. It will never happen again.'

She looked at him, drinking in all of his manliness. She had told him a little white lie when she'd described the aftermath of the scuffle. She had protected his identity not for him, or even for Jayden, but for her. Because having him in her flat, and in her life, was, despite the crazy drama, making her feel more alive than she had in a long time. And a text from Allan had helped confirm that it wasn't such an odd realisation to have.

Be nice to Ray. You know as well as I do that that brute deserved everything he got. I like Ray. I like him a lot. And I've heard from a very reliable source that there is NO truth to those rumours in the press. Live, my darling. Simon would want you to live xxx

'Well, I've been writing, while you weren't here,' Ray continued. 'For your show. OK, it's a little bit out there. It's based on Jona Lewie's "Stop the Cavalry". I've called it... wait for it... "Can't We Have A Carvery?".'

Emily couldn't stop the smile from forming on her lips.

'Because, I figured, not everyone has the whole Charles Dickens kind of Christmas, do they? Some kids, they'll be wanting something else, won't they? I'll play it to you if you like.' He stopped then and looked at her, as if to gauge her reaction.

'OK,' she answered, for the moment satisfied that the world was indeed still turning. 'I'll make hot chocolates.'

Thirty-Eight

Barnard Park, Islington

A Week Later

'This is better, isn't it?' Ray asked her, patting the bench next to him, encouraging her to join him. He breathed in the wintry air like it was food for his soul. Then he began playing his acoustic guitar, simply getting straight in to the song they were still trying to perfect a week on.

'It's cold,' Emily replied, teeth juddering. 'The flat was warm.' She shuffled forward, boots kicking late fallen leaves on the park ground. It was close to eleven o'clock at night. It was now December. Most people, more *sensible* people were inside in these temperatures, going to bed or catching up on the latest Facebook news. They weren't sitting on a park bench with a guitarist who was wearing sunglasses in the pitch black.

'The flat was killing our creativity,' Ray answered. 'It happens sometimes. You get to a certain place and you need a change. A shift in location. New air.' He patted the bench again. 'Come on, sit down. We're going to sing through that verse again.'

'Here?' Emily asked. 'In public?'

Ray took his hands away from his guitar and spread them wide, indicating the rather empty parkland. There were a few teenagers over by the adventure playground getting up to-who knew-what, but they were far enough away not to bother them or hopefully hear them. The only other occupants of the space were the frosty boughs of the trees above and around them and the stars in the night sky.

'There's no one here,' Ray told her. 'And when you're me, that's a great thing. So, come on, sit down with me before a reporter pops out of the bushes or something.' He looked up at her. 'Besides, you are gonna have to sing these songs in public at the show. To more people than the holy God squad.'

As if she really needed reminding...

'I know,' she sighed sitting down next to him.

'What are you afraid of?' he asked, strumming a chord, then stopping, hand flat on the strings. With his other hand he took off his sunglasses, positioning them on top of his beanie hat-covered head.

'Nothing.' That really translated as *everything*. And she knew, she wasn't fooling Ray at all. They had started to get to know each other quite well already. She now knew he definitely wasn't a morning person. That he made coffee and put the milk in first. He also wasn't really a TV-watcher. He played music all the time. On his guitar. On his phone. And he whistled, rather brilliantly. She was a little bit envious.

'Good,' he answered. 'Because, I keep telling you, you have a great voice.'

And he never stopped reiterating that. Each time they got down to the business of songwriting and rehearsing he would tell her how good she was. There was now a tiny, tiny part of her that was starting to believe it a little.

'Sing the first verse,' Ray encouraged.

'On my own?' Emily exclaimed as if Ray had told her to walk the Great Wall of China unaccompanied and in heels.

'Well,' Ray said, casting his gaze around the park. 'We could ask those guys over there to join in if you want, but they seem pretty engrossed in the swings.'

She could do this. Why couldn't she do this? Ray was right. She was going to have to sing out loud and proud with her children in a few weeks. She needed all the rehearsal she could get.

'OK,' she answered, shivering as a wave of cold air seemed to chill her bones. 'Play the introduction.'

'Yes, Miss Parker,' Ray answered with a grin.

She held her breath – and her nerve – as Ray strummed the acoustic guitar for the beginning of their altered version of 'Stop the Cavalry' by Jona Lewie. She started to sing:

Mum is peeling sprouts, sister selfie pouts
The cat is climbing up the Christmas tree
Auntie's on the wine, will dinner be on time?
Santa's late again, misery
Where's the Roses tin? Put that in the bin!
Can't we have a carvery?

'Yes!' Ray announced, stopping his playing and smiling at her. 'That was great! You nailed the phrasing. The kids are going to pick that up no problem.'

'Do you really think so?' Emily asked. She hoped so. She didn't want her children to feel under any of the pressure she was, but she did want them to care enough to put on the best show they could. But for them to enjoy it and have fun was, of course, the most important thing.

'Yeah, I really think so,' Ray told her. He played another chord. 'So, did you sing with Simon?'

Emily laughed then. 'God, no. Simon wasn't really into music. He was more of a reader. Thrillers and mysteries, the occasional biography if it was a rugby player he admired.'

'You never sang to him?' Ray asked. He nudged her arm. 'Never did any karaoke? Because, I'm telling you, I could see you up there, you know, doing a little Alanis Morrisette, or maybe Adele.'

'I don't think so.' She swallowed, nervous butterflies nesting in her stomach.

'Hey, I've done karaoke,' Ray admitted. 'You know, I think it's more terrifying singing along to lyrics on a screen in front of a pub full of pissed people, trying to emulate Michael Jackson when you're pissed yourself, than it is doing your own gig singing your own songs.'

She turned her head to look at him. 'You sang Michael Jackson at karaoke?'

'Is that judgement I'm hearing?' Ray asked, nudging up close to her again.

'No, I'm just trying to think what Michael Jackson song you would choose to sing.'

'Guess,' Ray said, his tone teasing.

'"Beat It"?'

He laughed. 'No.'

'"Thriller"?'

'Are these serious guesses, Emily? Or are you taking the piss now?'

'No!' She laughed and dug her elbow into his ribs, budging him up the bench.

'If you say "Billie Jean" next I'm not sure we can stay friends.'

'Well, I'm running out of MJ songs here.'

'OK,' Ray said. 'Enough guessing. I'll play it for you.'

And just like that, Ray started to make music with the guitar, almost a beat-box sound, fingers moving over the strings then tapping the wooden body of the instrument. She instantly recognised it as Michael Jackson's 'Remember the Time'. She should have guessed that was much more Ray's style. Over the last week she had listened to his songs on Spotify – on the Tube on her way to school, in the staff room at lunchtime – enjoying every note. It was so hard to try to correlate the soft, honeyed tones mixed with something also so raw and deep, with the man the press was still trying to condemn and the other tender, easy-going individual who sat on her sofa every night.

Emily watched him intently. His long fingers moving over the fret board, his hair falling out from under his hat, those full lips forming the words as he sang about falling in love and holding hands and looking into each other's eyes…

She shivered, hard, and Ray stopped playing immediately.

'Hey, what's up?'

'Nothing,' she answered, through teeth that suddenly wouldn't stop juddering.

'You're cold,' Ray said, lifting the guitar up and off his body, placing it on the floor and leaning it up against the bench.

'I... can't feel my fingers,' Emily admitted with a laugh. She started rubbing her hands together. 'I should have brought my gloves.'

'Here,' Ray said. He took hold of her hands, linking her fingers together, then cupped them both with his large hands.

His hands were so much bigger than hers. They were warm from his guitar-playing and hers had all but disappeared inside.

'Better?' Ray asked.

'A... bit.' She still couldn't seem to stop shaking.

'Here, let me try something.' Ray brought their joined hands up to his mouth and opened his fingers a little before putting his lips to the gap. Emily was already tingling from the close contact and then... he blew. Hot breath tickled over her fingers and suddenly her digits weren't the only things that were heating up... Slowly, he breathed a bit more, a little deeper, and as he let the breath go into their joined hands, their eyes connected.

Emily's head was spinning now. She should look away. She should focus on the Christmas lights she could see far across the park, or the youths on the play drawbridge, or the frost-coated grass. She should not carry on looking into Ray's dark amber eyes as he delivered central heating to her fingertips. What was it with his skills in bringing her temperature up?

'I should...' He cleared his throat. 'We should... go through the song again,' Ray said, suddenly letting go of her hands. 'Before you get cold all over.'

She wondered what part of her he would blow on first if more than her hands froze up... She quickly regrouped and nodded, rubbing her hands together. 'Yes.'

'From the top then,' Ray said. She watched him pick the guitar back up and strike a chord.

Thirty-Nine

Harley Street, Marylebone

Ray was running through 'Can't We Have A Carvery?' in his mind while Dr Crichton shone two types of torch down his throat. He began to sing the lyrics in his head…

'What on earth are you doing?' Dr Crichton asked, springing up from his throat inspection and hitting Ray with more evil eye than a Marilyn Manson video.

'Having a torch put down my throat that's actually heating up my tonsils?' he answered.

'You were singing,' Dr Crichton exclaimed. 'I told you specifically not to sing.'

'Er…' The doctor had obviously gone mad. Perhaps he needed to check in with one of his psych counterparts. 'I don't know anyone who can sing without singing… except those people on YouTube who sort of sing like they're trapped in a box.'

'Ray, I am a very specific doctor. You know that. That's why you're on my books. You were singing. Your throat was moving while I was looking at it.'

Wow, that was impressive. His throat moved of its own accord while he was *mentally* singing. Although Dr Crichton was not making this sound like a good thing.

'And I believe you've been singing since our last appointment despite my warnings to you.'

What could he say? His doctor was an expert in his field. He wasn't going to be duped. He obviously *had* been singing, more than ever over the past week or so. As well as the work he and Emily had been doing for the Stretton Park Christmas show he had spent two whole days in the studio recording tracks for his new album and putting together a small set of songs to perform at Ronnie Scott's. Finally, he had a little money – Saturn Records had caved once they'd seen the beginnings of results – and Deborah had really been pulling things together for him since their meeting with Ida. The press had been fed photos of him going to and from the studio – fresh-faced, alcohol-free – and the performance at the renowned jazz venue was going to be full of supporters – his fan club members and social media followers as well as hand-picked journalists promising feel-good articles. But he still needed to put on the best show of his life. Any chink in his voice or hesitance in his piano-playing and he knew the tables would turn once more. Being in the spotlight was a constant carousel. You never knew which way it was going to turn the from one minute to the next...

'Ray,' Dr Crichton said again. 'You can't sing.'

'With all due respect,' Ray replied. 'I can't *not* sing right now.'

'I know it may feel like that. I know all about the pressures you vocal musicians are under but...'

'Do you?' Ray interrupted. 'Do you really? Because I see a doctor making a lot of money from the fact that we *have* to sing. I mean, if we didn't sing, if we *didn't* fuck up our voices, you'd basically be out of a job.' He didn't really know how much sense he was making, but he couldn't stop now. 'So, really, you should be *encouraging* me to sing, to make sure you've got enough in the bank to get your daughter that Porsche she keeps coveting on Instagram.'

Dr Crichton leaned against the edge of his desk and flicked his torch on, then off, then on again. Ray swallowed. What was he saying? This man was only trying to help him.

'Sorry,' Ray apologised. 'That was total crap.'

'Hmm,' Dr Crichton mused.

'I am sorry, honestly. It's just difficult. How things are for me right now.'

'And it's difficult for me also,' Dr Crichton said. 'I don't want to be the guy who tells you you can't do the job you need to do. But, more seriously, I don't want to be the guy who has to tell you that you can never sing again. *At all.* Because you haven't followed my instructions.'

Yeah, there was that. That would definitely be worse.

'You need an operation, Ray, I told you that.'

And that was the real problem. His other fear. The one that crept up on him in nightmares. The one that harked back to his childhood. The one where his mum was supposed to get better and then didn't. He needed to work out his priorities. A life possibly without his career. Or a life.

'I know,' he breathed. 'But, you're the best there is. There must be something you can give me. Is there *anything* you can give me to see me through the next few weeks?'

Dr Crichton rolled his eyes and put his hands down on

the desk next to him, as if ready to spring off, grab the nearest paperweight and slug him in the head with it.

'Please, Dr Crichton, I'm begging you. I'll do all the exercises, I'll minimise studio time and singing before a performance, I promise. But help me out here.'

The doctor shook his head. 'There's no magic medicine, Ray.'

'I know. But you know I'm going to walk out of here and sing. We both know that, right? So, I'm asking for your help to minimise the damage continuing to sing might do.'

'You are by far my most exasperating client,' Dr Crichton said, moving from the desk and returning to his big chair.

'And your most talented?' Ray suggested with a smile. The doctor was now writing on a pad. Was there some special remedy he could take that was going to take the worry away from him? Lately, any change in his tone, any rasp in his voice had him downing as much Evian as he could get his hands on.

'More water,' Dr Crichton said. 'No throat-clearing and breathe moist air.'

'Moist air?' Ray queried. 'You mean I should sit in a steam room or something?'

'That would be excellent. But a hot bath would also work in between times.' Dr Crichton passed him the piece of paper he had made notes on.

'Great,' Ray said, poised to take it.

'But, seriously, Ray, I wouldn't be doing my job properly if I didn't reiterate that you are putting your voice and your whole career at risk if you carry on singing. I want you in for that operation before Christmas, or over Christmas, I'm not going anywhere this year… apparently I have a Porsche to buy.'

Ray nodded. 'Yeah,' he said. 'I hear you.' He stood up.

'One more thing,' Dr Crichton said, parting the blinds over his office window.

'Yeah?'

'It might be wise to take the back exit when you go. There seem to be a few journalists outside the front door.' He turned back to Ray and smiled. 'Now, I don't know if they are here for you or Not-Ariana but—'

Ray sucked in a breath. The last thing he needed was the reporters knowing he was here. 'OK,' he answered. 'Thanks.'

Forty

Stretton Park Primary School

'No, Joseph, we can't have a takeaway from Dar's Delhi Delights tonight, even though they have a special offer for buy one meal get one half price, with a free onion bhaji starter and 10 per cent off drinks. If I have a curry, it's going to bring on the baby, and we have to get to Bethlehem!'

'Well, Mary, how about we have an extra-large fillet of cod from Ralph's Plaice at 97 The High Street, Stretton Park. And hand-dipped chips with no trace of palm oil *and* the best crispy battered sausage this side of Jerusalem.'

'Oh my Jesus,' Dennis commented to Emily, poking a white chocolate mouse into his mouth as he watched the Year Sixes on stage.

'What are you doing here?' Emily asked him, trying to listen to her children speaking their lines. 'You never seem to be with your class.'

'Ah, well, today Years Four and Five have the firefighter in for a talk so Mrs Rossiter and Amy are watching them.'

'So, you thought you'd come to the hall and put off my students instead.'

'I'm not putting them off,' Dennis insisted. 'I'm showing support. I'm just not sure about this script.'

'You and me both,' Emily said, sighing. 'But with Mr Dar and Ralph Rossiter both trying to out pledge each other for advertising space, I don't have a lot of choice. I'm just hoping none of the other eateries on the high street want to jump in too. I mean the money is lovely, we're getting some great costumes from Amazon and this cool smoke machine that omits dry ice that won't make everyone choke, but do you know how hard it is to write something heart-warming, funny and Church of England friendly, while slipping in promotions for discounted dahl and half-price hake?'

'Miss Parker!' It was Alice shouting from the stage. 'Joseph just said he was going to eat a lamb tikka masala. He can't say that because the shepherds are going to come on with lambs later and the audience will think they are going to die.'

'I think you're doing wonderfully,' Dennis remarked. 'Really.'

'Alice, please call everyone by their real names and not by their character names or it's going to get very confusing. Joseph – I mean, Matthew – could you cross out the word "lamb" on your script and put the word "prawn".'

'Porn?' Matthew shouted loudly, a thick black pen in his hand, his Joseph bandana falling over his eyes.

Half the class started laughing and Emily really *really* hoped they were the members of chess club...

'Prawn,' Emily repeated. 'P-R-A-W-N. They live in the sea.'

'My mum's actual allergic to prawns,' Cherry announced,

waving a magic wand she insisted she needed to be an angel. 'If she even eats *one*, her face blows up and she's sick everywhere.'

'Like *you* were in front of the bishop,' Angelica teased.

'That's enough, Angelica. Now, where did we get to?' Emily asked.

'You said "porn",' Matthew repeated.

'Makenzie, could you please write "p-r-a-w-n" on Matthew's sheet for him please? And everyone else, please do the same on your scripts.'

'On his sheet?' Makenzie queried, adjusting his donkey ears.

'What's wrong with you today, Year Six? Did you stay up too late watching *Home Alone* last night?'

'I watched it!'

'And me!'

Dennis grinned at Emily. 'I actually watched *Bad Santa*. It reminded me of the "What Christmas Means to Me" afternoon. Who won the best tableau competition in the end by the way? Because I'm sure everyone was far more interested in the Claus versus Jackson bout.'

'Frema won,' Emily informed. 'Her interpretative dance based on Hanukkah and the storyboard of King Herod trying to kill the Baby Jesus were both very powerful.'

'Miss Parker!' Alice shouted again.

'What's the matter, Alice?'

'Makenzie is writing with pen on Matthew's costume!'

'Makenzie,' Emily said forcefully, striding forward to the stage. 'What are you doing?!'

'You told me to, Miss Parker. You said I had to write "prawn" on Matthew's sheet.'

Emily closed her eyes and looked at the large letters 'p' and 'r' now Sharpie-d on her Joseph's cloak. Today wasn't going well and tonight she had the get together with her parents. All in all, she had had much better Fridays... long ago... probably almost in days BC.

'I meant write it on Matthew's *script*. You know, the paper you're reading the lines from,' she told Makenzie with a sigh.

'You did say "sheet", Miss Parker,' Lucas informed.

'Sheet! Sheet!' added Felix.

'Yes, you're right,' Emily agreed. 'I did. It's my fault. OK... where's Rashid?' She looked around the stage, mentally ticking off her children. Rashid definitely wasn't among them.

'Has anyone seen Rashid?' Emily called, louder.

'He said he was going to the shed for something for his Nazareth villager costume,' Charlie said.

There was nothing in the shed that could be used for costumes. She had been through the shed again and got another padlock, after the Olivia Colman incident.

'Dennis,' Emily said, turning to her still-munching colleague. 'Could you supervise?'

'Well... I...'

'Thanks.'

Emily left the hall and began the walk up the pathway to the playground, heading to the shed at the very perimeter of the boundary. She could already see Rashid and he wasn't by the shed. Instead he was at the school gate, his striped villager costume blowing in the winter breeze. Emily quickened her pace. He was talking to someone. What was he doing? Out of her class and talking to someone outside of school? How had she not noticed? If Susan found out… As she got closer, she saw it wasn't an adult he was conversing with, but a girl. She had long, dark hair, was sitting astride a bicycle and wearing the distinctive uniform of Stretton Park Senior.

'Rashid,' Emily said, arriving at the gate. 'What are you doing out here?'

The boy turned around, a petrified expression on his face. 'Miss, I was…'

'I was giving him his books back,' the teenager responded with all the confidence of a seasoned US president.

'I see,' Emily answered. 'Thank you for that. And why do you have Rashid's books exactly?'

'I borrowed them,' the girl answered. 'There's no law against lending books to people, is there? I think they call it a *library*.'

Oh, this girl had *all* the sass and Emily wasn't going to be fooled for a minute. 'GCSE books,' she said, looking at the thick volumes in her student's hands.

'Yeah,' the girl said. 'Rashid's gonna be a doctor.'

'I've heard,' Emily said. 'So, what are you hiding from me under your coat there?'

Now the girl didn't look quite so confident and Emily could swear she sucked in a breath and held her stomach in tight.

'Nothing,' the girl answered. 'Had too much to eat at lunchtime, didn't I?'

'Undo your coat,' Emily ordered.

'What?!' the girl said. 'You can't get me to do that.'

'Either you undo the coat now, or I take you inside and we go and see the Head and you can explain to her why you're outside Stretton Park Primary talking to one of my students.'

'Miss Parker...' Rashid began. 'It's my fault.' His voice was wobbling, and he actually appeared tearful.

'Open your jacket or, as well as my Head, I'll be phoning yours,' Emily threatened. 'And I know Mr Walker *very well*.' She didn't actually know the head of Stretton Park Senior personally at all, but she did know he was well-known for being a beast on the local council...

The girl huffed and puffed and muttered close-to-expletives under her breath before she unzipped her coat and produced a four pack of bottles of alcopop, three sharing-sized bags of Kettle Chips and two packets of Wispa Bites. The price labels indicated these were from the shop across the road from her school. Emily put all this together in her mind and came to only the one conclusion.

'Right, you're both coming inside with me,' Emily said to the girl.

'But you said!' the girl exclaimed.

'It's either inside with me now or I'm calling the police. And, I can't guarantee that isn't going to happen anyway.'

Rashid let out a sob.

Forty-One

'Argh!' Emily exclaimed, looking at herself in the mirror of her bedroom. Nothing she was putting on to wear was right for this night with her parents. It went without saying that absolutely nothing was *ever* right for an evening with her parents, but she had long since given up trying to please her mother in the fashion stakes since she'd tried and apparently failed to rock a 'must-have' that Emma Willis had been pictured in.

There was a gentle knock on her door and she gasped, quickly slipping a jade green houndstooth patterned blouse on, hurrying to do up the buttons. Before she could quite get it fastened all the way, the door opened and Ray popped his head round.

'Are you OK? Whoa... sorry.' He started to close the door again.

'No, it's OK,' Emily breathed, finishing the last button.

He opened the door again. 'I heard you scream and I

thought you were… I don't know… under the wardrobe or something.'

'No,' Emily said. 'Just, having a fashion crisis.' She probably shouldn't have admitted that. Men weren't often interested in fashion. Well, Jonah and Allan were but that was different.

'Really?' Ray asked. 'Because you always look great.' He cleared his throat. 'I mean, your clothes look great… and you do… in them.'

'Oh… well… thanks.' Now her cheeks were on fire and she was worried that she had missed a couple of buttons on the blouse. As that thought was running through her mind, her elbow caught the wardrobe door and it fell open, revealing her secret stash from a year's worth of grieving. Three pairs of boots fell to the boards and the cupboard seemed to audibly sigh and expand, dresses and three-quarter-length 1950s trousers that had seemed such a good idea and perfect in the summer, now looked ridiculously whimsical.

'Wow,' Ray remarked, stepping into the room and surveying more clothes than a New Look warehouse. 'If the wardrobe had fallen on you, you'd have been dead for sure.'

'My mother would be horrified,' Emily admitted, picking up one pair of the boots and admiring them. Bright red, shiny, thick black heel, 1960s. She was never likely to go anywhere to wear them.

'Wouldn't she be ultimately devastated?' Ray suggested. 'If you died.'

Emily smiled at him, putting the boots back in the wardrobe with difficulty. It took three hard shoves. 'I think the shame that her daughter's vintage obsession killed her would hit her harder than my actual demise.'

'I don't believe that,' Ray replied. He picked up one of the other pairs of boots and looked at them. 'These are nice,' he said. 'I don't think they're my size though.'

'So funny,' Emily said, taking them from him.

'So, you've got a date tonight?' he asked, putting his hands into the pockets of a rather nice pair of dark grey trousers she hadn't seen him wear before. Not that she noticed the clothes he wore on a daily basis or had visions of that night in the park when he'd blown on her fingers. Plus, there was Allan's text message she had never known how to reply to.

I like Ray. I like him a lot. Live, my darling. Simon would want you to live.

'A date with destiny,' Emily answered with a sigh. 'My parents.'

'You don't see them very often?' Ray asked. 'Do they live outside of London?'

'Ha,' Emily said, unable to stop the laugh as she pushed her clothes collection back into the limited space. 'No, they live in the thick of London, they just have very busy lives, so I see them once, maybe two or three times a year.'

'I get it,' Ray said, nodding.

'It's the same with your parents?' Emily asked. 'Because I'm used to Jonah and his parents who are virtually joined at the hip. They phone each other every day and text all the time and every Bank Holiday they're arranging barbeques and sorting out who is going to marinade the chicken in what sauce etc. Jonah doesn't get my non-relationship with my mother and father.'

'Oh, I get it,' Ray said nodding. He picked up the last pair of boots, running his hands over them as if deep in thought. 'I just found out my dad has a new girlfriend.'

'Oh, wow, Ray, I'm sorry.' Emily swallowed. 'Does your mum know?'

'No... um... it's not like that... it's... well...'

Emily didn't know quite what was coming next, but Ray seemed to be really struggling with it. She kept silent and waited.

'My mum died.'

Ray's eyes were on the boots, but his mind was back there, to when he was a child and the only constant in his life had been taken away so suddenly. Veronica Stone had been so far from perfect, some people might have thought it was a blessing she left when she did, but he had never thought that, ever. She was his mum. Yes, she had had faults – a myriad of them – but amid the misery and desperate ache inside her no one truly understood, there *had* been love. He might not have felt it 100 per cent of the time, but he *had* felt it.

'Oh, Ray, I had no idea,' Emily said.

He heard her feet move on the bare boards of floor and he instantly held out the boots to her, not wanting the sympathy he knew was coming.

'Yeah, well, you know, it was a long time ago now. I just,

I don't know, I didn't think my dad would date anyone else.' He took a deep breath and finally raised his head to Emily's kind, beautiful eyes. 'I sound so pathetic right about now.' He shook his head. 'Her name's Brenda. She seems nice.' He didn't know her at all. He'd had one conversation about kebabs. 'I think she likes clothes too.' If the sparkly dress was anything to go by.

'I like clothes,' Emily stated. 'But usually not quite this much.' She sighed. 'I fell into a bit of a rut after Simon died and trawling the shops and the markets was the only thing that stopped me from going insane... or taking up vaping.' Another sigh. 'I needed something to keep me busy, so I shopped. Am still shopping... but not as much. I hate to say it, but the Christmas show is actually helping to distract me. I'm doing more shopping on Amazon for crowns and shepherd's crooks that can't be used to decapitate anyone, than I am for Lindy Bop dresses.'

'How did the new song go down today?' Ray asked. He felt almost as enthusiastic about writing new lyrics to 'Stop the Cavalry' as he did about new music of his own.

Emily grinned wildly. 'It was brilliant. The kids loved it. Especially the ones who don't celebrate Christmas in the Church of England sense. I mean it will have to get Mrs Clark's approval, but she's currently leaving us to it while the diocese is all glowing over our last performance.'

'That's great,' Ray said. Seeing her smile and become animated like this was so much better than the Emily he'd seen distraught in the hallway a week or so ago. And her voice was terrific. He was enjoying bringing out some confidence in her.

'Yes, that is great.' She took a breath. 'But what isn't

so great is having to deal with underage drinking and shoplifting.'

'Whoa, one of your children did that?'

'I can't say anything else. It's a delicate matter at the moment and investigations are on-going.'

'And you're worried about dinner with your parents?' Ray remarked.

'Oh, it's not dinner,' Emily said quickly. 'It's just drinks. Lots of drinks. And I'll come up with a super fundraising idea along the lines of this year's theme – that they will have made up between the lots of drinks – and I'll escape as quickly as I can and eat chips on the way home.' She rolled her eyes. 'It's at this pretentious wine bar called Clean Martini. The name is meant to be funny. A play on dirty martini.'

'I know it,' Ray said. 'I played piano there a few years ago, before the whole TV show thing. I was busking and labouring in the daytime and a couple of nights a week I played cocktail piano there.'

'Wow,' Emily said. 'I've been going there for a good few years now. Maybe you were playing piano while I was undergoing this yearly ritual.'

'Maybe,' Ray agreed. Although he would like to think that he would have remembered her…

'You should come with me,' Emily said suddenly. She shut the wardrobe doors, pushing her weight against them as they refused to correctly meet.

'Really?' Ray asked. 'Because you've made it sound like the worst night ever.'

'Well… it is… but, you know, if I had someone with me to help field the upper-class BS, it might not be as bad.'

Ray laughed.

'But it's Friday night. You probably have all sorts of plans. Sorry! The minute I get another flatmate I become all overbearing.'

'No,' Ray said. 'I mean, I don't have any other plans. I'm in the studio for another session early tomorrow morning.'

'Well, the offer's there and if you get fed up of my parents there's always the piano,' Emily said.

'OK,' Ray replied.

'OK?'

'Yeah,' Ray answered. 'Why not? Wait,' he said. 'Hang on.'

'What's wrong?' Emily asked.

'Have you got anything in that wardrobe I can wear? I've heard the fashion stakes are high.'

'So not funny!' Emily said as he ducked out of the door.

Forty-Two

Clean Martini Bar, Soho

Emily could hear her mother from the entrance of the ultra-modern bar and she wondered why on earth she had decided this would be an event to invite company to. She had never suggested that Jonah came with her. But then her mother didn't really like Jonah. Alegra didn't understand him or his love of where he'd come from and grown up. Alegra did love Jonah's food and culinary talents though, but she thought he had crawled up through the ranks to *polish off* his working-class tarnish, not to make good but then revel in and still enjoy being exactly the same.

There was a bright white Christmas tree in the lobby, it's only decorations black sequinned stars. It was neither festive nor stylish in Emily's opinion. It looked like something that would only fit at the funeral of a chintz-loving celebrity.

'Emily,' Ray said. He put his mouth to her ear. 'I'm not sure, but I think there's a reporter across the street so maybe we could head inside?'

'Oh, yes, of course, let's go in.' Emily said, stepping forward quickly.

'Would you like a drink?'

'I'd love a tonic water. The clementine flavour one if they have it.'

'Emily! Emily, darling! Mummy's here!'

Emily closed her eyes as her mother's voice grew even louder. She turned, looking through the supposedly arty terracotta roof tiles, made into circles and stacked into a square of space like a room divider. Alegra was finding the gaps, waving through one, then the other, laughing hysterically.

'Ray, listen, perhaps this was a mistake.' Emily turned to him.

'A mistake?' he queried.

Emily nodded. 'My mother's already deep into the wine. Nothing good can come from this. You should escape now. Get chips without me and head back to the flat. Or somewhere else. Anywhere else.'

Ray smiled at her. 'And miss all the fun?'

She gave a nervous laugh. 'Fun. Hmm.'

'Hey,' Ray said. 'From what I know about people and alcohol, and I have deep personal experience…' He took a breath. 'The ones drinking are never the ones in control of the situation.' He nudged her elbow with his. 'This could be a great opportunity to voice your ideas about their charity work and receive little resistance.'

He did have a point. A very good point. Her mother was far easier to manipulate – no, not manipulate, that was too harsh a word – easier to guide down a certain path, once she'd had a shed load of wine.

'I'll get us some drinks,' Ray said, moving up to the bar.

'Emily! Mummy and Daddy are over here!' Alegra called again.

'Thanks, Ray,' Emily said, turning and facing the inevitable.

Smiling desperately, she headed into the main body of the room, all aglow with those large lightbulbs on ropes and all manner of ode to steampunk. There were pistons and what looked like bicycle chains on the mock stone walls – all covered in tinsel and a dusting of fake snow. And there were her parents, seated at a chunky wooden, meant-to-look-straight-out-of-an-eighteenth-century-workshed table with the usual four others. Bill and Ben – no, seriously – Damien and Dana. The tabletop was already covered with wine bottles and pint glasses. What time had they all finished work?

'Hello,' Emily greeted them.

'Here she is!' her dad, William said, already ruby-faced, his thinning hair revealed under the light of one of the giant bulbs. 'Do we have enough seats?' He raised a hand in the air and began clicking his fingers seeking assistance. 'Another chair! Over here!'

Emily swallowed. No please. No thank you. Just a demand. She strode to an empty table and picked up a chair, carrying it over herself.

Alegra gasped. 'What are you doing, Emily? Put that down!'

'I'm getting a seat,' she answered, dropping the rustic mismatched chair down next to her mother.

'You don't carry seats like that! People here get paid to do that for you!' Alegra looked to her colleagues. 'I'm so, so sorry about my daughter, Dana, she works at a primary school.'

The words 'primary school' had been half-whispered like a) Dana had never met Emily before and b) this news was as secret as a minority country's nuclear program. Nothing changed.

Emily turned away again.

'Emily!' Alegra hissed. 'What are you doing now?'

'I'm getting another chair,' she answered. 'I've brought someone with me.'

Alegra stood then, looking around the room. 'What do you mean you've brought someone?' She tittered. 'One of your little teacher friends?'

'No,' Emily said, putting the other chair next to hers.

'Not... *a man?*' Alegra laughed again, smiling at Dana. Then she stopped smiling and looked put out. 'Please say it isn't Jonah.'

'It's not Jonah,' Emily answered. 'Jonah probably wouldn't come even if I paid him.'

'Oh, I'm sure he would then,' Alegra replied.

'Can we make a start?' William called down the table. 'Bill and Ben can't stay all night. They've been invited to the opening of a new all-flavours gin and cheese bar.'

'Not jealous at all. Are we, William?' Alegra said.

'Not at all,' William answered, slurping from a large glass of red wine. 'All I can say is, your ideas for the community day... feta brie good.'

Emily held her breath. As much as she loved cheese it was so corny. It was the corniest. And her parents and their colleagues all fell about laughing. Honestly, if the judges could see them all now, none of them would ever be allowed in a court room again.

'Evening, everyone.'

Emily looked up to see Ray at her side, a bottle of beer in one hand, her tonic water in the other. He passed her the glass.

'Good God!' Alegra exclaimed. 'It's that man from the front page of the *Daily Mail*!'

'No idea,' William replied.

'Yes!' Bill shouted, standing up and pointing a finger. 'I recognise him. He's a singer. You're a singer, aren't you?'

Emily sighed and looked to Ray. 'I'm so sorry about them. They aren't usually drunk when I get here. That bit ordinarily only happens later on in the evening when they suddenly all realise they've actually got to *do* some charity work.'

'Are you talking to him, Emily?' Alegra asked. 'Why are you talking to him?'

'Mum, Dad, Bill, Ben, Damien and Dana, this is Ray. He's my... friend... and he's going to help with tonight's brainstorming.'

'Hey,' Ray greeted, raising his beer bottle.

Emily looked to her mother and watched her literally turn a Brussel sprout shade of green.

Forty-Three

'I blame myself,' Alegra said, sucking on a cigarette outside the bar. 'I should have insisted on booking you in to see my counsellor. This is what I was afraid of when you turned up at the chambers the other day... in that same army coat.'

Emily shook her head and fastened another button on her jacket. 'Mother, what are we doing out here? It's freezing and everyone is waiting for us to get on with this evening of brainstorming.'

'This isn't like you,' Alegra continued, as if Emily hadn't even spoken. 'It's not like you at all.'

'What isn't like me?' Emily asked.

'This outlandish behaviour. This coming here, with a man... like that.'

'A man like what?' Emily said. She knew all too well her mother's prejudices but smoking, wanting to discuss it out on the street underneath a pulsating effigy of Santa Claus, was out-there even for Alegra.

'*I* wouldn't even represent that man,' Alegra said, blowing smoke out into the cold air.

'You didn't even know his name, Mother,' Emily reminded her. 'You don't know anything about him!'

'Piers Morgan called him a wife-beater,' Alegra stated. 'That *is* him, isn't it? The singer everyone has been talking about but not for his singing.'

'Mother, Piers Morgan once said "flaws should not be celebrated" and had just about everybody up in arms about it.'

'Well,' Alegra stated coolly. 'He was right about that. Who doesn't want to iron out their creases or straighten their curls? And he's right about this too!'

'You don't know Ray, at all.'

'And do you?' Alegra yelled. 'Because I don't remember you telling me anything about a new lodger the last time we spoke.' Alegra gasped then, both hands going to her face. 'Has he got some sort of hold over you? Is that why you've brought him here tonight? Because you need Mummy and Daddy to help you… escape.' She looked over her shoulder as if the entire Secret Service were queuing up behind them to make notes.

Emily shook her head. 'Do you remember the last time we spoke?'

'Don't be ridiculous, Emily. Of course, I remember. You turned up outside chambers in this shabby outdoorsy disaster.' She poked her cigarette towards Emily's coat as if she wanted to tarnish the outfit.

'And the time before that?'

'I telephoned you. About tonight. You insisted on having some futile discussion about pencils.'

'And the time before that?'

Emily folded her arms across her chest now and waited. This should be interesting. *She* knew the last time she had spoken to her mother before the invite to Clean Martini but she could almost guarantee her mother wouldn't.

Alegra flapped her fag-holding hand as if dismissing the subject completely. 'This is ridiculous. We are out here so I can inhale as much nicotine as I need to get over the shock of you turning up with a near-felon. *A reality TV show contestant.*' She shuddered. 'You do know what's next for him, don't you? It would be *Big Brother* if that hadn't ended, so it's either *Love Island* or… *Dancing on Ice.*'

'You don't remember, do you?' Emily said.

'Emily, for God's sake. *I'm* not the one embarrassing the family here.'

'Embarrassing the family!' Emily exclaimed, lungs bursting. 'Did you say "embarrassing the family"?'

'I invite you here every year because you excel at all this do-gooding. I have no idea where you get those qualities from. I can only assume that the teaching degree had something to do with it, but then again, there was that half-drowned butterfly you insisted on saving in Morocco… or was that in Algiers… and of course there was Jonah.'

Emily shook her head, her blood boiling. 'You don't remember the last time you spoke to me because every conversation with me is inconsequential in your life.'

'*Dancing on Ice*, Emily. Did you hear me? *Dancing on Ice*!'

'Everything is about you! It's always about you! You only phone me when you need something and that's never very often because you rarely need anything when you own two houses, two lavish cars you don't even use and more stocks and shares than... than *Dancing on Ice* has sequins.'

'Emily, you're getting hysterical,' Alegra stated. 'Calm yourself down.'

'No!' Emily said, with even more force and volume. 'I won't calm down. *I* don't want to be here, but I'm here because you're my parents and because, if I didn't come every year, I probably wouldn't see you at all.'

'That's not true.' There was less exasperation in her mother's tone now and she dropped the cigarette to the floor and crushed it out with the sole of her designer heel.

'It *is* true.' Emily drew in a breath, the hurt squeezing her chest. 'I've stopped inviting you to things, events I care about, like the summer fête at Stretton Park and Jonah's birthday party on the roof terrace where we had a Wimbledon theme and I covered the deck in Astroturf, and the Christmas when Simon cooked goose instead of turkey and it was really *really* horrible but we didn't care because we ate six Yorkshire puddings each and a whole packet of pigs in blankets.'

'Emily...'

'The last time you spoke to me, was when I told you Simon had died.' She swallowed, the memories clogging up her windpipe as she attempted to get her point across. 'And do you remember what you said? Because I do.'

Alegra shook her head.

'You said you were sorry,' Emily said. 'And then you asked when the funeral would be as you had a very packed schedule coming up. And then you said was it likely to be a wearing black affair or a new-fangled wearing bright colours to signify joy event, because if it was the latter then you should really have your indigo-coloured dress dry-cleaned.'

Emily really wanted to cry again, some of the same tumult she'd given into in the hallway of her home when Ray had held her close and hugged her emotion away – but she was not going to break down in front of Alegra. Weakness was, after all, the eighth deadly sin...

She watched her mother's mouth open, then close again. Alegra looked uncomfortable and that wasn't an expression she usually showed. Ever.

'Mum,' Emily began, softer now. 'I may be a grown woman doing a job you haven't ever supported or approved of, but I'm still your daughter and now and then, it might be nice if you valued me. For me. Not just for what I can bring to a fundraising planning meeting to impress your friends when it suits you.'

'You're making me sound colder than Rosemary West.'

'I'm here to see you and Dad, to catch up,' Emily carried on. 'As much as I'm here to help you with your project. And Ray is my guest. You need to respect him too.'

'Emily, darling, I just worry that you don't know anything about him. People in the public eye are a very different breed. They...'

'I know all I need to know,' Emily interrupted. 'And what I know hasn't come from the pages of a newspaper or... Twitter.' It had come from the delicate handling of a hedgehog, mending shelves and a heating system, holding her close while she cried, warming her hands in his... 'You need to trust my instincts.'

'I've had too much to drink,' Alegra admitted with a hiccup.

'You always have too much to drink on this night,' Emily replied.

Alegra sighed. 'Because I'm no good at it! I'm used to creating defence for the accused, not making happy places for the impoverished.'

Emily couldn't help but smile at her mother's expression when she'd said the word 'impoverished'. It was like the word had turned into an incurable disease that was going to infect her.

'I know, Mum,' Emily said, putting her arm through Alegra's and turning them both back towards the entrance of Clean Martini. 'But that's why you have your impoverished daughter to help you.'

'Darling, you only have to ask if you need anything! How many times have I told you that Daddy is always keen to write you a cheque?'

Emily sighed. 'If Dad wants to write a cheque get him to write it to your chosen charity this year. Kickstart your fundraising with a personal donation.' Emily nudged her mother. 'Wouldn't that be a lovely beginning?'

'Hmm,' Alegra mused. 'I really would rather watch you spend a vast sum on clothes that aren't second-hand than give it away to charity.' She edged herself away from Emily as if touching the military-style coat would taint her own outerwear.

'I know you would,' Emily answered. 'But let's not say that out loud... and absolutely never in a press release.'

Forty-Four

The low-alcohol beer really wasn't cutting it when having to converse with this crowd. Ray wondered exactly how many low-alcohol beers you had to drink for them to accumulate into enough units for you to be pissed. He was now on his fourth and Emily's dad kept trying to get him to drink red wine. As much as he wanted to be mellow around the edges, he had started to really notice what it did to people. And it was an escape he was no longer as interested in. What had his mother always found there that she couldn't find somewhere else?

He shook his head. The cocktail pianist was also getting on his nerves because Ray remembered all the standard tunes he'd once had to play himself. It was almost all in the same order.

'So,' Emily said, pen hovering above paper. 'What is your charity this year?'

She had come prepared like she might be about to teach a lesson to her Year Six pupils. When she and Alegra had re-joined the table, Emily had drawn a leather-bound portfolio out of her bag and started the discussion with the group.

'Ugh!' Alegra grunted, re-filling her wineglass. 'There are three.'

'It was put to a vote, Alegra,' William reminded. 'You were there.'

'I wasn't there! I was listening to the endless falsehoods of that woman from Carnegie's over the worst eggs benedict I've ever digested... well, I say digested, I'm not sure that actually fully occurred.'

'And the charities are?' Emily asked again.

Ray smiled at her. She really did have her work cut out with half-cut barristers completely uninterested in their own planning.

'Don't ask me,' Alegra said, picking at the bowl of artisan snacks that had been brought over with the last round of drinks. She fingered the chickpeas and flaked rice but none of them went near her lips. 'I wasn't there.'

'Who was it, Ben?' William asked his colleague. 'Do you remember?'

'One of them definitely involved animals, I remember that,' Dana answered. She had got very red-faced and seemed to be balanced rather precariously on the edge of her seat.

'Llamas!' Williams exclaimed, bouncing up from his seat. 'I distinctly remember llamas.' He shrugged back down again. 'Or was it alpacas?'

'Right, well,' Emily said, pen unmoved. 'Whatever the charities are, you can remind yourselves at the office tomorrow, has anyone got any thoughts as to what you would like to do this summer?'

'Emily,' Alegra slurred. 'You ask us that every year.'

'She does,' William agreed, then turned to Emily. 'You do.'

'I know,' Emily answered. 'And every year I hope you're going to come up with some fantastic and inspiring ideas.'

Dana and Damien burst into impromptu laughter like Emily had morphed into Michael McIntyre.

'What format does it usually take?' Ray asked Emily.

'Well…' Emily went to reply.

'The very first year,' Alegra interrupted. 'We had a lovely little medieval gala with pigs on spits and a jousting contest. We charged an absolute fortune for tickets and it was sold out. Then we gave all the proceeds to the hospital. We should do something like that again.'

'Yes, but, we decided that wasn't wholly in the spirit of reaching out to the wider community, which is one of the aims, isn't it?' Emily reminded. She looked to Ray. 'We changed the format a bit a few years ago. Now, with a budget from donations from clients as well as a large sum from St Martin's Chambers, a team goes into a local community and enhances the area in some way. They've made a garden, a playpark and even a lido thanks to cooperation with the council.'

'But there are only so many open spaces to fill with do-gooding equipment for all… and a client of mine is desperate for a prime spot to build luxury apartments.'

'Mother!'

'What?'

'How about you do something that fits both criteria,' Ray suggested. 'An event, but one that benefits everyone and brings the whole community together.'

Alegra rolled her eyes. 'You mean an England football match on a big screen, don't you? I couldn't stand it! Men and women wrapped in the St George's Cross, throwing beer into the air...'

'I mean, maybe a music festival,' Ray said.

'What?!' Bill exclaimed, almost knocking over one of the empty bottles of wine.

'Interesting concept,' William mused, putting fingers to his chin. 'I'm rather partial to a picnic with an orchestra, as long as one doesn't have to sit on the ground.'

Ray wondered what sort of a picnic involved *not* being sat on the ground. Perhaps he was stepping out of his initial remit as Emily's solidarity. Maybe he should get another low-alcohol beer and keep quiet.

'I think that's a fantastic idea!' Emily said, scribbling away on her notepad. 'It doesn't have to be something permanent to improve the community, it can be one wonderful day that everyone from the area can enjoy together. There can be music of all kinds from classical to rock and everything in between. A bouncy castle for the children and face-painting and... maybe a juggler... or magician. We could make it free to attend and then send buckets around for donations to the chosen charities or do a raffle.'

'There will be plenty of artists who will give their time for free in exchange for the publicity,' Ray told her.

'Would you play?' Emily asked him. 'Be the headline act?'

'Er, well...' He hadn't thought this through. But, why

couldn't he? Provided he survived the operation he was still trying to avoid, there was nothing lined up in his schedule for the summer yet. And this *was* to help Emily...

'Ray,' Emily said. 'Come on, you can't suggest a music festival and then not be a big part of it.'

'Ha!' Alegra commented. 'As long as Emily doesn't have to sing. Although, people might pay to *not* hear that, mightn't they, darling?'

'I'm not listening, Mother,' Emily said, taking a hefty swig of her drink.

'No,' Ray said. 'But I am.' He looked to Alegra, her fingers still in the bowl of snacks, perfect nails swirling the pieces around. 'Why would you say that? Emily has a great voice.'

'Ray,' Emily said, drinking some more. 'It's fine.'

'No,' he continued. 'It's not fine.'

'Ray, honestly, let's get on and workshop some more ideas for the community music festival. It's a really *really* good idea. I love it.'

Ray stood up. 'No, I think we'll do something else before that. Come on.'

Emily looked up from her pad of paper and saw Ray had extended his hand to her. What was he doing? Why was he holding out his hand? He lowered his head towards her ear and whispered, 'I could do with the practice. You'd be doing me a favour.'

'Ray, I don't know what you're talking about, but everyone is looking at me. My *mother and father* are looking at me.'

'So, they should be. Come on.'

He wasn't holding his hand out anymore; he had *taken* her hand and was pulling her up out of her seat.

'You weren't wrong about them being a handful, were you?' Ray whispered to her.

'I did say.'

'Then let's get away from the table. Have a time-out.'

'A time-out is what we give the reception class when they can't behave.'

'Then we'll pretend that's what we're giving your parents.' He smiled at the group of barristers and addressed them. 'We'll be approximately four minutes.'

He started walking, taking her with him, and it was only when they got deeper into the bowels of the room, where long tables turned into more intimate round ones, the décor changing to all muted uplighters and half-woven baskets on the walls, that Emily saw the grand piano. She had heard the music throughout the evening, a mixture of classics and songs from the movies, but she hadn't seen the pianist. She saw him now though, a petite man with thick black glasses on his face, dressed in a tuxedo.

'Ray, what are we doing?' Emily said.

'We're going to play the bar a song.'

'Wait. What? Oh no! No, don't be silly!'

He was smiling at her now, approaching the man who was sitting at the piano stool and still holding her hand, his grip insistent but not quite vice-like. She could let go... maybe.

'Come on, it'll be fun. And I'm sort of sick of listening to him play the *Titanic* theme tune.'

'He has played that quite a bit,' Emily admitted. What was she saying? She didn't really care if this pianist – employed by Clean Martini – played 'My Heart Will Go On' for all of eternity. It was better than Ray's other suggestion. Him singing? Fine. *Her* singing? No. Singing in a deserted park or at school with the children was one thing but here, in a crowded bar, on a Friday night, with her parents and their colleagues watching?!

'Hey there,' Ray said to the pianist who was currently paused, looking through sheet music. 'Would you mind if I played something?'

'Well, I...' the man began.

'Great,' Ray said, plumping down onto the oblong piano stool next to him. He scooted close to the man. 'We'll be as long as it takes to play "O, Holy Night". Come on, Emily, you sit next to me, I'll teach you the chords.'

'Ray, this is ridiculous.' She looked at the pianist who was getting up from the stool, hoping for the man to show some stance of possession over his seat – and his job – but it seemed that he was retreating.

'I thought we'd been through the "what are you afraid of" scenario,' he told her.

'Well, singing in the park isn't singing in a bar to a crowd of people and my parents and their co-workers.'

'Is that it?'

'Did you not hear "singing in a bar to a crowd of people and my parents and their co-workers"?'

'Sit down, Emily,' Ray urged, patting the space on the stool next to him.

She shook her head, in a "no" and also a sign of utter

frustration. What choice did she have? She didn't want to slope back to the table with her mother, despite their earlier conversation, ready to pick at her abilities.

Ray began to play the piano, his fingers flitting over the keys like it was the most natural thing in the world. He made it look effortless. He had no music, his digits simply found each note, like an accomplished touch-typist, not needing to look where they landed, simply *knowing*.

'So, you place your hand here,' Ray said. He took her hand in his again and hovered it over the piano. 'Here for the first bit and then it goes here for the next bit, then here and then... here.' He adjusted her position. His hand was warm in hers. Warm, solid, firm, sexy...

'Ray, I don't know how to play the piano. My mother tried to get me to learn the violin but that was... horrendous and I didn't learn any other instruments after that.' She sighed. 'Because you said recorders don't count.'

She was talking too much because focusing on sitting under a spotlight surrounded by patrons who seemed like they had stopped all conversation was really unnerving.

'Trust me,' Ray told her. 'You'll pick it up.' He was still holding her hand. 'Here... here... then here and... here.' He manoeuvred her fingers across the notes, showing her which three to press. It looked impossible.

'I can't.'

'Says the woman who told me she's a last grain in the sand-timer kind of person?' He stood up then, clearing his throat. 'Good evening, ladies and gentlemen. I hope you don't mind the interruption, but I haven't heard one festive song all night and we're all looking forward to Christmas, right?'

He'd told her he hated Christmas! Emily swallowed, looking out into the dark at faces she couldn't clearly see. There was some murmur of agreement amongst them. *Great!*

'So, we're going to play you "O, Holy Night". Thanks for listening.'

Ray sat back down on the piano stool and looked at her, those amber eyes connecting with hers, their bodies tight together on the seat really made for one...

'Absolutely and completely not ready,' Emily answered, a rush of breath leaving her.

'Terrifying, isn't it?' he said with a laugh. 'But exhilarating too.' He paused for a beat. 'Like singing karaoke.' He grinned, then finally he started to play the introduction and Emily held her breath, her chest and stomach both contracting together. Ray nodded to her and she played the first chord with trembling fingers. She'd got it right! Well, it sounded right to her untrained ear...

And then they began to sing, the traditional words, not the Stretton Park remix, and Emily started to feel the terror change. It started to turn into something else, something quite different. Finding the notes on the piano, feeling the power of the instrument underneath her fingertips, singing out loud with Ray, a rich, warm, deeply exciting bubble manifested itself in the outer echelons of her body and started to dance and whirl its way through the whole of her. With every chord she hit correctly, with every note she sang, her confidence grew and the fact she was being heard, and being watched, by a Friday night crowd in a packed bar quickly became secondary to the fact she was making music with this man no one in her life thought very much of, but who was making a habit of being there exactly when she needed him...

Emily belted out the highest note with enthusiasm and unfettered abandon then smiled as Ray nudged her. He smiled back as he continued to sing with that beautiful voice – deep and powerful when it required it, then a whispered soft high. They brought the song to its close and tears came immediately to Emily's eyes as the poignancy caught up with her. Life was going on. It had never stopped. She dropped her head a little, caught in the moment, and she felt Ray put an arm around her, drawing her into his body. His breath was warm in her hair, and there was that woodland scent of his aftershave, the heat from his body. She leaned into all of it.

'You OK?' he whispered, his fingers on her back making her skin tingle through the silk shirt as they rubbed over her shoulders, as if sensing her mood.

She looked up at him then and the world jolted like someone had pulled on a handbrake. His firm jaw peppered with a little stubble now, that slightly fuller bottom lip, those eyes... The unstoppable attraction she felt was hitting her like she was Tyson Fury's punchbag. She liked him. She *liked* him. Like *that*. The way half the country *liked* Tom Hardy...

It was at that moment she realised they weren't alone in her apartment, or on her roof terrace, or in Barnard Park. They were in a bar. In *public*. She shifted quickly, to the very edge of the piano seat, almost falling off. And it was then she heard the applause.

'We should bow,' Ray told her, catching her hand in his. Every touch was sending fizzes of heat over her skin now.

She should retract. She should tune in to the sensible part of her that knew having feelings like this was completely mad. But the non-sensible part of her craved more touches, closer contact...

She bowed, smiling out into the audience as Ray drew their hands up and down and they moved together to accept the clapping. And then she saw her mother and father, standing together with Damien, Dana, Bill and Ben, all frantically applauding with their hands actually making contact with each other – not the half-hearted fake clapping they usually did at ballet performances. And her mother was smiling with more than a hint of pride in her eyes.

'You were amazing,' Ray told her softly. 'And, I promise you, your mother, she'll never criticise your singing ever again.'

Forty-Five

Crowland Terrace, Canonbury, Islington

The roof terrace was definitely the best bet for not-getting-too-close while eating kebabs. Once they had finally been able to leave the charity-planning evening, when Emily had packed her inebriated parents into a luxury Addison Lee car, Ray had taken them to a Turkish restaurant he knew. Then, cradling the wrapped-up kebabs, swerving the attentions of a couple of women who had recognised Ray and wanted photos, they had taken the Tube back home. Now she was furiously switching on the patio heaters to warm up the space. She was not going to light candles. The lighting of candles would give the outside area a romantic glow and now her vagina seemed to be bouncing to a hip-hop rhythm whenever Ray was in close proximity, she thought it was better to let the rather too bright outside light illuminate the space instead. Ray was getting them drinks. She had suggested camomile tea in the hope it would calm down her inner workings. At least outside she had a fantastic excuse for keeping her coat on and fully buttoned up...

'It's no good,' Ray said, striding out onto the decking. 'I can't wait any longer. You shouldn't either.'

Oh God! What was he talking about? He couldn't have sensed what she was feeling, could he? And it was ridiculous to think he felt anywhere near the same. He was Ray Stone. She was Emily Parker not Emily Blunt...

'Emily,' Ray said, thumping two steaming mugs down on the table. 'Come and eat your kebab. I'm telling you, it's going to be the best you've ever tasted.'

The food. Of course, he was talking about the food. She looked at the two-seater 'sofa' made out of pallets Ray had plumped down on. No! That was the only seating she had put cushions down on. She either sat next to him and had her insides pulsing, or she braved the cold, bare wood. Or she went in and got another cushion from the cupboard.

'God! This is sooo good! Mmm!' Ray moaned loudly and Emily looked at him. His eyes were closed, his mouth full, chewing hard, breathing through his nose, his lips slick with what looked like chilli sauce. He still looked sexy. How was that even possible? And then his eyes snapped open and he was looking at her... looking at him.

'Eat the kebab,' he told her again. 'Or I won't headline at the music festival.'

'Well,' Emily said. 'When you put it like that.' The 'sofa' it had to be. She picked the paper wrapper up from the table and sat down next to Ray, unfolding the sheet until she found the pitta-wrapped meat. She had to admit, as kebabs went, this did look particularly magnificent. She turned her head to see that Ray had stopped eating and was studying her instead.

'What?' she asked as her stomach did a tumble turn worthy of Michael Phelps.

'I really want to know what you think of the food.'

'You're going to watch me eat it?' she asked. Apart from pizza with its stringy, messy, melted cheese she would have been bound to get all over her chin, the kebab was probably the next worst thing for eating with company.

'Just the first bite,' Ray replied.

Emily picked up the meat-filled bread and sunk her teeth into it, fearing for the succulent tomato pieces she was bound to drop down her shirt. But, all her concerns drifted away the moment the *sish* hit her senses. She hadn't realised quite how hungry she was, and the delicious concoction of lamb, salad, sauce and bread was the ultimate appetite appeaser.

'Oh, my goodness!' she exclaimed, in between chews. 'This is simply…'

'Heaven,' Ray said. 'Isn't it?'

'Absolutely heaven,' she agreed, munching. 'How did you find the place?'

Going into Mehmet's restaurant had given Ray all the feels from his childhood when they'd picked up the takeaway. From the delicious fragrance of the lamb and pork sizzling on the grill to the ancient television still showing Eastern European football. Then there was Mehmet himself, a little older – 110? – but with the same grin and happy-go-lucky attitude. It was like a time rewind.

'I used to go there when I was a kid,' Ray answered her.

'That's why the owner knew you,' Emily remarked.

He nodded. 'I used to go there with my parents. We went there a lot.' He grinned. 'My mum wasn't much of a cook.'

'Mine neither,' Emily admitted. 'One time, for a whole month, Jamie Oliver's restaurant used to deliver meals. And I didn't think they were anywhere near as delicious as this.' She took another bite of her food. 'I wonder who she gets to deliver her dinners now?'

It was now or never. He had known that when he had taken Emily to Mehmet's. He wanted to tell her about his mum. All evening something had started to change inside of him. It had begun when Emily had invited him to the night with her parents, it had carried on as he watched her handle the ostentatious and annoying barristers, and it had reached a peak when Alegra had insulted Emily's singing. Emotion had flooded him. Down and dirty sexual attraction, plus an overwhelming need to protect her had made him take her up to that piano. And then she'd sung and played along with him and all he'd wanted to do was feel her lips on his.

'My mother was an alcoholic,' Ray said, fast. There. He had said it. It was out there. He could feel his heart pumping in his neck.

'Oh,' Emily replied immediately. 'Goodness, I…'

'It's OK,' Ray stated. 'You don't have to say anything to try and make me feel better. It was a long time ago and it is what it is, you know.' He pulled some meat from his kebab and popped it into his mouth. 'A lot of people thought that being an alcoholic made her a bad person, but she wasn't a bad person. She was… I don't know… lost somehow.'

He swallowed. This was so difficult. He didn't talk about it. He hadn't ever talked about it with Ida. Ida had known his mum had died when he was young, but she had never asked the details and he hadn't offered them. Emily was looking at him now like she wanted to know more. He wasn't sure what he had to say.

'I don't know,' Ray began again. 'Some people just can't find their place in life for some reason. I feel now that maybe that's what happened with her.' He sniffed. 'She didn't have a career to get passionate about. She didn't have any hobbies. Apart from me and my dad, she just had the booze.'

'When did she pass away?' Emily asked.

'I was thirteen,' Ray said, blowing out a breath as the memories came back. 'She died on the operating table during a liver transplant.' And it was that that hurt the most. His mother's liver, damaged by years and years of abuse, had all but given up. She had needed a transplant to save her life and she had got one. It had been a miracle. But Ray knew, and his mother had been honest from the beginning, she was never going to be able to give up drinking.

'She didn't deserve the transplant and she knew it,' Ray stated. 'She decided she needed alcohol more than she needed me and my dad and all the other things in her life. And no one really knew why. I still don't know why.' He took a breath. 'Just like I don't know why she would sometimes forget to pick me up from school... or buy the wrong colour trousers for my uniform... or drink too much wine at the school fête and puke up in front of everyone. Sometimes she would apologise, sometimes not. Mainly not, nearer the end.'

'But, couldn't she have got help?' Emily said, putting her food back on the table and turning a little towards him.

'We tried. My dad, he tried so hard to make her see sense.

He shouted and bawled and when that didn't work, he cried and pleaded… but she was always absent somehow. Adrift.'

And there were times in his life when he felt something like the same. Except, *he* had music. Music kept him centred and the thought that his throat issues could take that from him scared the hell out him. What did he have then? What would be left?

'Every time I get drunk, I think about her and try to really drill down into what it is about drinking that would make someone want that more than *anything*. You know, more than being with the people you care about, more than, I don't know, walking in the park in the summer or seeing snow on the rooftops or… eating Mehmet's kebabs.'

'And do you ever find any answers?' Emily asked softly.

He shook his head. 'No. I just end up with a splitting headache and my rough-looking mug spread all over the newspapers.' He looked into the mid-distance. 'I don't know what alcohol gave her. No one did. I don't think *she* even knew for sure. She was just too scared to find out what life could be like without it.'

Emily picked up a mug of coffee and handed it to him.

'Thanks,' he answered, taking a sip, his food balanced on his lap. 'Sorry, I'm really oversharing.'

'No,' Emily said. 'Not at all.'

'I loved her, you know, despite everything. She was my mum. She drank too much. I need to accept that and move on.'

Emily nodded, unspeaking. He watched her pick up her cup of tea and take a drink.

'Listen,' Ray said. 'I didn't mean to kill the mood. I

just… wanted to tell you. That's all.' What else was there to say? That he hadn't really told anyone the depth of it before. That he had wanted *her* to be the one to know everything?

'Anyway, we should really be celebrating. We brought Christmas to Clean Martini. And you know how I feel about Christmas. I don't *do* Christmas, Miss Parker. That's your fault.'

Emily smiled a little.

'Hey,' Ray said, nudging his knee against hers. 'You've gone quiet on me.'

'Because… after you saying all that about your mum,' she sighed. 'I really…want to tell *you* something,' Emily answered.

'Anything,' Ray whispered. 'I'm here.'

She took a deep breath as if she was really deliberating what came next. 'The reason I *don't* drink alcohol,' Emily started, voice quaking a little. 'Is because… Simon died because of it.' She took a breath. 'He was hit by a car, coming home from work and… the man who knocked him down… he was drunk.' She closed her eyes briefly before opening them up again and continuing. 'This man… his name was Jonathan Stansfield… he had been at an office lunch that turned into an all afternoon affair… and then he got into his car and he drove. He was three times over the legal limit.'

'Oh, Emily,' Ray said, putting his arm around her and drawing her close.

'I know it's silly to correlate my drinking with his drinking, and I know my mother thinks it's ridiculous, which was why she kept trying to put wine into my tonic water and insisted on telling me life goes on... but I can't stomach it. I don't want to feel anything like Jonathan did when he ran over the person I thought I was going to be spending my life with.'

'I don't think it's silly,' Ray told her firmly. 'I think it makes perfect sense. I get it. Completely.'

'Jonathan Stansfield's life is ruined and, as glad as I was at the beginning that he went to prison... after seeing him myself, I know that whether he drinks again or not, I'm certain he will never get behind the wheel of a car after drinking again.'

'You went to see him?' Ray asked. 'In prison?'

Emily nodded. 'I had to.' She swallowed. 'In the courtroom I looked him in the eye and I wanted to see this unremorseful monster who had taken Simon away and I wanted to hate him and feel that his two years in prison was revenge for the damage he'd caused me. But he sobbed from the second the opening statements were read, until they took him into custody, and I realised then that he'd lost everything too. His girlfriend, his job... He hated himself. And I needed to go there, to see him, to talk to him, face to face and... to say that I forgive him.'

Ray shook his head, almost unable to comprehend the strength Emily had shown.

'He wasn't someone who had set out to kill that day. He was just someone who made a mistake. A horrible, catastrophic mistake and one he is absolutely paying for. But we all make mistakes, don't we?'

'Wow,' Ray said softly. 'You are... so incredible, Emily. I don't know how you could find it in your heart to do that.'

He couldn't help himself, he reached up and brushed her fringe from her forehead a little.

Emily shivered as his fingers grazed her forehead. Here Ray was again, doing that thing he always seemed to be so wonderfully adept at doing – supporting her, with his actions and with his words. No one had done that for her since Simon's accident. Not even Jonah. The trouble was, everyone around her at the time had maybe been too close. Ray hadn't known Simon. Ray was only getting to know *her*. Single her. Not one-of-a-couple her.

'I'm not a saint,' Emily insisted. 'And I do really miss gin.'

Ray smiled. 'Never been a fan of gin. Tried it. Didn't get it.'

'It's ordinarily my mother's favourite drink. The one thing we had in common.' She took a breath. 'But there are definitely more important things than that.'

'I don't know, some parents seem to think that their children are going to come out and automatically be a carbon copy of them. My dad still thinks I should be an engineer, even now.'

'Well, you did fix my central heating. You obviously have skills.'

'I think he's just fearful that I'll fall like my mother fell. Obviously in the music industry there's easy access to every kind of excess but, you know, my mother didn't need a VIP pass to drink herself to an early grave.'

'And do you understand his fear?' Was that too forward of her to ask?

'We don't see a lot of each other. I think, thinking on it, he stays distant because he doesn't want to lose me. And I know that sounds crazy but, maybe he feels if you're not tight with someone, that if you do lose them, somehow it will be easier.'

'I understand.'

'And I'm the same. I don't see him enough, I know that. But that doesn't mean I don't care. And then there's all this stuff with Ida…'

Emily really wanted to know more. But at the same time, she really didn't. Because she had already formed her opinion of him, based on the facts she'd experienced, not something she had read or someone had told her.

'I saw her the other day,' Ray began. 'My agent set up a meeting and it… it just went the way I knew it was going to go.' He picked up his coffee again and took a gulp. 'She's no different. She still wants the same things.'

Emily held her breath, waiting for Ray to continue.

'I can't give her what she wants. I don't think anyone is ever going to be able to give her what she wants.' He sighed. 'Sorry, TMI, right?'

'No, I… I don't know.' She took a breath. 'Everyone needs to express themselves, don't they?'

What the hell did that even mean? Everyone needs to express themselves?! Why couldn't she offer some support? Get the right words like he seemed to be able to do with her…

'She certainly always did that,' Ray replied.

'Are things resolved now?' Emily asked, tentatively.

'I don't know,' he answered. 'Ida needs to make a change and, a little bit like my mother, it's going to be hard and she doesn't want to do it. She seems to want to try to go back instead of forward.'

Emily shivered, the cold of the night filtering through her coat despite the warmth from the heaters above them.

'I wanted to help her, I really did,' Ray continued. 'But I couldn't stay. Not any longer. It was… damaging.'

Emily looked at him, cradling the mug in his hands, looking into the depths of the creamy coffee, his mind definitely elsewhere. 'Well,' she said, 'I've heard you've landed a spare room in a very exclusive area of London. Yes, it may have a very small kitchen, but it does have a full bathtub and a roof terrace with views of the cheese grater, if you stand on one leg… and lean over a little.'

Ray turned to look at her then, blinking those unusual-coloured eyes. 'Really?'

'No,' Emily answered. 'I lied about the cheese grater view.'

He smiled then and took a deep breath, looking away from her and gazing out at the night sky and the rooftops surrounding them. Then he put his kebab on the table and stood up. 'Stand on one leg you said.' He walked to the edge of the space.

'No,' Emily said, immediately nervous. 'I was kidding. I said so. I lied about that.'

'OK, so what *will* I be able to see if I stand really close and lean out on one leg?'

'Ray, don't,' Emily said, jumping up and stepping after him.

'God, I can see Christmas lights,' he told her. 'All the colours.' He leaned a little, his shoes right up against the low wall, his body stretching out.

'Ray, please, don't do that.' She was frantic. It was slippery up here, a near frost on the ground…

'I think you can just see the edge of something if I lean a bit more...'

She couldn't bear it any longer. She grabbed him with every bit of strength she had and all the strength she didn't know she had, hauling him away from the edge and pushing him to the ground. She landed on top of him with a thump.

'Whoa!' he exclaimed, breathing like the wind had been knocked out of him.

Emily was packed out with adrenaline, her heart racing, her mind flooded with all the horrible eventualities that could have occurred but thankfully hadn't. Now, basically straddling her new lodger, she realised that she had probably overreacted. But that knowledge didn't stop tears from springing to her eyes as the fright still rolled over her.

'Why did you do that?!' she said crossly. 'It was really stupid! So, so stupid!' She thumped his chest as tears streamed down her face.

'I'm sorry,' Ray said quickly. 'I'm really, really sorry. I don't know what I was thinking. I shouldn't have been such a dick.'

'I couldn't bear it,' Emily replied, the tears tumbling still. 'If you... if anything... happened to you.'

What had she just said? Why was her heart refusing to slow down? Why was she still lying on top of him? Because she cared. She cared a little too much. And somehow, she couldn't move. She was frozen in place, looking down at him as he looked back at her. She could feel the warmth of his breath on her face and then she could feel his fingertips gently grazing her scalp as one of his hands moved into her hair. What was happening? Why was she not getting up? Why was she closing her eyes and dipping her head into the palm of his hand? She opened her eyes then, looking down at him, searching for all the answers in his expression. But all she saw there was soul-nudging desire...

'Emily,' Ray said. 'I don't want to do the wrong thing here.'

She swallowed. He was a gentleman. Despite what everyone thought about him, he *was* a good person. She trusted her instincts when it came to judging his character... but what about *her* instincts on the path forward right now?

'I... don't know what the right thing is,' Emily whispered to him, hands moving to his shoulders, bearing a little of her weight. 'But I think... I'd like you to kiss me.'

His body moved beneath her hands and she saw the recognition come alive on his face. Her heart was hammering now. No longer fear, instead it was pure rapture.

'You think?' Ray asked softly.

Still he was holding back. Like a sensible, good person. He was giving her time to back away and get up, to change her mind. Should she? Was this really and truly what she wanted? He was giving her all the choices.

She shook her head. 'No,' she answered. 'I don't think. I *know* I'd like you to kiss me.'

The millisecond her words hit the air Ray was up off the floor, catching her in his arms and turning her over. It was her turn now for the breath to leave her body. Now he was lying over her, looking down at her, his chest rising and falling quickly. Should she watch and wait? Or should she make the first move? It had been so long since she'd had feelings like this. It was like starting from the beginning...

*

What was he doing? Ray had wanted to kiss her on the piano stool at the cocktail bar. Despite the patrons watching, the applause, he had felt like they were in their own sealed bubble, completely alone, totally in the now. But common sense had won out and the moment had gone. But now, here, the feeling was deeper, overwhelming even. Emily was a special person. He didn't want to hurt her. And he didn't want to *be hurt* either. How could he trust this? Or did he need to? They had both been through so much, did it have to be something that was analysed? Could it not just be a kiss?

She reached up then, putting her palm to his face and her touch sent a thousand tiny sparks fizzing under his skin. He moved towards her, centimetre by slow centimetre, his lips almost already tasting hers. He was nervous. This was so special. He saw her shiver and he kissed her then, their mouths meeting, softly, gently, exploring delicately, still a little hesitant. And then more deeply, wider, passion increased, their lips a tangle of sexy, their hands reaching out, holding, desperate for even more of a connection.

And then suddenly Emily broke away, her throat making a sound that ripped through his panting arousal. She shifted, out from underneath him, leaving him, getting to her feet, brushing down her coat with her fingers.

'I... we... it's late,' she said unable to meet his eyes.

He stood up too. He shouldn't have kissed her. She wasn't ready. And he wasn't ready either, despite the physical signs his body was offering up. It was a mistake.

'Yeah,' he answered as coolly as he was able. It didn't sound cool. He sounded like someone who had just experienced the most beautiful kiss of his life and then had a bucket of cold water poured all over him. 'You're right.

I have a big day in the studio tomorrow and you have…'

'Shopping,' Emily answered. 'Christmas shopping with Jonah.'

'Well, we should definitely call it a night in that case,' he said, nodding.

'We should turn off the heaters and…' Emily began.

'I can do that,' he said, wanting this awkwardness to be over. 'Why don't you head in?'

'Are you sure?' she asked.

'Yeah, I'm sure,' he answered.

'OK,' she said. 'Goodnight, Ray.'

'Goodnight, Emily.'

He watched her leave, rushing away because she couldn't face what had happened between them. What *had* happened? From his point of view what had happened was what *always* happened. The girl realised that who he was simply wasn't what she wanted.

Forty-Six

Hyde Park, Winter Wonderland

'Ooo, we must have a go on the helter-skelter! I haven't been on one of those in years!' Allan was already munching on a mustard-covered bratwurst he'd insisted on getting the second they arrived at London's premier Christmas extravaganza.

Every year Emily and Jonah went out looking for Christmas gifts and ended up here instead. Not that the Winter Wonderland didn't have plenty to buy. There were cute little Bavarian-style chalets selling gorgeous hand-made gifts from unique jewellery to artisan preserves but Jonah (and now Two L's) were easily distracted by the fairground attractions and many, *many* eateries. It *was* a beautiful, Christmassy arena though, with a big wheel and ice-skating and acrobatic shows to watch, all sitting amid ice white lights and warm, glowing bars offering mulled wine and mince pies or chocolate calzones and beer. It was impossible not to feel the festive spirit in these surroundings, nestling in with other smiling shoppers all partaking in the season of goodwill.

'I need to get my mum a nutcracker,' Jonah remarked. He was reading from a gift list on the notes section of his mobile phone.

'Everyone loves a man in uniform,' Allan replied, grinning. 'Or a Christmas jumper.' He pulled the bright red, green and gold reindeer motif sweater away from his body.

'I don't mean the soldier,' Jonah replied. 'I mean an actual nutcracker. To crack nuts.' He turned to Emily as they meandered through the park, bracing themselves against the chill wind as well as the crowds. 'Every year since I was little, my mum's borrowed a nutcracker from Hilda at number fourteen. And every year, since I was about ten, I've asked her why she doesn't buy one of her own. And she always says the same thing.' Jonah took a breath then spoke in a thick West Indies accent. '"Jonah, I only have nuts to crack once a year, at Christmas, why would I buy something I'll only use once a year?"'

'I'm always so impressed by that excellent impression,' Allan said, biting into his sausage.

'I want to finally get her one,' Jonah said. 'So, I don't have to have the same conversation for the next twenty or so years. A nice one, silver maybe.'

Emily nodded, her gloved hands in the pockets of her coat. It was really cold today. Even colder than the icy atmosphere in her apartment that morning. The heating wasn't on the blink again, it was how things were with her and Ray. She felt the absolute epitome of awkward after their kiss on the roof terrace but, in the shower, she had also closed her eyes as the water sprinkled all over her bare body and relived every stomach-turning sultry second of it. They bumped into each other over making breakfast, literally. Ray had stepped towards the fridge just as she had wanted to get something from the top cupboard and his face had all but ended up in her armpit... luckily *after* her shower. Things were now so stilted, they were both behaving like a divorced couple forced to move back in with each other and not remembering anything they used to have in common. It was eating her up. She couldn't concentrate. She had no notes about gifts like Jonah. She was even considering buying her mother the cheapest gin she could find on Amazon to make a point...

'Emily, what do you think?' Jonah asked her.

Oh God. She hadn't been listening properly. Had the conversation moved on from silver nutcrackers? She could hazard a guess or she could...

'Ray kissed me,' she blurted out.

Allan made a horrendous noise like a cross between someone choking and a hiccupping camel.

'Allan, are you OK?' Jonah asked, thumping his partner on the back as his eyes began to bulge and he attempted to catch his breath.

'Fine!' Allan inhaled, clutching at his throat. 'Not the first time I've had too much sausage down my throat... but that's a conversation for another time. Emily! Wow! I'm so thrilled for you!'

'Hang on a second,' Jonah interrupted. 'She just said Ray kissed her. Was it something you didn't want? Because if he did that then...'

Emily shook her head, drawing their walking to a halt

and putting fingers to her fringe that was being crucified by the slightly too-tight yellow woollen hat she was wearing. Not all vintage was worn-in enough. 'No, it wasn't like that. Of course, it wasn't like that.' Ray wasn't like that.

'Then what was it like?' Jonah wanted to know.

'Yes,' Allan carried on. 'Tell us what it was like, all the details, don't leave anything out. Was it all hot and steamy… did you walk in on him in the shower again? Did your eyes meet amid a cloud of sexy condensation—?'

'Did you just ask if she walked in on him the shower *again*? Why don't I know about the first time?' Jonah wailed.

'I think we need mulled wine for this,' Allan said, gobbling the last of the bratwurst then linking arms with Emily. 'Come on, let's go and settle in one of those little huts and get comfortable.'

'A non-alcoholic version for me,' Emily reminded, letting herself be tugged forward.

The oompah music rose above the excited chatter of patrons indulging in huge glasses of beer and Emily was glad of the lively atmosphere here in this Oktoberfest-style marquee. The roof was illuminated by strings of lights and the bench seating, together with the German tunes, gave it a Christmas party atmosphere. She sipped at her alcohol-free mulled wine and realised that Jonah and Allan were both staring at her waiting for her to re-start the conversation.

'The wine is lovely, all spicy,' Emily remarked with a smile and another little sip.

'I'm not drinking a drop until you tell us what happened,' Jonah said.

'And I'm saving drinking mine until the really juicy bits,' Allan answered, all grins.

'Well,' Emily began. 'I took Ray to the charity planning evening with my parents.'

'What?!' Jonah exclaimed.

'God, he went to *that*,' Allan stated. 'The man is a saint.'

'Yes,' Emily said with a nervous nod. 'And my parents, well my mother really, was really rude to him. And then my mother insulted my singing and then, I don't really know what happened, but Ray got up and he took me with him, and we played the piano and sang "Oh, Holy Night" to the whole entire bar.'

'Sweet Jesus!' Allan inhaled a mouthful of wine.

'And then we got kebabs and he told me all about his mum who died when he was young, and I told him... I told him how Simon died and about why I don't drink and about Jonathan Stansfield, and then I thought he was going to fall off the roof and we ended up on the floor together and... then... then... I asked him to kiss me.' She picked up her drink and downed half of it.

'Mother Mary!' Allan gasped.

Jonah wasn't saying anything now. Emily knew he was worried about her, but she still wanted her best friend to say something, *anything*, even if their opinions were opposing.

'And did he?' Allan asked. 'I'm guessing he did! Right there? On the floor of the roof terrace? Were you clothed at the time? Because you didn't mention anything coming off and...'

'Fully-clothed,' Emily said. 'In coats.'

'God!' Allan said, pulling a face. 'That's not romantic at all.'

Jonah still hadn't said anything. His hands were wrapped around his cup of mulled wine and his body language seemed to be questioning her sanity. She supposed it was a real change to her persona from what everyone had got used to since Simon's death. But it wasn't so far removed from the Emily she'd been before that fateful evening. Drinks, laughter and love on the roof terrace had been staple weekend entertainment for all of them before life got shadowed.

She looked towards the Christmas tree near the entrance, its festive glow kick-starting reverie. 'It was... wonderful... yet crazy and impulsive and...'

'You're going to be a couple and buy padlocks and keys and clip your initials to Tower Bridge for all eternity,' Allan suggested, leaning a little over the table towards her.

'No,' Emily said. 'Not that... not any of it. Because I stopped the kiss and now I'm wondering if it was all...' She didn't know how she wanted to end the sentence. 'A mistake,' she breathed. 'You know...wrong.'

'Does Ray think it was a mistake?' Allan asked softly.

'I expect so,' Emily said.

'You don't know? You didn't discuss it?' Allan said.

'I said it was late and he said he had to be up early too for a session in the studio and I went to bed.' She sighed. 'Then this morning we tip-toed around each other in my kitchen and it was so uncomfortable. It was like we'd lost all the camaraderie we'd built up and that's the worst thing, feeling like that... because I've enjoyed getting to know him and he's been fantastic helping with the Christmas show and... I should have thought of all those things before I asked him to kiss me.'

Still Jonah remained quiet. Emily watched him, his eyes looking into the cup of mulled wine, not meeting hers, not offering the best friend advice she so badly wanted to hear, no matter what it was... Perhaps she needed to be more direct.

'I don't know what to do,' she admitted. 'Tell me, what do I do?'

Allan went to reply but then he stopped himself. He reached for Jonah's hand and placed it on top of Emily's. 'What do *you* think she should do, Jonah?'

With accordions and trombones sounding out a noisy polka, Emily wondered if Jonah was actually going to reply at all, even now Allan had tried to force his hand. But then Jonah gave her hand a squeeze and started talking.

'Well, Em,' Jonah began. 'The way I see it, you have two options. Depending on how you want things to go.' He squeezed her hand again. 'So, if you simply want the awkwardness to go away... you either give it time, or you face it head on and you talk to him. You say it was a mistake and you both put it down to the... tonic water.'

'And if it wasn't a mistake?' Allan asked, nudging Jonah with his elbow.

'Well, if it wasn't a mistake,' Jonah said, 'then, Em, you should tell him how you feel and you should suggest... maybe... going on a date or something...' He took a breath. 'But don't put yourself under too much pressure. He's in the spotlight right now, there's lots of forces at work, and Christmas, it's an emotional time of year and you're living in the same space and...'

Allan interrupted. 'What Jonah is trying to say, very badly, is that if you only think the *timing* was off, or it's a case of needing to get your head around the situation, and not that the *whole thing* is a mistake, then talk to him, clear the air and find out how he's feeling.' Allan smiled. 'It could be that you're on the same page, you're just both too stupid to say it.'

Jonah squeezed Emily's hand again. 'What Two L's said.'

'Really?' Emily asked, wanting so much for her best friend to understand.

'I think I knew this was going to happen,' Jonah admitted. 'It was my fault. Trying to force-feed you men *I* find attractive and thinking you would too.'

'I beg your pardon!' Allan exclaimed. 'You've been picking housemates for Emily based on *your own* criteria.' He rolled his eyes. 'Did they all have a Hispanic look, tight black jeans and a snug vest like Enrique in the "Hero" video?'

Emily laughed. 'Well…'

'I'm not listening,' Jonah answered.

'No? Well, perhaps we need to buy two nutcrackers today,' Allan suggested. 'And the walnuts I'm thinking of breaking apart don't come in a net from Waitrose.'

Talk to Ray. They had both said it. *Jonah* had said it. But was it all easier said than done?

'Now,' Allan said. 'I think it's high time we all started acting like the grown-ups we're meant to be.'

'Says the man who wanted to go on the helter-skelter no more than thirty minutes ago…' Jonah said.

'Be strong, Emily,' Allan said, slurping at his mulled wine. 'Like I'm going to be over that strudel over there I can practically taste but can't try because I've not long had a German sausage.'

'Just be you, Em,' Jonah told her. 'Take it one step at a time. One conversation at a time. One—'

'Quality Street at a time… no, cancel that, that's just ridiculous. One handful of Quality Street at a time.'

'Thanks, guys,' Emily said, picking up her plastic glass.

'What?' Allan exclaimed. 'That's it? We've imparted all our worldly advice and you're not going to give us any details of this lip-locking that took place?' He inhaled, leaning over the wooden table and gazing at Emily. 'Was he good? Was his tongue like crushed velvet or sandpaper? I'm not telling you my preference…'

'Allan!' Jonah exclaimed.

'What?!' Allan replied, leaning back again. 'Just because Ray doesn't have an urban, *favela* vibe.'

Emily laughed, a soft, cosy feeling rising up in her belly. She felt happy. *Really* happy. For the first time in a long time. Contentedly she sighed, glancing around the marquee and taking in the frivolity and carefree ambience anew. Christmas was coming and she was no longer too sad to look forward to it.

Forty-Seven

MP Free Studio, Islington

'Are we good to go again? Ray?'

It was his producer, Leyland, calling through from the sound desk, wanting another take of the last song Ray thought had been pretty much perfect. His voice was hurting after two hours hard at it. But not in the scary way it had been before. This felt more like tiredness, or lack of practice, or the fact he hadn't done his vocal exercises enough. He was going to try a hot bath later, breathe in some of that steam Dr Crichton had recommended. Taking a sip from his bottle of water, he looked up from the piano keys to Leyland's face through the glass. Ray spoke into the microphone. 'Yeah, we can go again. Can you turn up my headphones a bit?'

He adjusted the headphones then put his fingers back to the piano. In between takes he'd been thinking about lyrics for another festive song for Emily's show. They currently had another three songs, together with 'O, Holy Night', but he couldn't get the tune of 'I Saw Mommy Kissing Santa Claus' out of his head. It was probably down to the fact that he had kissed Emily last night. It had been magical, *everything*, until it hadn't, and then this morning he had been scared to breathe too heavily in case he touched any part of her in the tiny kitchen. Neither of them had mentioned it at all. He needed to find a way to break the ice somehow.

'You OK, Ray?' Leyland asked again.

He nodded. 'Yeah, I'm good. Let's go again.'

He listened to the intro begin in the headphones over his ears and got ready to play. But, as he put fingers to keys, the door of the studio burst open and Ida was there, right in front of him, the angriest look on her face. Right away, his heart began to race like one of the horses his dad put bets on...

'What's going on, Ray?' Ida stalked towards the grand piano. 'I mean, what *the fuck* is going on?!'

He pulled his headphones off, dropping them to the top of the piano, then leaped up off the stool, needing to be standing tall when she got to him. She didn't just look angry. She looked crazy – eyes frenzied, hair untamed, loose-fitting cardigan way too big for her small frame. Now he was really concerned.

'Hey, Ida, what are you doing here?' He swallowed, trying to stand still and strong. He needed to be calm. In control and cool.

She struck out, thumping him hard on the shoulder. 'Don't fucking ask me that?! What else did you expect me to do? Where else could I possibly be after you do *this* to me?!'

'Leyland, can we get a couple of coffees?' Ray called. Right at that moment, a security officer barrelled through the door looking like he was in some sort of pursuit of the interloper and Ray hurried to wave him back before Ida noticed. Ida didn't deal with figures of authority particularly well. In this state, Ida didn't deal with *anyone* particularly well.

'Coffee!' Ida exploded. 'You think you can fob me off with coffee? Or those macarons and that *bitch* Deborah?! I always hated her. I don't trust her. I've never trusted her. She never listens to me. No one *ever* listens to me!'

'Hey, Ida, it's OK,' Ray said. 'Calm down.' Ordinarily, before everything, he would have held her, put a steadying hand to each shoulder, try to get her to focus, look into his eyes and take deep breaths. But he shouldn't now. *Couldn't.* Instead he just put his hands out and up, palms vertical and flat like he might be expecting a double high-five. He wasn't. He was expecting much worse.

'Don't tell me to calm down! How could you?! How could you!'

'Shall we sit down?' He looked over the room, seeking out the safest place for them to settle. The huge Christmas tree dominated the space in this more intimate of the three studios and the bright white icicles hanging from it looked like they could be sharp. All at once came a memory of a large piece of broken glass...

There were no chairs in here, only stools, one behind the drum kit and two others on the large oriental rug sat behind microphones.

'Who is she?!' Ida screamed. 'Who is this woman you're with?!' She rifled through the large bag on her shoulder, hands scrabbling, her whole body trembling.

Ray's heart jolted. What was Ida talking about? Then, striking out again, her phone was thrust into his sightline, a photo displayed on the screen. He looked at the image of him and Emily, sitting at the piano at Clean Martini. People were stood up applauding, they were under the spotlight, sitting so close on the piano stool... He began to remember exactly how he had felt at that moment. Full of heat. Filled with pride in Emily. *Beautiful Emily.* He hurriedly regrouped and gave Ida a smile.

'Is this what's getting you so upset?' Ray asked. 'A photo of me with someone I plucked from the audience?' Where had she even got the photo from? Was this making small column inches somewhere? Or had Ida been there that night? No, he didn't believe that. If Ida had been there that night, she wouldn't have been able to stop herself from making a scene at the bar, like she was making a scene now.

'Someone you plucked from the audience?' Ida's voice had thankfully dropped a degree of unhinged. He was saying the right things. He just needed to keep that up.

'Yes, Ida, I used to work there, remember? They asked me to play something festive for them. This girl... this woman... she just came right up with me,' he explained. 'I think she was the daughter of the owner or something, I don't know, we just played a song and everyone liked it and... that's it.'

'That's it,' Ida repeated. Her shoulders were rolling forward now, the anger dying down, the dangerous, ugly force diminishing before his eyes. But he knew from experience that could change in an instant.

'Who took this photo?' Ray asked as Ida dropped the phone away from his view.

'I... no one...' Ida stopped talking, then fixed him with a

stare. 'So, you don't know her? You don't know this woman at all?'

Ray shook his head. 'No, Ida. I don't even know her name.' What was he saying? If he fed her too many untruths and she found out he was lying later then who knew what would happen?

'Have you thought about what I said?' Ida asked, her voice sweet now, heading towards calm. She reached out and began running her hands over the sleeves of his shirt, cupping his biceps and moving her body closer. She might be petite but there was strength there.

'Ida,' Ray said, stepping back out of reach. He had to make his point loud and clear now. 'This is never going to work. Ida, we tried. It didn't happen. And you know I can't do it anymore. You know why.' He had to be firm. Straight-talking but not angry or harsh. Simply stating the facts to make her realise – again – that there was no going back.

'I know you say that, Ray, but we have worked through things before, haven't we? You know we have. And things were good before, weren't they? They can be good again, I know they can.' She was moving closer to him again using that expression she had always used to try to make him see her how he had first seen her when they'd met. Except he really didn't see her like that anymore. He hadn't seen her that way for a long time. How could he?

'Ida, I have to work right now,' he told her. He spread his arms wide, to distract her as well as to highlight the setting they were in. The music studio, the large, black, glossy piano, the other instruments and the small group of people watching them from behind the glass.

'You're making new music,' Ida said, twirling around in a dance.

Ray watched her, immediately perturbed. He knew he hadn't seen her for a while before all this press attention, but she looked as manic now as she had ever been. Perhaps he needed to do more. But it was hard. And he definitely didn't want her to come to depend on him again.

'I was always your muse, wasn't I?' Ida said, laughing as she danced across the wooden floor. 'I could be your muse again. I would sit, really *really* quietly, listening and I could give you inspiration for new songs that everyone will love.' She smiled, wide, unnatural. 'They can be about us.'

'Ida, have you spoken to your mother recently?' He had to ask, despite knowing it was usually awkward territory. Ida wasn't his responsibility. Her mother should be stepping up. He knew Victoria probably didn't know the extent of Ida's issues but maybe it was time she did.

Ida immediately snapped to attention, her expression changing from joyful to wretched as she rounded on him. 'Why would you ask that? Why would I have spoken to *that woman*? She's far, far away in Leeds living her perfect little suburban life without me. Don't you remember? Don't *you* listen to me either now? Just like all the rest!' She was biting her mouth now, her bottom teeth grazing the flesh on her lower lip.

'Why not give her a call?' Ray suggested as casually as he was able. He used a faint shuffled sidestep to the right, kind of like a move a sheepdog would make, to try to corral Ida towards the door.

'Why not give her a call,' Ida mimicked, her face screwed up again. Another mask. A mask he'd seen often.

'Ida, please,' Ray said. 'You need someone. You need...' He so desperately wanted to say the word 'help', but he knew that wasn't the best word for this situation.

'I need *you*, Ray. I've only ever needed you.' She stepped towards him quickly, arms open. For a moment she again looked so weak and vulnerable. He didn't want her to be living this life. He wanted her to be happy. Truly happy. But it was impossible for him to achieve. Because Ida wasn't at that stage yet. She needed to reach acceptance of what had gone before, and her turning up at the studio, knowing he was going to be here, holding a photo of him and Emily at Clean Martini, were not signs that acceptance was even close.

'Ida, you need to go now,' Ray said as kindly as he could. He raised his head a fraction, caught the eye of the security guard who was looking through the small glass panel of the door. 'I don't have that long left of my studio time today and you know how it is. I always overrun and...'

Ray didn't even see it coming. Before he could say another word, before he even had a chance to think another thought, or take another step, Ida had snapped her fist out and punched him square on the jaw. The pain was instant, and his reaction was too. He did nothing. He stood his ground. He watched her eyes, dark, rage-filled, then in a matter of milliseconds the tide turned, the regret, the pain and sadness.

The security guard was already through the door and Ray knew there was nothing left for him to do right now.

'Ray, I... didn't mean that. I don't know why I did that. You know I don't know why I did that. It's OK. It's OK. It will be OK, won't it? Won't it, Ray?'

The security man took hold of Ida's arm and she tried desperately to pull it back, flapping her limbs like that frightened, damaged bird from her painting. Ray wanted to tell the guy to be gentle, but he couldn't show any affection to her now. Not now. It was all far too late…

'Ray! Don't let them take me away!' Ida shouted as she was marched to the exit. 'Ray! I love you! I still love you! Even after everything! I love you, Ray! Ray, you know I love you, don't you? Ray!'

He closed his eyes, fingertips on his sore jaw, unable to watch another second. Time was rewinding in his mind. He was somewhere else, somewhere darker, somewhere he thought he might never escape from…

'Ray, are you OK?' Leyland asked, appearing at the door.

He opened his eyes and took a breath, his throat tightening. 'Yeah,' he answered, voice ragged.

'Listen, Ray, we all saw what happened in here.'

'Nothing happened in here,' Ray said quickly.

'She's the one in the media, isn't she?' Leyland continued. 'Talking to the press.'

'Ley, listen to me, please,' Ray begged. 'Nothing happened in here, OK? Just leave it. Please, just leave it.'

'But—'

'Let's break for a coffee,' Ray said. 'I'll go out and get coffee.'

'Sam can get the coffees,' Leyland replied. 'You come and have a seat. We can listen back to…'

Ray was already shrugging his shoulders into his coat. He really needed some air.

Forty-Eight

Emily hit the glockenspiel with force and closed her eyes. She was sitting on the roof terrace under one of the patio heaters, coat on, hat on, but enjoying the strong winter sunshine that was currently warming up the outside space. Was that the right note? She hit play on Spotify and listened again to the chorus of 'Last Christmas' by Wham. That song had been a suggestion for her show from Allan and Jonah as they walked around Hyde Park earlier. In fact, when the two guys had both said the song title in unison, they had shared a look of togetherness that had warmed Emily's heart. She was so happy her best friend had found someone he was truly connected with in every way. And it *really wasn't* that show of deep affection that had sent her scurrying to one of her favourite vintage boutiques after she'd left the happy couple.

The amber dress had spoken to her through the window. It had been pinned to a coffee-coloured mannequin in the front display, it's light gauzy material completely inappropriate for the current London temperatures, but the shade had reminded her of Ray's eyes. Before she had time to dwell on the significance of that, her boots were on the steps to the entrance and she was pushing at the door. It was knee-length, cut on the bias and it was as if it had been fashioned for her and her alone. Looking in the mirror she had turned one way and then the other, and felt like a princess. It was totally her style, not elaborate, simple in its structure, pure, gentle elegance…

She hit another note on the glockenspiel and cringed. That definitely didn't sound right. Were her children going to be able to play along to this? Granted, they were all more talented with the instrument than she was…

'What are you doing? Is it a pigeon deterrent?'

Emily grabbed her chest, the stick she was holding jabbing the skin. 'Gosh, Ray, I didn't hear you.'

'I got that,' he replied. 'You were making noise.'

'Music,' Emily interrupted. 'Don't turn into my mother and slate my abilities.'

'I apologise,' Ray replied. 'You're absolutely right.' He sat down next to her and instantly she was back to last night and the slightly more intimate setting – stars above, fairy lights, rolling around on the floor…

'What are you working on?' he asked her, picking up the piece of paper she was making notes on. '"Last Christmas"?'

'It was Jonah and Allan's idea, but a good one I think. The children definitely know this song. I'm just trying to come up with some new words and the notes for a glockenspiel instrumental.'

'What have you got so far?' Ray asked, holding the notepaper in the space between them.

'I think I've got a couple of lines nailed,' Emily answered.

'Sing it to me,' Ray told her.

'Oh… well… I…' Why was she hesitating *again*? Maybe because although she had sung to him plenty of times, the other times had been mainly lyrics of his creation and none of those times had been after kissing him like they were the uplifting finale of a Lifetime movie…

Ray picked up her phone and she watched him move the cursor on the app back to the beginning of the song. The opening bars began to play and Emily cleared her throat in preparation, before starting to sing.

'Last Christmas. You let me cook. Then on Boxing Day. I read a book.'

Emily stopped singing and smiled, her cheeks blushing. 'That's all I've got at the moment.'

'O–K,' Ray replied.

'Gosh, it's rubbish, isn't it? I mean it's supposed to *mean* something and it doesn't mean anything and I don't know where to go from "cook" or "book" and then it's got to have at least three mentions of God according to Susan and I tried to go from "book" to "the Bible", but it doesn't rhyme and I can't *make it* rhyme or fit with the song.' Emily let out a screech of annoyance and put her head in her hands.

'More God lines,' Ray said, nodding.

'And more meaning. And super-funny. But nothing rude. My children have to know what they're singing about… but it's OK to throw a few jokes the parents will get in there. I've done that in the script.' And the play was almost complete. She very nearly had a whole performance based around a modern-day version of the Nativity incorporating some of the suggestions her Year Six pupils had made. She still hadn't quite worked out what Rashid and Frema were going to do. She didn't want to offend anyone and these days that was a near-on impossible task. Frema had ideas of a dual costume, one side representing the Jewish faith, the other Christianity. When the girl had pitched that idea, high on her 'What Christmas Means to Me' competition win, she had turned one way, then the other, first speaking Hebrew, then transforming seamlessly into a vicar...

'OK,' Ray said, moving the cursor on her phone again.

The intro played and then Ray started to sing.

'Last Christmas. You... gave me some myrrh. But on Boxing Day, you gave it to her.' He tapped his fingers to his head as the music continued. 'This year. To not break my heart. I'll give it to... Baby Jesus.'

Emily's mouth dropped open. 'How do you do that? Seriously, how? I've been sitting here for over an hour now and I came up with "book" and "cook".'

Ray smiled. 'Shall I write the words down?'

'Yes,' Emily said, passing him a pen. 'Yes please.'

The music was carrying on. George Michael crooning away and those jingling bells speaking of sleighs and snow rides. It was so easy to imagine sitting underneath a fleecy blanket with Ray, dashing through the snow while his lips worked over hers... She shook her head and spoke quickly. 'How was your time in the studio?'

'It was good,' Ray said, nodding. 'We laid down two whole tracks. The record is really starting to shape up.'

Ray tried to concentrate on writing the lyrics he had just made up as the Christmas song continued to play. He wasn't going to tell Emily that Ida had burst into his session and rattled him so much that he hadn't been able to carry on. He'd had three sweet coffees after the interruption, but his mood had been killed and his voice was aching no matter how much he'd tried to relax it. Dr Crichton's warnings about carrying on singing had been ringing in his ears. He really did need that bath for some hot mist therapy.

'Listen, Ray…' Emily began.

And he knew exactly what she was going to say next. She was going to try and talk about last night. Here was the moment where the only good thing that was happening in his life right now disappeared into the air like smoke from the chimney stacks he could see from here, stretching across the city.

'How was your day with Jonah and Allan?' he interrupted. He couldn't bear to hear it. Not yet. He wanted to listen to Emily's sweet voice, talking about her day, describing something much better than fighting in a music studio.

'It was good,' Emily answered with a smile. 'The Hyde Park Winter Wonderland is always amazing. Every year we go there thinking we've seen it all and there's always something new to surprise us or make us laugh.' She smiled even more broadly then. 'This year we laughed when Allan got stuck on the helter-skelter. His jeans got caught beneath the wood somehow and he was suspended there, halfway round a bend, calling out "999 denim malfunction".'

Ray laughed. 'He couldn't just say "help"?' There was that word again.

'You've met Allan,' Emily said.

'You're right,' Ray answered. 'I've met Allan. I can actually hear him saying "denim malfunction".'

The song playing on Emily's phone came to an end and a Bing Crosby number kicked in. Immediately it intensified the mood and Ray knew Emily was going to use this opportunity to tell him that last night was all a mistake and she had never regretted something more in her entire life.

'Listen,' he said quickly, turning a little on the wooden seating and facing her. 'Are you…' He paused before continuing. 'Are you doing anything tonight?'

'Well,' Emily said. 'I don't have any plans to go out if that's what you mean. I was going to try and get some more of this song worked out but…' She clapped her hands to her face. 'Gosh, sorry, you need the apartment for something. To invite someone over. That's fine! Absolutely fine! I can go out. Jonah will be working, but Allan might want someone to watch re-runs of *Vera* with.'

'It's not that,' Ray said. 'I don't want to invite anyone over at all.' He took a breath. 'I was thinking… maybe… that I could take you out.' God, his heart was beating a rhythm harder and faster than any session drummer he'd ever worked with.

'Oh, I see.'

'Hey, listen, I know that you're probably thinking that last night was a bad move and a big mistake because, let's face it, why *wouldn't* you think that?' He sighed. Was he even in with a shot here? 'And, Emily, I know I'm not someone your friends, or your parents, or, in particular, Jayden's dad have warmed to, but the fact is… Emily, I really like you. And I really like spending time with you. And, for me anyway, I feel this connection with you that I've never felt with anyone else before and—'

'I'd love to go out with you,' Emily responded.

It felt like a doctor had taken off a clamp that had been restricting his blood flow. Suddenly Ray's entire body was flooding with heat and his insides were performing all kinds of street-dance. 'You would? Wow, I... really wasn't expecting that.'

Emily laughed. 'But you asked anyway.'

Ray shrugged. 'I figured that when you've got nothing to lose you only have everything to gain.'

'Well,' Emily began, 'you might also be surprised that I wasn't going to say that I thought it was all a big mistake.'

'No?'

'No, I was going to say that I wasn't sure what it was or where I currently am with my feelings... but that the one thing I do know is that life has become a little bit better since you've moved in.'

'It has?' Ray said, looking at her and taking in her beautiful petite features, her fringe falling over her forehead, her cheeks pink from the heat lamps.

'The apartment is warm again,' Emily said, then quickly followed it up. 'And I don't just mean the heating.' She laughed, sounding a little nervous. 'What I mean is, it's nice to have someone to share things with again.'

'Yeah,' Ray agreed. 'I like that too.'

'So,' Emily said, eyes bright. 'Where are we going tonight?'

'Ah,' Ray said. 'You'll have to wait and see.'

Forty-Nine

Leadenhall Market

Emily wasn't going to lie. It felt a little weird. *She was going on a date.* This was not two platonic flatmates sharing an evening together because they didn't have another offer. This was two people *going on a date.* They might not know exactly where their feelings were at, but there *were* feelings. And they were definitely of the non-platonic kind...

'Wow!' Emily exclaimed as they stopped at the entrance to Leadenhall Market. There were cobbles on the ground and the air of a Victorian Christmas all around. A gigantic Christmas tree stood at the far end of the old-fashioned arcade, reaching almost the full height, top branches grazing the decorative glass roof. 'I thought the pub we came from looked like something from Diagon Alley but this...'

'Ah,' Ray said, standing close to her, so close she could feel the warmth of his breath. 'This market was actually used in one of the Harry Potter films *as* Diagon Alley.'

'No!' Emily exclaimed. 'Really?'

'Really,' Ray replied.

She took in the painted red and gold signage of well-known shops and restaurants, all in keeping with the age of everything around it. Ancient columns, iron lanterns, delicate carvings, it really was like stepping back in time. As in the pub earlier. They had wound down a dark narrow alley and Emily had wondered where on earth it was leading, until a building that wouldn't have looked out of place on the edge of a stormy Cornish cliff-edge had appeared. It had been all deep-coloured wood décor and mysterious corners, serving ale out of wooden barrels.

'I've never been here,' Emily breathed. 'It's so beautiful. Like another world.' She wanted to step onto the cobbles and marvel at every little nuance. It was all so intricate, so detailed, like some kind of working museum. And who would have thought it? All this, here in the heart of London's financial district.

'Want to know where we're going to eat?'

She wasn't sure Ray could take her anywhere better than here. She'd be happy with another drink, in the midst of all this, sitting outside but inside, beneath heat lamps that were omitting a red glow over patrons sipping wine and nibbling on olives.

'I...' she began.

'Right over there,' Ray said, pointing to an establishment mere strides away.

Emily read the sign and smiled with excitement. 'Cheese! We're going to eat cheese?!'

Ray laughed and nodded. 'We're going to eat cheese. Is that alright? I've booked a tasting for us. Ten different types of cheese to sample. You can choose what styles you want to try and I don't think it's like a wine tasting. I think you actually taste it and eat it rather than push it round your mouth and spit it out.'

'I'd never, ever spit cheese out, no matter what anyone said,' Emily told him.

'That's good to know,' Ray replied. 'So, shall we go and sit down?'

Emily found his hand and held it in hers. Those long fingers, his large, strong palms felt so good to touch. 'Ray, this is just so... me. I really *really* can't wait.'

They had been shown to their table outside Cheese at Leadenhall, not at the very edge of the seating where the world – including fans or paparazzi – could see them but tucked in the corner. Yet here they were still very much able to look out onto the thoroughfare of the arcade. It was private and intimate, but with a great view of the goings-on and the plump Christmas tree twinkling with a myriad of traditional dressings. And now the cheese had arrived. Gorgeous portions of internationally produced dairy products rested on black slates and each serving was explained to them by their host. They'd also been given a list of their choices to refer to as they sampled. But it wasn't the cheese Ray was really excited to look at. Emily had taken off her coat and revealed the most perfect dress he'd ever seen. He was no women's fashion expert, but the colour made her skin glow and her eyes come alive. It wasn't tight, it didn't cling to her curves, it just enhanced her pure, beautiful simplicity. It was 100 per cent giving him the Emily Parker that so enchanted him.

'You should have wine,' Emily remarked, taking a sip of her tonic water.

'Why?' Ray asked.

'Because red wine goes beautifully with cheese.' Emily sighed a little sadly.

'Well,' Ray said. 'I've heard real cheese lovers think only more cheese goes beautifully with cheese.'

She laughed then, smiling at him.

'What?' he asked, enjoying her delight.

'Thank you,' she said. 'For the show of solidarity. But, I don't want you to think that you have to be tee-total because I am.'

'I don't think that,' Ray replied. 'Really.' He lowered his voice to a near-whisper. 'Don't tell anyone but I'm enjoying finding out what life is like without any enhancement. And, apparently, as well as wrecking your liver, too much alcohol can also dull your taste buds. Did you know that?'

'God!' Emily exclaimed. 'No, I didn't know that. How awful!' She sat forward on her chair, eager. 'Can we start trying the cheese now?'

Ray laughed at her enthusiasm and watched her cut a small section of the first cheese. The list said it was Bath Soft Cheese. She placed the morsel into her mouth and closed her eyes.

'Oh goodness!' Emily remarked, mouth moving slowly. 'This is so good. I mean, it's really, *really* good.'

Ray swallowed, watching her lips taking their time to completely savour every second of the cheese-eating. It was making him a little hot under the collar if he was honest...

'You aren't trying it,' Emily admonished.

Her eyes were open now and she was looking straight at him. 'Sorry,' he answered. 'I was enjoying watching you enjoy it.' *Probably a little too much*. He cut himself a piece and put it in his mouth. Wow, Emily was right, it really was a divine taste.

'Isn't it amazing?' Emily asked, cutting herself another section.

'It's amazing,' he agreed. 'It's soft and... creamy and so light on your tongue.'

'So,' Emily said, grinning. 'You're a cheese lover too.'

He shook his head. 'I like it, but I don't know much about it if I'm honest. Cheddar is still where it's at, right?'

Emily laughed. 'There are many kinds of cheddar.'

'The yellow one,' Ray said. 'Goes good on a sandwich.'

Emily smiled. 'We always had a wide variety of cheese at Christmas. Maybe that's where I get the love of it from.' She popped another piece into her mouth. 'So, I know you're not a fan of the whole Christmas thing but, when you were little, before you lost your mum, how did you celebrate it? What sort of things did you do?'

He picked up his pint of lime and lemonade and took a sip before answering. 'Well... usually my dad would leave buying a tree to the absolute last minute.' He adopted a thick, breathy Cockney accent. 'That's when you get the best bargains, son, never mind late-night shopping, this is never-too-late shopping.'

Emily laughed, taking a sip of her drink.

'And every tree he got was always miles too tall, or miles too wide, with a bare trunk and missing boughs or some other tree defect. But he enjoyed getting it on the cheap and my mum used to enjoy moaning about it. But she'd be smiling as she grumbled about it, knowing, no matter what, it was going to be exactly the same the next year.' His mum had generally seemed happy at Christmas time. Maybe because his dad had some time away from work and they were together as a family. Plus, everyone started drinking at breakfast time on Christmas Day, didn't they? Maybe, for her, it was a day off having to hide things. And maybe the reason he didn't like it now, was because, without her, the happier, more smiley version of her, Christmas didn't feel anything like it used to.

'Well,' Emily said, 'the Parker family always had a real tree and we always got it early. Another one of my parents' status things. Get the tree as early as possible to have the best pick *and* to ensure that every December drinks party they hosted was accompanied by the scent of pine and spruce. *And* all matching decorations, naturally, whatever colour was in that season.'

'What's in season this season?' Ray asked.

'I have absolutely no idea,' Emily answered. 'And no desire to know either. I got all my decorations from charity shops or fairs I went to. Simon…'

She stopped talking and dipped her head as if suddenly finding her slate of cheese needed closer inspection. 'Sorry,' she whispered.

'Hey,' Ray said, leaning forward a little and, putting his index finger to her chin, he encouraged it upwards. 'What are you apologising for?'

'I don't want to keep bringing him up.'

'Emily, Simon, he was a huge part of your life. You loved him. I think it would be crazy if you *didn't* bring him up.'

'Really?' Emily said, looking back him.

'Of course,' Ray answered. 'People we care about aren't suddenly erased when they leave us.' He sighed. 'In fact, the memories get stronger and more vivid. Especially the good ones.' He smiled. 'For the love of God, tell me Simon liked cheese the way you do.'

'Ah,' Emily began, holding a finger in the air. 'He actually liked cheese the way you do. Plain cheddar on white sliced bread, toasted under the grill.'

'Now you're talking,' Ray answered. 'Good on him.'

Emily shook her head, but her mouth was upturned in a beam. 'You are both cheese heathens. How did that happen to me?'

'What's the next cheese?' Ray asked. 'I'm prepared to be educated.'

'Oh,' Emily said, looking to her piece of paper. 'It's called Golden Cross. I think this is the one the lady said was goaty and grassy and actually rolled in ash.'

'I remember she said the texture of that one was like eating ice cream,' Ray said. 'I'm going to think of it that way.'

Before he could cut himself a sliver of the cheese, Emily reached out and touched his hand. Her small fingers rested on his and he looked over at her. Her auburn hair loose and tumbling down to lightly kiss her shoulders, her blue eyes full of intent…

'Thank you, Ray, for bringing me here. It's the most wonderful place for a first date.'

He moved his hand and cupped hers, gently holding on, her fingers so small compared to his. 'Is this what this is? A first date?' he asked. 'Because, for me, the kiss on the roof terrace… well, that felt a lot like a date to me.'

Emily smiled. 'A second date already. Wow. Who knows, by the time Christmas Day gets here we might be—'

'Proficient on the recorder and glockenspiel,' he interrupted.

'Absolutely,' Emily agreed, nodding. 'Or signed up to write songs for the next Broadway extravaganza.' She gasped. 'Of course, you could actually do that, because you have all the songwriting talent.'

All at once Ray was distracted. Despite their slightly guarded position at the back of the outside seating, he had noticed a group of people gathering in the arcade, mobile phones trained in their direction. He dropped his head a little lower, even though he knew it was no doubt too little too late. He was thankful that Emily had her back to them. At least, hopefully, she wasn't going to be brought into the middle of his chaos just yet...

'Are you OK?' Emily asked him softly.

'Yeah,' he answered, forcing a smile.

'What is it?' Emily wanted to know. She made to turn around, to look where he had looked and he caught her hand in his, holding it tight.

'Don't,' he begged. 'Just... ignore them.' He took a breath. 'Just keep looking at me.' He squeezed gently, protective. 'I like you looking at me.'

'Is it journalists?' she whispered, keeping her gaze on his.

'Not yet,' he answered. 'It's just people. Being people. It's OK.'

'It's not OK,' Emily responded. 'Really, it isn't.'

'Hey,' Ray said, rubbing his thumb over her fingers. 'No one is going to spoil our kind-of second date, right?'

She didn't say anything, and he knew how she must be feeling. Suddenly under scrutiny. Spied on.

'No,' Emily said with a determined nod. 'No one is going to spoil our second date.'

'It could be worse,' Ray remarked. 'They could be a lot closer and they could be asking me to sing.'

He should tell Emily, here, now, about the issue with his voice, about his fear of having the operation. But, in a corner of his mind was the reminder of everything that had happened with Ida. And he *so* didn't want to appear weak to Emily. Their friendship that had happened so unexpectedly, this move forward to something that could be more than friendship, was his chance for a new beginning. He so longed to try and find the person he used to be before he'd got into a relationship that had altered his perception of everything. And Emily – beautiful, sweet, strong and determined Emily – she already had her hands so full with everything going on in her world… he really didn't want to end up letting her down. Not now, on this second date, or, in fact, ever.

'Well,' Emily said, 'let's taste the cheese before they do.' She picked up a sliver of the Golden Cross and put it in her mouth. Ray watched again as she closed her eyes and the sensations hit her taste buds.

'Good?' he asked, already sensing the answer that was coming.

'So good,' she breathed. 'Like… the sweetest savoury cream and sunshine and sky…' Her eyes opened and she gasped, her head turning to face the end of the arcade and the archway they'd walked through.

'Oh goodness, Ray, look!' Emily exclaimed, completely animated in her seat. 'It's snowing.'

His gaze followed hers then and he watched the lightest specks of snow begin to gently float down from the dark sky. Looking back to Emily he saw the complete joy in her expression, like this weather change was a precious gift that had relegated curious members of the public to way down the pecking order and enhanced her everything.

'You like snow,' Ray said, making it a statement rather than a question.

'I *love* snow,' she answered. 'Can we go for a walk after here? It might have settled by then.'

He wasn't going to tell her that it really didn't look like it was going to amount to anything significant; in fact, seeing her joy in it, he was mentally willing the snowfall to speed up and thicken.

'Absolutely,' he answered. 'Maybe there'll be enough to make a snowman.'

'Wow,' Emily said, smiling at him. 'The man who doesn't like Christmas would help me make a snowman?'

He nodded, suddenly overwhelmed with sentimentality. 'Sure. I'll even ask here if they can give us a carrot for his nose.'

Fifty

London Bridge

The snowfall *had* sped up and the flakes were now super-sized, but the pavements were damp and there was little chance of there being more than a crisp topping on the ground unless things changed overnight. Ray and Emily walked across London Bridge, taking in the usual sparkling lights of England's capital, coupled with all the festive enhancements. Colour shone across the city – reds, electric blues, gold and bright greens – in December celebration mode, the vibe laid-back, but also buoyant, exciting and expectant.

'I do love London at night,' Emily said, a shiver running through her as she delved her hands a little deeper into her pockets. 'There's no other city quite like it.'

'Have you been to many other cities?' Ray asked.

'Edinburgh. Edinburgh was lovely,' Emily said. 'Paris. Paris was beautiful. We went in the summer. It was chic and the Eiffel Tower was even more astonishing than it looks on the internet. I didn't think I was going to make it all the way to the top, but I did and it was so worth it.'

'You went there with Simon?' Ray inquired.

'No,' Emily replied. 'I went there with my mother. It was years ago. One of her friends dropped out of what was meant to be a gastronomy experience, so I stepped in. She didn't climb the Eiffel Tower – she nibbled at *tarte flambé* and guzzled *vin rouge*. I didn't have long enough to see everything I really wanted to see.'

'What would you have liked to see?'

Emily stopped walking and leaned on the bridge's wall, overlooking the dark, fast-flowing Thames. 'All of it,' she answered. 'The Arc De Triomphe. The Louvre. The Sacré Coeur. Notre Dame.' She sighed. 'That was so sad. To see it destroyed by the fire.'

'I saw Notre Dame,' Ray said, standing next to her. 'I went there. I actually wrote a song outside, sitting on the floor, surrounded by pigeons.'

'Really?' Emily said, turning to look at him.

'Yeah,' he replied. 'Within a few minutes someone took me for a busker and gave me five Euro.' He smiled at her. 'True story. And rather ironic given I spent a long time busking in London. And it always took until lunchtime for more than the odd 50p to arrive.'

'Was Notre Dame amazing?' Emily asked him, nestling a little into his side.

He nodded. 'Yeah, it really was. I mean, London has more than its fair share of spectacular buildings, but there was something about Notre Dame from the second I walked in. I don't know. It was like… spiritual or something. Nothing like where I'm from. I guess you can take the boy out of New North Road but...'

Emily took a breath of the snowy air and relished the flakes hitting her cheeks, some touching her lips. 'Did you go to Paris with Ida?'

She looked away from the river, facing Ray fully. He hadn't answered immediately and she wondered if she should have brought Ida up. He might have said he was cool with her talking about Simon, but maybe he didn't want to talk about the woman who had ensured his face was all over the newspapers.

'Yeah,' he replied. 'Ida took part in an exhibition. It was a big thing for her. She'd never exhibited outside of the UK before.'

'Wow, that sounds amazing. So, she's an artist?'

'Yeah,' he answered.

'She must be really good to be showing her work somewhere like Paris.'

Ray nodded. 'She's very talented. She just...' He stopped talking then. 'I don't know. She seems to have some sort of self-destruct mode she switches into even when things are going well for her.'

This was as much as she had been able to get from him about his ex-girlfriend. Emily swallowed. 'Are things not going so well for her now?'

'I don't know,' Ray said shaking his head. 'And I don't want to know.' He took a harried breath. 'I can't know.'

She turned back to the river. She shouldn't have pushed. It was still none of her business. They were on a second date, taking things slowly and she was being way too nosy.

'I'm sorry,' Ray apologised. 'I'm sorry if that came out

harsh.' He took another breath. 'Ida, she is… that is… it's… complicated… and that's why I haven't been able to say too much in answer to her stories in the press.' He let go of a heavy sigh. 'It wasn't an easy relationship in the end.'

Emily observed his expression. It was almost like he was somewhere else. The snow was falling into his dark hair and she found herself wanting to reach up and touch it, run her fingers through it, coax out the flakes, then trail a hand to the line of his jaw…

'I don't know, maybe one day, I'll be able to use my experience to write a kick-ass number one song and get it all out of my system.' He smiled, seemingly back in the moment again.

'Ah yes,' Emily answered. 'I need to be careful, don't I? Writers always use their experiences for novels or songs or poems.'

'Only the really, really good stuff,' Ray told her. 'Or the really, really bad stuff.'

'Then I should keep on going with my mediocre and I'll be fine,' she said with a smile.

'What?' Ray asked, pulling his hand from his pocket and touching her arm. 'Emily, there's nothing about you that's mediocre. That wasn't what I meant at all.'

She felt suddenly much warmer, her cheeks igniting, and she was unable to look him in the eye.

'If you want me to be honest, I think you've spent a lifetime feeling like you're underachieving because of how your parents treat you. They look down on anyone who isn't like them. And you're not like them. And, believe me, that's a good thing.' His voice softened, slowed, deepened. 'Emily, you're the most wonderful, the most kind, most giving, genuine, honest person I've ever met.'

She gave an awkward half-laugh. She didn't know how to respond. She had never been comfortable taking compliments. And then Ray's finger was under her chin again, cajoling her face upwards, forcing her to draw her gaze away from the top buttons of her coat and focus entirely on him.

'You're beautiful, Emily,' he continued, his voice a little rough now, his finger delicately brushing the slight bump on her chin she didn't like too much. 'Outside and in. I don't know how meeting a hedgehog and spending a night in a shed led me to finding you, but my God, I can't imagine any place I'd rather be right now.'

He palmed her cheek then, his breathing intensifying, his unique eyes holding hers captive like time was standing still.

'Emily, whatever this is between us. Whatever happens next. I want you to know that this time with you... well...' The briefest of pauses seemed to hang in the air for an age until he carried on. 'I don't remember a time when I was happier.' He drew in a long, latent breath. 'I really mean that.'

'Oh, Ray, I feel all that too,' she said as tears began to fall from her eyes. She could sense his total sincerity in his touch as well as in his words.

'Hey,' he said. 'No tears.' His lips met her cheeks, one by one, gently pressing the saltwater off her skin. She closed her eyes, relishing the feather-light feel of his mouth as he gently brushed her fringe with his forefingers, looking at her as if taking her in anew. Emily knew what she wanted from this moment, without any doubt. She leaned forward, pressing her mouth to his, connecting their lips and drawing their bodies together. All the emotions she'd felt on the roof terrace came rushing back like the most tumultuous of snowstorms, but it was a storm she was welcoming and one she was completely and utterly in charge of. Ray deepened their connection, backing her up to the bridge's wall, one arm around her body, protective. He tasted of cheese and snowflakes and masculinity and it was divine. It was the most heavenly of kisses and Emily began to wish she could stop the world, make this evening stretch as long as possible, delay tomorrow coming around.

Ray finally edged back, breaking their lips, but keeping his eyes locked on hers. And Emily carried on looking too. He'd said she was kind and giving and honest. He'd said she was beautiful. She was also not going to be fearful of this connection she was enjoying so very much. None of the circumstances were perhaps perfect, but life *wasn't* perfect. And she knew that more than most.

'God,' he breathed. 'You really are amazing, Emily Parker.'

'I know,' she answered as more soft snowflakes fluttered through her vision. 'But you should also know that you're pretty special too, Ray Stone.'

He wrapped his arms around her then, so warm and solid and utterly sexy and she held on tight and watched the glowing lights of a riverboat pass on the water beneath them.

Fifty-One

'Listen, Jonah, I've got to go. There was a delay on the Tube and I only have ten minutes before the whistle goes and I really need a coffee before I get into it with Rashid's parents this morning.' Emily adjusted the phone she had clamped to her ear. She was out of breath from powering from the Tube station in one of the pairs of vintage boots she hadn't worn before. Big mistake. They were chewing up her heels like a dog gnawing at rawhide.

'Wait! You can't leave it there,' Jonah told her. 'So you kissed on London Bridge and it was all snowy and romantic and then...'

'Well, then someone came and asked for Ray's autograph and a selfie and I wondered how long they had actually been there and whether they'd been watching us, you know, kissing.'

'Oh, Emily,' Jonah said with a slight laugh. 'Welcome to the celebrity life. No more buying discounted tins in the supermarket. Your basket is going to be heavily scrutinised from now on and probably posted on Instagram.'

'Don't say that.'

'Just warning you.'

'Right, I'm going now.' She began walking down the path leading to the school building, gingerly stepping as she saw the weekend flurry of light snowfall had crisped up after the minus temperatures of the previous night.

'Wait, hang on, we haven't got to the bit when you and Ray got back to the flat.'

'Jonah, I have to go,' Emily reminded.

'Emily! Did you...'

'For Christ's sake, Emily!' It was Allan's voice now. 'Did you *do it*?! We want to know if you *did it!*'

'Jonah! Am I on speakerphone? Please tell me you're not in the hotel or Allan's office or anywhere public!'

'She did it!' Allan exclaimed hysterically. 'They did it!'

'We did not,' Emily replied quickly. 'Not that it's any of your business, but Ray is a perfect gentleman. We got in and we worked on the songs for the school show and then we went to bed... alone... in separate rooms.'

'Oh no!' Allan exclaimed. 'How utterly boring!'

'Well, I think it's very sensible and grown up,' Jonah replied to Allan not Emily.

'Like I said,' Allan replied. 'Boring!'

'Listen, you two can talk all you want about how boring we are *between yourselves*. I've got a meeting to get to.'

'Hang on! Emily, wait! The reason I phoned was because we're getting tickets for the Christmas show at the Albert Hall, you know, like we always do. And we wanted to know if we should get three or, you know... four?'

Emily stopped walking and thought for a moment. Ray didn't really like Christmas, but the night of songs at one of London's most iconic venues always gave her goose bumps and never failed to get her in the festive spirit. 'Get four,' she answered. If Ray didn't want to come along then maybe she could ask Dennis... or her mother... or Dennis's mother...

'Maybe you will have done it by then!' Allan shouted.

'I really am going now,' Emily replied.

She ended the call and hurried towards the school building.

'Are you sure you wouldn't like a cup of tea or coffee, Mr and Mrs Dar?'

Susan Clark had asked this question three times since the Dars had arrived in her office. She had also talked about the snowfall – more was expected, apparently – *The X Factor*, and the hearty shepherd's pie she was making for dinner that night. Emily could see that, like her, the Dars wanted to get this meeting over with. The point needed to be got to.

'We are sure,' Ahmer Dar responded for him and apparently his wife. 'We aren't quite sure what this meeting is about. I mean, I thought, that is, we *both* thought that we had sorted out this issue with the alcohol from the shop. I went to see the owner, I explained that Rashid had been coerced by this older girl from the senior school and—'

'Well,' Emily interrupted, 'I'm afraid it goes a little bit deeper than that. Which is why we've asked you to come in today.' Emily looked to Susan, waiting for her to continue. But the Head simply sat there, eyes on the open folder on her desk. Emily, sat next to Mr and Mrs Dar, suddenly felt the weight of both their gazes. This wasn't the plan. In her talk with Susan, before the Dars arrived, the headteacher had insisted *she* would be taking the lead. What was she supposed to do now? Susan finally raised her head and made big, almost pleading eyes at Emily.

'Right, well, if one of you could tell us what's going on that would be helpful,' Ahmer said.

Emily sat a little forward on her chair. 'Rashid was actually taking the alcohol, sweets and other items from the shop to repay Rhiannon for work she had done for him.'

'What?' Ahmer gasped.

'What do you mean work?' Mrs Dar asked.

Emily looked to Susan. Was the Head really going to leave all this to her? Then again, perhaps this was a test. To see how she would cope taking meetings such as this if she was made deputy.

'Rhiannon was helping Rashid with the GCSE work you've been giving to him. It's my understanding that he isn't coping with this advanced work and that he didn't want to disappoint you. Therefore, he was getting someone else, someone in Year Eleven, to do the work for him.'

Ahmer tutted loudly and dropped his head, shaking it as if in complete despondency. There was no movement from Mrs Dar… *or* Susan who had simply adopted an expression she probably thought showed compassion. It actually looked like she had indigestion.

'Taking this all into account, and also the fact that I have had to call Rashid up a couple of times for his behaviour towards one of his peers recently, well, to be honest, I'm very worried about him,' Emily told the family. 'I think he's under a lot of pressure for a ten-year-old and I think it's having a profound effect on every part of his life.'

'Ahmer,' Mrs Dar said to her husband. 'Do you think this is true?'

'It can't be true,' Ahmer answered her. 'He's a bright boy. I would know if the work wasn't his. And what is all this about other behaviour now? Why has nothing been said about this before?'

'Well,' Emily started, 'I decided it was something I would try and deal with personally, but, if it had accelerated, of course I would have brought it to your attention then.'

'I told you you were pushing him too hard,' Mrs Dar mumbled.

'*You* want him to become a doctor!' Ahmer exclaimed.

Susan picked up her cup of coffee and took a sip. OK, this was definitely a test. It was time for Emily to move things forward.

'OK,' she interjected with authority. 'This is the time where we talk about making positive steps, not get into blame, or back track on how things might have been done differently.' She spoke calmly but with utter authority. 'What's happened has happened. We all need to work together now to move ahead.' Wow, that sounded exactly like a Deputy Head. Perhaps she would get the promotion *before* Christmas…

'And what exactly are you proposing?' Ahmer asked. He had turned a little in his seat, was looking directly at Emily. For a second, she could only focus on the fact she hoped her children were going to get his ad for Dar's Delhi Delights word perfect in the show. She swallowed. She could do this.

'Mr Dar, Rashid *is* a bright boy. But he isn't bright enough to be doing GCSE level work right now. He's only ten. And, it's my professional opinion that the last year of primary school is difficult enough as it is, without having additional things to worry about. It's a time of complete change for them. The children are growing up, they're becoming independent and trying to push goalposts. Moving up to senior school is daunting. It's going to take them some time to get used to new routines, make new friendships. I think in these last couple of terms at Stretton Park you should encourage Rashid in learning other valuable *life* lessons, not academic ones.'

'What kind of other life lessons, Miss Parker?' Mrs Dar wanted to know.

'Kindess,' Emily stated. 'Tolerance. Difference. I have thirty-three children in my class, and they are of all different faiths and backgrounds. Some have everything, others have absolutely nothing, but what they *all* have in common is opportunity.' She took a breath. 'I always try to teach every child that they can be anything they want to be. And it doesn't matter, at ten years old, whether that dream is to be a doctor or a... dustbin collector. At this age they should be free to explore whatever their heart desires and learn to be accepting of the dreams of others. I know, without any doubt at all, that you love Rashid very much and I know that you want Rashid to be happy.'

'Of course we do,' Mrs Dar stated. 'Don't we, Ahmer?'

'Of course,' Mr Dar answered softly.

'Then I'd like to discuss a plan I have,' Emily said. 'Because, Mr and Mrs Dar, I'd really like Rashid to be one of the stars of our Christmas show.'

*

As soon as the Dars had left the office, Emily took a deep breath. Her palms were sweaty. Susan always had the heating on too high and with four people in the snug office it had turned into a mini-sauna, plus it had been stressful. You never wanted to be telling parents uncomfortable things they would rather not hear, but now everything was out in the open they could move on, exactly like she'd told the family.

'Right,' Emily said, stepping towards the door. 'I'd better get back to my class, we have a lot of work still to do for the show.'

'One minute, Emily,' Susan said, standing up and coming around her desk. 'I'd like to have a word.'

Was this it? Was this the moment Emily was going to be given her promotion? She wasn't sure she was ready. It was quite possible she could cry.

'I've read the script for the show you gave me,' Susan said, leaning her bulk against her desk.

'Yes?' Emily said. 'What did you think?'

'It's rather short.'

'Oh,' Emily said. 'Well, that's because we haven't put in all the songs yet. We're still working on them, but they're almost there, we just need one more for the final nativity tableau and then I thought, after that breath-stealing scene we could have a different act showing all the ways Stretton Park families will be celebrating the holidays.'

'No,' Susan said abruptly. 'That won't work. I told you what the diocese wants and they are paying for most of it. There needs to be much more God.'

'To be honest, Mrs Clark, there is stable-to-stable God at the moment. There's a song about the Three Kings, except we made it the Three Queens because none of the boys wanted to be the Kings. There's "O, Holy Night", and the bishop loved that one when he heard it and...'

'You start the play with Mary and Joseph's journey to Bethlehem,' Susan said.

'Yes, well, that's when everything starts, isn't it? They have to go there for the census.'

'I think you should start it off when Mary gets the visit from Angel Gabriel who tells her she's going to bear the Son of God.'

Emily didn't know what to say. For some of her children the nativity story wasn't part of their lives at all. She was trying her best to make compromises, tick every box, keep everyone happy... as well as throwing in references to local restaurants and their money-off deals...

'Right,' she said flatly.

Susan smiled. 'You know I have absolute faith in you, Emily. Absolute faith.'

Emily forced a smile and wondered just how long she could wait for the promotion she craved. Perhaps, regrettably, it was time to look for another school after all.

'Positivity all round today I think,' Susan said, easing herself off the desk. 'Apparently Mr Jackson has moved out of the family flat. Mrs Jackson left a message on the answerphone.'

Fifty-Two

MP Free Studio, Islington

'That sounded amazing!' Deborah passed Ray a coffee in the chill-out area of the studio. Over the weekend someone had filled this spot with Christmas too. There was a real tree, a small one, in a red and white pot on a corner table and strings with Christmas cards pegged to them hanging across the ceiling. He and Deborah were sitting on the large leather sofa, Ray taking a break from what had been a hard morning. His throat was actually killing him now and what he really needed more than the coffee was a gallon of water and a packet of Strepsils.

'Thanks,' he croaked out. He took a sip of the coffee. Definite twangs of cinnamon in this one...

'Whoa, is there something wrong with your voice?' Deborah asked, suddenly looking like BBC News had announced a zombie apocalypse.

Here was his chance to confess about his visits to Dr Crichton and the possibility of surgery...

'Because you have the show at Ronnie Scott's coming up,

Ray, you need to be in top form for that. It's probably one of the most important shows of your career so far,' Deborah continued.

And how could he mention it now? He nodded. 'It's fine.' God, his voice sounded even worse now. Perhaps he had pushed it a little too much in the morning's session *and* he was heading to Stretton Park later to sing through songs with Emily and her children. He couldn't let her down either, despite stress being no good for his larynx...

'OK, well, there's something else we need to deal with today,' Deborah said, putting her coffee on the table and getting her phone out of her portfolio bag.

'Not another story?' he breathed. Was this going to be Ida's revenge after the other day in this very building?

'Not yet,' Deborah stated on an out breath. 'But it could be.' She showed Ray the screen of her phone. He swallowed as he looked at the image. It was him and Emily, kissing in the snow on London Bridge. Instantly he was flooded with all the feelings that had engulfed him in that moment. It had been sexy and sultry, also slow and soft, Emily's slightly tentative sweetness soaking into him. He couldn't remember ever feeling the same way before...

'Want to tell me about this?' Deborah asked.

'I don't know,' Ray admitted.

'Ray, everyone is entitled to a personal life, but your personal life is of public interest, you know that.'

'Yeah, I know that.'

'So, I need the heads-up on things like this if I'm going to be doing the best job I can for you. Now, Nigel – he's the editor who happened upon this image – is going to hold off printing it for now. But I can't guarantee his source isn't going to try and sell this picture to another of the tabloids.'

'OK,' Ray answered with a nod.

'I'm just thinking of you and… I'm thinking of Ida,' Deborah said. 'She wasn't in the best place the other day and…'

'And she came here, to the studio, agitated.' He wasn't going to mention he thought Ida may have got someone to stalk him, seeing as she had a photo of him and Emily at Clean Martini. He also wasn't going to mention the physical altercation, because that would only open up a whole different can of worms.

'Did she?' Deborah asked. 'When? Do you think we ought to think about getting some kind of restraining order?'

He shook his head. 'No.' He had always thought that was the very last resort. He didn't want to take things that far. But when was it going to end if he didn't do *something*?

'I'm serious, Ray. If money didn't work as an incentive for her to back down… and she seemed so intent on trying to rekindle your relationship. I'm worried this might turn into something bigger. Something… *Fatal Attraction*… and no one wants that.'

And his agent really didn't know the half of it…

'*I* don't want that,' Deborah carried on. 'I can't get caught in any cross-fire that might lead to me taking time off work now I've signed up for Dog Behavioural School: The Second Season.'

'Wow,' Ray replied.

'I know. If Oscar knew how much those lessons cost, he'd insist on tickets for the FA Cup final next year. In a hospitality box.'

'OK,' Ray replied. 'I'll do something.' There was really only one other option left before they took the action that Deborah was suggesting. 'I'll call her mum.'

'You think that will work?'

He didn't know for sure. With Ida's mum living in Yorkshire and them not being close... But she *was* the only family Ida had. Ray had only met Victoria once and it had been an odd affair. Ida had dressed up like a fairy princess, as if she was channelling childhood times gone by, and Victoria had sat quietly for the most part at their meal at The Ivy. Ida had insisted they go to the celebrity hangout to impress her mother. Whether Victoria had been impressed or not hadn't been apparent. The day had ended with Victoria heading back on a coach saying she would call in a month or so. Conversation had been polite but staid. It was almost as if they were talking but not actually saying anything at all.

'I can try,' Ray answered.

'OK, good,' Deborah answered, seeming somewhat appeased. 'Right, so, tell me, who is the girl in the photo?'

Ray couldn't help smiling. Simply thinking about Emily brightened everything. 'Her name's Emily,' he informed. 'I fixed her central heating and she gave me her spare room.'

Fifty-Three

'It's snowing again! Wow! Look how big the flakes are!'

'My dads say that in America it snows so much sometimes even the snowploughs get stuck!'

'My granny doesn't go out in the snow in case she falls over.'

'If your granny fell over do you think she would die?'

Emily watched her children, faces pressed against the windows of the assembly hall, looking out onto the playground as another light flurry of the white stuff descended from the clouds. Unfortunately, it wasn't the only thing that had fallen from above in the past hour. Some of the Sellotape that had been holding the festive decorations across the ceiling had come unstuck and Emily had been forced to climb on another unstable stool in order to reinforce everything with Blu Tack. Luckily, this time, with no Ray to save her, she had managed to ascend and descend without incident. Now, they all needed to get on with the play rehearsal to be ready for when Ray got there to perfect the songs. She was going to have to break it to him that they needed *even more* God…

'Children, we need to get on with rehearsing the play now so please come away from the windows and get into position on the stage.'

'Snow! Snow!' Felix announced, his eyes bulging.

'I'm going to build a snowman when I get home,' Lucas announced, sniffing a descending bogey back into his nose.

'It's actually a snow-*person*,' Makenzie corrected. 'Because you can't ask the snow-*person* what gender they are, and you shouldn't assume.'

'I'm going to make snowballs and throw them at my sister,' Angelica said, taking aim with an imaginary missile.

'I'm going to eat the snow. It tastes like a Slush Puppy without the flavours,' Matthew told the class.

'Ugh!'

'Year Six!' Emily shouted at full volume. She struck the pose of Jesus standing over Rio.

The children all jumped in shock and Emily felt immediately guilty for raising her voice quite so much. She might be feeling under pressure, but the children shouldn't be. They were enjoying the play, as they should be, it was only *her* dreams of promotion that were on the line. Suddenly, looking across the room to those innocent faces – and the faces that weren't quite so innocent all of the time – Emily had an epiphany that had nothing to do with Wise Men. *Fun. The holidays.* Whatever that meant to her class. Just like her project. *That* was exactly what this show should represent. It didn't matter what the diocese wanted. The diocese should *really* want what was best for the children.

She wanted what was best for the children. And she knew them better than anyone else at Stretton Park.

'OK,' Emily breathed. 'Right, now, let's all be nice to one another, listen to one another and get ready to make this show the best that Stretton Park has ever seen, yes?'

'Yes, Miss Parker,' the group all replied.

'OK, everyone on the stage and take your places for the opening scene. Except... Rashid and Jayden. I want you two to come over to me for a second.'

Emily watched most of her class scurry off, rushing up the steps of the stage and Rashid and Jayden, looking less than happy about being 'singled' out trooped towards her, dragging their feet.

'Am I in trouble again?' Rashid asked as he reached Emily.

'Have you done anything to *be* in trouble?' Emily asked, raising an eyebrow.

'I caught Alice's plaits in a ring binder earlier, but it was an accident,' Rashid said, a note of worry in his tone.

'It *wasn't* an accident, Miss Parker,' Jayden said. 'But it wasn't Rashid's fault. Alice said she wanted to see what it would feel like.'

'No one is in trouble,' Emily reassured. 'Quite the opposite. I would like you two boys to work together on a song for the show.'

The two ten-year-olds eyed each other a little warily. Emily knew this was a risk. They were far from friends, but she suspected, given their mutual appreciation of all things football *and* the fact that both of them were working through some tough times, that they might find common ground with this project. She had everything crossed.

'What song?' Jayden asked.

'Well,' Emily said. 'I don't quite know yet, but I thought it might be nice if you worked on a song about your mums. Because I've met both your mums recently and they are both very strong women who work so hard in their jobs and with you two at home. I thought it might be nice to surprise them both with a song about them at the show. What do you think?'

'It will be hard to write a song like that,' Rashid commented. 'And I wouldn't want it to be about Jesus.'

'No!' Emily exclaimed, hand to her chest. 'No, definitely not about Jesus, or anything about the nativity story. I want this song to be all about the things your mums do in the holidays that *isn't* to do with the Christian Christmas story.' She looked at them both. 'I wouldn't ask you two if I didn't think you could do it. And it can be the same as we've done with the other songs. You can pick a Christmas song and simply change the words. Make it about your mums.' Emily smiled. 'What do we think? Do we think we can manage that?'

She watched Jayden look at Rashid and Rashid look at Jayden and both boys gave a slow nod that was, at least, promising.

'Great! Well, why don't you have a quick think about the things your mums do and we can go from there.'

Suddenly the door of the hall opened and Emily watched as Ray rushed in, his hands once again full of hedgehog.

'Ray! It's Ray Stone again!'

'It's Olivia Colman! She's come back!'

Emily rushed towards him, her class all descending back down from the stage and hurrying across the floor to the advancing singer and the animal.

'Is Olivia Colman sick again? Is she going to die this time?' Alice asked, reaching out a hand to the hedgehog.

'What's going on?' Emily asked Ray. 'I thought the hedgehog was safe at the sanctuary.'

'It's not the same one,' Ray said. 'But… I think this one is pregnant.'

'Good grief!' Emily exclaimed. 'How can you tell? Wait, no, please don't answer that.' All her children were now far more interested in the animal than they were in getting on with the play practice. Ray was having to shield the hedgehog from hands keen to stroke and eyes desperate to catch a peek.

'Is she going to have babies now?' Lucas asked.

'Ugh! That's gross!'

'Hey, listen,' Ray said with calm authority. 'Let's give her some space for a minute.' He looked to Emily. 'Have you got a box we can put her in?'

'Let's call her Idris Elba,' Makenzie suggested brightly.

'Idris Elba is a boy! You can't call her a boy's name!' Cherry announced.

'My dads say that you can be anything you want to be and you can have any name you want. Makenzie can be used for a boy *or* a girl so why can't we call her Idris Elba?' Makenzie asked. 'We don't *actually know* the gender.'

'I can't see a willy or a foo-foo! She's too curled up!'

'I'll find a box,' Emily said quickly.

Fifty-Four

We Three Queens
– to the tune of 'Last Christmas' by Wham

Last Christmas I gave you some myrrh
But on Boxing Day you gave it to her
This year to not break my heart
I'll give it to Baby Jesus... x2

Ray thundered at the piano, mouthing along to the children and Emily singing the song they had adapted. Emily had projected the lyrics on the wall at the far end of the hall, but it seemed to Ray that the Year Sixes were close to perfection already. He smiled as the queens performed their dance break before moving onto the verse...

You broke my heart, I don't know why
I didn't get that you were someone else's guy
Tell me maybe, did you really like me?

Or was it just because I'm part of the monarchy?

Happy Christmas, I'll give it to the baby
With some gold and nappies bought from Sainsbury's
Now I know what love can mean, I finally realise how
* crazy stupid I've been*

He wanted to join in and sing so much. The kids had obviously worked hard on this, but earlier his voice had given out completely when he'd hit a tricky run of notes in the studio. Thankfully, Deborah had been gone by that stage and he'd been able to suggest to Leyland that it was just tiredness, that a good night's sleep would restore things. He wasn't really sure how long he could keep that up, but he knew he had to put on an outstanding performance at Ronnie Scott's. And, currently, that one night and Emily's Christmas show was all he could think about. That and his concerns about Ida. What was the right thing to do? The only thing he knew was that whatever he did it wasn't going to be easy.

Two more choruses sung with even more confidence, projecting their vocals to the back row of chairs like he'd told them earlier, then some flossing and dancing the Hype before the next part of the song...

Sandy desert, no more mince pies
Hiding from you and your Insta lies
Good gosh I thought you were someone really super,
But hey, I guess you still weren't Bradley Cooper

Faced with three camels who do nothing but fart

*We're queens on a mission, stop the world from falling
  apart*
*O-oo, now we've found our real calling we won't need
  you again*

Ray played on to the final choruses and outro and
watched Emily directing the children to their positions for
the ending with one hand and beckoning on the participants
for the next scene with the other. How she was pulling this
all together with limited resources and time he didn't know.
But what he did know was that playing this music with
the children and their teacher was a departure for him and
there was something so raw and pure about it. He was back
to enjoying songs again, relishing the children's reaction to
the music...

Suddenly, the doors of the hall flew open and Emily's
boss, Mrs Clark strutted in, an unamused look on her face.

'Miss Parker, what is going on?' Susan Clark demanded
to know. Her hands were on her hips now and Ray couldn't
help but sink a little down into the piano stool. He had
signed in as a legitimate guest today. He wasn't wearing
that Father Christmas costume ever again...

'Mrs Clark,' Emily said, walking to the front of the stage
and straightening one of the camel's tails. 'We were just
running through the show and...'

'Why is there another hedgehog in the school? In the
staff room.'

'Ah, well... that is...' Emily began.

'It's Idris Elba,' Makenzie announced loudly and proudly.
'And they are going to have babies.'

Susan Clark shook her head like someone who couldn't

quite believe what they were being told. He should take ownership of it. Help Emily out. He stood up from the piano. 'I brought in the hedgehog.'

'And you are?' It seemed to take the headteacher a few moments for realisation to dawn and Ray wasn't sure whether the penny quickly dropping was concerning his singer status or whether she recognised him as the Santa who Chinese-burned a parent. He had never wanted it to be the former more than now...

'You... you are that person in the news. Lorraine Kelly talked about you on morning television. She wasn't very complimentary. Because they were saying that...'

He put his hands in the pockets of his jeans, seeing the judgement all over the woman's face.

'Mrs Clark,' Emily interrupted. 'Ray is here to play the piano. No one at school can play the piano and the things that have been reported in the news, they're not true and...'

'Why didn't I know you were hiring a pianist? Why don't I know that you're bringing someone *like this* into school?' Mrs Clark hissed. 'I can't have anyone who isn't checked, working at the school, you know that.'

'He *is* checked,' Emily replied. 'He's worked in schools before and—'

'Listen, I'll go,' Ray said, taking a step away from the piano.

There was a moan of despair from the class of children followed by calls of:

'Don't go, Ray!'

'Miss Parker isn't very good on the glockenspiel.'

'We can't do it properly without you.'

He turned to the stage full of children and smiled at them.

'Listen, guys, you've got this. You're going to be amazing. Miss Parker doesn't need me to make you great. You're all already great. Really great.'

'Susan,' Emily said, looking pleadingly at her superior. 'We need a pianist for the show and the children need to practise. We—'

'I'll call Mr Jarvis,' Susan said tightly, arms clamping over her bosom. 'He's been itching for something more than his allotment since he retired.'

Ray looked to Emily who was still on the stage. 'I'll see you.' This was his past with Ida coming back to haunt him, haunt *them*, spoil things for these children who only deserved the best.

'Ray, listen, we'll work this out,' Emily said, voice shaking. 'You're part of the show. You *have* to be part of the show.'

'It's OK,' Ray answered her. 'It's your show. And it's going to be fantastic.'

'This isn't fair!' Frema announced, stamping her foot. 'Ray knows all the right notes to play in the right time when I turn from rabbi to vicar! Mr Jarvis won't.'

Ray stepped out of the door.

'To the left,' Susan ordered him. 'You can take the hedgehog with you.'

Fifty-Five

'No!' Emily roared. She didn't head for the stairs to get herself off the stage, she sat down on it and propelled herself forward, feet meeting wooden floor in what probably could have been an ankle-breaking manoeuvre but thankfully wasn't. 'Ray, stop! Don't go anywhere!' She was moving across the room to Susan now and could only imagine the expression on her children's faces. What was she doing? Probably kissing goodbye to any hopes of promotion, but hadn't she always told her children to stand up for what they believed to be right? She wouldn't be being true to that mantra if she didn't make a stand now, no matter what it cost her.

Ray was standing in the doorway, his back to one of the swing doors, neither in nor out. She wasn't going to let him be rubbished like this. He had been nothing but supportive to her since they had met in the playground on that very first frosty day...

'Miss Parker,' Susan began. 'I suggest you return to the stage and get on with your rehearsal.'

'I can't rehearse the show without a pianist,' Emily said defiantly.

'I've just told you I will telephone Mr Jarvis.'

'I need someone who can play more than an off key "He's Got The Whole World In His Hands".'

The children erupted into fits of laughter, their palms finding their lips but actually muffling nothing.

'That is,' Emily continued, 'if you want this show to be a roaring success to impress the diocese *and* get the future funding we all so desperately need.'

Susan withdrew the arms that were clamping her breasts and suddenly seemed to bloat herself out like an engorged pheasant in a show of authority. 'That sounds a little like blackmail to me. Is that really where we are at, Miss Parker?'

'Of course not, Mrs Clark,' Emily replied. 'It's just that you put *me* in charge of the Christmas show and that means that *I* have ordered the costumes and *I* have painted most of the set and *I* have written the script and had to insert all kinds of ridiculous lines about "buy one poppadum get one free" and "pensioners haddock special every Wednesday" and the children have worked tirelessly to learn lines for songs that *Ray* has written in his spare time to help us make this show the best Stretton Park has ever seen.'

'That does not change the fact that the children's welfare is my responsibility and—'

'You would be letting an accomplished musician, someone who has had an enhanced DBS check already, continue to help me and Year Six with this show. So that we can all celebrate this winter term and look forward to buying new equipment come January.'

Susan was still looking very dour, yet Emily knew there was no stopping now. This was the right thing to do.

'I too have the children's best interests at heart, Mrs Clark, and I would never, *ever* put them at risk. Plus, I am always telling the children what a magnificent leader you are. How you always treat people equally and fairly no matter who they are or where they come from. I would hate for that not to be the case simply because you listened to a rumour Lorraine Kelly's show helped to fuel.'

Perhaps that last statement had been a little too blackmail-y. There was standing up for something you believed in and then there was coercion… Emily didn't say any more and she watched Susan adjust her stance a little and then turn her gaze to Ray. Ray looked awkward and she felt for him. She had put him in this situation when he already had enough on his plate. Maybe it would be better for him if he did bow out. She swallowed. But very selfishly, for the school and her long-forgotten libido, she really wanted him in. Heart-to-heart in the chorus line…

Susan shook her head before speaking again. 'If I wasn't under so much financial pressure from the council then this would be ending quite a different way. I can assure you of that.'

'You won't be calling Mr Jarvis?' Emily clarified.

'You will not leave the children alone for a second,' Susan said firmly. 'Is that clear?'

'Absolutely,' Emily answered.

'And this show,' Susan breathed, 'better be worthy of the

West End. And I mean one of the good shows... not *Viva Forever*.'

'Understood,' Emily replied.

Next, Susan looked directly at Ray. 'And you! Please, please stop bringing wildlife into my school!'

He nodded. 'I'll make sure Idris gets to the rescue centre tonight.'

Susan bustled out of the hall, Ray took a step back inside and the whole class let out a huge cheer.

'And now, Angelica, you run in a circle, run, hands in the air, looking excited because the baby is *coming*. Good!' Emily directed, flicking through her pages of the script. 'And then we will all get into the stable to sing the big nativity finale song and...'

'What is the actual big nativity final song?' Cherry asked.

'We haven't quite got that yet,' Emily answered.

'But we don't have many days left,' Lucas reminded.

'And we need to learn the words,' Matthew added.

'And we have the final *final* song to do too, remember?' Emily said. 'The song Ray is writing especially for us.'

'Is that finished yet?' Charlie wanted to know.

'Not quite,' Ray answered, writing something down on his script. He was stationed back at the piano but had been very quiet since Susan Clark's comments of earlier. Emily hoped she had done the right thing standing up to Susan. Maybe Ray resented her stepping in and making a spectacle of him. Despite being known for standing on stage keeping audiences in raptures, he really didn't like the attention his fame gave to his every day. She would talk to him later, maybe they could get the kebabs he liked from the Turkish grill house and eat them on the roof terrace…

'Miss Parker,' Jayden called.

'Yes, Jayden.'

'Me and Rashid know what we want to sing about, you know, to our mums.'

'Oh, really?' Emily said. 'Brilliant. What is it?'

'They both play Candy Crush,' Rashid announced. 'All the time.'

'My mum plays it with one hand while she stirs dinner with the other one,' Jayden said.

'And my mum plays it in the car when my dad is driving. He says she never listens to him when she's playing that,' Rashid added.

'Right,' Emily said. 'Let's go and talk to Ray, see if we can all think of a song that works around Candy Crush.'

'Hey,' Ray greeted, suddenly by her side. 'Listen, I've got to go. I got this weird text from my dad. He says he needs to see me. He never texts. He never needs to see me so… I have to go.'

'Of course,' Emily said. 'You go. I will see you when you get home.' God, she hadn't meant to say 'home' in front of Jayden and Rashid. 'I mean, I will see you later, for rehearsing and things.'

'OK,' Ray said, slipping on his coat.

'I hope everything's OK,' Emily said softly.

'Me too.'

Fifty-Six

New North Road, N1

'Hello, love, come in out of the cold. Your dad's let me put the actual heating on today, not just the wavy fake flames that are meant to make you feel warmer just by looking at them.'

'Is my dad OK?' Ray asked Brenda as she ushered him through the front door like a hefty security person desperate to move on a crowd. Today she was wearing a bright red all-in-one with gold boots on her feet. She looked like a cross between a superhero and a bit part in *Star Trek*.

'Yes, love, he's fine.'

'But the message he sent me…' Ray found he had to duck his head to enter the living room now, as there was a giant glittering ball that seemed to be making shadow Father Christmases and reindeers dance all over the opposite wall. There was also a myriad of festive animals dotted around the cosy room all looking like they could perform Christmas boogying if set to 'on'.

'Oh, you know,' Brenda said, wafting a hand in the air.

'I told him not to be so dramatic. I said you'd worry and there's really... you know... not that much to worry about.'

Not that much didn't sound very convincing. Now he was imagining all sorts. Was his dad ill? Was he hiding an operation he sorely needed just like Ray was? Had smoking most of his life finally caught up with him? It was unusual in itself that Ray was standing in the lounge and Len wasn't sitting in his favourite old chair...

'Is he... not here?' Ray asked, suddenly fearful. Perhaps it would have been more sensible to call, or message back, not dive straight over here. And he had abandoned Emily's rehearsal...

'Oh, yes he is here, love,' Brenda said quickly. 'He's in your room... the spare room... I was just going to make some tea. Would you like a cup? Or I've got some of those fancy sachets of coffee if that's more your thing. They were on special offer this week.'

His room. Why would Len be in Ray's room? Not that it was theoretically his room anymore. It hadn't been his room for some years, but it had never been a place his dad usually hung out. Only that one time, when they had both drunk whisky, well before he was eighteen, and talked about his mum...

'Go on,' Brenda urged, giving him a gentle shove. 'Go and see him and I'll make the fancy coffee.'

'Just normal coffee,' Ray croaked out. 'I'd rather have normal coffee. If that's OK.'

'Perfect,' Brenda answered. 'Because I haven't been able to make the fancy coffee without getting lumps in it yet.'

Ray stepped towards the hallway.

When he pushed open the door of his room there was an outcry.

'Ow! Hang on! Give me a minute!'

'Dad? Are you alright?'

'Yep, fine, the ladder's moved that's all. I just need to shift it over a bit and...' The door opened wider and there was Len, cigarette hanging from his lips, flecks of paint on his face, a cap covering his balding head.

'You alright?' Ray asked, stepping into the room.

'You know how I love decorating,' Len said with a scoff. 'Brenda's got a vision of this becoming a purple grotto before Christmas Eve. Her sister's coming down to stay and the woodchip won't do.' Len suddenly looked concerned. 'You don't mind, do you? Me, you know, changing your room.'

'No, Dad,' Ray answered. 'It's not been my room for years.' Except only a few weeks ago he had been here asking for the bed back.

'I know,' Len answered. 'But, you still, you know, kept some of your stuff here, didn't you?'

'Well, there was a guitar I said you could have and...' He stopped talking and straightaway a chill ran over his whole body, like someone had opened up the meant-to-be-unopenable-window and the icy wind had blasted in. He suddenly didn't feel so steady on his feet. He put a hand on the stepladder and tried to remain composed. There was only one other thing he had left here, one time after a visit, and he'd hidden it behind the skirting board.

'Sit down, Ray,' Len urged.

'I... don't want to sit down. If you're OK and you're

obviously OK if you're here painting and climbing ladders and…'

'You're not OK though,' Len stated brutally. 'Are you, lad?'

'I'm fine. I'm good. I'm…' His throat was hurting badly now. The stress and strain moving up and down with every attempt to get the words out. He needed to keep calm. His larynx needed serenity or the Ronnie Scott's show wasn't going to happen.

'I found it,' Len stated simply. 'I found it. And I've seen it.' He huffed a sigh. 'I don't know how to work these things. These chips you stick into computers. Chips into computers! The only place chips should be is bubbling in cooking oil.' He laughed briefly, then his expression reverted to concerned. 'But Brenda's got a laptop she got on the shopping channel and she knows how to use them. We thought it would be videos or pictures or something, of you singing. It was Brenda's idea.'

Ray knew then that the game was up, and his world began to swim before his eyes. This was the worst thing. The very worst thing. He took a step backwards, wanting to leave. His dad was fine. He wasn't ill or in trouble, or anything like that, therefore he could go. He really, really didn't want to face this. Not now. Not ever.

'Don't you even think about leaving, lad,' Len warned. 'I think all this nonsense has been going on too long.'

'Dad,' Ray began.

'Sit down,' Len ordered. 'We need to talk.'

The need to run was taking over, simmering under his surface, his everything crying out to retreat and escape. But equally he was paralysed.

'Sit down,' Len said again.

The single bed was warping and moving amid his blurry eyes, suddenly becoming the biggest thing in the room. Its uncovered mattress was calling out to support him. But sitting down on it meant staying. And staying meant talking.

'Sit down,' Len repeated. 'Please, lad.'

Ray could no longer look at his father. Shame and failure were taunting him like bullies, ready to take over.

'Is what I've seen on those videos the real truth? The truth you've not told anyone despite them all slagging you down on the telly and in the papers?' Len asked.

Ray cast his eyes to the carpet, the seventies swirls the council had put in long ago that he had once recreated for an art project. 'That depends what videos you've seen.' Still now he hoped it was something else. Or perhaps he simply needed Len to be the one to say the words out loud.

Len made a noise of exasperation and Ray didn't blame him. But Ray couldn't say the words. That was the crux of this whole issue. He had never been able to say the words. He felt the weight of his father's body lower down next to him on the bed.

'What I've seen is a terrified young man talking to a camera, saying he is in fear of his life... while he mops up deep cuts and ices fresh bruises, while someone hammers on the bathroom door screaming like they're possessed by the Devil.'

Ray dropped his head even lower, eyes focusing on the green and blue patterns in the carpet that had always looked a little bit solar system to him. Right now, he wished he was there, flying out of this atmosphere, suspended in space and heading for a faraway intergalactic destination.

'Ray,' Len said, 'all this time people have been thinking and saying you're some sort of girlfriend batterer and... it was her. It was all her.' Len took a breath. 'It was this Ida woman. It was her... attacking *you*.'

'She's not well,' Ray said immediately. 'I don't know whether it's her upbringing. I think it's probably that.' He sniffed. 'Her mother is distant, and she doesn't even know her father at all and—'

'Ray,' Len interrupted.

'Or, I don't know, maybe it was me,' Ray continued. The videos he had made when he was alone and desperate, locked in the bathroom tending his wounds while Ida raged outside, were now all running through his mind. He didn't even know why he had made them. Self-preservation? A diary to share his feelings with while he believed there was no one else he could confide in? Evidence? If he was ever going to be brave enough to admit what he was going through? 'Maybe *I* did something or said something that made her act that way?'

'No!' Len said furiously, slamming a hand down onto the mattress. 'Don't you dare say that.' His dad's voice was choked up now and Len removed the cigarette, stubbing it out hard into the ashtray on Ray's old school desk. 'It killed me to watch it. To see you in pain like that. And I don't mean from where she hit you or... whatever she did to you...' Len shook his head, the emotion making his voice quake. 'I mean, pain in your gut.' Len struck his own midriff with his hand. 'In your heart and your soul. I could hear it coming from you and... it broke me in two.'

Ray couldn't stop the tears now. He cried out in the deepest anguish. Everything he had suffered with Ida over the years was all spilling from him in a torrent of despair. Len drew him into a hug he'd never felt from his father before, his dad's strength undiminished despite his age, holding him tightly as they both shed equal emotion.

'I'm sorry, son,' Len whispered. 'I should have been there for you. I should have known there was something wrong. That there was more to it than what that ponce Piers Morgan was saying.'

Ray shook his head. 'I didn't want anyone to know. I *don't* want anyone to know.' He sniffed back his tears, wiped the back of his hand over his nose.

'Listen to me, you have to tell someone,' Len told him. 'You have to tell *everyone*. Then they'll all see that it wasn't *ever* you. It was her. And she made up all these lies the papers have bought, to hide the truth about herself. She has to be stopped.'

'She's not well,' Ray repeated.

'I agree!' Len said. 'But that don't mean she's not responsible.' He put a hand to Ray's coat, parting it and pulling at the collar of his jumper.

'What are you doing?' Ray asked, shifting on the mattress and trying to escape his dad's grip.

Len tugged the jumper down from Ray's shoulder and revealed the jagged scar that lay there, a hoarse breath escaping his lips. 'You have to look at that every day in the mirror and be reminded of what she did to you. What's she gonna do next? To someone else? Someone not as strong as you? Or someone who might fight back? Where will things be then?'

'What are you saying?' Ray asked, dragging his clothing out of Len's grasp.

'I'm saying, son, you need to do the right thing for *you* this time. Not what you think the right thing is for this woman... or for your career. For you. For Ray Stone. For my son.' Len's voice weakened on the last phrase and Ray felt his insides curdle at the love that lay there.

'I'm scared, Dad,' he admitted.

'Of what?' Len asked. 'Because *I'm* here for you. And Brenda can't wait to be here for you since I told her you loved Australian soap operas. We are gonna be right by your side.'

'People will think I'm weak,' Ray stated. 'That I somehow made this happen. That maybe it all started with me and Ida was... defending herself.'

'That's not what the videos tell me,' Len said. 'And that's not what they're gonna say to anyone else either.' He took a breath before continuing. 'People said I was crazy to stay with your mum, you know that. They saw how she was with us when she went to her bad places with the booze... but I loved her. *We* loved her, didn't we? Because no matter how bad things were, she would never have hurt us like this woman hurt you. Never.' Len swallowed. 'And if she was here now, to see you like you were on the video...'

'Don't,' Ray begged. 'Please.' He remembered almost every line he had spoken the days he had recorded what had happened to him, plus the other clips recorded while Ida was ranting and smashing and thumping him with anything she could get her hands on. Every scene was imprinted on his memory and he didn't want to relive another second of it.

'I'll do something,' Ray breathed. 'I was going to call Ida's mother, but I think I need to call someone else too. She'll know what to do.'

Len shook his head then put fingers to his eyes and padded away unspent tears. 'It breaks my heart you went through this and you didn't come to me.'

'I'm sorry, Dad,' Ray said, their shoulders touching as they sat on the mattress.

'Don't you be sorry, lad. I should be the one who's sorry.'

Ray shook his head. 'Dad, there's something else I haven't told you. And I should have, in case... in case it all goes wrong.'

'What is it?' Len asked him, expression back to worried.

Ray took a deep breath and looked directly at his dad. 'I've got to have an operation, on my vocal cords, and... I'm... I'm absolutely fucking terrified.'

Len's mouth fixed into a firm line and he gave one single nod of defiance. 'Right, well, now you listen to me, son. I understand but... what you don't know is last year I had to have a general for an ingrown toenail and I almost wept when the appointment letter came through. But Brenda, she bucked me up, and then she told me real statistics of mortality rates for operations and, well, I went through with it and here I still am, minus that toenail.' He smiled. 'Your mother died because she drank too much. She didn't deserve that transplant as much as it hurts me to say it. She knew that too. I always believed it was the resignation that killed her in the end. She just gave up,' Len told him. 'If the surgery had been a success she would have simply given up when she got home.' He put his arm around Ray's shoulders again. 'You're not someone who gives up. You never have been. That's why you're singing and not working on boilers,' Len said. 'You've got everything going for you, son. Everything. And if you want your room here back, I'll return the purple paint and you can have it any colour you want.'

Ray blew out a breath as gradually, very slowly, the weight of all the fears he was facing began to gently ease.

'Right, well, we need a plan, don't we? You need to phone who you need to phone to put things right, and I need an excuse not to start painting until tomorrow. Want to stay for some tea?'

'Yeah,' Ray answered. 'I'd really like that.'

Fifty-Seven

Crowland Terrace, Canonbury, Islington

Emily paused YouTube on her phone and clicked over onto her texts. *Nothing.* Maybe she should text Ray and see if he was OK. But, then again, if things were bad with his father he would let her know, wouldn't he? Or maybe he was in the thick of things at a hospital or worse... She clicked back into YouTube and returned to listening to 'Shallow' from *A Star is Born.* This was what she was working on, curled up on the corner of her sofa, trying to draw inspiration from the night sky and all those twinkling stars across the London skyline she could see from her vantage point. She was trying to create the Christmas song for the nativity section finale, making festive lyrics to a non-festive song the children all knew the tune to. So far she had the first couple of lines of the first verse.

Will he be born tonight? Lying underneath a star so bright?
Or will it take some time? Will Mary wish she'd had a glass of wine?

She wasn't really as adept at this songwriting business as Ray. But, then again, she was a schoolteacher and he was a professional songwriter. It was quite possible that Ray couldn't teach a lesson on deforestation... But her skills with lyrics *had* developed since they had begun this school show mission.

Her phone made a noise, dulling Bradley Cooper's vocals for an instant and Emily clicked over to her messages, hoping it was Ray. It wasn't. It was her mother.

Darling, when is your little show at school? Daddy and I are going to see if we can squeeze it into our schedules. What is the dress code? And when do tickets go on sale? I don't suppose there's a VIP section...

Emily shook her head at her mother's message. There was the usual 'We are so uber-busy, if Donald Trump popped over for a visit we would have to decline' but at the core of the text was the sentiment that her parents wanted to attend the Stretton Park show. It was unheard of. They had never been to any of her events at school. Her mother had loosely said she might come to one of the summer fairs, but in the end she donated 'An hour with a barrister' for the raffle instead.

Should she text back? Or do her usual of ignoring it for a few days to pretend she was also uber-busy? No, that wouldn't work right now. She wouldn't be able to get on with re-writing 'Shallow' with that hanging over her. She texted a speedy reply.

Tickets are usually free, but a donation to the school

would be very much appreciated. It's 20 December at 6 p.m.

Emily's thumb hovered over the 'send' icon and then she added another line.

Everyone is dressing up as their favourite Christmas character. I think Dad would make a wonderful King Herod

Now she clicked send. Within seconds her mother would come back with a sarcastic response about her attempt at hilarity. The phone buzzed again before Emily could even switch back to YouTube. What quip had her mother made about outfit choices now? But, looking at the screen, Emily saw that it wasn't from her mum, this one was from Ray.

I want to talk to you so much but, right now, I can't do it. Emily. Gorgeous, sweet, beautiful, kind, Emily. No one has stood up for me like you did today at the school. You turned warrior right before my eyes and I have to admit, it was incredible and… really, really hot. But there are things going on now that I have to deal with before I can move forward.

You are going to hear some things about me in the press over the next few hours and days and, as much as I don't want this to be out there, there's no way around it now. I have to do the right thing. And that means I have to stay here with my dad, for a while, and I also have to… not sing. No Ronnie Scott's show. No humming in the shower even. No singing at all. I'm terrified about the enormity of that last sentence because I can't remember a moment when I haven't sung, but more than that I'm terrified that I've already hurt you by starting something you are going to want to finish as soon as this news is out there.

I've been closed when you've been so open about everything and it kills me that I haven't been able to be truly honest with you. But I want you to know that you're the only person I've told even a fraction of anything to – about my mum, about Ida. If I could be the man you deserve, Emily, I would be there in a heartbeat, but you deserve so much better, someone so much stronger, someone who's not too much of a coward to pick up a phone and instead wears out his thumbs typing a text.

I'm sorry. I'm so, so sorry for promising you things I can't deliver on or, at least, alluding to them by kissing you in the snow… and feeding you cheese… and finding hedgehogs. God, I walked out on Idris. I hope he/she is OK.

Anyway, this is really hard and way too long but, honestly, you've got this Christmas show nailed. It's going to be amazing and, by the way, I wouldn't leave you with that Mr Jarvis fella if he really can't even play 'He's Got The Whole World In His Hands'. I'm going to finish the song I promised I'd write for you and I'll get the music and the lyrics sent to the school. And I'm going to get a pianist from the studio to take my place for any rehearsals you need and for show night. I would love to be there, I've loved every second of these crazy few weeks, but it's better that I'm not there, for everyone. The show's spotlight should be on the children and on you, Emily, the amazing, most wonderful person who believes anyone can achieve anything.

I just want to say that I think, if the timing was better, I'd be telling you I love you. Can I still say it? Even if it's in a goodbye? I don't know why I'm asking. Here it is. I loved you, Emily Parker and I'm so grateful for every second we got to spend together. Ray x

The tears had been falling from Emily's eyes by the second paragraph and they quickened and thickened until she could no longer see the screen of her phone that was wobbling in her shaking hand. What had happened? Between this afternoon at Stretton Park and now, just a few hours later? It was a goodbye. And she didn't really understand it. How could she? The message said everything and nothing. What was she going to hear in the press? Had Ida's claims been right all along? She didn't believe that. Even Jonah was coming around to Ray now or he wouldn't have asked how many tickets she wanted for the Albert Hall show… None of it made sense and Emily had no idea what to do. But she had to do something. She had to speak to him. Text back? Call? See him in person? She didn't know his dad's address. She was up off the sofa now, YouTube forgotten, pacing the bare boards of her lounge and trying to think logically. This couldn't be the end of things between them, not when

things were only just beginning. It couldn't be because…
she was in love with him too.

Her eyes went to the cardboard box in the corner of the
room and she walked towards it, full of determination.
Perhaps it was time to use the power of a hedgehog.

Fifty-Eight

'I don't know why, but just Googling this is making me feel really really dirty,' Allan said, screwing up his face as he typed into his laptop. 'How to make pregnant hedgehogs give birth. Ugh!'

Emily's face was reddened from sobbing but, after sharing the contents of Ray's text with Jonah and Allan over the phone, and again when they arrived at her flat, she was now feeling less pathetically desperate and more desperately determined.

'Here you go,' Jonah said, handing Emily one of his very special caramel and coconut hot chocolates he only ever made on special occasions – *Eurovision*, royal weddings and season finales of *How to Get Away with Murder*. 'Are we really sure this is the best course of action? I mean, I know you say you can't phone him or text him back, and you don't know where his dad lives, but there must be something else you can do other than inducing the birth of hedgehog babies.' Jonah looked at Idris Elba who was currently snoring, wrapped up in a blanket in the cardboard box.

'Jonah!' Allan hissed. 'Can't you see how upset Emily is?'

'I know she's upset. I've made caramel and coconut hot chocolate, haven't I? I'm simply saying that trying to find out where Ray's dad lives and seeing him in person, talking to him face-to-face might be a better option than... this.'

'I've tried to find out where his dad lives,' Emily said, sniffing back the gooey muck of after-crying that was clogging all her much-needed breathing tubes. 'But it's impossible.'

'Is his real name "Stone" because sometimes they have stage names, don't they? For their Equity card or whatever. We need to Wiki Ray and find out all the info on him from there. Sometimes they have where they're born and their real name and who they've had kids with... not that I'm saying he's got kids,' Allan said, talking fast but his eyes on the screen. 'Ew! We are not doing *that* to a hedgehog.'

'There's nothing helpful on Wikipedia, or on Facebook, or Twitter... or Instagram. He doesn't use social media much. It's someone from his record company doing his posts,' Emily replied.

'Did you know,' Allan began. 'That hedgehogs are only pregnant for about thirty-five days, so, we might strike it lucky and this one might be due imminently or...'

'Or worst-case scenario, we have to sit here for thirty-four days?' Jonah asked.

'Well, I'm sure it will only really be maybe a week or so? I mean, she does look rather well-rounded.'

'I can't wait a week,' Emily said. 'I need to action something now. Because Ray *will* come if there's an emergency with Idris Elba. I know he will.'

And that was her grand plan. To force him to come here under false pretences. That wasn't like her at all. What was this situation doing to her?

'How does she really look to you?' Emily asked, peering at the hedgehog who seemed nothing but peaceful and sleepy. Was that a sign of imminent childbirth? Or was it simply slipping into hibernation like it really should be in December?

'You're saying that like you're talking to two wildlife experts. I might have had a season of my hair looking like a funky ginger Chris Packham, but the only wildlife I've ever really been interested in hung out in bars in Soho,' Two L's said.

'And you know most of the creatures in my neck of the woods were rats… and that was just some of the neighbours,' Jonah added.

Emily let out a desperate sigh and sank back into the sofa feeling defeated. What was she doing? Trying to make a maybe-pregnant may-not-be pregnant hedgehog go into labour simply so she had a genuine excuse to contact Ray. If she wanted to contact Ray, she should contact Ray. But that would involve talking about how she felt about Ray *to* Ray and the thought of doing that was terrifying her. And, maybe it didn't even matter how she felt. The text was goodbye. As clear as it got. Except he had also said he loved her and most of his large rucksack, his two guitars and the tool bags were still in his room. *His* room. Not the spare room. Not Jonah's room anymore. Now thought of as only Ray's.

'This is silly, isn't it?' Emily said, fingers in her fringe. 'What am I doing? I should be taking Idris to the sanctuary, not trying to get her to push babies out.'

'You said the sanctuary is closed,' Jonah reminded.

'It is.'

'So, what do you want to do, darling?' Allan asked her, fingers poised over the keyboard of his laptop. 'Do you want Jonah and me to continue looking at ways to make this little one start heaving and grunting and delivering young? Or shall we, instead, talk about the real issue here?'

Emily shook her head. Googling the habits of pregnant spiky females was distracting. While she had a stupid crusade, she didn't have a yearning for gin or a hurting heart.

'Perhaps, if you give Ray a little time and space then things will work themselves out,' Jonah suggested, slipping an arm around Emily's shoulders.

'Are you mad? I know I thought this skit with the pre-newborn kits was crazy, but Emily has the right idea to *not* give him space. Time doesn't heal everything, it simply increases distance. And the longer the distance stretches, the further away you get. Like an endless journey on a Virgin.'

'Allan, you're talking rubbish.'

'Well, you've never really been on board with Emily and Ray.'

'That's not true,' Jonah answered. 'I admit, at the start, I was unsure about the set-up, but now... I can see how much you like him and he... grew on me.'

'He's not a foot fungus, Jonah. He's a nice slightly-rough-around-the-edges guy with a gorgeous voice and quite a nice arse.'

'Allan!'

'He does wear jeans well, you have to admit that.'

'I do like him,' Emily said. She got to her feet and moved

to stand at the full-width windows overlooking the rooftops of her neighbourhood. The sky was clear and filled with a thousand stars. Like it had been when she and Ray had sat drinking hot chocolate and finding out about each other. Before they'd rolled around on the floor of the terrace…

'I like him a lot.' Her mind was telling her there was much more than 'like' going on. Why was that so hard to admit, even to herself? 'I like him,' she started again, 'in a way I didn't think I would ever like anyone again after Simon.'

'Oh, Em,' Jonah said.

'Well, then,' Allan began forcefully. 'If you feel like that then I want to know what on earth this "news" you're going to hear about over the next few hours-slash-days is? I mean, it has to be pretty major for him to message you something like that, out of the blue, with no warning at all.'

'I don't know,' Emily breathed. 'And… do I really want to know?'

'Of course you do,' Allan answered. 'Tell her, Jonah.'

'Em, if you feel that strongly about Ray, like you might feel as strongly for him as you did about Simon, then you need to know,' Jonah told her. 'I hate to say it but… you don't think there was some element of truth to the newspaper articles after all?'

Emily shook her head defiantly. 'No. I'm sure of that. Ray wouldn't hurt anyone.' She thought of Mr Jackson. Ray *had* hurt him, but only to save Jayden. Her eyes went to Idris. 'He's saved two hedgehogs in the space of a few of weeks.' And Ray had cradled them despite their prickly exterior, holding them close, caring, worrying, making sure they were OK. 'Someone like that wouldn't do what the press is suggesting.'

'Despite the Chinese burn incident which we *all* thought was necessary, I agree,' Allan said. 'And I have a natural talent for reading people. I'm like that Patrick Jane from *The Mentalist*, without the three-piece suit, but with all of the ginger hotness.'

Suddenly three mobile phones all made a noise simultaneously. The BBC News Breaking News alert that sounded like the beginnings of a dramatic action movie. The one Emily still, somehow, couldn't mute.

Allan was the first to reach for his. 'Another royal baby announcement? Or Prince Philip getting his driving licence back and getting a job as a cabbie?'

Emily picked her phone up from the coffee table, all fingers and thumbs. She didn't need to unlock the screen to read the headline.

'Oh my God!' Jonah remarked.

'Why does this thing say there's breaking news and when you go in to read it there's no other information!' Allan screeched. 'Damn you Huw Edwards and your digital news colleagues. Oh, Emily!' He leaped over to her, putting his arms around her and squeezing so tight it felt like she was being juiced. But over Allan's shoulder, her eyes blurry with newly-formed tears, the sparkle refracted from all the timeless ornaments on the Christmas tree she'd decorated with Ray. And in her hand was her phone, still locked, but the headline bold.

Breaking News: Musician Ray Stone makes domestic abuse claim against former partner

Fifty-Nine

Harley Street, Marylebone

'How soon can you get him in?'

Ray was sitting in his usual chair of choice at Dr Crichton's office, watching the evil-looking black fish, while Deborah took control. He had seen all sides of his agent over the past few days and he was starting to feel he knew exactly how her less-than-obedient dog, Tucker, probably felt. Deborah might not have asked him to jump through hoops or sit but he would have been more than happy if she'd suggested he begged, all things considered. She had simply made clear that she was now the one in charge of this situation and he was going to have to toe the line if he wanted to come out of it completely intact. He had learned a lot over the past few days: who was going to be there for him, who cared... and the fact that Soot's demise hadn't been down to his escape from the cage, but because his mum had accidently filled his water bowl with Smirnoff...

The press had been buzzing around his dad's flat since the news broke and Gio had called him, hysterically shouting in that Italian way, that the new tenant in Ray's ex-rental was complaining of photographers trying to scale the main gate. Ray was surprised the journalists had attempted that. He had tried to scale it a couple of times when he'd forgotten the gate code and it absolutely wasn't a drop you wanted to fall from. It had taken a diversion tactic from Brenda – running screaming down the external corridor shouting that a car was on fire – to get the press away from the front door in order for him to leave for Harley Street without being tailed. And now he was here, feeling as shell-shocked with life as he had ever been.

'Realistically, if I move a few things around, next Thursday.'

Next Thursday. He was going to have an operation next week. He opened his mouth, ready to say it was an impossibility. Despite everything he had agreed with Deborah, a part of him still wanted that gig at Ronnie Scott's… And he still *really* wanted to be playing the piano at a primary school in Islington on the 20th too. He closed his mouth again and said nothing. In truth, all he could think about was Emily and that harder-than-harsh text he had sent her when he thought he was doing the right thing. Why hadn't he picked up the phone? Or gone to the apartment? He had to go there at some stage to, at least, pick up his things…

'Ray,' Deborah said, loudly, close to his ear. 'Did you hear what the doctor said?'

Had he missed something after talk of 'next Thursday'? He shook his head. 'Sorry, I…'

'Next Thursday,' Deborah recapped. 'Dr Crichton can do your operation next week. So, you'll go into the private wing under the cover of darkness on Wednesday night, then...'

Ray shook his head. 'I can't do next Thursday.' What was coming out of his mouth now? Ida had tried to call him after the news had broken. He'd expected it and he had done what he knew he had to do. He had ignored her. He just hoped the conversation he had had with Victoria, before Deborah had contacted the news agencies, had made her realise the severity of the situation with her daughter. Victoria hadn't said very much. Ray hadn't said very much. It was hard enough to talk about everything that had happened without going into the finer details that still very much hurt him. But he had been clear. He wanted Ida to get help. He wasn't in a position to implement her care. It had to come from somewhere else, someone else. And it was time her mum stepped up before it was too late.

'Ray, what do you mean you can't do next Thursday?' Deborah asked. 'We talked about this. We made a plan. The current news is going to cover up the fact there's something wrong with your voice. We can now postpone the gig at Ronnie Scott's and tell everyone you need a time-out to get over this trauma and then it's back to the studio in say, six weeks' time, to complete your new album.' She took a breath. 'Then, when we're absolutely sure you're recovered, we can do the comeback concert, perhaps at a much bigger venue, and everything will be back on track, including your vocals.'

What wasn't sitting well with him? Which part of this whole life-altering scenario wasn't working? He knew this was the right thing to do. He couldn't avoid this operation. Dr Crichton had made it clear that steam and readjusting his technique was not going to cut it long term. And his dad and Brenda had already been talking about the pros of getting this sorted now compared to the likelihood of throat cancer when he hit his sixties... The irony was, they rattled this out from stories on the web while Len smoked his way through a packet of Marlboro Lights.

'The 21st,' Ray suddenly stated.

'What?' Deborah said, her thick portfolio almost falling off her knee.

'Can you do 21st December instead of next Thursday?' Ray asked Dr Crichton directly.

'Ray,' Deborah said. 'That's another week away.'

It was the day after the Stretton Park Christmas show. And that was all he could think about. He might not be able to sing, but he could still play. He couldn't send a session pianist to Emily's school, to play for those kids he'd got to know, to perform the songs he'd helped them all transform. He had been selfish. He had made this situation entirely about him, when what he really should have done was been braver in those moments before he'd sent the text. The world didn't revolve for him alone. Yes, Emily deserved more than him in her personal life. Someone without any of the press attention. Someone strong and sensitive who wasn't living in such a crazy situation. But what Emily and the children needed on 20th December was confidence. And confidence for them came from familiarity, not change. The kids needed a performance they were going to remember for years to come. And they needed him to help with that.

'I need to be somewhere on 20th December,' Ray said firmly.

'Ray, there is nowhere you need to be any time right now except an operating theatre,' Deborah insisted.

Ray watched Dr Crichton looking to the screen of his iPad, touching icons, bringing up different views. He had the doctor's attention at least.

'Ray,' Deborah stated again, sounding irritated.

'This one date isn't up for discussion, Deborah,' Ray told her firmly. 'Please, I promise I'll do everything you say with everything else, I just need that one day.'

'What for?' Deborah asked.

'I...' What could he say? He had told Deborah Emily's name and that he liked her, after the photo of them kissing in the snow, but he hadn't told her anything about his work with the Stretton Park production. Whether it was a good look or not, whether it might help with his career resurrection, he didn't want the limelight heading his way with regard to this. It was Emily's show. It was Year Six's time to shine. 'I can't tell you.'

Deborah closed her eyes tight and seemed to inhale from right down into the soles of her shoes. He didn't blame her for trying to inject a little meditation into proceedings. She was currently working harder than the Conservative party spin-doctors...

'I can do the 21st,' Dr Crichton piped up. He lifted his head from the iPad and looked at them both.

'Great,' Ray answered. 'I mean, as great as it can be to be having an operation.' He swallowed. And the fear was still there. Simply the thought of gowning up and having pre-meds and lying on a table having his control taken from him was raising his heart rate. Not to mention the thought of the six to eight weeks before he could sing again.

'I'm not sure that will work,' Deborah said, flipping pages of her paper diary back and forth and forth and back. 'That means I have to keep you "anguished" for longer.' She took a breath. '*And* we have that photo Nigel is still holding back on. It's going to be really poor timing if that leaks now.'

Ray shook his head, a seed of annoyance starting to ferment. How long had he sat on this? How long had he kept what Ida had done buried so deep? Was his previous – admittedly slightly misguided – determination to protect Ida going to screw things up even more?

'No more lying,' Ray said on an outbreath. 'For once, let's be straight with everyone.'

'Ray, I'm telling you now, if you tell the world about this operation now then...' Deborah started.

'Then?' Ray asked, sitting forward on his chair. 'Then what? The London Eye stops turning? Oxford Street takes down all its festive lights? Jules's Hootenanny is called off?' He stood then, picking up Dr Crichton's glass paperweight from his desk and crushing it into his palm. 'I want to be honest. This is me. This is Ray Stone going through the shittiest time of his life while everything around this city turns into a fucking grotto.' He glared at Dr Crichton's medical skeleton in the corner of the room that was now bedecked with tinsel, its skull covered by a Santa hat. 'But there's good news. A chink of light. Because people with issues like Ida get help. People whose vocal cords aren't doing what they should, they get help too.' He looked to his doctor. 'No one's going to die, right? No one's going to come close to dying, if we admit I'm having an operation, am I right?'

No one answered him. Deborah looked like she might

want to. Either that or she was silently writing her resignation letter in her mind. He thumped the paperweight into his opposing palm just like his doctor did when he was pissed off.

'I'm not saying we have to set off another breaking news alert with this, but no more sneaking around. No lying. No covering things up. My career. My life,' Ray told them both. 'My decision.'

Still the room was eerie quiet until finally Dr Crichton spoke up. 'So, the 21st, yes?'

'Yeah,' Ray answered. 'The 21st. It's a date.' The adrenaline rush at insisting on being the master of his own destiny was starting to fade already. He needed to speak to Emily. And a text he had got from Jonah this morning meant it had to be tonight...

Sixty

Stretton Park Primary School

The scent of Dennis's liquorice allsorts was turning Emily's stomach. And why was he here again in the hall while she rehearsed the Christmas show? There couldn't be another visit from a firefighter surely!

'Tell me, Emily, do you really think they had a larger-than-life carrot in the stable in Bethlehem?' Dennis smirked, chewing away like her rehearsal was a much-talked-about blockbuster at the Odeon he was watching and he had got in half-price.

She didn't bother to disguise her eye-roll. 'It's the only costume that Felix likes. His auntie bought it for him. Donkeys eat carrots. A donkey was definitely, undeniably used in the stable in Bethlehem. There. Got it?'

'You sound a little on edge today,' Dennis remarked, his eyes not leaving the stage. 'Nothing wrong is there? No more pilfering from the corner shop or fights over football cards or Santa-slapping weighing on your mind?'

Emily really didn't have time for Dennis winding her up

today. She had been late for this morning's assembly because she'd got a cab to the wildlife sanctuary and dropped Idris Elba into their care. She'd been slightly worried over the past few days when he/she/they had refused to even sniff the water she'd put out for it, but equally she was glad she, Jonah and Allan hadn't ever tried to get it to drink raspberry leaf tea to induce birth. And every time she thought about that night and her decided course of action she felt ridiculous. Exactly how old was she? And then the news about Ida had hit and she realised what Ray was *really* going through and she couldn't for a second even start to comprehend it. The main lines from those first news articles came back to her now. *Years of physical and mental abuse. Ray hopes Ida receives the help she needs.* Still, after everything the reports had said he had been through – in very vague detail – Ray (the real victim) was worrying about his abuser. That was the person she had been getting to know. That was the man who had chipped away at the barriers over her heart. And, she still didn't know what to do. He'd asked for space when all she wanted to do was hold him close. She longed to say he was crazy for thinking she would feel any differently about him now she knew about this. But he had been hurt. He was still hurting. And all she really wanted to do was wrap her arms around him and tell him everything was going to be OK...

'It was a Chinese burn,' Emily said with a sigh. 'Not a slap. And, if you didn't know already, Jayden's father has moved out.'

'Well,' Dennis said, mid-munch. 'In case *you* don't know already, Penny *is* pregnant. Twins. She told Linda in the staffroom yesterday, but it isn't common knowledge so keep it under your shepherd's headdress,' Dennis said.

'Did you eavesdrop on a private conversation?' Emily asked, astounded.

'It isn't my fault,' Dennis moaned. 'They all think that microwave is louder than it actually is. Anyway, the main point is, they're going to have to advertise for the job while she's on maternity leave and Mother is delighted. She says this opening could be the new lease of life she's been waiting for.'

Emily closed her eyes, trying to envisage a woman in her eighties dealing with the rather boisterous lunch queue. Never mind the amount of food that seemed to need to be produced to feed the Stretton Park children who had hot dinners.

'Miss Parker! Miss Parker!' It was Felix, his bright red face clashing wonderfully with his orange carrot costume.

'What is it, Felix?' she asked, stepping towards the stage.

'Ray! Ray!'

Emily swallowed. The children had already asked when Ray was coming in to play the piano today, several times. She'd managed to tip-toe around the questioning and then she'd linked her phone to the speaker to play YouTube karaoke versions of the Christmas songs for them to sing along to. But it wasn't anything like the same.

'Felix means we need to sing the actual song when Jesus is pushed out of Mary that we haven't got the actual words for yet!' Cherry shouted, her hands either side of her mouth.

'Oh dear,' Dennis said, doffing his head at Emily. 'I hope there's not trouble in Palestine.'

'That isn't remotely funny, Dennis,' Emily snapped. 'None of this is.' The enormity of everything was suddenly washing over her like she was standing static in a car wash being pushed and pulled by the heavy rollers, soaked with soapy water that was stinging her eyes. 'Do you know anyone who can play the piano? Except...'

'Mr Jarvis is the only pianist I know,' Dennis interjected. 'Apart from Jamie Cullum. And I've heard he's a bit of a prima donna.'

'Ray! Ray!'

That had been the only word Felix had said all morning except 'carrot' when Emily had tried to get him to change out of the suit for the 'everyone in their favourite clothes' scenes at the end of the play that they'd had to practise first because Lucas had had to go for a dentist appointment.

'OK, well, I'm working on that song. It's to the tune of "Shallow". You all know that one, so we'll just sing the original words and pretend they're Christmassy so we practise the timing, and then, when I've finished the other words, we can do it again.' She tapped on her phone to call up YouTube again.

'But we don't have very many practices left,' Makenzie called.

'My mum and dad have been making videos of me practising at home,' Frema said. 'They say I'm going to be one of the only girls who celebrates Christmas *and* Hanukkah and they're going to send all the clips and the video of the whole play to all their relatives as a gift.'

This show was getting real. She was going to have parents and grandparents, aunts, uncles, the diocese and Susan Clark, all here, watching, committing the scenes to video for uploading to social media. Her show. Her script. Mainly Ray's lyrics. Palpitations pounded her chest.

'We haven't got a song about Candy Crush yet either,' Jayden called.

'My mum was playing it again last night,' Rashid answered. 'She's like some super-gamer on that app.'

'Mine too,' Jayden agreed.

'Allsort?' Dennis asked, offering Emily his bag.

She shook her head as her phone bleeped the arrival of a text message.

'The cavalry?' Dennis said, trying to look over at her screen. 'Someone who can tinkle your ivories?'

It was from Jonah.

Hiya! Change of plan for the Albert Hall show tonight. Allan's got to stay later at work and give a pep-talk to his new minions. Meet you at the usual entrance at 7 p.m. Xx

The Christmas concert at the Albert Hall. The one thing that had kept her going through this week while she pretended not to wait for Ray to walk through her front door, if only to pick up his things. Usually the three of them, plus Simon, would have an early dinner, somewhere swish near the venue and get slightly fuzzy on mulled wine. Now it would be a Mug Shot meal and tonic water and a cab or the Tube on her own...

'Right, Year Six, let's have you all in the stable now,' Emily ordered with a lot more confidence than she felt.

Sixty-One

Why, oh why did inspiration have to strike when she needed to get ready? In her bedroom, half inside a black dress swirled with gold thread, hair untamed, fringe in her eyes, Emily put the pen between her lips like it was an already gnawed at chicken wing and started the music on her phone again. She had a whole verse of the adapted words to 'Shallow' that she'd loosely entitled 'In the Stable'. Now she was getting flooded with words for the chorus. Who knew that in a few weeks she would have become almost adept at song-composition? It was extraordinary.

And then, above the strains of Lady Gaga coming from the phone speaker, she heard the sound of her front door opening. Jonah? Allan had managed to finish work earlier after all? She paused the song and shoved her other arm into the dress, hauling the fabric up and over her shoulder. If they wanted to go out to dinner now, when she'd already eaten, not a Mug Shot but a best-before-yesterday panini and a Peperami, she was going to be irritated.

'Hello? Jonah?' She put her feet into lovely shoes she'd found one day in Brixton – black crocodile print with a gold block on the toes – and picked up her hairbrush. She'd planned to pin it up, but she wasn't going to have time for that. And no sound was forthcoming from the entrance. It *had* sounded like an unforced entrance, hadn't it? Not a break-in. She stilled then, gripping the hairbrush tight. Should she stay here? Wait for whatever was going to happen next? Or…

She lost her breath when a shadow was cast in the doorway. A vision in black tie attire. Ray was standing there, just a few metres away from her, never having looked more gorgeous. There were already tears in her eyes, but she took him in anew. His height, his broad frame, the faint shadow of beard over his jawline, those exquisite eyes…

'Hey,' he greeted.

Hey. Simple. Absolutely the Ray she knew. Emily swallowed, feeling suddenly all kinds of self-conscious and not really knowing why. She hadn't expected him. She had always expected him?

'Hello,' she answered. 'I thought you were Jonah. Or Allan. Or…' She was running out of people who had keys to her flat. She might be soon forced to say something sensible. 'Have you come for your things?' That wasn't anything like what she wanted to say. She had envisaged this scenario a million times over between Ray's last text and Idris Elba…

'No,' he said, taking a step closer to her. 'I've come for you.'

Her heartrate picked up as he drew nearer still. She didn't know what to say at all now.

'If it's not too late,' Ray continued. 'If I haven't fucked it up. If you haven't come to the conclusion that I'm actually as weak and pathetic as my last message to you was. Which I definitely am by the way, but I'm hoping I can make a change with that, you know, going forward.'

He was standing right opposite her now, barely room to swing a piece of tinsel between them. Emily hadn't ever thought she would be this close to him again.

'Damn, that sounded terrible.' He sighed.

'I don't think you're weak,' Emily said boldly. 'I think you're the bravest person I've ever met.' A sob left her throat before she could stop it. 'What you've been through…'

'Sshh,' Ray begged, reaching out and touching her hair. 'I want to tell you about it.' He paused as if deliberating what to say next. 'I want to tell you everything but… we have a Christmas extravaganza to get to.'

Emily let out a laugh. Ray had said 'extravaganza' in the tone of Allan and she knew then that her two friends had somehow been involved in Ray being here. For the moment she didn't care how that had occurred, she was simply glad he *was* here.

'I know I don't deserve it but… will you come to the Christmas show with me?' Ray asked her softly, his fingers grazing her jawline.

'Give me a minute,' she said, her eyes mirroring his. 'Is this Ray Stone, the self-confessed Grinch, asking me to go to the big band Christmas at the Albert Hall?'

He put his hand to his chest and breathed deeply. 'You did just say I was brave,' Ray reminded.

Emily laughed. 'I absolutely did.' She slipped her arms around his waist, drawing him towards her. 'And I meant every word.' She stilled in his arms, relishing being close to him again.

He brushed his lips against her cheek and she closed her eyes, the feather-light touch gentle, like a whisper of a promise. And then Ray stepped back, taking both her hands in his.

'Are you ready?' he asked. 'I hear we've got seats right under where they release the fake snow at the end.'

Emily smiled. 'I'm ready.'

Sixty-Two

The Albert Hall

'Well, this has never happened before,' Allan announced as they waited outside the iconic building to show their tickets and be searched by security.

'I'm really, really sorry,' Ray answered, putting his arm around Emily and shielding her from the cold wind that was curling around the perimeter of the building.

He was apologising because this was all his fault. They had pretty much been followed by photographers since they had left Emily's apartment and now, as they waited to get into the hall, more journalists had arrived and there was snapping of pictures and questions he was doing his very best to ignore. If they didn't get inside soon he was considering walking to the front and asking for a little VIP assistance, something he ordinarily hated doing.

'Do you think we'll be on the *News at Ten*?' Allan asked, every statement he made being accompanied by a pout to whoever's camera was trained on them at the time.

'I really hope not,' Ray said, moving forward as the queue surged a little.

'It's OK,' Emily whispered to him. 'You don't have to worry about me.'

He *was* worrying about her. She was the only person he was really worried about, because she hadn't asked for any of this attention and here she was, in the absolute thick of it. This was what he was going to bring to her life. Celebrity chaos. Was that fair? He brushed the thought away and looked to the Grade I listed building all lit up, its red bricks a-glow, the one star at the top of the Christmas tree they had walked past still visible. What wasn't fair was even now he had told the truth it was still no better for him. The journalists were still here. Still wanting a story.

'Ray, have you spoken to Ida about the allegations?' a reporter called.

He closed his eyes and wished them all away. It was best not to say anything at all. If he gave any answer it could be turned against him. 'Do they have popcorn at these things?' he asked the group.

'Ice cream,' Allan answered. 'Gorgeous ice cream. And I know you're thinking, baby, it's a little cold outside for ice cream, but believe me, under all those lights, next to all those people singing and swaying and getting festive, you're going to want a vanilla tub in the interval.'

'Great,' Ray said with a nod.

'And the other good news is,' Jonah began. 'I'm sure none of these reporters have tickets to the show.'

'Let's hope not,' he answered.

*

Emily squeezed Ray's hand as they found their seats about ten rows back from where the band were going to be playing. She loved coming to the Albert Hall. It was such a magnificent building with its plush red seats and ornate décor curling round its circular interior. The swags and bows in front of the boxes and the arches around the gallery all made it look like they had transported into an era long ago. It was grand and majestic and decked out with full-on Christmas lights. Emily really thought it was more spectacular than anywhere else.

'It's amazing, isn't it?' Emily breathed, her eyes still tracking around the hall, looking at every little thing, soaking up every trace of its ambience.

'It's a beautiful building,' Ray admitted. 'And it has great acoustics.'

'Have you played here?' Emily asked suddenly.

'God, no,' Ray said straightaway, shaking his head. 'No, you have to be pretty special to get a gig here.'

'Well,' Emily said. 'One day.'

'Yeah,' Ray answered. 'Maybe one day.' He smiled at her. 'Listen, Emily, there is something I need to tell you, before the show.'

'I thought we were going to talk later,' she reminded.

'Yeah, I know,' he said. 'We are. It's just...'

She didn't know what he was going to say now. What could it be that it couldn't wait just for a few hours? Surely they deserved to put the world on hold for a while and regroup, indulging in the Rat Pack's Christmas finest.

'The press outside,' Ray began.

'I told you. It's OK,' Emily reassured. 'I get it. It's part of your life and there's nothing you can do about it. If it's a choice between you being here with them outside and you not being here at all then...'

'I know,' he interrupted. 'I get that. I appreciate you saying that but... the thing is...' He swallowed before carrying on. 'A newspaper has a photo of us, us on London Bridge... you know, when we...'

He didn't even need to say the word 'kissed', because Emily was already reliving every single sexy second of it. Wrapped up in that magical, spine-tingling moment, she hadn't thought about who could be watching. Hadn't cared. She nodded her head now. 'OK.'

'OK?' Ray asked her. 'Because the way I'm splashed over everything at the moment they're going to use it for something at some time.' He sighed. 'And although I've tried my best to keep it from being out there, there's only so much I can do.'

'You tried to keep it from being printed?' Emily asked him. The seats were filling up now, the audience filing in and getting ready for the start of the show. A gentle Christmas instrumental was echoing around the concert hall.

'Yeah,' Ray answered. 'I didn't want any of my flack being directed at you. And... I didn't want Ida to know you either.' He stopped talking then, an unbearably sad expression on his face. 'She's with her mum now. She's gone up to Leeds. Apparently, she's got a place in a facility up there for assessment.'

'That's good.'

Emily didn't know what else to say, so instead she slipped her hand into his and held on tight. 'Have you seen this picture of us on London Bridge?'

'Yeah,' Ray answered. 'Deborah showed it to me. I think

the fact she slept with the editor at college one time is the only thing that's stopping it from being published.'

'And how do I look?' Emily asked. 'Front page material or just worthy of the tiniest of thumbnails?'

Ray squeezed her hand. 'Full colour supplement, Miss Parker. Without a doubt.'

'Good,' Emily answered. 'Then I'm sure my mother will absolutely love it.'

Sixty-Three

MP Free Studio, Islington

'Oh, wasn't it amazing?' Emily exclaimed as Ray opened the door of the building and they stepped in out of the cold. 'All those instruments! Those Christmas songs! Saxophones and trumpets and the over enthusiastic conductor. And don't think I didn't notice you singing along, Ray Stone.'

Ray smiled at her, shrugging off his coat and unfastening his bow tie. He hadn't sung aloud, but he had mouthed the words. He couldn't remember the last time he had ever sung along to a festive song. But in that arena, it had been hard not to get wrapped up in the moment when thousands of others all around were high on the heady atmosphere of the season. Plus, there had been Christmas trees and reindeers and every light show imaginable, all culminating in an outpouring of synthetic snow from the ceiling of the magnificent hall. Allan and Jonah had been in fine voice throughout the entire performance and had sung most of the way to the Tube station until they split to head home. Under the influence of two vanilla ice creams, Emily had told him that she *really* needed a piano and, apart from sneaking onto the stage at the Albert Hall and commandeering theirs, the studio was the best closest option.

'Come on,' Emily said as Ray opened the door to Studio Two, his favourite. 'Admit it. You enjoyed it tonight.'

He flicked on the lights, glad no one was here, and smiled at her. 'It was fantastic,' he admitted. 'I do actually feel a little festive.' He whispered. 'But don't tell anyone.'

She laughed. 'That's good.' She stepped in after him and began gazing around at his workspace. 'Because I need your help finishing my new song.'

'Have you even started it?' Ray asked, throwing his coat down on the sofa.

'Yes, I have actually!'

'Does it have the words "cook" and "book" in it?'

Emily's mouth dropped open. 'So cheeky! That was my very first tentative step into songwriting.'

'I'm sorry,' Ray apologised. 'Let's hear it.'

'Can I have my pianist?' she asked.

He looked at the sleek black grand piano, its stool a place where he had felt so comfortable for so long now. Swallowing, he took it in afresh, its body gleaming under the studio lights. Was he going to come through this operation OK? Would he still be able to reach those notes he was famous for? Or was this the end of the road, the time where Sam Smith really did takeover all the airplay and stadium tours...

He shook himself and strode forward. He had to live for the moment. That was what life was about. 'Come and sit with me.' He pulled at the leather seat and sat down, beckoning Emily to join him. And then he began to play, something he had been working on before this current nightmare had started.

'The last time I sat on a piano stool with you, you made me sing in front of a bar full of people,' Emily reminded, brushing hands over the front of her dress then plumping down next to him.

'I remember,' Ray replied, playing quietly, but looking at her, and not the keys his hands were caressing. 'It was the most intimate public moment of my life.'

'It was…' Emily began.

He was holding his breath now, wondering what she was going to say. What did he want it to have meant to her?

She sighed, deeply. 'It was at that moment I realised I was falling for you.'

Her eyes met with his and suddenly his fingers weren't finding all the right notes now. One finger was simply pressing down on middle C, over and over again. Oh, so slowly, slower still, until he stopped.

'Ray,' Emily started.

'Wait,' he breathed, taking his hands off the keyboard and turning a little so they were almost facing each other. 'There's one more thing I have to get out there. About what I said in that message I sent you.' He had rehearsed this in his mind a hundred times today. *Be honest. Say the words. The truth can't ever really hurt you.*

'What is it?' Emily wanted to know, her beautiful eyes studying him. 'You can tell me anything. I want you to know that, now more than ever.'

But it still felt uncomfortable inside of him. Because no one knew how it was going to turn out. He took her hands in his. 'The reason I said I couldn't play with you for the show… the reason I was going to get another pianist… is because… coming up…' He took a slow breath. 'For a while… I'm not going to be able to sing… at all.'

His throat was aching with the stress of this conversation and he desperately wanted to clear it… which Dr Crichton had all but banned. He paused, taking another breath, before carrying on.

'I've got to have an operation.' He quickened his pace. 'Basically, my vocal cords are pretty shot and my specialist wants me in as soon as possible.'

'Oh, Ray!' Emily exclaimed, squeezing his hands in shock.

'And I don't know what I'm more afraid of, you know. Having an operation, like my mum did… and not coming out of that hospital again. Or making it through the operation and not getting my voice back.'

'Ray, you have to think positive. You're going to be fine,' Emily reassured.

'Statistics say you're probably right. My dad and Brenda believe statistics but… I've got a ghost in my mind telling me that shit happens and… currently shit happens to me.'

'Well, what's the very worst thing you can imagine happening?' Emily asked him.

It should have been obvious but somehow it wasn't. He needed to think. He needed to give her the answer he truly believed.

'That I'll die,' he answered. No life at all was definitely worse than a life without his career. His view of the world had never been as skewed as his mother's. Life was precious. Life was something you held on to no matter what your struggles.

'There we go,' Emily said softly.

'O–K,' Ray replied.

'You have to trust that your specialist isn't going to kill you,' Emily stated in a matter of fact manner. 'And worrying about whether he's going to kill you or not isn't going to change the outcome. You'll just have spent the time you could have been living your best life worrying about something that probably won't happen.'

'Probably,' Ray said with a sigh. 'It's not a great word.'

'Ray, do you think Simon spent time worrying that maybe one day, when he was walking out of work to catch the Tube he might possibly be run over by a drunk-driver?'

When she put it like that, he sounded like a lunatic for even starting this conversation. What was the matter with him?

'Hey,' Ray said quickly. 'I didn't mean to correlate any of that to Simon. I'm not looking for sympathy here. I… really don't know what I'm looking for. Probably someone to end this conversation right now so I don't carry on making an arse of myself.'

'Listen to me,' Emily said solidly, still holding onto his hands, strength in those petite fingers, dwarfed by his. 'I trust that the universe is not going to deliver you to the shed at my school, make me fall for you and then take you away from me. That really would mean my life was a horrible twisted rom-com Paramount would never touch.'

Her words drew a smile and he felt himself relax a little.

'When are you going into hospital?' she asked him.

'That's the thing,' Ray said. 'Emily, I really couldn't bear to think that someone else was playing the piano for you.' He took a breath. 'I want to see the kids do their thing. I want to see you do *your* thing. I was crazy to think I could miss it.' He smiled. 'I told them I can't go in until the 21st. I might be in there for Christmas Day, but you know, I'm not all that struck on Christmas Day anyway.'

'And here was I thinking I'd turned opinion tonight.'

'You've done more than turn opinion, Emily Parker,' Ray breathed. 'You've turned my world back the right way.'

He could feel his heart beating in his chest. Her hands were in his, her body so close... was it too soon to share everything?

'Play for me?' Emily begged. 'And this time, if you need me to, I'll do all the singing.'

Sixty-Four

In the Stable
– to the tune of 'Shallow' by Lady Gaga & Bradley Cooper

Will he be born tonight?
Lying underneath a star so bright
Or will it take some time?
Will Mary wish she'd had a glass of wine?
God's calling
My son is coming, it's time to stop and listen
We all need change
Time for a new start to turn the page

The shepherds bring their flock
The Three Kings tire but they do not stop
Mary's trying hard
Joseph's there for her, a constant guard
God's calling
The hour is nearing, it's time for destiny

We all pray
And when he comes alive the earth will cry

Here in this stable
A baby will scream out
His life will save the world
Conquering evil, bring us together
We'll never feel the fear

Chorus

He's in the manger, manger
In the manger m-m-m-manger
In the manger, manger
We're all in the stable now
Oh oh oh oh...

Jesus is born now
Look at his cuteness
He's sweeter than Meghan and Harry's son
A king for the whole world, marking a new dawn
We're all in the stable now

He's in the manger, manger
In the manger m-m-m-manger
In the manger, manger
We're all in the stable now

Ray hadn't been able to stop himself from joining in with Emily. They had spent the past hour putting this song together and the ideas had sprung mainly from her. He had seen it in her eyes. She was thinking about her class of children and making this show special for them. In the beginning it might have been about creating a spectacle for her boss to try and earn promotion, but right now, it was about those kids she cared so much about. This was the perfect song to end the nativity tableau scene in Stretton Park's play.

He played the final chords and then he looked at Emily. He was shaking, the emotion of what they had created simply blowing his mind. Their legs were touching, and he could feel it from her too. He was too scared to speak, for fear of breaking the connection that was pulsing in the air between them. Energy, sparks, tension, those few centimetres had it all going on. But how long could they sit this close and not say anything? Action was out of the question, wasn't it? They should go slow given the current situation...

'Ray,' Emily breathed, her voice ragged.

'Yeah.' He didn't trust himself to say anything else.

'You said something else in that message you sent me,' she carried on, her body seeming to get *even* closer to his.

'Yeah,' he replied. He remembered all the stupid things he had said in that message. Which one was she wanting to talk about now? Now, when desire was sprinting through him.

'You said,' she paused, wetting her lips with her tongue. 'You said you loved me.'

Her voice whispered to him, those words falling first on his skin, then quickly beginning to soak inside him. *That* part of the message hadn't been stupid. That sentiment he had meant with every fibre of him.

'Yeah,' he replied. 'I remember.' If he thought he was

scared about his upcoming operation, then this moment was something else entirely. He currently felt like someone was churning up his insides with a blender. *He loved her.* He had let his heart accept that feeling, admit to it, now he had to decide whether he wanted to own it. He knew the answer but, what was more important was how Emily felt.

'Did you mean it?' she asked him.

He finally took his hands from the keys of the piano. They were shaking, like every nerve-ending. He put his palms to the flat of his thighs, nervous. But then he looked directly at her, drinking her in, taking a little time to admire every soft line and delicate edge. That auburn hair framing her features, that cute chin she'd told him she didn't like, her lips he already knew every contour of...

'I meant it,' he finally said, exhaling a breath and all the emotion that was quickly gathering.

'Tell me again,' Emily said, putting her hands to the lapels of his dinner jacket, smoothing down the fabric then holding it captive.

Ray swallowed, feeling his heart throbbing in his throat, desperately trying to control his breath. 'I love you.'

'Say it again,' Emily whispered, shifting even closer to him, fully connecting their bodies on the piano stool.

There was no hesitation this time, but his voice was even thicker with desire. 'I love you, Emily.'

A rush had been building inside Emily since they'd started singing the song together. Here in this intimate studio, the gorgeous Christmas tree making the moment even more festively romantic, Emily had completely lost her heart to him. Through these past weeks she had gone from feeling that she was never going to get over Simon, let alone love again, and here she was, experiencing unchartered territory but, now, unafraid to venture forth and explore.

She pressed herself to him but held back from connecting their lips. She wanted to look into those eyes again, see what was expressed amid that sparkling amber. It was hard to stop her body from shaking, simply keep still and be, but, although she was sure about what *she* wanted to happen next, she wanted to give Ray that time. Ensure he was certain about the next step.

'Ray,' she whispered, finally reaching up and putting her fingers to his hair. She watched him close his eyes as she toyed with the strands, tucking them behind his ear.

'Yeah,' he answered in a deep rumble, eyelids opening.

'I love you too.'

She watched his reaction to her words, saw the realisation in those eyes, the pupils reacting. It set fire to her soul. She kissed him then, firm but slow, then with *all* the force of the passion she was feeling in this moment.

Ray kissed her back, his mouth responding to hers, hungry, fast and she edged his jacket from his shoulders as the stool became suddenly too small to host this embrace. He shrugged a little, lips still locked with hers, helping her to remove the shirt as they continued the kiss.

And then Emily's fingers were pulling away the loosened bow tie and working on the buttons of his white dress shirt. She stood up, losing his mouth for a second, then quickly reconnecting as she hurried to undress him.

'Hey,' Ray said, drawing his mouth away from hers as he stood too, pushing the stool back from the piano with his knee and giving them a little more room.

'What?' Emily asked, successfully unfastening another two of his shirt buttons.

'Taking off my shirt,' he breathed. 'I mean... are you sure?'

Emily answered him by undoing the last of the buttons and parting the cotton, her hands moving over his torso, across his abs and up over his chest. When she reached his clavicle she stopped, her fingers finding the scar on his right shoulder. Running her index finger over the small knot of scar tissue, she looked deep into his eyes. And then she took her hands away and put them to her black and gold dress, gently easing the figure-hugging fabric up her body, all the while keeping her gaze on him, this gorgeous man standing in front of her. She pulled it up, over her breasts, over her head and then off, finally standing before him in just her underwear. It was cream silk, circa 1950, something she'd never worn before.

'I'm sure,' she answered, shivering as she watched his eyes appraise her.

She gasped as Ray kissed her then, his arms coming around her and lifting her up, over the piano keys, and up again, onto the very top of the grand piano. She watched him, moving to lean over her, still seeming uncertain whether this was what she wanted. Perhaps she needed to be clearer still.

'Make love to me,' Emily begged him. 'Make love to me, Ray.'

It was all the cue he seemed to need, and Emily pulled him towards her, knowing that any crescendo they had made during the performance of their song was about to be eclipsed by the music their bodies were going to make when they finally came together.

Sixty-Five

Stretton Park Primary School

20th December

Emily wasn't usually a nail-biter, but her nails were currently down to the quick. She was blaming a combination of Olivia Colman plus her pre-show nerves. She had taken her class on a visit to see Idris, Idris's babies and Olivia yesterday. All were doing ridiculously well for hedgehogs who should be hibernating. It couldn't be explained. One of the animal welfare volunteers had suggested it was climate change, but seeing as London had been as cold as always this winter, Emily was sceptical. Anyway, as she had gently petted Olivia Colman's nose, the creature had nibbled at one of Emily's nails, thus starting the downfall of the rest of them. Who cared? She was too busy for handshaking with the bishop and his suffragans. She had props and scenery that were falling apart and Allan hysterically shouting 'you're another meme' approximately every six seconds. Since the photo of her and Ray kissing on London Bridge had been printed, she had been made into a gif a day. It had been enough for even her and Ray to get bored of it and they'd decided that kissing in a few other places might mix things up a bit. So, they'd gone on a tour, ignoring the presence of reporters and simply enjoying the beginnings of their relationship. On a moonlight cruise up the Thames. By the locks at Camden. Christmas markets for gifts. New North Road. Emily had met Len and Brenda and had been treated to three hours of *Home and Away* episodes that Ray seemed to be frighteningly excited by, and they had been guests of honour at the unveiling of the new purple spare room that really was something to behold. She hoped Brenda's sister was bringing sunglasses with her when she came to visit.

'Felix!' Emily hissed. 'Come away from the curtain. We don't want any of the audience to see you before the start of the show, do we? We don't want to spoil the surprise.'

'Surprise! Surprise!' the carrot-coated boy chanted, still ruffling the thick red stage curtain with his orange arms.

'Felix,' Cherry called, her Queen Number Two costume ironed to pristine and looking like it was so starched and stiff she was going to have trouble walking. 'Come away from the curtain until the actual performance!'

'Thank you, Cherry,' Emily said. 'But I'm still the teacher here until you get your degree.' She swallowed. She needed to try and calm down. Each and every one of her performers was in varying degrees of anxiety and had been the whole day. Rashid was uncharacteristically quiet. Alice hadn't mentioned death once. Makenzie hadn't corrected anyone on their wrong use of gender. Matthew hadn't twirled his hair around his finger. Charlie hadn't picked his nose...

'Hey.'

Emily looked up to Ray and couldn't help the smile that seemed to instantly break out whenever he was around. She didn't hesitate. She threw her arms around him, holding him tight, inhaling the scent of musk and winter spice and something uniquely Ray that seemed to just rise up from his skin and catch her unawares.

'Woooooo!' every member of Year Six cooed, laughing, some of them clapping.

Emily suddenly came to, remembering where she was and she stepped out of Ray's embrace, brushing down her smartest red and blue striped dress with the fabric belt that tied in the middle. To her it had always shouted 'Deputy Head' when she got it out of her wardrobe. No news on that promotion and unlikely to be for the foreseeable future. It was apparently one thing to have worked your socks off for weeks maintaining equilibrium in the classroom as well as managing the equivalent of West End Kids Week, but another to have done all that *and* turned the Head's head...

'Thank you, Year Six. Now let's concentrate on remembering our lines and the words to the songs now there's only—' Emily looked at her watch '—fifteen minutes to go.' She literally felt her complexion blanch. 'Oh my goodness, there's only fifteen minutes to go! And there's so much I need to do! Frema!'

'Yes, Miss Parker,' Frema called, half of her dressed as a vicar, the other half rabbi, a line drawn down the middle of her face in a sparkling gold. She did look tremendous.

'Can you check the llama is OK?'

'You have a llama?' Ray said, laughing.

'Don't ask,' Emily begged. 'We had a last-minute sponsorship for the "after party" from Lakeside Llama Petting Zoo. Guess who had to squeeze *that* mention into the script about an hour ago?' She sighed, wringing her hands together nervously. 'Dennis is going to be laughing for at least the rest of the school year.'

'Well,' Ray said, taking hold of her hands. 'There's something else you need to do before any of that.'

'Oh God!' She put a hand to her mouth and side-eyed the children. 'I mean, oh goodness, what's happened in the auditorium? Those decorations haven't fallen off the ceiling again, have they? Ray, they can't fall down because some of them are quite heavy and Lucas's grandma turned eighty today. Having a Harvester meal and coming here is her big celebration. I can't kill her! And how old is the bishop? Is he wearing his big hat?'

'Take a breath,' Ray ordered, squeezing her hands.

'I haven't got time for breathing. Breathing has been scheduled for around an hour and half's time when this is all over.'

'Hey,' Ray said, forcing her to look into his eyes. She both loved and loathed when he did that. It was like being hypnotised in the sexiest of ways...

'Living in the moment, right? We talked about it.'

They had talked about it. They had talked about it a lot in between teasing the paparazzi on festive riverboats and having sex on pianos. And tomorrow Ray was going into a private hospital for surgery that could change everything. But Emily believed the only change would be a positive one. Ray's vocal cords would be stronger. His voice fixed, maybe even improved. They hadn't talked about the nitty gritty of his operation, she had focused on making plans for when he came out of it, starting with Christmas Day. If he was out of hospital, they were going to have a relaxed dinner with Jonah and Allan, plus Jonah's parents and Allan's parents, followed by sandwiches and cakes with Len and Brenda at teatime. If he *wasn't* out of hospital, she was going to bring turkey and all the trimmings to him and annoy him intensely with Christmas music exactly as she had been doing from the very start of their relationship.

'We did talk about it,' Emily answered with a nod.

'So, you need to come now and help with a situation with... your parents,' Ray told her.

'My parents?' She was completely astounded that Alegra and William were *actually* here. She had truly expected them to not turn up like usual, even after them making inquiries about ticketing options.

'Yeah,' Ray said. 'Just come with me a second.'

'But, I need to stay with the children,' Emily told him.

'Jayden,' Ray called.

'Yes,' the boy answered, toying with his innkeeper waistcoat. His hair was freshly washed and tamped down with a lovely smelling product Emily definitely recognised the scent of from somewhere.

'You're in charge for two minutes,' Ray said seriously. 'Be nice. Be cool. And don't set fire to anything.'

'Wait! What?' Emily said as Ray pulled her to the stairs that led the way off the stage.

Emily held her breath as she reached the floor of the hall. The whole space was packed with people, almost every chair filled, and the other teachers were setting up more chairs in every-not-governed-by-fire-regulations-space for the last-minute influx. There had never been this many people at a Stretton Park show before. The pressure to get this right suddenly rose inside of her.

'Emily!'

It was her mother's voice and it was an agitated cat-hiss of the highest order. And then Emily actually looked at her mother properly. She was standing next to her dad and it became immediately apparent why this had been classed as a 'situation'. Her mother was dressed elaborately as something akin to Cleopatra, a short white tunic, gold sandals despite the freezing temperatures outside, complete with black wig, headdress and thick winged eyeliner. William was a definite King Herod with what looked like a very realistic crown and a tabard that was a little too tight.

'Emily! Why is no one dressed up?! You specifically told me it was fancy dress!' Alegra exclaimed.

The text her mother had sent! The night Ray's news had broken! The joke message she had returned! She had meant to follow it up with something sensible later. Emily hadn't even thought about it again. There had been too much going on. Laughter was bubbling up inside her now, but she shouldn't. She couldn't. Could she?

'Emily! What's going on?' Alegra continued to wail. 'No one is dressed in costume! No one!'

'That's not actually true,' Emily said quickly. 'There are thirty-three children behind that red curtain on stage all dressed in costume.' She took her mother's arm and turned her slightly so she was facing the other end of the room. Was that one of Felix's arms she could see poking out of the drapes? Ray shouldn't have left Jayden in charge...

'But I'm not part of the show!' Alegra squealed. 'I'm part of the audience.'

'Would you *like* to be part of the show?' Emily asked. 'Because Nazareth had many, many villagers.'

William scoffed, his fingers going to the crown on his

head. 'I don't know if you've noticed, Emily, but your father is in fact the king.'

'You look great,' Ray told him. 'Where did you get that crown from? The queens have crowns from eBay, but yours looks really *really* authentic.'

'Well,' William said, removing the headwear and showing it to Ray. 'I borrowed it from a friend. Prince Michael said it was just hanging around in a display cabinet.' He smiled. 'Rubies *and* sapphires.'

Her dad was literally wearing the Crown Jewels to her school's Christmas show.

'Emily!' Alegra whined. 'This is unacceptable. What are we supposed to do?'

'Well, you could sit down and enjoy the show knowing that, dressed in costume, you will be having an almost fully immersive experience... or I could find you a tabard the children wear for painting... or an apron Penny wears for cooking the school dinners.'

Alegra looked like she might weep.

'I quite like being a king,' William announced, putting the crown back on his head. 'Do you remember Tintagel, Alegra?'

Emily watched her mother's features soften a little.

'It was all high jinks that weekend, culminating in that drama we put on. You were my Guinevere that night.' William slipped an arm around his wife's shoulders. 'And tonight, you're my Cleopatra. I do believe she was the fifth wife of Herod.'

And apparently her dad had done his historical research for cos-play at her school... Could this evening get any more bizarre?

'Well,' Alegra said, leaning a little into William's arms. 'When you put it like that.'

'Good,' Emily said, clapping her hands together. 'Find seats. I have a show to direct. Ray, come on, you should be checking the piano right now.'

Sixty-Six

'OK, everybody, you're doing so, so well!' Emily said to her class as they took a second behind the curtain while scenery was moved. 'You're all singing beautifully and loudly, and no one's forgotten any lines.'

'I forgot to mention the battered sausage,' Angelica said, tears springing into her eyes.

'It doesn't matter,' Emily reassured.

'But it was supposed to be "and Mary loves a battered sausage with Ralph of an evening" at the end and I forgot,' Angelica continued.

'It was probably a good thing,' Emily answered, tying a cloak around Cherry. She didn't quite know what she had been thinking when she wrote that line. It was quite close to the mark. She hadn't wanted to turn the children into Frankie Boyle.

There was that hair product smell again. Where was Jayden?

'We have forty seconds!' Matthew announced, the stopwatch Emily had put him in charge of in his hand.

'Thirty-nine, thirty-eight...'

'Jonah!' Emily exclaimed. Her best friend was behind the scenes, putting hair clay into Jayden's hair. 'What are you doing here? You're meant to be watching.'

'I have been watching,' Jonah answered. 'It's brilliant, Em! Absolutely brilliant! I just noticed, under the lights, Jayden's hair needed a bit more magic so...'

That's why she knew the scent! Jonah's hair products...

'I smell of coconuts now,' Jayden informed with a grin.

'All the England footballers wear this in their hair, you know,' Jonah informed.

'I've got forty seconds before the next scene,' Emily informed, pulling a stray piece of cotton from Jayden's waistcoat.

'Thirty-two!' Matthew piped up. 'Thirty-one, thirty...'

'How is it being received by the bishop and his suffragans?' Emily asked Jonah. 'I can't really see very much from the wings.'

'One of them pulled out a bag of popcorn,' Jonah informed. 'Literally from under his robe. Even Allan was appalled.'

'That has to be a good thing though, doesn't it?'

'Of course it is,' Jonah said. He put a clay-covered hand on Emily's shoulder. 'How could they not enjoy this show? It's like a cross between a hilarious version of *Songs of Praise* and *Ant and Dec's Saturday Night Takeaway*.'

'And they haven't even seen the llama yet,' Emily said taking a deep breath.

'There's a llama?!' Jonah exclaimed, his expression a picture of astonishment.

'Currently leaving the contents of its bowel in a makeshift litter tray,' Emily answered. 'Thank Jesus for shredded paper and sand.'

'Twenty seconds!' Matthew yelled. 'Nineteen, eighteen…'

'OK, queens! Are you ready for your big song? Everyone get ready to find their places when the curtain goes back,' Emily instructed.

'Miss Parker,' Jayden said suddenly.

'Yes, Jayden.'

'I like it that you don't look sad anymore,' he told her.

She swallowed away emotion as his words settled on her. She *was* happy. Amid the stress of this performance she was actually happier than she had ever been.

'I like it that you don't look sad anymore too, Jayden,' she said, quickly regrouping.

'It's quieter now my dad's gone,' he admitted. 'Mum says she's gonna try and get a better place with a garden.'

'That's fantastic news,' Emily told him.

'Oh, Jayden,' Jonah said ruffling his hair a little more. 'Don't make me emotional. I can't style hair if I'm emotional.'

Emily smiled at her student, hoping and praying that this December was going to bring a new start for everyone. 'Come on, Mr Innkeeper, it's time for you to make room in that stable.'

We Three Queens
– to the tune of 'Last Christmas' by Wham!

Last Christmas I gave you some myrrh
But on Boxing Day you gave it to her

This year to not break my heart
I'll give it to Baby Jesus... x2

Dance break*

You broke my heart, I don't know why
I didn't get that you were someone else's guy
Tell me maybe, did you really like me?
Or was it just because I'm part of the monarchy?

Happy Christmas, I'll give it to the baby
With some gold and nappies bought from Sainsbury's
Now I know what love can mean, I finally realise how
    crazy stupid I've been

Chorus x 2
Dance break*

Sandy desert, no more mince pies
Hiding from you and your Insta lies
Good gosh I thought you were someone really super,
But hey, I guess you still weren't Bradley Cooper

Faced with three camels who do nothing but fart
We're queens on a mission, stop the world from falling apart
Ooo, now we've found our real calling we won't need
    you again

Chorus x 2

Faced with three camels...

Emily stared out into the darkness as the audience burst into another round of applause and cheers. It was one of her favourite songs of the entire performance and Alice, Angelica and Cherry made fantastic queens, with all the dance moves completely nailed. She watched them curtseying and bowing and soaking up the clapping... and getting completely out of character.

'Into the stable!' Emily hissed from the wings. 'Stop bowing!'

'The baby is here!' Jayden called out over the audience's reaction, signalling that the time for moving the show on had arrived.

'It's not here yet!' Jennifer, Emily's Mary called. 'One... more... push!' She let out a gut-wrenching grunt even better and more realistic than in any rehearsal and the baby doll flew out from under her gown faster that anyone had anticipated.

'Baby Jesus! Baby Jesus!' It was Felix the carrot who caught the doll before it catapulted off the stage and he kissed it on the face before dropping it head-first into the manger.

'The baby was born, and the last visitor arrived to see the new King of Kings. A cute and cuddly llama came all the way from Lakeside Llama Petting Zoo. This llama won't harm ya! Hours of family-friendly fluffy fun at Lakeside!'

Emily said a silent thank you that Charlie had remembered the new words he'd had literally minutes to learn. Now she simply had to hope the llama wasn't going to make a drama out of its performance.

'Llama! Llama!'

What was Felix doing with the llama? Leading the llama

on was Frema's job. Emily looked across the stage and saw that her carrot-costumed boy was sitting on the llama's back and Frema was having trouble making the poor thing join the tableau. What did llamas like to eat best? What could she entice it with?

'Come on, Mr Llama!' Angelica called loudly. 'If you're a good boy you might get a battered sausage from Ralph's Plaice. Mary loves a sausage at the weekend.'

Emily closed her eyes and willed the earth to part and for her to disappear down into the ground. Then, just as quickly, she opened her eyes and directed her gaze to Ray at the piano. Finally Frema was making some headway with getting the animal to comply, while, still aboard, Felix threw his orange arms around like he was a cowboy at a rodeo.

'And lo! There is rejoicing! We are all in the stable now!'

The lights were dimmed, leaving only the strings of fairy lights around the stable to illuminate the actors. Ray began to play the introduction to 'In the Stable'.

Emily's heart soared as her children sang the song so beautifully and she was brought back to the night when she and Ray perfected the new lyrics in his studio. She had been giddy with her feelings for him then. She was still giddy now. Utterly and undeniably in love with him. She watched him playing the old school piano, nothing like the beautiful grand pianos he was used to. But as his fingers hit the ebony and ivory, he was watching the children too, mouthing the words, making sure they didn't falter, like this was the most important performance of his life. And he was doing this all for her, the evening before he went in for surgery. It had to be OK for him. For *them*. It just had to be.

'We're all in the stable now,' the children finished, holding on to the note like they had practised. Finally, Ray ended the tune and the audience erupted louder than ever.

Sixty-Seven

'Year Six!' Emily shouted above the excited hubbub backstage. She adopted her usual pose, Rio De Janeiro stretching out in front of her, waiting for calm.

The children stopped talked immediately and their wide, excited eyes were all directed at her.

She smiled then. 'You were amazing! Honestly, so amazing. And I am so proud of all of you. Each and every one of you.'

'But not the llama,' Frema said, a cross expression on both the vicar side of her face and the rabbi side. 'You can't be proud of the llama because he pooped on my new shoes.'

A few of the children laughed, but quickly stopped when Frema's look darkened further.

'Listen,' Emily told them. 'The hard part is over. The last section of the show is all about you and having fun.' Her eyes moved over each of her class in turn. They were all so different, so unique and that was a wonderful, *wonderful* thing. She hoped they stayed that way for ever and never let anyone tell them what to think, or how to feel, or who or what to be. Emotion was thickening now and she needed to hold it together. She needed to hold it together for tonight for her children and for tomorrow for Ray. Then, hopefully, they could all look forward to Christmas Day and whatever the new year was going to bring.

'I want you to go out there and show your mums and dads, and dads and dads, and mums and mums, and step-parents, and brothers and sisters, and nans and grandads, and aunts and uncles, and godparents, and friends and...'

'My hamster Gordon,' Lucas interrupted.

Emily didn't know what to say. Had Lucas's parents really brought his hamster to the show? Were they taking it to the Harvester? She shook her head. 'Show Mrs Clark and the bishop and the...'

'Suffragettes,' Alice added.

'Suffra*gans*,' Emily corrected.

'Are they different things?' Alice asked.

She didn't have time to go into this now. 'Year Six, go out there and show the audience how much fun we have in our class. Show them what the winter holidays mean to you.' She caught the gaze of two boys who had had the most challenging of weeks. 'Rashid, Jayden, are you ready for your moment in the spotlight?'

'I feel a bit sick,' Rashid told her.

He did look a little wan. She stepped forward, ready to put a hand to his forehead and check for a temperature but Jayden beat her to it. He clapped a hand onto Rashid's shoulder.

'You're alright, mate. Come on. Our mums are gonna love our song.'

Rashid visibly brightened at Jayden's show of companionship and he gave a small smile.

'Right,' Emily said. 'Let's go!'

I Saw Mummy Playing Candy Crush
– to the tune of 'I Saw Mommy Kissing Santa Claus'
by Jackson 5

*Rashid (spoken): Oooo! Mummy's playing Candy
     Crush*
Jayden (sung): I saw Mummy playing Candy Crush
Sitting on the sofa late one night
Her fingers moved so quick, like lightning they did slick
*Across the screen as she matched up the sweets to win
     her game*

*Rashid (sung): When I saw Mummy playing Candy
     Crush*
Her face was filled with pure and utter glee
*And when she didn't win the round, her smile turned
     upside down*
But she still loves playing Candy Crush

*Both (sung): I saw Mummy playing, playing, playing
     Candy Crush*
*Both (spoken): It's all true! It is! I did see Mummy
     playing Candy Crush!*
And I think she's really cool!

Instrumental (recorders and glockenspiels)

Both (sung): Next I saw Mummy put down Candy
  Crush
And turn the TV on to Game of Thrones
Rashid (sung): Oh, how mad my Dad would be
To know she's on Season Three
When he hasn't got past Season One

Both (sung): Oh how very glad we'll be
To see Mummy so happy
When she's playing Candy Crush tonight!
Both (spoken): It's all true! I did see Mummy playing
  Candy Crush. I swear!

As the lights came up on the audience, Emily leaned out of the wings and looked to Mrs Jackson and Mrs Dar, seated on the same row, but a few seats away from each other. They were both clapping madly, tears in their eyes, as Jayden and Rashid took bows after their outstanding performance. She had done everything she could for these two boys. She just hoped their parents and the boys themselves would continue to be kinder to one another and see what was really important at ten years old.

'Right, everyone in their places for "Can't We Have A Carvery"!' Emily called.

Can't We Have A Carvery
– to the tune of 'Stop the Cavalry' by Jona Lewie

Mum is peeling sprouts, sister selfie pouts
The cat is climbing up the Christmas tree

Auntie's on the wine, will dinner be on time?
Santa's late again, misery
Where's the Roses tin? Put that in the bin!
Can't we have a carvery?

Instrumental

Stress is through the roof, shouting is the proof
Can you find the batteries?
Oh no I feel sick, get a bucket quick
We should have had a carvery!

The gifts have all been opened now, the turkey's
   smelling really foul
Wish I'd got a drone not socks, or endless packets of
   Barbie frocks

Not another James Bond, not another James Bond,
Another James Bond, not another one x 2
Wish we were at Toby for Christmas

Instrumental (glockenspiels)

Bored of things to play, shopping Boxing Day
Going to see what's gone half price
Kindles in the sale, a really big discount rail
If you buy one you get one free
Scoffing After Eights, before their use by dates
Can't we have a carvery?

Not another Strictly, not another Strictly, another

Strictly, not another one x 2
Wish we were at Toby for Christmas

Wish I could be remembering, all the dates for recycling
Will the bin men ever come? How many dustbins?
Forty-one.
Wish we were at Toby for Christmas

'Can't we do it again?' Cherry moaned, a suspicious brown mark on her cheek as they convened backstage before the final song. Either she had been tucking into the tub of Celebrations Emily had said they could only have access to at the end of the show, or it was something from the llama. She wasn't sure at this stage if she wanted to find out.

'I want to do it all again too,' Angelica agreed.

'Can't we say that was a practice and do it actually again?' Cherry carried on.

Emily didn't want to do it again. Emily was exhausted and was wondering how she was still standing. She picked up her bottle of water and took a much-needed suck.

'I don't want to do it again,' Makenzie announced. 'My dads are going to take me to McDonald's for tea. And I'm never usually allowed to go to McDonald's.'

'Listen, Year Six, we have one more song to perform and it's our most special song, isn't it?' Emily reminded. 'The one Ray wrote just for us.'

Ray had played it for them only a few days ago, here in the hall, and she had had a job to contain her tears. As soon as she had dismissed the children into the playground, she sobbed a whole river full and had to wave away Ray's attempts to console her. It was beautiful. Every single line was perfect. The lyrics said so much and she really hoped it would resonate with their audience.

'OK, has everyone got their mobile phones ready?' Emily whispered. The hall seemed to have fallen silent which was exactly what was called for in this moment.

'Yes, Miss Parker,' the children whispered back.

'Right then,' Emily said, wiping at Cherry's cheek with a tissue. 'Frema, take your shoes off. And let's go.'

The children quietly filed onto the stage and once they were in position they switched on the torches of their mobile phones and held them above their heads as Ray began to play the piano.

One Christmas Star by Ray Stone

Reaching for that tinsel, holding out a hand
Trying to remember how close it is we stand
Part of the same world, we're moving now as one
Our first steps to the future, our journeys just begun

Chorus

There's not one Christmas star
It didn't make us who we are
We grew because of you and learn from the things
    you do
We are all Christmas stars
No matter who we are
Our love can reach forever, if we make kind together

We need strong, we don't need broken
With open hearts we are awoken
Believe in helping, giving not taking
A better world we are creating

Chorus

We are all unique, it's true, but we're also all the same
All we want is love and peace to win this tough life
game
Joining forces, as one team, it's Stretton Park united
No matter how you celebrate it's time to get excited!

Chorus

We are all bright Christmas stars...

Sixty-Eight

Ray played the last note of the final song of the show and looked to the stage and the children he had got to know over the past few weeks. They were all special, each and every one of them and they had worked so hard for this night. The momentary silence was shattered by an eruption from the crowd. Louder than any of the earlier applause, this was nearly greater in volume than his sell-out shows at the O2. Everyone was on their feet, the bishop clearly visible – his hat higher than William's crown – whooping and cheering and celebrating the enormous success of this performance. The children had been incredible and focused for the entire night and they deserved every second of this adoration from their loved ones. But there was someone else who also deserved a whole lot of appreciation. And he was going to be the one to make sure that happened...

'Ladies and gentlemen, could I have your attention for a minute?' He took his microphone out of the stand and stood up from the piano as the crowd finally began to settle down. Emily was most probably going to kill him later, but, as he was going in for surgery tomorrow, that fact was pretty irrelevant.

'Weren't the Year Sixes fantastic tonight?' Ray asked as he made his way up the steps and onto the stage. That question was answered with another round of thunderous applause and some loud whistles of appreciation. The children all began to put their hands up in the air for high-fives from Ray, like they had after rehearsals, as he joined them in the spotlight. He made his way down the line, connecting palms with everyone, being careful not to miss anyone out. The last to slap his hand was Jayden, his eye finally healed, the biggest smile at last reaching his eyes.

'You were all fantastic,' Ray spoke into the microphone. 'Really fantastic.'

The llama made a noise from backstage and the children burst into fits of laughter.

'Listen,' Ray said, 'I'm sure you'll appreciate that for a show like this to happen, a lot of work has to go into it. And I want you to know that there is one person in particular who put her heart and soul into this performance so that your children could really shine tonight.'

Emily wanted to get on the llama, who was currently eating a mini-Bounty bar, and trot off to the petting zoo never to be seen again. She didn't want the limelight. She had enough of that with her lip-locking with Ray spread all over Twitter. This was about her class, not her.

'And that person,' Ray continued, 'is Miss Emily Parker.'

Emily closed her eyes, wanting to bury her head in the llama's fur. She held her breath. *What to do? What to do?*

'Come on, Miss Parker,' Rashid said, taking hold of her arm.

'Yes, come on,' Cherry bossed. 'Makenzie won't get to McDonald's before his bedtime if we don't actually hurry up.' Cherry gripped her other arm. When had her ten-year-olds got so strong?

'I...' Emily began, really not wanting to go.

'*I'll* look after the llama, Miss Parker,' Alice told her.

Now going seemed definitely preferable to staying...

She finally let the members of her class lead her out onto the stage and, as soon as her feet hit the boards, she was dazzled by the lighting and the refraction from all the festive tinsel, baubles, garlands, coat hangers and lanterns she had decorated the room with. Ray was grinning at her, looking so super-sexy in those jeans that fitted him so well and a plain black shirt. She froze for a moment, then slowly, slightly pushed by Rashid and Cherry, she made her way over to him. Before she could think or do anything else Ray had handed her the microphone. It was either take it or let go of it and perform the worst mic-drop in history...

'Hello everyone,' Emily said tentatively. 'I'm Emily Parker... Miss Parker.'

The children let out a collective laugh, presumably at her awkwardness. Who could blame them? She needed to focus on something out there in the darkness. Maybe her mother in a toga... Spurred on by that mental image she carried on.

'I just want to say... how proud I am to be the teacher of this year's Year Six class.' She drew in a breath. 'Your children come into my class every day full of enthusiasm and bursting at the seams with excitement for the world. And I know, for us as adults, it's sometimes hard to feel the same sense of joy that these children do.' She gathered her thoughts. 'Life… life is hard. And, all of us, we are all going through different situations, all navigating the fast pace of living in today's society.' She took another breath, clasping her second hand to the microphone. 'But, every morning, when I look at the hopeful, expectant faces of your children, I'm encouraged.' She looked to her class then. Those sweet faces, growing up so fast. '*They* inspire *me*. They *all* inspire me. And, tonight, I hope they have all inspired you too.' Emily smiled again at her children. 'Thank you.'

Another rip-roaring applause rushed through the room and as it echoed back and forth, someone came bursting out of the audience. Susan Clark was making her way through the auditorium and Emily stepped back a little, quickly passing the microphone back to Ray.

'She doesn't look happy,' Emily whispered to him. 'And she really likes to be the one in charge of microphones.'

'Am I going to get detention?' Ray asked.

'That's not funny.'

'Should I give it over to her?' Ray asked, looking at the microphone like it might be about to explode.

'I think she's coming to take it,' Emily answered. 'Or else she's coming to fire me. Or both.'

The audience were still clapping when Susan mounted the stage and she bustled her way to the centre. Emily held her breath and Ray offered up the microphone which Susan duly snatched without delay.

'Parents and governors,' Susan began, her voice loud and calling for quiet. 'Esteemed members of the clergy, children...' She did a side-eye towards Ray. 'Pianist...' She straightened the amber beads holding her glasses around her neck. 'Thank you so much for attending our annual Christmas show here at Stretton Park and for providing so much support to our little school since the beginning of September.' She drew in a breath, gazing out into the crowd. 'I too would like to extend my heartfelt thanks to Miss Parker for her absolutely sterling work on the performance this year. I think you will agree that we haven't laughed quite so much in any previous years and, I can safely say that we've never had as many animals in Stretton Park as we have had this term. Llamas... hedgehogs...'

'Hamsters,' Lucas called out.

Emily put at arm around him and drew him to stand a little closer to her, pressing a finger to her lips in a 'sshh'.

'But, as well as all the joy I feel about this night, it is tinged with sadness... because, in the New Year... in February, I will be stepping down from my role here at Stretton Park.'

There was an intake of breath from the audience, but it was Emily's heart that virtually stopped. What had Susan just said? She was leaving? She was no longer going to be the Head of the school? This was bad news. This meant there would be someone new, someone who didn't know anything about anyone, someone who might promote Dennis to Deputy Head. Dennis! Who she had been able to hear crunching on an everlasting gobstopper throughout the entire play. This was not what she had been expecting at all. Or, actually, ever.

'My husband has been offered a new position, in Scotland no less, so I will be taking early retirement and becoming a lady of leisure in a brand-new country.'

There was a note of real sadness to Susan's voice and Emily suddenly realised that although Susan was firm at times, she had, for the most part, always been fair. Grumpy most of the time, but fair nonetheless.

'New beginnings,' Susan continued. 'That's what I wish for Stretton Park. That and a new leader who will continue the fantastic work the current teaching staff do here. And, I for one, hope very much that that new leader will be... Emily Parker.'

Suddenly, Emily's legs wanted to give way and it had nothing to do with vintage brogues that were killing her toes. She found she had to lean on both Lucas and Ray. What had the headteacher said? Her? The new leader? The new Head of the school?

'Obviously,' Susan continued, 'we have to comply with employment law and advertise the position... blah blah blah.' She laughed. 'I don't believe I said "blah blah blah".' She waved a hand in front of her face, tears springing to her eyes. 'But I really think Miss Parker is the best person for the job and I would really like it if you would all support her application. Governors, teachers, parents and guardians.' She pointed a finger out into the audience as if trying to locate someone. 'And you, your Excellency, because I don't know how Miss Parker managed to do it, but we had all the Christianity I ordered, and we had a touch of Hanukkah and Eid and we had... real life. Real Stretton Park life and... of course, a carrot.'

'Carrot! Carrot!' Felix called, cheeks rosy, eyes bright.

'So, let's have one last round of applause for a wonderful, heart-warming, seasonal show.'

As the crowd showed their appreciation once more, no

one's expression was more joyous than Emily's. Susan had faith in her. She had *always* had faith in her. And, as the lights went up in the assembly hall and Emily gazed out into the audience, her lower limbs still wobbly, her heart overflowing, the people she could see clapping harder than all the rest were her parents.

'You OK?' Ray whispered, slipping an arm around her waist and continuing to prop her up a little.

'I don't know,' Emily admitted, her voice a little uncontrolled. 'What just happened?'

'Well,' Ray said, drawing her close. 'I've heard about this thing called a Christmas miracle and I've never really believed in it before but...'

She turned her head to look up at him then. 'But?'

'It's what you've done,' he told her. 'And, with these kids, it's what you do every single day.'

She wanted to kiss him, right there on the stage, but if she was going to apply for the position of Head then decorum needed to be maintained. She reached for his hand and, interlocking their fingers, she squeezed tight. 'Here's to more miracles,' she whispered. 'Starting tomorrow.'

Ray smiled down at her. 'Amen to that.'

Sixty-Nine

Christmas Day

Ray didn't want to be here. It was four days after his surgery, and he was craving normality. But his reluctance to be here he was actually classing as an improvement. The day of the operation, in recovery, he had wept because he was alive *and* because his coming-out-of-anaesthesia very real nightmare that James Morrison's comeback album was at number one had finally ended. The day *after* surgery everything had felt sore and tight and he still wasn't used to not being able to speak and kept dropping either the Sharpie or the notepad – sometimes both at the same time. Day Three and Brenda and his dad had bought kebabs from Mehmet's he couldn't face eating no matter how good they smelled. And here they were, Day Four, Christmas Day. He had never wished for a sofa and *James Bond* re-runs more than he did right now. His gaze went to the Christmas tree Emily had insisted on bringing in for the duration of his stay. It was the one Jonah had put in the living room that she had never liked, but she had decorated it with some of the traditional ornaments from the other tree in her apartment. And he liked it. He liked it because Emily liked it and she had put it there for him. He just couldn't wait until he got his voice back and he could tell her again exactly how much he loved her.

The door banged open and suddenly his room was like the pub at turfing out time. People rushed in and he had a job to quickly distinguish who was who amid the arms, parcels, hats, coats and... a dog?

'Merry Christmas! I can't stop long! Tucker's halfway through his walk and needs a pee and although I've part-trained him not to do it in front of polite company, he's still a little sketchy on the polite company part.' Deborah grinned then made a tighter grab for the lead attached to her pet as he went to investigate under the bed. 'I bought you something. Didn't have time to wrap it. It's one of those electronic notepads. I know you won't be without voice for long, but I couldn't bear to think about all those trees being murdered while you're writing notes.' She deposited the cardboard box on Ray's bed. 'Got to dash. I've left Oscar in charge of the Brussel sprouts. Merry Christmas, Ray.' She leaned forward, kissed Ray on the cheek and, before he even had a chance to pick up his pen, she was gone.

'Our turn!' Allan announced, bouncing forward and delivering a beautifully gift-wrapped parcel onto Ray's bed. 'It's a scarf!'

'Allan!' Jonah exclaimed. 'You've ruined the surprise!'

'Well, we do have to be at your mum and dad's in twenty minutes or your cousins are going to eat my share of everything and who knows what burnt-out vehicle is going to be residing in the communal areas of the estate for us to navigate around today!' Allan grinned at Ray as he sat down on the edge of his bed. 'It's a very nice scarf. Designer. I picked it. And it's stretchy enough that if you're being pursued by the paparazzi you can pull it up over your face as a kind of mask. A two-in-one gift.'

'What Allan means is,' Jonah began, edging closer, 'while you're recovering it will keep your throat warm and after that you can—'

'Use it to tie Emily up in the master bedroom,' Allan interrupted, clapping his hands together and laughing. 'Three-in-one gift!'

'Two L's!'

It was Emily admonishing now and Ray gave her all his attention. She looked so beautiful, hair under a woollen hat, fresh-faced from the winter weather, unfastening her coat, snowflakes falling to the hospital floor.

'Well,' Allan said, 'a little bird told me Ray's moved out of the spare room.'

'How…' Emily began. Ray smiled and watched her look to her best friend. 'Jonah, I knew things in my kitchen had moved around!'

'I popped in. I had a whisk emergency at work. I happened to notice a touch of maleness in your bedroom and nothing but two guitars in my old room.'

Ray began writing on his notepad.

'Ooo, he's going to speak,' Allan announced. 'I mean "write". He's writing!'

'He can hear you, you know,' Emily reminded, whipping off her hat and going to stand by the side of the bed.

Ray held up his notepad. It read:-

She still won't give me space in her wardrobes!

'Ha!' Allan announced. 'No, good luck with that. Jonah said it's been brimming with all things deeply retro for a while.'

'*I* can hear too, you know!' Emily exclaimed.

'Well, we'd better go,' Jonah said. 'Allan's right. My cousins will devour everything if we don't get to dinner on time.' He smiled. 'Merry Christmas you two.' He held his hand out to Ray and Ray took it, drawing the man into a hug.

'Aww, they're hugging,' Allan announced, sounding delighted.

'Merry Christmas,' Emily said catching them both up in a cuddle before they headed out of the room.

Ray began to write on his pad again.

Dad and Brenda came this morning. They're going for a carvery. Ironic!

'Are they coming back later? I can go back home and get the presents,' Emily replied, looking like she was going to leave.

Ray grabbed her hand with his right hand then quickly swapped, holding her with his left hand and scribbling with his right.

Emily read the words.

Don't go anywhere...

'Ooo, that sounds a little possessive for Christmas Day but... I quite like it.' She sat down on the edge of his bed as he continued to write. This type of communication was getting him down. He had been using a laptop, until he'd discovered he was actually quicker at handwriting than he was at typing.

I hate not being able to talk to you. Dr Crichton says a few more days. I don't know what I will sound like. I'm hoping not Joe Pasquale... I did not spell that right, did I?

Emily laughed as she read the words. 'I'm not sure if you spelt it right, but I know who you mean and what he sounds like. I'll pray.'

He tried to make his hands move faster across the page. Maybe he should open Deborah's gift and get started with it. He wrote another couple of lines and turned the paper towards her.

Despite being in a hospital bed for Christmas this is the happiest I've ever been. Things are going to be good from now on. I feel it

He watched a whole range of feelings filter over Emily's expression and he squeezed her hand in his.

'I feel it too,' she replied, her voice catching a little.

He released his hand from hers to turn the paper back around and began to write again.

There's a present for you under the tree you hate

She laughed. 'I don't hate the tree.' She stood up and Ray wrote again.

Yes, you do

'No, I don't.'

He offered the same piece of paper again, pressing it forward and shaking it about. He watched her scoop up the small, neatly wrapped gift box, bringing it back to the bed and sitting down with a sigh.

'You didn't need to get me anything.'

He wrote quickly.

It's not cheese

She laughed. 'Damn, I might not even open it.'

Get on with it or I'll give it to the nurse that likes me. His name's Blake

Emily carefully peeled back the paper and revealed a red velvet box, slightly worn at the edges. This wasn't anything like throwaway cardboard or something from H Samuel, this was chunky and aged and she couldn't wait to see what was inside. She looked to Ray before she lifted the lid. He had been through so much and yet here he was, strong, immovable, resilient. She hoped this operation had been successful and his recovery was going to signal the start of a whole new journey, for him as an artist and for them as a couple...

She eased back the lid and it opened with a hefty and satisfying clunk. Gasping, Emily put a hand to her chest, as she gazed first at the brooch inside and then back at Ray.

'Ray... this is... it's so, so beautiful.' She didn't have

the words to describe how elegant the gift was or how absolutely *her*. It was a stunning silver star, gleaming with encrusted diamonds, or fake diamonds, or another clear-coloured stone she didn't know the name of. She didn't care what it was made of, because what it had been given with was so much thought and feeling… and love. When she had finished marvelling at its beauty there was another message from Ray waiting on the notepad.

The man at the shop said it was art-deco. I don't know whether that's true but he seemed legit. I bought it because it reminded me of you and the Stretton Park kids and that show we made that brought us together. It's our Christmas star

'Our Christmas star,' Emily said, eyes leaking tears as she gazed at the man who had taught her how to love again. 'The biggest and brightest and craziest and maddest one of all.' She kissed him then, softly, slowly, slightly concerned she might break him, before smiling again. 'I love you, Ray Stone.'

This time his words were written large, at speed and with zero hesitation.

I love you, Miss Parker. Merry Christmas xx

Epilogue

The Freedom Music Festival

Seven months later – summer

It was an absolutely picture-perfect summer's day in London and Emily was so thankful for that. Blue skies, that fragrant scent of ice cream, freshly cut grass, sun cream and barbeque filling the air. And good weather meant that the turn-out for her parents' chambers charity day was high and even more money was going to be raised for the three charities. It was obviously a little sad that she wasn't going to get to see Alegra and William in their Hunter wellies, knee-deep in mud like a really soggy Glastonbury festival, but charity was more important than her own personal need for a laugh. Besides, her parents had been slightly less absent since Christmas. They had even invited her and Ray *to the house*, and not just to form part of a dinner party missing the down-to-earth element. Alegra had even cooked. Herself. And the lemon chicken had been so terrible William had begged her never to cook again. Emily had helped him order Dominos from an app she installed on his phone. Granted they had eaten the pizzas with knives and forks, but her dad had called the meal 'most agreeable'.

'Thank you so much,' Emily said as a concert-going family dropped some coins into her charity bucket. She popped it down on the grass for a moment while she tied the bottom of her Ray Stone T-shirt into a knot at her waist. Ray had laughed when she'd got dressed in it that morning and said it was almost a kissing deterrent, having to look at a shadow of his profile across her chest whenever they got close. Emily had insisted it was great publicity for the festival *and* his upcoming tour and she actually really liked the design Deborah had signed off on.

'Hey,' Ray greeted, his voice close to her ear, hands slipping around the waistband of her denim cut-offs. She loved his 'heys' more than ever, remembering those ten days with limited talking, digital notepads and Post-it notes and even, at one point... Maltesers to shape words.

'Hey,' Emily answered, turning to face him. Ripped jeans, boots, a muscle-fit vest he had no right to look so good in... Gone were the long sleeves of winter and his self-confidence was mended enough for him to be almost comfortable with that scar on his shoulder. His beard was short and his brown hair was verging on that scruffy side of sexy she loved.

'Argh! You're still wearing my face!' he exclaimed, covering his eyes with his hands.

'I hope you don't react that way to *all* your fans,' Emily said, smoothing her fingers over the picture on her top.

'What way?' Ray asked, removing his hands and stepping closer to her. 'This way?' He kissed her lips. 'Or this way?' He kissed her again, deeper this time. He tasted of sugary lemonade, the meadow and... was that Haribos? She stepped away from him, looking amid the growing crowd getting the best spots for picnics, others moving close to the stage, enjoying the first performers. 'Is Dennis here?'

'He is,' Ray answered. 'With his mum. He gave me some sweets. He's just there, setting up a parasol.'

Emily shielded her eyes from the sun and looked where Ray was pointing. Her first sighting of the elusive Mrs Murray. One of her first jobs since being appointed Head at Stretton Park, was finding Penny's replacement for her maternity leave. Dennis's mother had applied for the position but failed to turn up for interview citing 'other commitments' as her excuse. Emily had been beginning to think Mrs Murray didn't actually exist and perhaps Dennis had a Norman Bates thing going on. But here, it seemed, she was.

'Miss Parker!'

Emily turned around to see some of her children running across the grass towards her. Except they weren't *her* children anymore. Her Year Sixes had spent the past six months learning and growing at a rate of knots and they were all off to secondary schools in September. She smiled brightly at them. Jayden with Rashid, Alice, Cherry, Angelica, Felix – who was dressed as an astronaut which probably wasn't the smartest idea on one of the hottest days of the year so far – Makenzie wearing a bright rainbow T-shirt and pink shorts, Matthew, Charlie, Frema and Lucas.

'Ray! Ray!' Felix chanted before realising it might be better if he opened the visor of his helmet to speak. 'Ray! Ray!'

'Oh, it's so good to see you all,' Emily greeted, ruffling heads of hair and high-fiving others. 'Thank you for coming. Thank your parents for bringing you and letting you come.'

'We've adopted two of Idris Elba's babies,' Matthew informed. 'The man at the sanctuary said that they wouldn't be able to go back into the wild and survive so they're living with us now.'

'That's amazing,' Emily said. 'What have you called them?'

'Mine's called Taylor,' Charlie said with a grin.

'And mine's called Swift,' Matthew told.

This earned laughter all round from the group.

'Great names,' Ray agreed.

'So, have any of you been on the helter-skelter yet?' Emily asked them. 'You'd better make sure you have a go because my friend Allan has been hogging it since the gates opened.'

And Jonah was trying out a brand-new venture today. As much as he loved his work at the hotel, he really wanted to be able to put his own unique spin on his cooking and sticking to a rather restricted menu was all but killing his creative flair. He had a stall at the festival, with one of his sous chefs helping, serving up his mother's old wholesome Caribbean recipes alongside more contemporary dishes of his own creation. Emily knew he was road-testing the idea with a view to starting his own restaurant and she had no doubt he was going to make a success of it.

'I've been on the bouncy castle,' Angelica announced.

'Jayden and me kicked goals against someone called David Seaman. My dad said he used to be famous,' Rashid said. 'I scored three of mine.'

'And I scored four,' Jayden added.

'What time are we singing again, Ray?' Alice asked.

'Ah, um, yeah... about that...' Ray replied. He looked at his watch and Emily sensed his edge of uncomfortable.

'It was supposed to be a surprise, Alice!' Makenzie exclaimed in irritation.

'Sorry!' Alice snapped back. 'But no one's died!' An eye-roll ensued.

'You're singing?' Emily asked.

'I got parental consent,' Ray told her. 'All above board. I couldn't risk the wrath of the headteacher, I hear she can be really raw when it comes down to it.'

'Is that so?' Emily said, stepping closer to him.

'Eww, they're going to kiss!' Matthew stated, putting a hand over his eyes.

'Kiss! Kiss!' Felix shouted.

The daytime part of the festival had been a roaring success and, as the evening arrived, and the temperatures dropped, it was time for the headline act to take to the stage. It was Ray's first big performance since his surgery, but it wasn't his first test. After his convalescence, he *had* sung at Ronnie Scott's, a small, intimate, yet sell-out show to prove that his voice was still perfection and that he was coming back with a vengeance and a hunger to produce new music. His album was now complete and set to launch next month, when he would also take to stages around the country to promote it. He couldn't wait to get back out there, living his songwriting and performing dream, but he was going to miss not waking up with Emily every day. Which was why he was calling in the big guns, Year Six, to help him in this moment.

'Good evening everyone,' Ray greeted the crowd from the seat at the grand piano. 'I'm Ray Stone.' There was loud applause from the hundreds of festival goers. 'And these are my awesome friends from Stretton Park Primary School.'

'We've made thousands,' Alegra stated, plumping down a charity bucket next to Emily in the VIP area of the crowd. 'I am most probably heaving around hundreds of pounds in tiny coins.' She looked into the bucket. 'I've never even seen those little silver ones before.'

'5ps?' Emily queried.

'Tiny!' Alegra commented. 'Tinier than pennies! How does that work?' She let out a sigh. 'Your father has bought another hat. This one has a ridiculous feather. I don't know what it is with him lately. It's like he's experiencing a middle-age crisis that only millinery can solve. Have you ever heard of a condition like that?'

'No, Mum,' Emily replied. 'But sshh, Ray and the children are going to sing.'

'Don't you think I know that?' Alegra asked. 'That's why I'm here.'

'We haven't missed it, have we? Len had to have a go at the coconut shy, didn't he? I told him I don't even like coconuts, but he wouldn't listen.' It was Brenda, red-faced and panting like she had run the London Marathon. Her summer dress was slightly too short and every time she breathed Emily caught sight of her bright lime green knickers. Once seen they couldn't be unseen...

'Coconut's good for you,' Len announced, arriving too. 'Unless you've got an allergy. Then I guess it's fucking bad for you.' He wheezed a laugh.

'Candy floss?' Allan offered. A bright pink swirl of fluff was pushed into Emily's orbit.

'Or Caribbean salt cod fritters?' Jonah suggested. He

was holding a box with the most delicious-smelling food inside.

'Can I have both?' Emily asked. 'But after Ray and the children have sung! Sshh!'

'I'm loving the VIP section.' It was Dennis now invading her space. She really just wanted to hear Ray's opening number and with her children there it was all the more special...

'Dennis, please have some free water and M&Ms but let me listen to the music!'

'I need to talk to you about Mother.'

'Oh, Dennis, can't it wait until after the holidays?' Emily asked. She was getting completely frustrated now.

'Well, that's not the mark of a true leader,' Dennis replied. 'Susan always listened.'

'Susan always made budget cuts,' Emily reminded. 'Not that that was *all* her fault.' She was having trouble managing their spending too, but was juggling funding as best she could.

'Well, that might be something you no longer have to worry about,' Dennis continued. 'Budgets should be dealt with by an assistant.' He smiled. 'Mother thinks the cooking was beneath her. She wants to apply to be Deputy Head.'

Emily opened her mouth to make reply but was stopped by a call from the stage.

'Emily, will you come up and join us?'

Jonah nudged Emily hard, Allan grabbed her shoulders and spun her towards the exit to the stage and suddenly she was being propelled away from her friends and family towards those bright lights again. The bright lights she did her best to avoid despite her relationship with one of the

UK's top talents. Ray's job might mean fame. Her job meant using a red pen a lot...

'Let's hear it for my girl, Miss Emily Parker,' Ray spoke into the microphone.

His girl. Yes, she was his girl. And he was her man. And seven months down the line they were as strong as two people in a relationship could be. Like every couple they were trying to live in the moment, feeling their way into a future no one could predict, but they had so much honesty and hope in their hearts.

'What are you doing?' Emily whispered to him as she got onto the stage, the crowd whooping and clapping her arrival.

'Starting a night of music,' Ray told her.

'With me?'

'Never without you,' Ray answered with a smile. 'Sit down right here.' He patted the piano stool with room enough for two.

'Oh, Ray, no, you know my playing the piano was a one-off and...' Emily began. She could feel her cheeks heating up from the crowd attention and a little sunburn she'd got earlier.

'You don't have to play this time,' Ray told her. 'Just listen.' He smiled at her, those eyes that looked like autumn leaves matching hers for a moment, before looking back to the children. 'Ready?' he asked them.

They all nodded, stepping up to their microphones. Then Ray began to play, the drums kicked in and his sweet voice started the opening bars of Jason Derulo's 'Marry Me'.

★

Tears were flashing down her face and there was nothing Emily could do to stop them. Ray and the children had sung a marriage proposal and now, on the ivory keys of the piano in front of her, rested the most gorgeous gold ring, two diamond hearts intertwined. It was like time had stopped and she and Ray were in a moment just for them.

'It's Edwardian,' Ray told her, a nervousness to his voice. 'Maybe. Possibly.'

'I don't know what to say,' Emily answered, tears still flowing.

'Say something,' Ray begged. 'Even if it's "No. Are you mad? You're no way good enough for me."'

'Oh, goodness, Ray, that can't be what you think!'

'I think… if you say yes… I'm going to be the luckiest man alive.' He swallowed. 'And I'm not picking that ring up again. So, if it's a no, I'm going to have to work around it for the rest of my set.'

Emily wiped her eyes with her fingers. 'Pick the ring up.'

'Really?'

She nodded and held out her left hand to him.

His fingers were shaking as he picked the delicate ring from the keys and presented it towards her hand. He paused, his eyes fixing with hers. 'Emily Parker, will you marry me?' he whispered softly.

There was no doubt in her mind, or in her reply. 'Yes!' she gasped. 'I say, yes.'

Ray slipped the ring onto her finger and drew her into his embrace, the children clapping, hollering and jumping around like excited hedgehogs next to them.

Emily held him tight, living only in this one moment, letting the feeling of excitement, contentment and all-round euphoria surround her heart. And then she came to and realised there was something she had to do. She didn't want to leave the festival-goers, her friends, her family or the whole world in any doubt. She took hold of the microphone, her heart bursting.

'I said yes!' She beamed. 'Yes! We're getting married!'